The Greek Maiden and the English Lord

A Novel

Patty Apostolides

"The Greek Maiden and the English Lord," by Patty Apostolides. ISBN 978-1-60264-623-0 (softcover); 978-1-60264-624-7 (hardcover).

Published 2010, 2017 by Virtualbookworm.com Publishing Inc., P.O. Box 9949, College Station, TX 77842, US. ©2010, 2017 Patty Apostolides. All rights reserved. No part of this publication may be reproduced, stored in a retrieval system, or transmitted in any form or by any means, electronic, mechanical, recording or otherwise, without the prior written permission of Patty Apostolides.

Chapter 1

Lily exited the dark chamber of the bookseller's store clutching a small book in her grubby hands, content with her purchase. Her voice was hoarse from selling trinkets all day. She was tired and hungry, yet her victory was not in the number of coins in her pocket, but the leather-bound book in her hand.

A sigh escaped her lips when she spied the crescent glow of the setting sun peaking behind the crown of the stone building she faced. She was late.

It was the first day of the festival in Caen and the town's square was bustling with activity. Lily's bare feet skimmed past the spice-filled barrels with their wild profusion of rich scents, followed by the pungent smell of leather and freshly baked bread. She hugged her book close to her as she passed the tight crowds that were watching musicians singing and performing juggling acts, while nearby food vendors competed for attention with their chaotic shouting, as they bargained and sold French cheese, sausages, and brioche. Jumping over carpets brimming with an assortment of textiles, handcrafted goods, and tools, Lily ran to the edge of the square, and then turned into a dark alley.

It was quiet here, except for the steady pitter-patter of her feet hitting the cobblestoned pavement, and the rhythmic sound of her heavy breathing. Lily could see her grandmother's tent, which always stood on the outskirts of the towns they visited, and would be removed by the end of the day. It was round and dirty white, with tiny tears from constant use and had two openings, one in the front and one in the back. A small line of people, mostly women, had formed in the front.

Lily flipped the back flap of the tent and stepped inside. Grandmother Mirela sat at the table with her crystal ball and two lit candles on each side. Plump and middle-aged, with round gold earrings, she wore flashy apparel and a purple turban on her head. Her closed eyes suggested that she was meditating.

"Your earnings were good enough to afford that book?" Mirela spoke without opening her eyes.

"Yes, Grandmother. I earned more than Sultana and Fifi, and the other girls."

Mirela's dark, heavy lidded eyes slid open. She gazed with interest at Lily's wide, blue-green eyes.

Lily strode toward her and pulled out the shiny coins from her pocket, dropping them into her outreached fat palm. She showed her the book. "It is a new French novel and--"

"You can tell me another time. Now go and wait for my cue. Take some candles with you."

Lily grabbed a few tallow candles and slipped out the back. She slithered the black wig off her sweating head like a snake casting off its skin. Her grandmother had wanted her to wear the piece in public so she wouldn't stand out from the other gypsies, but she never could get used to it. With anticipation coursing through her sixteen-year-old body, Lily sat down on the small stool, lit the candle and began to read her book. It would be several minutes before she would be needed to escort the customer out the back.

Grandmother Mirela had taught her to read and write English, Greek, and French, although reading was not an acceptable practice of the gypsies. Her friends often teased her when they spied her reading. She would shrug her shoulders and toss her head. They could not understand her.

The sun had already set when Gertrude Charleton entered Mirela's tent. Hiking her blue walking dress up so as not to sully it on the dirt floor, she walked into the dimly lit tent. With a flourish, she sat down on the hard chair. "I am so glad I found you," she said, removing her snug-fitting gloves. "So much has happened since I saw you two years ago in Paris, when you read my future."

"I have been expecting you." Mirela spoke in English. Her voice was calm and dusky.

"After you told me about Mr. Penbroke, I checked up on him, and you were right. He had gambled away everything he had. I married Sir Douglas Charleton after all." Gertrude showed her the ring on her finger.

"You are to be commended for your wise choice, Lady Charleton."

"With help from you, of course. I will always be in your debt. If you ever need assistance in anything--"

Mirela's eyes flashed open. "Later, we can talk. Let us begin." She fixed her gaze on the gleaming ball for a few moments, and then looked up. "What brings you to France, Lady Charleton?"

"My husband's cotton textiles business." Gertrude twisted her gloves. "He doesn't need the money. Mind you, he inherited quite a bit from his late father. He just likes to make more." She appeared guilty. "Although trade is not quite accepted by the *ton*."

"Maybe trade is not, but money *is*, and trade brings money."

Gertrude appeared pleased. "We recently were in Lyon, where we bought silk fabric. We will be leaving tomorrow with our packet ship for England. Is silk right for us at this time?"

"I do not see anything wrong with the choice, but I do see machines, many of them, for the cotton. The looms will help your business grow."

Lady Charleton thanked Mirela. A shadow flitted over her features. "My husband's uncle is quite ill with consumption. The doctors claim he does not have much time left."

"A change of climate could help his condition."

"His son is returning to England from his trip abroad, and now my younger sister Charlotte, has confided in me that she is in love with him," Gertrude said with lowered voice.

Lily's long, honey-blonde braids brushed the pages of the book as she labored over the words. With one ear cocked toward the tent, she listened to the conversation and waited for the cue to usher Lady Charleton out the back.

"Charlotte recently turned twenty-one," Gertrude was saying to Mirela, "I am not surprised of her interest for Edward. Indeed, he is wealthy and quite handsome. Even I had a crush on him at one time, but that was so long ago." She tittered.

"Hmm, and you want to know whether they are right for each other." Mirela's eyes narrowed as her hands hovered above the ball. "Yes, I sense a woman next to him. She is attractive and brightly clothed, and appears to be important in his life, for they are holding hands."

"Oh, that sounds like her. Is there anything more you can tell me? Will there be a wedding?"

Two drops of candle wax landed on the page that Lily was reading. Disgusted, she moved the book to the side, not wanting to damage it, and turned her gaze on the shadows in the tent. Mirela's turbaned head was close to the woman's plumed head. She gave an inaudible response.

Lily could easily imagine what they were discussing, filling in the blank spots. Each city they visited was different, but the people were alike, with similar emotions, aspirations, and dreams. The hushed conversation inside the tent was no different; it included a possible marriage, illness, and impending death.

The rattling sound of a carriage caught Lily's attention. It was unusual for carriages to come through the narrow alley and besides, they were quite expensive and only the rich rode in them. The clattering sound stopped.

Lily arose and hurried toward the alley with her candle to see who it was. She peered down the pitch-black lane, shifting the sputtering tallow candle towards that direction. Unable to see anything, she leaned forward. Her lit candle revealed a closed carriage and horses.

The scene before her reminded her of a story she had once read, where the handsome prince drove up in his plush carriage to rescue the maiden in distress, but where was the maiden? She shook her head, realizing that she was becoming too fanciful. It must be Lady Charleton's carriage, she was sure of it.

A crackling sound followed by the smell of stark, pungent smoke interrupted her daydreaming. She glanced down in alarm at the flames soaring through her hair. Her heart jumped to her throat. She dropped the candle and cried out, but nothing came out of her mouth except a croaking sound. *What is wrong with me?*

What came next happened so quickly that it would remain a blur in Lily's memory. Someone pushed her to the ground, rolling her in a thick, scratchy fabric. The scent of sandalwood and spice replaced the smell of smoke.

"*Ne vous enquietez pas, ma petite,*" said a man's voice, deep and soothing.

Lily struggled to be free, for she did not want to be a captive in his arms, whoever he was. The warm wool was lifted from her. She arose, trembling like a leaf, and feeling the coldness of the evening press upon her. The tall shape of the man kept a respectful distance as she swiped at her face and clothes. She felt stronger by the minute.

"*Merci, Monsieur,*" Lily rasped. Her throat still felt raw from the smoke. "I do not know what I would have done without your help."

"Ah, so you also speak English."

Lily remained silent, feeling unsure as to how to reply to this man's gentle probing. If he found out she was a gypsy, who spoke several languages, he would turn his heel, checking his pockets to make sure she did not steal something.

"I was in that carriage when I saw your head glowing like a ball of fire in the night," he said. "I used my coat to put the flames out. You should be more careful in the future."

Lily was touched by his words. His gentle tone was that of a father addressing a child. A *gadjo* speaking in such a manner was unusual.

"Good-bye!" Mirela announced from inside the tent.

Lily's head swiveled in the direction of her grandmother's call. It could not be ignored. "I must go!"

She dashed back to the tent, thankful for the candlelight inside the tent guiding her way. She threw the black wig on her head and pulled the flap open to reveal the small frame of Lady Charleton standing there.

Lily curtsied, her head low. "Please follow me, my Lady," she said, grabbing her gloved arm and leading her towards the direction of the street.

Lady Charleton pulled her arm away. "I can find my way."

Lily watched the woman glide forward. She wondered if the man would still be there. Maybe he was the lady's coachman. As if reading her mind, the man's tall shape materialized.

"Hello, Gertrude."

"What a surprise to see you here," Lady Charleton exclaimed. She clung to him as they walked away, their dark shapes blending into the night.

Lily stared at their retreating shadows, feeling deflated. She did not even know the name of her rescuer.

❦❦❦

Gertrude sank into the plush seat of the carriage. "I was expecting Douglas to collect me. You can imagine my surprise when you showed up instead! I suppose my husband was still busy finishing up with his transaction?"

"He duly sends his apologies."

"I thank you for playing the gallant," Gertrude replied, laughing. "We were expecting you earlier in the day."

"I arrived an hour ago. Our ship struck inclement weather just as it was departing from Italy, which made for an arduous journey."

"I'll have you know that delays in shipping are common these days. Indeed, our textiles are always late for some reason or another. So, Edward, how were your travels? You must tell me all about your trip."

"Extraordinary, and always something new to see or do." He discussed a few highlights of the countries he visited.

"You took so long in returning, we thought you might have met some beautiful exotic woman and decided to live on some secluded island with her for the rest of your life."

Edward laughed. "It was not like that at all. I assure you, I am still a free man."

"That is good. There are some people besides your father and we who are glad that you are returning to England."

❦❦❦

After the last customer left, Lily dragged her sore and tired body into the tent. She pulled off her ragged black wig and combed her fingers through her singed hair, thinking about the tall stranger who saved her from the fire. Perfumed scents from the female customers clung in the air as she greeted her grandmother, whose head was bent over the table as she counted the coins.

"We did very well today." Mirela looked up at Lily and blinked. "What happened to your hair?"

"It was nothing. My braid got caught in the candle," Lily mumbled.

"Come, sit down. There is something important I must say to you." Mirela's fleshy hand sought Lily's hand, guiding her to the stool. "I had a dream last night, a prophetic vision, where a young woman I knew came and took you away. I woke up feeling terrified and did not know what it meant until this evening when Lady Charleton appeared."

"Lady Charleton? What are you saying?"

"The time has come for you to leave us, Lily, and the reason? It is here, a lie that I have lived with for a decade, that has been knocking on my heart heavily, seeking to be free." Mirela pounded her chest. "You *must* know that I am not your real grandmother."

Lily sat motionless, stunned into silence. How could this be? Mirela was all the family she had.

"You always wondered why you stood out from the other gypsies, your tall height, your fair hair and blue eyes and I told you lies. They were all lies." Mirela sighed once more. "Your parents were not gypsies. Your mother was not my daughter. You are a *gadjo*."

Chapter 2

The tent seemed too small for Lily. She stood up with the urgent need to rush out into the night and breathe deeply. She'd do anything to get away from the terrible feeling she was experiencing. Raised to believe that *gadjos* were foreign to them, to be avoided except for business only, she had a difficult time accepting the fact that she was one of *them*. She held her ground, her hands clenched, trembling with emotion. "How can this be?"

"Your mother was Greek and your father English."

"I do not believe it!"

"You must believe it," Mirela insisted. "Ten years ago, in March, we were staying on the outskirts of the Greek city of Patras." She looked out into the distance, her eyes hooded. "The night before, I had a disturbing dream about the city. A prophetic dream that it would glow like the sun."

Lily heard about how Sultana and her sister, Fifi, had found her wandering the streets of Patras with her doll. The two gypsy girls snatched the doll from her hands and she chased them into the woods, losing them. The girls went and confessed to their mother, Babushka, about what happened, and she alerted the others. The men searched for Lily, and brought her to the camp.

"Why was I not taken back to my parents?"

"It was too late. The Turks had already set fire to the homes in Patras and the smoke had come up to the hills. I could smell death in the air and urged Petroff that we leave right away." She shook her head emphatically. "The fierce fighting between the Greeks and the Turks marked the beginning of the war. Later, we learned of the atrocities committed by the Turks, and how they took the children and women as slaves. It is good you came with us."

"Is that why you always spoke to me in Greek? Is that why I was always afraid of fire?"

Mirela nodded. "I remember them carrying you back to the camp. You were beautiful, just like your doll, with your large, blue eyes, blond curls and pink dress. You said your name was Lily, and that is what we called you. Petroff entrusted you to my care." There was a faraway look on her face. "We had just lost our own daughter to an illness, and there was a huge void. I loved her dearly." She turned towards Lily. "You came into my life at the right time."

"How did you find out about my parents?"

"You wore a locket around your neck and carried a purse in your pocket that revealed your true identity." Mirela pulled out a green silk purse from her pocket. "Count Igor got a hold of this after my Petroff passed away. Today, I took it while he was at the festival. He does not know I have it. It truly belongs to you." She retrieved a folded paper from the purse, and then a gold locket, handing it to her. "Open it."

As Lily struggled with the latch, a discomforting feeling tugged inside of her. This simple act reminded her of something buried deep in the past. A cry of joy escaped her lips when she succeeded. It revealed the miniature portraits of her parents. Her mother was beautiful and her father was blonde-haired and blue-eyed.

"Quickly, read this. Count Igor will be here soon," Mirela said, shoving the paper into her hand.

The paper identified her as Judith Evangelia Montgomery, daughter of Frederick C. Montgomery and Penelope S. Mavroditis. She was born in London, England on March 23, 1815. It stated that if she were lost, she was to be taken to the Clemence and Hartford law office in London, where this document was to be submitted. The lawyer would take the appropriate action to secure her place. The signature on the paper was that of Frederick Montgomery, her father.

Lily brushed the tears from her eyes. "Why was I never returned to my parents?"

"If we took you back to Patras, the Turks would have captured you and taken you as a slave. If we took you to England, they would have thought we stole you and would have put us in prison. Each year that passed, the idea of returning you to England became more painful to me. When I became a widow, you became even more important in my life. I did not want to part with you. I wanted to teach you fortune-telling, to make you follow my foot-steps, but that is not to be." Mirela's shoulders sagged.

Lily felt mixed emotions. On the one hand, she felt sad for the loss of her real parents, and at the same time, guilty. How ungrateful she must appear to her grandmother. She stood up, clutching the paper. "Why should I go after all these years? No one came for me. No one cared to find me." She paced the small tent, flailing her thin arms around. "How do I know whether or not my parents are alive? What if no one is there to take me?"

"There is another reason I want you to leave. Now that you are sixteen, of marriageable age, Count Igor plans to take you as his wife so he could claim your inheritance from your English relatives."

Lily recoiled from the news. Count Igor was the leader of the gypsy caravan. She had known him ever since she was a child. He was darkly handsome, but so much older. Her friend Sultana had spoken openly about her feelings of adoration for him. "Are you sure about this? I do not want to marry him! Sultana wants him."

"Why do you think he never married?" Mirela hissed. "He should have had a family by now. Instead, he has been waiting all these years for you to grow up. He plans to leave for Germany after the festival ends."

"Germany?"

"There, he will meet with his cousin's caravan and the two caravans will become one, leaving Count Igor free to take you to England and marry you there. After your marriage, he wants to take you to the attorney's office and claim your inheritance. I cannot allow this to happen."

"How can that be?" Lily cried.

"I have seen the future. You are not meant to marry Count Igor." She stopped, not wanting to go further. "I will deal with him when the time comes. He will listen to me."

Lily stared at her feet, a tight feeling forming in her chest. She did not want to leave her grandmother. She was the only family she had.

Mirela rose, her arms outstretched. "*Ela etho*. Come here." Lily ran into her open arms. "Things will be all right, my dear, you will see," she crooned, stroking Lily's head.

The sound of the men's voices outside was loud and boisterous. Count Igor and his band of musicians had arrived and apparently had a few rounds of drinks before coming here.

Mirela scrambled up, grabbing her lit candle. "Stay here." She hurried outside.

Lily stuffed the purse into her skirt pocket and threw the wig on her head, and then pushed the front flap of the tent to the side, peeking out into the breezy night. Emilian and Iakov, members of the band, were descending from the wagon, while Count Igor stood in front of his horse talking to Mirela. Mirela handed him a pouch of coins.

"Where is Lily?" Count Igor asked Mirela. He glanced at the tent.

Lily dropped the flap and withdrew back into the safety of the tent, feeling guilty at eavesdropping.

"She is inside getting things ready."

Lily busied herself with preparations. Emilian and Iakov entered the tent, greeting her cheerfully. They transported the furniture to the cart. Within minutes, they were dismantling the tent. No one seemed to notice her pensive face. They were too happy.

"It was a wonderful day," Emilian announced. "Everyone made good money at the fair."

Lily learned that Count Igor had sold his black stallion, *Night Dust*. He had made a bundle. Soon, they were heading to the camp. Lily and her grandmother sat quietly in the back of the wagon while the men sang with gusto.

Strains of violin music greeted their ears as they entered the gypsy camp. Several gypsies danced with abandon around the campfire, accompanied by whooping sounds and clapping. Lily's friends, Sultana and Fifi were among those dancing. Even the children were still up, playing and running around.

Babushka sat in the middle of the camp, stirring the large pot over the campfire. "There is plenty of stew left," she called out to them.

Mirela excused herself, feigning tiredness, and Lily did the same. She followed her grandmother's footsteps down the path, away from the group, and into the dark, safe haven of their round tent. She did not feel like eating anything or conversing with any of her friends. Too much turmoil weighed her young heart down, and she worried that they would eventually tease the truth out of her.

She did not want them to know that she was a *gadjo*.

With a determination that was to help her later in life, Lily lit a candle, and then retrieved the knife. "Come, *Yiayia*. Help me cut off the burned edges of my hair."

With a steady hand, Mirela sliced off the offending chunks of singed hair. "Do not worry, it will grow back again. Life is that way. You lose some and you win some."

As each long strand fell, Lily felt as if she were relinquishing her innocence, her naïve existence, and allowing a new life to begin. With a solemn air, she bent down and retrieved a lock of her silky flaxen hair from the small heap on the floor. "Please, take this to remember me."

Mirela took the strand. "I will always remember my dear Lily."

Lily dug a hole in the ground next to the black trunk. She buried her hair, covering it with dirt. She rose and wiped her dirty hands. "How shall I prepare for the trip?"

"Look in that black trunk. It has English clothes. I kept them all these years, thinking they might be needed one day."

Lily opened the chest. It held folded dresses. "How did you get these?"

"Do you think I was always a gypsy?" Mirela asked with a doleful shake of her head. "I was born in England a long time ago, to a squire."

Lily was astonished to hear this.

"I was the oldest of five children, and when I was seventeen, my father died and we had to work," Mirela continued. "I became a personal maid to Mrs. Evermore. She gave me these clothes. When I was nineteen, I met Petroff at the town fair. He was singing and dancing with his group. We fell in love and once we married, I became a gypsy."

Feeling bewildered, Lily had always assumed that her grandmother was born a gypsy.

"I know what you are thinking," Mirela commented. "You are probably wondering why I did not tell you sooner." She shook her head. "There was no reason for me to tell you this story. Not until now."

"What was it like, becoming a gypsy?"

"At first, it was wild and beautiful, and free, and so different from English life, but soon I noticed there were problems. Wherever we went, I was dismayed at how poorly people treated us. There was no respect for us. There was a bad stigma attached to the gypsies. Even though we made an honest living, it made no difference to them."

Lily thought about Mirela's words as she dipped her fingers into the cold water from the basin. She wiped her hands and chose a gray, muslin dress from the trunk. Her fingers smoothed the wrinkled fabric. "I wonder what happened to Mrs. Evermore."

"She is resting," Mirela said cryptically. "There are also some shoes in there."

Lily slipped pair of black shoes on her feet and winced. "These are too tight." She tossed them to the side. "I will not wear them. I will just go bare--"

"No, you will not," Mirela scolded. "There are rules of society you will need to abide by in order to fit in. For instance, never take your shoes off in public. I will give you money to buy new ones in London, but until then, you must wear these."

"I do not like all these changes." Lily sighed. "What else do I need to know?"

"Do not speak unless spoken to, and never shout or swear." Mirela paused, as if thinking. "Never stay in a room alone with a man or speak to him alone, unless you are engaged or married to him. Else, you will be labeled as a loose woman. Always have a chaperone with you."

"What silly rules. Why is it a crime to speak to a man?"

"It just is. Oh, and do not wear any of your gold bracelets. They jingle too much and call attention to you. Keep them hidden in your bag. They can be exchanged for money."

Lily was thankful that it was so late and that no one had come by to interrupt them, including her friends who were too busy enjoying the festivities. They would have been shocked to see English ladies' clothes strewn all over the cots.

"Here, I almost forgot. Take these with you. You must use these to eat with, instead of your fingers," Mirela said, pulling out a silver spoon and a knife from the trunk and handing them to her.

Lily fingered them. "They must have cost you quite a bit."

"I did not pay for them. Grateful clients have made these possible," Mirela said, smiling. "Now finish your packing. We must get ready for bed. You have a big day tomorrow."

Chapter 3

Lily rose just before daybreak and tripping through the woods, she scampered down the hill headed for the nearby creek. Today was a turning point in her life. She was going to find her parents and live in a place she would call home, and stay there *forever* and leave the gypsy way of life *forever*.

The icy cold water of the creek refreshed her and afterwards, she strolled alongside its bank, her bare feet stepping on the dew-kissed grass. She listened to the gurgling sounds of the water and the birds chirping somewhere in the distance. A few minutes later, Lily stopped in an apple orchard to pluck apples off the branches. She had to reach high for the apples, for the lower branches had already been picked. A dog barked in the distance. Lily fled into the sheltering cover of the woods.

Before entering the tent, she visited her horse *Tsingana*. Tethered to a tree behind their tent, the black horse with the white spot on her forehead, bobbed her head and playfully nipped Lily's wet curls.

Lily laughed. "Oh, no. My hair is off limits. Here, have this instead." She fed her an apple, speaking quietly to her and patting her mane, and then slipped inside the tent.

"*Kalimera*," Mirela greeted her from the bed. "You washed down at the creek?"

Lily's fingers nervously ran through her wet crop of curls as she nodded.

"You did not want anyone to see your short hair, so you arose early. You are unsure of yourself, just like a little bird learning how to fly. Are you excited about the dance today? I know you have been looking forward to it."

Lily was silent. A few days ago, Sultana had asked her to be part of the dance group at the fair, and she was excited about the opportunity to dance today, but the thrill had been replaced last night by her grandmother's news.

"It is not so important now. What matters is for me to find my real parents."

"In the small trunk are the black wig and clothes to wear for the dance."

The wig engulfed Lily's head. She secured a wine-colored headscarf around her head to hold it in place. Minutes later, she was dressed in a bright yellow blouse and wide blue skirt with three layers of colorful skirts underneath. She tied an orange sash around her slim waist.

"I can smell the coffee. Go and get some before it is gone. *Ante.*"

Lily grabbed two cups and flew outside. By now, the camp was bustling, as everyone prepared for the festival; goods were being stuffed into the cart wagons, while the musicians practiced their music.

Babushka's heavy body sat placidly by the campfire as she stirred the morning porridge. "You are already dressed for the dance. Good. Is that a new hairpiece?" she asked, her eyes squinting.

Lily's hand flew to her wig. Even with her poor eyesight, Babushka never missed a thing. "Yes. *Tsingana* chewed holes in the other one."

Babushka laughed, her big belly jiggling. "That horse will eat anything. I caught her yesterday at the fair, chewing on a lady's hat." She continued stirring the porridge in the large pot, and then lifted the spoon. "Have some nice porridge."

Lily eyed the gray porridge with distaste. It was a fact that not only Babushka's eyesight was poor, but so was her cooking. The last time Lily ate Babushka's infamous fish soup, she almost choked on a small chicken bone that had mysteriously found its way into the soup.

"Not now. I came to fetch coffee." Lily handed her the mugs. "Are the girls up yet?"

Babushka chuckled. "When did you ever see Sultana and Fifi up before eight?"

"Count Igor said we should be dressed and ready to leave by eight so we could get an early spot before the others claim it," Lily announced.

"Don't you worry. He always says that, and no one is ever ready by then, not even him." Babushka chuckled as she handed her the mugs filled with coffee. "Here's your hot coffee. I made it strong."

Lily thanked her and hurried back to the tent. They drank the hot brew and munched on biscuits and apples.

"You will ride *Tsingana* down to the square," Mirela said. "Do not go with the other girls in the wagon. After the dancing, you will not help with the selling of trinkets, but will excuse yourself. Tell Count Igor I am too weak this morning and need your help. From there, we will proceed with the plan."

ৰ্জ্যৰ্জ্যৰ্জ্য

Later that morning, Edward entered the hotel dining area. His cousin, Sir Douglas Charleton, was already seated and eating. Edward joined him and helped himself to the food.

"The French make the best cuisine. Help yourself to this scrumptious feast, cousin," Sir Douglas said, slathering butter on his warm, crusty bread. "Gertrude sends her apologies, but as you know she is a late riser and will probably eat something in her room."

"Quite all right." Edward bit into a delicate croissant. "Did you buy the stallion?"

"Yes, and what a price! But he is worth it. He is truly of high caliber and in excellent condition. I can't wait to race him." Sir Douglas stopped chewing and stared at him. "Really, Edward, what happened to your clothes? They look positively--"

Edward winced. "The only good suit I had was damaged last night from some smoke, and Herman, my valet, offered me one of his own. The rest of my clothes had already been shipped to England".

"Sorry, I could not offer you any of my clothes to wear," Sir Douglas replied, smirking. "You always were taller and thinner than me."

"It is of no consequence. We will be in London soon and everything will return to normal."

After breakfast, they strolled outside. The festivities in Caen had continued for one more day. Strains of gypsy music, accompanied by shouts, could be heard in the distance.

"Sounds like the gypsies," Edward said. "Shall we attend?"

Bells from the nearby Saint-Sauveur le Vieux church chimed rhythmically as the two men joined the festivities.

⋘ ⋘ ⋘

In the square, Count Igor's bass voice crooned out a French love song, while the violin wailed and whined, and the dulcimer provided the necessary chords. Once the song finished, Count Igor bowed to his audience.

The crowd whistled and clapped with enthusiasm. "*Encore! Encore!*"

Lily and the other girls retrieved their tambourines, positioning themselves around Sultana. The next song was a mixture of contradictions, beginning with a yearning, mournful slow rhythm and ending with a happier, lively theme. The girls tapped and jiggled their tambourines, swaying around Sultana as she performed her famous solo dance. The pace quickened, and the girls became a vivid blur of colors as they twirled and danced passionately.

At some point, Lily sensed her scarf loosening, and slowed down. Her hand flew up to her wig and stayed there for the rest of the dance, causing Count Igor to stare at her with consternation. The pace picked up and they twirled faster and faster. Just when Lily thought she would drop from exhaustion, the music ended. Sultana laughed exultantly as she bowed to the sound of wild clapping.

After the dance, the gypsy girls dispersed into the crowd, jiggling their tambourines and collecting coins. Weaving through the crowd, receiving offerings, Lily approached two English speaking men. The stocky one had brown hair and wore a black, well-tailored suit with a white cravat and black hat, suggesting he was nobility, while the taller one was dressed in ill-fitting clothing, suggesting that he was the man's servant.

Lily jiggled her tambourine at the well-dressed man. "*Merci, Monsieur,*" she said, just as she had been told to do.

"Look what we have here," the well-dressed man drawled. He took his glass monocle from his pocket and peered from under it, his brown eye appearing hugely swollen. He turned to his servant. "This dancer has the audacity to thank me before I give her money. Edward, do you think she deserves to be rewarded?"

Lily was jolted back into reality by this man's questions. Until now, people would toss a coin in her tambourine and she would be off. Squaring her shoulders and jutting her chin, she turned her gaze defiantly at the servant. She blinked, for he was exceptionally handsome. He had shiny, black hair, broad shoulders and slim hips. He gazed at her with brilliant dark eyes.

"I'm afraid my knowledge in such matters is very limited, Sir Douglas, although I do think they danced well enough," he replied.

Sir Douglas cocked an arrogant eyebrow. "I am appalled that they allowed her to dance with Sultana's superb group. She is too thin, has no grace, and no style."

Lily stepped back, feeling agitated at the man's words. He must surely think she did not know English to be insulting her. She was about to move away when someone pushed into her from behind, causing her to lurch forward, ramming her head into a man's solid chest.

"*Oof,*" Lily muttered, ready to cry, feeling the heat of embarrassment creep up to her face. Strong arms grabbed her, helping her steady herself. She looked up, but could only see black. Her hairpiece had rotated on her head. Laughter burst forth around her as she stepped back, muttering and guiding her wig into its place. The handsome servant was staring at her in a mystified manner.

Lily turned on her heels and sped away from the crowd. At least she still had the other coins. Her eyes checked the tambourine for reassurance. She stopped in her tracks when she saw the empty tambourine. The coins must have fallen when someone pushed her from behind. How was she going to go back into that crowd and find that money? How was she going to face Count Igor? This was Lily's first time dancing with the girls, and she had failed. Her shoulders slumped forward.

Someone tapped her on the shoulder. Lily whirled and faced the handsome English servant.

"*Pour vous, Mademoiselle,*" he said, dropping several coins in her tambourine.

Lily looked up, about to thank him, but he had already disappeared into the crowd. Maybe the rich man repented what he had said about her and sent his servant to pay her.

Feeling much better, Lily hurried towards the other gypsy girls who were already in line handing their coins to Count Igor.

He nodded at her earnings and dropped a coin in her palm. He held her hand. "You have done well for your first time, although you must tell Mirela to get you another wig." His voice was low and he gazed at her intently. "I must speak to you."

Lily blushed, remembering what her grandmother had said about him. Even worse, Sultana was close enough to hear, and she was watching them. Lily withdrew her hand, dropping the coin inside her skirt. "I cannot stay, for Grandmother is ailing and needs me. She said it is important that I go to her right after the dancing."

Count Igor nodded, appearing skeptical. "We will speak tonight, then."

Lily rode *Tsingana* as fast as she could towards the camp. When she arrived, the camp was eerily quiet, as everyone had gone to the fair. She found her grandmother lying in bed, with reddened eyes. Lily wondered if she had been crying. English dresses lay on Lily's cot.

"How did everything go with the dancing?" Mirela asked, sitting up.

"Fine," Lily said, staring at the dresses on her bed. The reality of what she was about to do was finally sinking in. With great resolve not to cry, she turned her focus back to her grandmother's conversation. "Count Igor wanted to talk to me, but I told him I had to come to you."

"By the time that he returns from the fair tonight, you will be far away."

As Lily slipped into the gray, muslin dress, she was beginning to feel miserable.

"I almost forgot to tell you that Lady Charleton knows you by a fictitious name, a Miss Judith Montefrey. This way, no one will be able to trace you back to us."

"Miss Judith Montefrey," Lily said, rolling the name over her tongue.

"Also, you are to act sick. That way people will not want to start a conversation with you." Mirela retrieved a small jar from the trunk. "This is a special white paint, given to me by a rich patron. Your skin must be pale white if you are to act sick. Besides, ladies never have tans."

Lily watched in dismay as the mysterious, white paste was spread lavishly on her face.

సౖు సౖు సౖు

Much later that afternoon, Gertrude and Sir Douglas entered the lobby of the French hotel, talking in raised voices.

"Are you sure this girl is not deathly ill?" Sir Douglas asked.

"Dear, I only promised I would chaperone her to the attorney's office," Gertrude insisted. "Her family is supposed to collect her there."

Edward and his valet, Herman, and Mariette, Lady Charleton's maid, were waiting for them in the lobby.

"The carriage is ready," Edward announced. "Shall we go then?"

"Yes, but there is one other person coming with us," Gertrude declared. "I promised a friend that I would chaperone her cousin's daughter to London. She is very ill and the doctors here cannot help her."

"Why does her family not come for her?" Edward asked.

"Time is of essence, they say. Her family lives in York, and it would take them take too long to come here and get her. They plan to meet her in London. Hopefully, our doctors there can help her."

"That is commendable of you," Edward told Gertrude, smiling at her. He always liked to see acts of kindness towards others.

"She is probably outside this very minute, waiting for me. Mariette, please go and have a look."

Mariette peered outside, and then returned, shaking her head. "She is not here, my lady."

"I feel very uncomfortable traveling with a sick girl," Sir Douglas muttered, loosening his cravat nervously. "If the doctors here cannot help her, what makes you think ours can? It will probably be necessary to use a handkerchief to protect yourself."

Gertrude appeared flustered. "Indeed, I had not thought about it. Do you think she is that ill?"

"Just a precaution, my dear, just a precaution."

"Oh, well. A promise is a promise. Dear, you go on ahead with Edward," Gertrude said, sighing. She pulled out a handkerchief from her purse and held it to her nose, preparing to meet the girl. "She might not feel well enough to travel with all of us, either."

"I hope she shows up soon. I do not want us to be late," Sir Douglas grumbled as he left with Edward, heading for their packet ship.

Chapter 4

Lily hurried down the narrow, cobblestoned street, clutching her satchel with one hand and keeping her bonnet in check with the other hand. She was late, and hoped Lady Charleton hadn't left yet. The road broadened, and she continued past elegant, Caen stone homes, and several dignified looking buildings, and a tall church. The ornate hotel loomed up ahead. Lily slowed to a walk, trying to catch her breath. She had arrived.

Lady Charleton stood in front of the hotel, speaking to the coachman. She wore purple traveling clothes and a matching plumed hat. Lily's gloved hand nervously ran down her wrinkled, gray dress, trying to smooth it.

Lady Charleton turned and waved to her with a handkerchief. "Hello! You must be Miss Montefrey. I am Lady Charleton. You are quite late, my dear. My husband left already for the port twenty minutes ago!"

Lily curtsied, her heart clamoring. "Lady Charleton. I apologize for my lateness. I have been ill."

"Indeed, you look quite ill, my girl. Did you walk here? You seem out of breath. Where is your carriage?" She had covered her nose with the handkerchief and her voice sounded muffled as she peered around.

Lily panicked. Her grandmother had driven her with the wagon and dropped her off a few blocks away. They hadn't thought about having her come with a carriage. "Ahh, the carriage, it broke down, and instead of finding another one, I thought it would be quicker to walk."

"Oh, you poor dear. You really must not tax yourself. What is it that ails you?"

Lily coughed, playing the part. "I have been very tired, and my stomach hurts. The doctor has given me medicine for it," she whispered. She placed her hand on her stomach.

"I was told that you caught this disease at the French boarding school you were staying at. I believe it was from some foreign students there?"

Lily's eyes widened, wondering what else her grandmother had concocted. She swallowed, and then nodded. Lady Charleton was fishing for more information, but she remained silent.

"Well, we shall see what we can do to get you back home safely where you can be treated properly."

Another woman appeared, holding a handkerchief to her nose. She was introduced as Mariette, Lady Charleton's personal maid. "Is that all you will be taking with you, *Mademoiselle*?" Mariette asked, pointing to Lily's bag. "Fred, the coachman, can put it with the rest of the luggage."

Lily clutched the bulging satchel close to her chest. Almost everything she had was in there, including her clothing, silverware, jewelry, and the coins her grandmother gave her. "Please, may I keep it with me? My medicine is in it."

"As you wish."

Once inside the carriage, Lily sank into the red, velvet seat next to the window, easing her feet out of the tight shoes, and placing the bag in front of them. The carriage exuded wealth, from its rich interior decorations to the thick carpet. Lady Charleton pulled out a small bottle of French perfume and delicately dabbed her handkerchief with it, issuing feathery wisps of the fruitful scent into the air.

A momentary lapse of silence ensued as the carriage jolted forward. Lily stared out the window. She did not notice the church, with its ornately carved stone facade, as they passed it by, for her thoughts were in turmoil and her hands felt clammy. What was she getting herself into? She was sure that Lady Charleton would see through her thin disguise.

To her relief, Lady Charleton started a conversation with Mariette about French fashion. "Madame Tourdeau did a wonderful job on my new ball dress," she began, chatting about its details.

As they reached the intersection, Lily spied Mirela sitting in the wagon, waving sadly to her. She was about to wave back, and then stopped, not wanting to draw attention to her grandmother. Instead, her moist eyes remained riveted on the fading image of her grandmother until she was no longer in view. Lily's heart wept, shedding silent tears. With great difficulty, she turned her attention to the discussion in the carriage.

"Madame Tourdeau has such exquisite taste. There is no one like her. I tried to convince her to open a shop in London. We would provide the textiles for her, but she would hear nothing of it. All her family is in France, she says."

At one point, Lady Charleton's gaze settled on Lily's face. "Oh, dear." She covered her nose with the scented handkerchief and was silent.

"I am good friends with Suzette, her cousin," Mariette informed Lady Charleton, appearing smug. "She confided in me that Madame Tourdeau was recently commissioned by a French nobleman and his family for a considerable amount of money."

"That is why she was so reluctant to take on my sister's wedding dress!" Lady Charleton exclaimed. "I had to pay a pretty price before she would listen. It will be the best in London, with pearls and lace, and the finest silk available. I expect it to arrive in two weeks, but my sister does not know about the dress." She looked at Mariette meaningfully.

Mariette blushed. "You have my word on it, my lady. I will not tell a soul."

The sun was beginning to set when they reached the port. The workers bundled the last of the cargo onto the packet ship, casting their shadows in the golden glow.

Lily's fingers probed into her satchel for coins. "Lady Charleton, I would like to pay my fare to Portsmouth," she said.

"There is no need, Miss Montefrey. It's been taken care of."

A gust of cool air shot through the carriage as the coachman opened the door.

"There you are, Fred. Please take me to Sir Douglas." Lady Charleton turned to Mariette. "Stay here. The carriage will continue into the ship. I will send a servant to guide you to your quarters. Good night."

Once their carriage was securely inside the ship, a servant arrived. Lily and Mariette followed him into the bowels of the ship, down a flight of stairs, and through a dimly lit passageway to their room, which was near another stairwell.

The small room was dark, with two beds, a table and a round window.

"You can sleep here," Mariette said, pointing to the one bed. She arranged her hair, humming a gay French tune, and then excused herself to go and see her mistress. "She will need my services."

After her departure, Lily slipped out of her shoes and sank into her bed, unable to sleep. Her grandmother's makeup was working too well. Everyone was avoiding her, thinking she was ill, including Mariette. Lily was beginning to feel lonely. She had no one to share her thoughts with, and her anxiety had been mounting all day.

For the hundredth time that day, Lily wondered what she would find in London. Would her family accept her after all these years? Doubts assailed her. What if they thought she were only a gypsy, telling them lies? Her hand crept towards the satchel. She had the document and locket to prove her identity. That should suffice. *What if they still did not accept the truth? What would I do then?*

A loud horn sounded above, breaking Lily's thoughts. She shot up and peered out the window into the descending evening. There was much creaking, as if the ship was about to break apart. She shuddered at the idea of being inside that small room if anything serious happened. Lily ran barefoot up the stairs onto the deck. The black canvas of the night sky, sprinkled with tiny shining stars, reminded her of the times she sat outside at night with her friends and counted them. The ship rocked, and she held the rail firmly while the wind whipped her dress about her.

"All the passengers are in, then?"

Lily shrunk against the rail when she realized that the male voice was nearby.

"Then let us set sail."

The two men walked away and it wasn't long before the ship rolled and rocked from the strong waves. Lily stumbled downstairs to her room, then tripped over her shoes that lay on the floor and landed with acrobatic aplomb on her bed. Somewhere between feeling nausea and dozing off, in the recesses of her mind she could hear her grandmother scolding her for not wearing her shoes.

Mariette entered the dark room, humming. "*Mademoiselle, c'est temps pour dejeuner,*" she announced gaily.

Lily peeked at the shadowy scene from under her lashes as Mariette kit a candle. The aroma of some unknown food tickled Lily's nose, causing another bout of nausea to arise. A tray of food and a pitcher of wine had been deposited on the table. "I cannot eat. I feel so sick!"

Mariette clucked compassionately, and then appeared content enough to sit and eat all the fare on the tray. "I am blessed with a strong stomach," she said between mouthfuls.

The rocking of the ship and the stifling nature of the small room made for a fitful night of unrest for Lily.

Early the next morning, the sound of the ship's horn awakened Lily.

"Come, Mademoiselle. We must get ready." Mariette stared at her, and then sucked in her breath. "*Mon Dieu!*" she exclaimed.

Lily shot up from bed. "What is it?"

"Your face. You feel very ill, *n'est ce pas?*"

A short while later, a groggy Lily was assisted by a concerned Mariette down the ramp and on to the dock. The darkness was already beginning to fade as the promise of dawn appeared in the sky. The harbor in Portsmouth was a hive of activity, with much commotion. Streams of laborers, like worker ants, exited the ship, carrying supplies on their backs, and then placing them on to the merchants' horse-drawn wagons, amidst shouts and calls. Eager buyers milled around the merchants, haggling for the best price for materials.

Lily leaned against the rail, feeling suddenly weak.

"Can you stay here?" Mariette told Lily, appearing concerned. "I see Lady Charleton and must go to her, but I do not want you to walk too much."

She hurried away into the crowd.

Lily heard her tell someone, "The girl is very sick! She slept all the time. Her face is now patchy, with brown spots, and she did not eat anything throughout the whole trip. I do not know if she will make it to London."

"Oh, dear. I fear her situation is worse than we thought," Lady Charleton replied, with consternation in her voice. "I should have called for a doctor before taking her. I hope she makes it to her house."

"I will not allow you to travel with her to London!" Sir Douglas Charleton scolded his wife. "It might be contagious."

Lily's stomach did a nosedive as her hand fluttered to her face. She had no idea how she looked. The paste must have worn off in some areas when she slept, showing her sunburned skin underneath. Her feet, saddled with the tight shoes, inched away from the crowd. Maybe she should continue the rest of the journey by herself so as not to cause difficulties. A nagging problem presented itself. Where could she find a coach without calling attention to herself?

"*Mademoiselle!*"

Lily turned to see Mariette rushing towards her.

"I panicked when I did not find you where I left you. I thought you might have fallen into the water!" Mariette scolded her, gesturing wildly in the air. "Come, we are *tres* late."

"Where are we going?" Lily asked, feeling relieved, as Mariette dragged her away.

"We are to take the post chaise into London, you and I. Lady Charleton gives her regrets that she could not attend to you, but she has more pressing obligations."

∞∞∞

Edward and his valet, Herman, arrived mid-morning at Lord Peterborough's home in Grosvenor Square. Sir Douglas and

Lady Charleton lived a few blocks away and promised to stop by later, after they had arranged their affairs first.

Edward greeted the aging butler amiably. "Good morning, Samuel."

"Good morning, Mr. Grant," Samuel replied, bowing. "Welcome back."

"Indeed, it is good to be back," Edward said. "Did my luggage arrive from Italy?"

"Yes. Late last night. They are in your room. I also took the liberty of putting the calling cards along with your mail in your room."

"Good. See that a warm bath is prepared." Edward strode up the stairs with Herman following at his heels. Once in his bedroom, he read his mail and cards.

Herman poked through the valises with relish, pulling out a painting and a small Greek cap. "Mr. Grant, what do you want done with the paintings and these other items?"

"Check them for any damages. I have yet to decide where to put them."

An hour later, feeling refreshed from his wash and wearing a new change of clothes, Edward visited his father's room. The dark chamber smelled of illness. His father appeared to be asleep. The plump nurse sat to the side of his bed, slumbering.

Edward strode towards the window and swung the curtains open, flooding the room with sunlight. He could not bear to see his father in this way.

The nurse awoke with a start when she saw Edward, then introduced herself as Nurse Nellie.

Lord Peterborough's eyes fluttered open. "Who goes there?"

"It is Edward. I have just returned from my journey abroad."

Lord Peterborough's haggard face lit up. "You have arrived at last. Sit down and tell me your news." He stopped to cough in a series of rhythmic patterns, and then wiped his mouth with a weariness that had penetrated his soul. "I cannot get rid of this sticky cough. Once it begins, it does not want to go away. Nurse, get me the medicine."

Nurse Nellie arose and gave him his medicine. It seemed to help with his coughing.

"That is better," Lord Peterborough said, leaning back and sighing. "Now, tell me about your travels."

Edward complied. He told him about the various countries he visited, and their cultures. "Imagine my distress when I received your news about your illness. I left everything and came as soon as I could."

"Did you meet Douglas in France? He said he would meet you there."

"Yes. We traveled here together. They will be arriving shortly."

Lord Peterborough fixed his gaze on the nurse. "I want to speak with my son privately." He waited as she left the room. He turned his tired eyes on Edward. "My illness has progressed and I must speak to you about your responsibilities as heir."

Edward was to inherit everything, including the ten thousand-acre country manor house in York, with its school, rented cottages, farm and cattle, and the townhouse in London, as well as all the savings, stocks and bonds. He would have a seat in Parliament with a title of Baron, and his father's older sister, Mabel Grant, a spinster in her sixties, would be under his care.

"Your aunt prefers to stay in the country home rather than come to London," Lord Peterborough continued.

Edward nodded. Aunt Mabel was like a mother to him, after his mother passed away when he was twelve. "Do not worry. I am aware of my duties to everyone, including Aunt Mabel."

"I am pleased. You have always been a good son."

Edward asked him about Mr. Benton, who was the manager of the estate.

"We lost him two years ago to consumption. Yes, it was a sad affair."

"That is an unfortunate bit of news."

"I have not been able to keep up with the books due to my illness. Indeed, they are in need of a good going over. Now that you are here, you should become involved in the estate."

"Yes, Father."

"One more thing." Lord Peterborough started coughing again. His voice was raspy when he resumed talking. "You are aware that all our ancestors were blessed with healthy male heirs to pass on their title and inheritance. You are next in line and you must marry and beget a son. All the Grants have had sons." He stopped, wiping his mouth with the back of his unsteady hand. "You are in your prime, twenty-six years old. This is a good age to settle down. I want you to promise me that you will marry soon, before I die."

Edward felt the heat rise to his face, trying to control the agitation that arose in him. Marriage was not a topic he was ready to discuss. Not now. He arose, pacing the room. "You are asking me to promise you that I will marry a person who does not even exist." He gave his father a challenging look.

"What about Gertrude's sister, Charlotte?"

Edward stared at his father, feeling dumbstruck. He had known her since she was a young girl, and she had always been a troublemaker. He could not imagine her as wife material for anyone, let alone him. "We will talk about this at another time," he answered tensely. "I will leave you to rest."

Edward headed to the study. He sat brooding about his father's health and the future. He knew that eventually he would marry, yet the urgency of his father's request could not be ignored. How could he choose a life companion on such short notice? There was not enough time to court anyone seriously.

He had plenty of opportunities to marry in the past, with hopeful mothers vying for their daughters every chance they could get. But he had not been ready then. He wanted to travel the world, to become his own man first, and he did. Women easily came and went in his life, but to choose one woman above the rest to become his lifetime partner was a different matter. She would have to be perfect.

He wondered if he would ever be ready for marriage.

A knock on the door aroused Edward from his reflective mood. "Come in."

Sir Douglas entered the room. "I just visited your father. I am afraid his condition is getting worse." He sat down.

"I know," Edward said pensively. "Would you like something to drink?"

"I am feeling rather parched."

Edward poured him some cherry brandy. "Tell me, cousin. What do you think about Gertrude's sister, Lottie?"

Sir Douglas smirked. "As a spouse for you, or as a sister-in-law?"

"Both," Edward replied. "The last time I saw Lottie was when I returned one summer from college. She was barely a woman then, somewhat unrestrained, I remember. Tell me, how is she now?"

"Oh, I would say she is no longer the same Lottie, the one who always tagged around us, getting into mischief. Oh, no," Sir Douglas said, chuckling. "I would have you know that she does not like to be called Lottie anymore, but Charlotte. I admit that she has become quite an attractive woman."

"Yes, but is she kind and thoughtful to others?"

"She helps Gertrude in her charitable functions. That should be a consideration." Sir Douglas downed his drink. "I do know one thing. Every eligible bachelor in London has been calling on her, but she has not committed herself."

Edward was intrigued by the description.

Sir Douglas arose and stretched. "How about joining me at White's? I have told some old friends at the club about your arrival and they are eager to see you."

"All right then," Edward said.

Chapter 5

A guard dressed in scarlet livery stood in the back of the coach, blowing his brass horn, while the driver sat perched on top. Several passengers lined up like crows. Lily and Mariette hurried toward the maroon and black mail coach.

"We get to sit inside," Mariette informed Lily.

They entered the coach. The air was pungent from the smell of whiskey, tobacco, and body odor from the five people already inside. Once the passengers saw Lily, they all wanted to sit as far away from her as they could, arguing for the seat "nearest the window."

During the journey, Lily shut her eyes, pretending to sleep, not wanting to talk to anyone. After some time, the coach stopped at an inn.

"Would you like to come along and freshen up? Maybe take a breakfast of tea and warm rolls?" Mariette coaxed. "You might feel better."

Lily shook her head. She had considered the idea of washing at the inn, but was afraid it would reveal her tan. There would be questions asked. Instead, she slumped in her seat, shutting her eyes. She heard Mariette sigh as she left with the other passengers.

Not having slept the night before, Lily fell into a deep sleep. She was oblivious of the fact that at the inn, Mariette became the center of attention as she chatted with the other passengers, telling them that Lily had an "unknown" illness. "Even her chaperone became mysteriously ill and I had to come in her place. For all I know, I may already have it!"

There was much murmuring and raised eyebrows. When the coach resumed its journey, the remaining passengers chose to sit outside on the coach, holding on tightly through the rough road passages, rather than be inside with Lily and risk contracting a mysterious disease. Implicitly quarantined by the other passengers, Mariette contentedly stretched out on her seat, enjoying the rest of the ride.

Once in London, the coach stopped at the General Post Office. From there, they took a hackney to the Clemence and Hartford Law office. They passed a string of shops, including a candle shop, bookstore, bakery store, and shoe store. There was a bit of congestion as barouches, phaetons, carriages, and pedestrians all vied to use the same thoroughfare.

Dark clouds overhead suggested an upcoming downpour as the hackney stopped in front of the law office. Mariette told her that she could not stay because the rain would begin any minute. Her employer's dwelling was on the west side of town.

"I hope you feel better," Mariette sang out as she rode away.

It seemed that Grandmother Mirela's idea with the white paste worked too well. *Everyone is afraid of my illness, but I will remedy that soon.*

Lily entered the office and glanced around her. The room had very tall windows, expensive looking cherry furniture and landscape paintings. A man sat at a desk in the center of the room. He studiously wrote figures into a large book.

Ipatia cleared her throat. He looked up at her. He was thin, with a long, beak nose, and few wisps of hair on his head. A nervous twitch had formed in one of his bulging eyes and it seemed to get worse as he stared in horror at her face.

"Are you the attorney?"

"No. I am Mr. Watson, the clerk. Do you have an appointment?"

"No, but I am the lost daughter of Frederic Montgomery." Lily approached him and pulled out the document from her bag. She showed it to him. "Here is proof. I would like to speak with the attorney."

As he read it, she looked around her in naïve anticipation, wondering where the attorney was. He would save her and send her to her proper family.

"Mr. Hartford is the only one in today and he is a very busy man!" he snapped. He stared at her face. Now both of his eyes were twitching nervously.

Lily's stomach plummeted. She had expected a more welcoming reception. A long-lost daughter appearing out of nowhere was not something that occurred every day. "I must see him," she insisted. "I have nowhere else to go."

"Then you will have to wait. He is with other clients." Mr. Watson shook his head, pointing to the seats at the far end of the room, under the large windows.

The early overcast sky gave a rare appearance of the sun and its rays peeked through the window, basking her in its warmth.

"Excuse me, Mr. Watson, how can I get some water?" she asked. She touched her throat. "I am very thirsty, and am not feeling well at all."

"*Hmmf.* You certainly do look ill. People like you should be home in bed," Mr. Watson replied, his eyebrows wrinkled, having a difficult time hiding his disgust. "There is only tea for our clients."

"May I have some, please? I will be a client very soon."

Mr. Watson grudgingly pointed to the silver tea set located on a table in the far corner behind him. "Be careful that you do not break anything, for you will have to pay for it," he muttered. In no time, he was dipping his head back into his book, scribbling away with his quill pen.

Lily poured herself a cup of tea. The china felt small and dainty in her hands. She stood there, savoring the lukewarm tea. This was not the watered-down tea she had tasted all her life, but strong, wholesome tea.

She did not drink it all, but instead, retrieved a handkerchief from her pocket and dipped it into the remaining brew. Turning her back on Mr. Watson, she scrubbed her face clean with it. She discreetly stuffed her dirtied handkerchief into her pocket, and returned to her seat. She slipped her feet out of her tight shoes and stared out the window at the people walking by.

By the time the door to the back room opened, Lily had counted twenty-four women, six children, fifteen gentlemen, thirty-two carriages, and ten phaetons that had passed by the window. She suppressed a yawn. An older, well-dressed couple came out of the room and exited the office. Lily jumped into her shoes and shot up, anticipation coursing through her young body. She strode to Mr. Watson's desk and leaned forward expectantly. "*Now* may I go in?"

Mr. Watson fixed his gaze on her transformed face. He appeared shocked. "Your face, that tea. You drank it and it cleared--" He was unable to complete his sentence as he turned and stared at the tea set and then back at her tanned face. "Hmm. I will check if he is available." He scuffled through the door into the other room, muttering,
"I might try some of that tea. It might help my nervous twitch."

A moment later, he returned. "Mr. Hartford can only see you briefly. His next appointment is due any minute."

She entered the office. The elegantly furnished room smelled of tobacco. A rather stout, young man sat at the desk. Dressed in formal attire depicting the role of attorney, he had a fair constitution, with insipid blue eyes and a weak chin.

They exchanged greetings.

"How may I help you?"

Lily eagerly handed him her legal document. "I am seeking my parents."

As Mr. Hartford read it, his eyebrows furrowed, and he shook his head. "This paper is more than ten years old." He handed it back to her. "I have only been in the practice one year, and young Mr. Clemence, two years. Our fathers passed away several years ago. They were the signers of the document."

"Did they not leave any instructions? Are there no papers regarding this matter in the office?"

Mr. Hartford's lips pressed tightly together. "Unfortunately, a fire three years ago burned the building down. Some say it was due to vandalism." He shrugged his shoulders.

"In any case, everything was lost, including all legal documents and paperwork. The building had to be rebuilt."

Lily stared at Mr. Hartford, stunned by the news. "I came all this way, thinking that you could help me find my parents." With trembling fingers, she unclasped her locket and handed it to him. "Please, Mr. Hartford, please look at these pictures. Maybe you will remember the faces, if not the names. My mother was Greek."

He studied the miniature portraits in the locket. "Come to think of it, I remember a client of my father who married a Greek heiress. There was some family tragedy."

"Could you tell me how I can get a hold of my father?"

"I cannot help you, but I am sure that my mother can. She knew every client of my father's, and usually invited them to dinner every chance she got. She said it was good for business," Mr. Hartford said wryly. He scribbled something on a sheet of paper, and then sealed it with his wax seal and handed it to her. "You will give this paper to my mother. It has my seal on it." He gave her the directions to the house.

"I am very much obliged," Lily exclaimed.

As she left the office, she noticed Mr. Watson hunched over his desk slurping down a cup of tea.

Lily breezed past several shops with enthusiasm before her feet began to complain from the tight shoes. She stopped in front of a shoe store, gazing inside the window. The scent of freshly baked bread from a nearby bakery assailed her senses, reminding her of her hunger.

Out of nowhere, a flower girl sang out, thrusting a bunch of wilted flowers in her face. She looked so young and pathetic, with her stringy hair and grimy face. Lily's heart lurched from pity. Digging a coin out of her pocket, she dropped it in her lap, and was rewarded by a bright smile.

"Get yourself a decent meal," Lily told her.

Lily hurried into the shoe store. After much haggling, she bought a comfortable pair of shoes and resumed her journey. At some point, the sun vanished under the newly formed clouds. It was about to rain.

She entered a residential area filled with stately, red brick Georgian townhouses lined up on either side of the street. They all looked alike.

Mrs. Hartford's residence was at the end of the street, and when Lily reached it, the first raindrops landed on her head. She dashed up the steps, the rain pelting her, and knocked on the door's brass knocker. She leaned against the door, trying to stay dry.

The door swung open.

"Ow!" Lily cried, tottering forward and sprawling onto the floor. She gathered herself up, shaking the water off of her clothing, and then picked up her opened satchel, stuffing her belongings back into it.

A distinguished looking butler dressed in a waistcoat with horizontal stripes, and formal knee breeches and stockings, stared down at her.

"I am here to see Mrs. Hartford."

"Off to the back with you, if you are looking for a free meal."

"Oh! I am not here for a free meal. I came to see her on a business matter. I *must* see her." With wet fingers, Lily pulled out the sealed paper that Mr. Hartford gave her and handed it to the butler.

His eyes grew wide when he saw the paper. With deliberate composure, he gestured her in. "Please wait here." He took the paper with him as he climbed the carpeted stairs and disappeared.

Lily was on the verge of breaking down and crying. Nothing seemed to be working out today. She was going from one person to the next, and so far, no parent had emerged.

The butler returned shortly and led her upstairs and into a large drawing room. The room was decorated to the point of opulence, from the damask-lined walls to the matching curtains and flower-filled vases and statues. Lily felt that she should have bathed and changed into clean clothing before entering. The wood floors were polished, and in the center of the room was a large Oriental carpet, upon which several pieces of Chippendale furniture rested.

Mrs. Hartford's well-dressed, generous frame sat comfortably on the plush sofa, with her embroidery work resting on her lap. She wore a kind expression on her plump face. "Please come in and have a seat, my dear."

Lily strode toward the sofa and perched herself on the edge, afraid to dirty it, while Mrs. Hartford read her son's paper.

"I understand that my son sent you regarding some person he thought I might know, that you were inquiring about?"

"Yes. I am looking for information on a Mr. Frederick Montgomery."

"Oh, you must mean *Sir* Frederick Montgomery."

"*Sir* Frederick Montgomery?" Lily shook her head. "You must be mistaken."

"I assure you I am not. We have known the family for many years. A good family," Mrs. Hartford affirmed with the tone of someone who knew very well, what she was saying. "His father died five years ago, and last year, his poor mother, Judith, joined him. She was my *dearest* friend. Their son, Frederick, inherited his father's title of baronet and now goes by Sir Frederick." She stopped, as if thinking. "Sir Frederick Montgomery travels a lot. We hardly see him anymore. We hear about him through his cousin, Cecilia, I mean Mrs. Bennington."

"Is Sir Frederick Montgomery married?" Lily ventured, holding her breath.

"Yes. Well, he was, but now, I mean, oh dear, it is somewhat complicated. Let me start from the beginning." Mrs. Hartford took a deep breath. "While on his grand tour, he met a Greek heiress on Corfu, an island near Greece. They fell in love and would you believe it, they married in two weeks. It was such a romantic match. The whole town was talking about it." Her eyes twinkled.

Lily's heart soared when she heard about her parents.

"It took his family by surprise, it did. But she was the daughter of a wealthy Greek merchant and brought money into the family and that made it all right." Mrs. Hartford chuckled. She leaned toward Lily. "He brought her back with him and they married again in a grand style. It was for his family. Judith insisted that they have a proper wedding, although marrying in a

Greek church is as proper as any church here, I say. Anyway, Mrs. Montgomery was so beautiful, and so gracious. I am sure that whoever met her, couldn't help liking her. I remember her well."

Mrs. Hartford's chattering stopped and she became reflective.

"They had a beautiful daughter, like a doll, she was. When they visited here, she played with my son. He was a few years older, and she followed him everywhere. I would speak with my dear husband afterwards, and we always said what a nice match they would make." Mrs. Hartford shook her head. "But their happiness was not to last. Such a sad story. Very sad indeed." Her voice trailed off.

"What do you mean?" Lily's heart thudded in her chest.

"It happened a few years later. The mother and daughter were visiting her parents in Greece. I think it was Patras. Yes, Patras. Mr. Montgomery was away on business. While his wife was in Patras, there happened to be an uprising, some type of revolt by the Greeks against the Ottomans, and they perished in the fire. It was such a terrible loss! See, I still have tears remembering it." Mrs. Hartford sniffled, and took out a handkerchief from her pocket and blew into it.

Lily was stunned. *My mother had perished in the fire with the rest of my family.* The tears swelled in her eyes as images of her mother's anguish filled her young heart with sadness. Her lips trembled and she felt weak all over, as if she were going to faint. She wiped her wet face with her sleeve, trying to maintain her composure.

"Poor Mr. Montgomery made an attempt to enter Patras, but they had closed the port, you see, and would let no one in. When he arrived, everything had burned to the ground, including the family home. It was sad." Mrs. Hartford shook her head. "It left him a changed man. He never remarried. He was so much in love with her, he was. I presume his title will eventually go to a cousin, since he has no sons."

Lily sniffled. "How can I get a hold of my father, Sir Frederick?"

"You *father?*" Mrs. Hartford looked at her askance. "Why you, that little darling girl that we loved so much, she was *you?* It is hard to believe he is your father! You are so dark, so different from him. How can I put it?" Her hand fanned her flushed face. "Such a dignified looking man and in such a high position! Oh my! How can this be?"

Lily explained to her the story, showing her the document and locket. "I have my mother's coloring, but my father's blue eyes and blonde hair." She removed her bonnet and shook her head, letting the short golden curls loose. "They called me Lily. I *do* remember that. It is short for Evangelia."

"One might see some resemblance if one looked hard enough." Mrs. Hartford studied her. "Your eyes are more green than blue, and your hair is blonde, but you are *quite* dark."

"That is a tan. I spent much time out in the sun with the gypsies."

"Oh, dear!" Mrs. Hartford said, looking flustered.

Lily knew she had to convince her somehow. She desperately pulled out her legal document from the bag and showed it to her. "See, here. That is my name. That is my father's signature. I came to the law firm, hoping to find out how to get a hold of my father, but your son did not know anything. He sent me here in case you could help me."

Mrs. Hartford read the document and her face softened. "I believe you, my dear! This is quite something, indeed. Raised up by gypsies. Oh my! How romantic. It will be the talk of the town."

"Would you know how I could get a hold of my father?"

"Oh, dear, did I not tell you? He is away, I fear, on another trip to the East Indies. He dabbles in trade there. Spices, I heard."

"He is?" Lily asked, feeling as if her world was caving in on her. *Nothing is going right.* "Are you sure?"

"Quite sure. I know, because his cousin, Mrs. Bennington told me. About a month ago, my son and I bumped into her at the theatre. She told me the news. She is a widow, and has an eighteen-year-old daughter."

"So I have cousins," Lily said, feeling a ray of hope. She could depend on someone until her father arrived.

"Once her year of mourning was over a few months ago, she has been after Sir Frederick." Mrs. Hartford leaned towards Lily conspiratorially. "I know, because she said she came to London this year for her daughter's coming out and is staying at his London townhouse while he is away. You see, that was the excuse she gave, but I heard that, oh, I forgot. I should not mention these things. How old did you say you were?"

"Sixteen."

"Oh, dear, I thought you were at least eighteen. You present yourself in a mature manner, I might say," Mrs. Hartford tittered. She rang for service. "Would you like some tea?"

Lily gulped. She was feeling hungry, but her pride pushed her to say, "Thank you for your time, but I should be going. I have overstayed my visit." She stood up, unsure as where to proceed next.

"But where are you going? You cannot wander the streets alone, a young girl your age. No, it will not do!" Mrs. Hartford retorted. "You must stay here until we notify your cousin. She is the most likely person for you to go to until your father returns."

"How could I ever repay you for your kindness?"

"How could I not help the granddaughter of my *dearest* friend, Mrs. Montgomery? No, you must remain here until we hear from your relations. To think that you are the lost Lily who has returned to us from the dead. We must get a letter out to your cousin right away. They live close by."

"Oh!"

Mrs. Hartford went to the writing desk in the corner and scribbled some words on a piece of paper. She folded the letter, and then sealed it with the wax seal. "I think this is the best way to approach this. Besides, you need me to explain things to her. I will send it immediately with a servant. We should be receiving a call from her later today. Mark my words."

Mrs. Hartford winked and rang for the butler.

Chapter 6

Later that afternoon, as expected, Cecilia Bennington and her daughter Marianne, arrived in Mrs. Hartford's drawing room. Mrs. Bennington was attractive in a sleek way, with blue eyes and honey blonde hair piled high on her head. She wore a peach, silk walking dress and exuded an air of elegance in her demeanor. Marianne was just as fair, and dressed all in white, with a slimmer figure and a demure look.

Mrs. Hartford made the introductions.

"I was astonished when I learned the news," Mrs. Bennington murmured to Mrs. Hartford, removing her gloves.

"So was I, so was I. The poor dear!" Mrs. Hartford exclaimed.

Mrs. Bennington's eyebrows shot up. She stared at Lily. "Her face is rather dark for a Montgomery. Our family is fair and doesn't tan, we burn."

"Oh, but you must remember, her mother was Greek, all that olive skin and such. But have a look at those beautiful eyes, her delicate bone structure, and that blonde hair," Mrs. Hartford said in earnest, as if she were trying to sell a horse. "Just like a Montgomery, do you not think so, my dear?"

"Many people have blue eyes and blonde hair, but that does not make them a Montgomery. Is there any other proof of her identity?"

"Dear, show them your papers," Mrs. Hartford told Lily.

With sinking heart, Lily pulled both the paper and locket from her satchel and handed them to Mrs. Bennington.

Mrs. Bennington read the document and gazed at the locket in stony silence, then shrugged with elegant indifference, returning the items to Lily. "Assuming these were not stolen by the gypsies and they lied to you, it appears that there might be some truth to all of this."

Lily straightened her back and stiffened her upper lip by the woman's implicit accusation about the gypsies. *How dare she say that?*

"How was it like, living with those savages? I hear that gypsies steal and lie to make a living," Marianne said, wide-eyed. "How did you ever manage to escape?"

"It is not like that at all! They were the nicest people to me," Lily retorted. "They raised me and took care of me. I did not escape, as you put it. They let me go willingly."

"What a kind dear," Mrs. Hartford exclaimed, smoothing over Lily's unladylike outburst. "Miss Montgomery is so loyal, and I could never see her saying a negative thing about anyone, even the gypsies." She gestured towards the sofa. "We were just having tea. Would you like to join us, my dears?"

They sat in the drawing room, where Mrs. Hartford served tea and small cakes. Her garrulous talk helped smooth Lily's ruffled feathers.

Mrs. Hartford eventually brought up the topic about Lily's place of residence. "I would love to keep her here, but what would people say, knowing my son and Lily were under the same roof?"

"You need not say anything further on this topic," Mrs. Bennington said. "Miss Montgomery will come live with us until her father returns."

"Oh, how wonderful. And now Miss Bennington will also have a companion."

"Thank you for your kindness, Mrs. Bennington," Lily murmured, puzzled by the woman's gesture.

Mrs. Bennington bowed her head slightly in response.

"When is Sir Frederick expected back?" Mrs. Hartford asked.

Mrs. Bennington placed her teacup down. She was silent for a moment, appearing at a loss for words, which revealed a vulnerability that was not evident before. "It was to my understanding that he would have arrived by now. The last letter I received from him was in June, stating that he would journey back to England end of July. I have not heard from him since. That is somewhat unusual, since he sends us his news at least monthly."

"Maybe he was busy with his affairs," Mrs. Hartford said. She turned to Lily. "When your father returns, I am sure that he will take care of things."

As they were leaving, Mrs. Bennington turned toward Mrs. Hartford. "It would be good if some discretion was used in this matter. We would not want it to get around that a cousin of ours was raised up as a gypsy."

Mrs. Hartford's eyes were round as saucers. "Oh, of course, of course, if that is your wish."

⋅⋅⋅

Later that afternoon, Lily arrived with her cousins at her father's house. The brick town house looked similar to the others on the street, only it had a small courtyard to the right, which led to a back garden. The butler who opened the door was tall and gray-haired, with a beak nose.

They entered the hall.

"I am Miss Montgomery. Sir Frederick is my father," Lily informed him. She looked around at the elegant surroundings. "So this is my home."

The butler's eyes flared open. He stared at Lily for a moment, as if challenging her statement. "I beg your pardon, Miss."

"Miss Montgomery believes Sir Frederick is her father," Mrs. Bennington announced. "You will treat her as such until Sir Frederick arrives and verifies it. Please inform the others. Also, I need a maid up to the pink guest room with a tub of hot water."

"Right away, milady."

"Marianne, dear, show Lily around the house, and then take her up to the guest bedroom."

Lily's senses were fine-tuned as she followed Marianne, gazing at everything in wide-eyed wonder, and trying to imagine her parents living here.

"All the main rooms have gas-lighting. We still use candles in the bedrooms, though. Here is the drawing room."

Beams of sunlight from the tall windows coated the drawing room with a brilliant hue. Beige colored French furniture, matching honey-colored damask-lined walls, and a marble mantel fireplace with Grecian columns greeted Lily's eyes. An impressive looking marble female figure stood near the fireplace with a large, potted fern next to it. Lily stared at the sculpture, fascinated by its lifelike appearance. "That statue must be Greek."

"Mother says it is an original from Greece and must be thousands of years old. Sir Frederick was planning to ship it to the country home, but Mother talked him out of it. She thinks more people will see it here."

They entered the dining room next. Its walls were lined with blue silk and wainscoting, and its ceiling had an elaborate plaster design. The mahogany table seated fourteen people, with an elegant glass chandelier centered above the table.

"Mother likes to entertain important people. We have at least one or two dinner parties a week."

"Oh," Lily said. "Do I have to be there?"

"You are too young. You will probably have dinner in your room. I am eighteen, and already had my coming out, so I am expected to be there."

When they entered the library, Lily's senses reeled with pleasure at what greeted her. The carpeted room held innumerable leather-bound books that lined the shelved walls. She could picture herself reading all those books. A mahogany desk sat in the center of the room, facing the fireplace.

"Sir Frederick's bedroom connects through this door. He likes to read. Now let me show you to your room upstairs."

They walked up another flight of stairs and down the corridor.

"Above, is the attic and that is where the servant's quarters are." They stopped in front of a room. "You will sleep here."

Lily immediately liked the cheerful, pink room, from its creamy white carpet, to the pink bedcover with its roses, and rose-colored wallpaper. A cherry table and dainty chair sat by the tall window. In front of the fireplace was a tub filled with water and some towels and soap on the side. The soap's lavender scent permeated the room.

Marianne dipped her fingers into the water. "Better take your bath now before it gets too cold." As she tripped out the door, she called out, "Dinner will be at eight. A maid will come for you then."

Lily stared at the bathtub. Sleeping in this beautiful room was acceptable to her, but bathing in a tub was another matter. She had always bathed in a creek, which was a gypsy tradition, since sitting in stagnant water carried disease. She scratched her body, knowing very well that there was no creek in the vicinity and that this was the only option she had. Without another thought, she peeled off her travel stained clothes and jumped into the tub. Afterwards, she slipped into her clean brown dress, and then fastidiously washed her clothing.

At eight o'clock, a thin, older woman came for her, her keys jingling by her side.

"I am Mrs. Tippins, the housekeeper. I had to come see you for myself. You must be Miss Montgomery, bless your heart!" the woman said, curtsying. "When Mr. Tippins told me about you, I was so excited!"

"Nice to meet you," Lily replied, curtsying back. They walked down the corridor. She was conscious of Mrs. Tippins eyeing her.

"Excuse me saying, Miss, but I remember you when you were just a little baby. You were the prettiest thing."

"I am sorry, but I do not remember you."

"It was such a long time ago," Mrs. Tippins tittered, revealing crooked teeth.

"I also do not remember my parents."

Mrs. Tippins nodded, appearing delighted to be in the confidence of the Lord's daughter. "I reckon you wouldn't. They were a handsome couple. Half the year, they would come here, and the other half, they'd be in Corfu, an island near Greece, or in the country house in Yorkshire. 'Tis a shame what happened."

They reached the dining room. Mrs. Bennington and Marianne arrived at the same time and greeted Lily.

Mrs. Tippins glanced down, fumbling with the keys from her side, turning businesslike all of a sudden. "Well, I had better be getting back to my work."

"Thank you," Lily said, smiling at her.

"It's so good to have you back, Miss. Sir Frederick will be very pleased indeed to see you when he returns. Very pleased indeed." Mrs. Tippins hurried away.

Lily entered the dining room with Mrs. Bennington and Marianne. The table held a variety of meats, as well as fish, vegetables, fresh fruits, meat pies, puddings, and bread. Feeling ravished, Lily pounced on her food.

"My dear, a lady always eats bite-size morsels and never stuffs her plate, or her mouth, no matter how hungry she may be. Do not chomp down on it like a horse. See, watch me."

Mrs. Bennington chewed a small morsel of food as if she had all the time in the world, causing Lily to swallow in hungry anticipation.

"There, now you try it. Slowly. That's right, take your time."

After a few satisfactory attempts, Lily's improved eating habits restored Mrs. Bennington's faith that all was well with the world, and she resumed her eating.

"How is life here in London?" Lily asked, with her mouth full.

Mrs. Bennington stared at her. "Oh dear. I forgot to tell you. Never speak with your mouth full. I will wait until you have swallowed your food."

Lily blushed, gulping it down. After she wiped her mouth with her handkerchief, she repeated her question with a more subdued air.

Mrs. Bennington told her about the social events, the dinner parties, the theatre, and the exclusive Almack's Assembly Rooms for dancing that were very difficult to get an invitation to. There were evening promenades at Vauxhall and other pleasure gardens, and glittering balls, and much more.

"However, since you are only sixteen, you will not be allowed to mix with the adults until you have your coming out, when you are at least seventeen or eighteen. That is when you will be presented in court and a ball is given in your honor, and several male suitors are invited in the hopes of making a desirable match."

"Why do I need to be presented to the court?" Lily asked, feeling puzzled.

"Because you are presumably a daughter of a peer. Your father, Sir Frederick, inherited the title of baronet from his father, and your grandmother, Judith Gray, was the granddaughter of a Viscount. That makes them peer."

"Were you also presented in court?" Lily asked her.

"No, because the title always falls on the eldest son, Mrs. Bennington replied, appearing cross. "Your grandfather, Sir Frederick, was the eldest of four children, so he inherited the title. His younger siblings were Lucille, Henry, and Charles. Charles was my father. He was in trade and after he became wealthy, married a French noblewoman, Marianne de la Mordeaux. I was the first addition to the family, followed by my younger brother Charles. The only living male is my brother, so if anything happened to your father, my brother Charles would be the next heir."

"Quite a family," Lily said, wondering why Mrs. Bennington would mention anything about an heir, especially when her father was still alive. "How did you become Mrs. Bennington?"

Mrs. Bennington had a faraway look in her eyes. "I was married to Mr. Bennington when I was seventeen. He was landed gentry, much older, but quite attractive in his personality and very wealthy. Marianne was our only child. He loved her dearly. Is that not so, my love?"

Marianne nodded.

"Ah, life is too short. He passed away a few years ago. But I have my brother Charles, who lives with Mother in Bristol. He often visits when he is in town."

"He is wealthy and unmarried, and has not found a wife yet," Marianne added.

"Sshh!" Mrs. Bennington said. "That is no interest of Lily's."

Lily chewed her meal, her mind reeling from the news. She had no idea that there were so many relatives in her family. When she reached over to help herself to more food, her hand knocked over a bowl of cream, spilling the cream on her dress. She wiped the stain in dismay.

Marianne suppressed a giggle. "I think Lily needs another dress. I could give her some of my old ones."

"I really do not need--" Lily began, but was interrupted by an imperious look from Mrs. Bennington.

"Think nothing of it. Marianne can spare a dress or two for you. Besides, your dress is quite unfashionable."

The next morning, as Lily prepared her wardrobe, Marianne swept into her room, carrying a bundle of clothes. "Here you are. I chose them myself." She deposited everything on the bed. "Go on. Try them on."

A white dress with pink lace, several petticoats and accessories lay in the pile on the bed. Lily picked up what looked like bones held together by fabric. "What are these used for?" She scratched her back with them.

"They are called stays and are for your waist, silly girl. Here, let me show you how they work." Marianne wrapped them around Lily. "After Amanda finishes helping Mother, she comes and helps me dress. I can never do it by myself." She giggled as she tugged at the stays, tightening them.

Lily sucked in her breath. "Stop! I cannot breathe."

"You don't really need them. You are too thin," Marianne said, removing the stays. After she helped her dress, she plopped on the bed. "Tell me, Lily, how was it like growing up with the gypsies?"

Lily relaxed, remembering her past. "I was free to do whatever I wanted, ride, dance with my friends, and play with the children. But there were rules to follow, too. It was one large family and everyone had to help in some way. We all had to earn money." She told her about Mirela and her fortune telling.

"You came looking for your father because Mirela saw it in a dream?"

"Mirela is so wise. Anything she saw in a dream always came true."

"I do not believe in that!" Marianne scoffed. "I mean, I could say I had a dream, and if it happened to be true, then I would be wise, like Mirela?"

"It is true," Lily insisted. "Many things that she talked about came true." She fingered the soft and delicate pink lace on the white dress. "This is so beautiful."

"You act as if you never wore clothing before," Marianne teased her. "What did you wear?"

Lily retrieved her gypsy clothes from her bag. "These."

Marianne stroked the colorful fabric, her eyes gleaming. "These are quite different. May I keep them?"

Lily hesitated.

"I *did* give you a dress. The least you could do is give me one of yours," Marianne insisted.

"Oh, all right." Lily watched her cousin fumbling with the clothes. She laughed at her failed attempts. "No, you have to put the skirts on top of each other, like this." She showed her.

"One day you will have to teach me to dance," Marianne said, swaying and swinging her arms.

"Maybe, but something is missing," Lily said. "Your hair is too light for a gypsy." She reached into her bag and pulled out her black wig and the scarf. "This might make you look more like a gypsy."

There was much laughter and banter as Marianne placed the large wig on her head, and tied on the scarf.

After Marianne changed back into her clothing, they proceeded downstairs for breakfast, being in high spirits.

Mrs. Bennington greeted the girls in her usual calm manner, and then stared at Lily. "How remarkable a change when a proper dress is worn."

After breakfast, Mrs. Bennington excused herself. She had errands to attend.

"Mother will be away for at least two hours. She loves to shop at the Arcade and make calls. We can go for a walk together to Hyde Park," Marianne announced. "Amanda will chaperone us. You can tell me more about your gypsy life along the way."

Lily enjoyed the sunny, breezy day which made their walk a pleasant one. Along the way, Marianne chattered about her beaus, Harold, Freddy, and Artie. The three young men had proposed to her during the summer. By the time they reached the park, Lily knew what they wore, what they said, and how they said it. They passed other people strolling in the park, including nannies with little children.

"Do you know that I rejected all their proposals? Even though they were handsome enough, they were younger sons, which Mother did not approve of. They would not do, she said, if I wanted to get ahead in life. They had no money."

After they returned from their walk, Lily acquired two more dresses from Marianne, a pale blue walking dress and an even prettier white dress with pink lace and ribbons. Her cousin said that she shouldn't be seen in the same dress whenever they went walking outside together. In exchange, there was an implicit agreement that Lily would spend all her time devoted to Marianne.

That evening, Lily visited her father's library and browsed the books. She felt exhilarated at the extensive number of books and could imagine him sitting in this room, reading them. Curious about her Greek heritage, Lily chose a book about Socrates, and then took it to the drawing room to read. She found Marianne playing a pretty composition on the piano while Mrs. Bennington was doing some needlework.

"What do you have there?" Mrs. Bennington asked Lily curiously.

"A book about Socrates, a Greek philosopher," Lily said, showing it to her.

"Oh, dear. It is not ladylike to be reading books," Mrs. Bennington admonished her, appearing displeased.

Lily was puzzled. Mirela had always encouraged her to read. "I do not understand."

"Reading is the cause of all kinds of problems to women. It twists their thoughts and gives them wicked ideas. Please, return that book to the library at once."

Marianne stopped her playing and smirked. "Really, Lily. Mother is right. Besides, men do not like women who show any superiority in intelligence."

After that day, Lily did not read in front of her cousins.

Over time, Lily learned her cousins' ways and daily routines. She spent the days mostly with them, listening to Marianne's chatter and being obedient to Mrs. Bennington, and in the evenings when Mrs. Bennington entertained dinner guests or was out with Marianne attending social functions, Lily would dine alone in her room, reading one of the books from the library.

Chapter 7

One evening at Covent Garden, Edward sat with his cousin Sir Douglas, Lady Charleton, and her sister Charlotte, waiting for the curtains to rise.

Edward preferred to have remained with his father after seeing him have one of his coughing bouts, but his father insisted that he come. "I have my nurse to take care of me. Spend more time with Charlotte. Get to know her more," his father had commanded.

The theatre was packed with over three thousand people in its five tiers of boxes, the gallery and pit. He glanced at Charlotte next to him. She was a vision in that low cut, white and gold trimmed dress that hugged her body and exposed her creamy white skin. Her perfect features, slender neck, and elegant blonde curls that graced her delicate face made her irresistible, and he was falling under her spell.

Charlotte's eyes combed the theatre. She turned and whispered to her sister behind her fan. Edward tore his gaze from her and looked out into the sea of faces. He frowned. Several young males publicly ogled Charlotte. He remembered Douglas's words the other night. He had been right. There was every indication that she was the belle of the town.

"Marianne told me that Mrs. Hartford had invited them to sit with them tonight," Charlotte said to her sister, her fan pointing in the direction.

"I am surprised to see the Benningtons in the Hartford box."

"I think that Mr. Hartford will become another beau of Miss Bennington's," Charlotte remarked archly.

Edward followed the gaze of the two women. "Another beau? How many does Miss Bennington have?"

"Oh, several," Charlotte replied, and then looked at him. "Why, do you not think a girl should have more than one beau? Where have you been all these years?"

Edward raised an eyebrow. "Not in London."

"Oh, do not mind her, Edward," Gertrude remarked. "You know how Charlotte loves to tease you."

"Miss Bennington told me her cousin is visiting them," Charlotte informed him. "I hear she is a pretty little thing, but only sixteen. Mind you, I have not seen her yet, but Marianne raves about her. Says she has traveled the world with--"

"The performance has begun," Sir Douglas admonished her.

⚜⚜⚜

That same evening, as the sun settled behind the lonely tree in the back yard, Lily sat by her open window in her room, reading a novel. Her father's library had opened up many doors to the universe, and being a voracious reader, she spent most of her evenings reading by candlelight. Often, Lily pictured her father sitting at his desk in the library, examining one of the scholarly books in his collection or writing a letter.

A half-hour later, she finished the novel, satisfied that the heroine had reunited with her true love. Lily placed the book down on the table, daydreaming about having a similar fate, only in her case, she wanted to reunite with her parents. Her fingers touched the locket that lay there. She opened it and studied her parent's portraits. "*Mitera mou, Mitera mou,*" she whispered, seeing her mother's lovely face for the hundredth time, trying to remember her.

Lily felt troubled when she drew a blank, unable to conjure up any images from the recesses of her mind. Then she noticed the time. Her cousins would be back soon. "I must hurry."

Grabbing her book, Lily fled to the library. She had been careful about reading in her room after that one day when Mrs. Bennington caught her reading and threatened to send her to bed without dinner.

In the corridor, Lily saw Mrs. Tippins advancing toward her, carrying a stack of linen. Lily hesitated, remembering how eager the housekeeper had been in sharing news about her parents. "Good evening Mrs. Tippins. May I have a word with you?"

"Why of course."

"I would like to learn more about my parents."

"Oh, well," Mrs. Tippins said, beaming. "What is it that you wish to know?"

"I am curious about the house in Corfu. You mentioned that my family spent part of the year there?"

"Well, yes. The house was a dowry present from your mother's father to your parents. Your parents visited there yearly, I believe. I saw a painting of it done by your mother. The house was tall and white and tall, and sat on top of a hill, with bright red and yellow flowers surrounding it. It overlooked the blue sea. It was quite a beautiful picture."

"So my mother painted!"

"Oh, yes, Miss, she liked to paint, and I think she was very good at it. She also made miniature portraits." She sighed. "'Tis sad, it is. She was always writing to Sir Frederick, for he'd be away months at a time, and her face would always light up whenever she received one of his letters. They loved each other, truly they did. He hasn't gone back to Corfu, ever since, well, you know--" She paused. "He hasn't visited the country home in York in all these years either."

Lily understood her father's reluctance to return there. It probably evoked too many memories of her mother. "Would you know where my mother kept her paintings?"

Mrs. Tippins stepped closer, her eyes narrowed into slits. She glanced behind her down the dark corridor, as if expecting someone to appear any moment. "They're all gone, Miss, the ones that were framed and on the wall, and those that were on canvas," she whispered. "It happened a few months ago, when I was sick and laid up for a week or so. That's around the time when Mrs. Bennington moved in. When I returned to my duties, I noticed them missing, because I used to dust them regularly. She's put her own paintings in their place, she has."

"Did my father not notice their disappearance?"

"He hasn't been back yet to see what she did. I think she hid them."

Another servant was seen coming down the hallway.

"Thank you, Mrs. Tippins," Lily said, dismissing the housekeeper.

Once in the library, Lily sat down at the writing desk, thinking about all that Mrs. Tippins had said. She could sense her father's loneliness. She wondered if he corresponded with her mother when he was away, and where he would keep his personal letters. If her father used this room, where would he put his personal documents? She recalled reading in a novel that desks often held secret drawers.

Lily pulled the first drawer open. It contained writing paper and several quills. She searched each drawer, her fingers probing the back, looking for anything hidden. Nothing came up. She had reached the fifth and last drawer and it was empty, but her fingers brushed against what seemed like a knob. Her heart clamored as she pulled out the secret drawer. It was filled with papers. A noise coming from downstairs alerted her that her cousins had returned. With pounding heart, Lily shut the drawer and sped to her room.

It rained the next morning, and Lily and Marianne were confined inside.

Marianne gossiped about the people who attended the performance the night before at the theatre, what they wore, and with whom they came. "My friend, Charlotte Stanton was there with her family. I met her last summer, at my coming out ball. She is so beautiful and has many beaus, you know. Uncle Charles is one of them. He adores her. Anyway, tonight at the theatre she sat with a very handsome man. He probably is her latest beau for I have not seen him before. She was dressed in this heavenly, silk dress. It must have cost her a fortune. Oh, and Mr. Hartford hardly noticed the performance at all," she said, laughing. "He was too busy ogling Charlotte. I did see Harry and Artie, though."

"How was the show?"

"I do not know. I was too busy watching everyone else," Marianne admitted, laughing. "Mother hit me with the fan when she caught me looking. She thinks it is impolite to stare at people there."

That evening, after her cousins left for a dinner party, Lily visited the library. With anticipation, she searched the hidden drawer and pulled out the stack of folded papers, and then hurried back to her room, clutching them to her. She locked her door and settling on her bed, leafed through the pile.

A few papers were business letters from England to an Indian spice company. Her father had bought a considerable number of spices from India and sold them at a higher price in England. From the invoices, it appeared that her father was wealthy.

She discovered a letter at the bottom of the pile written by her mother to her father. Her hands felt clammy as she unfolded it. It appeared to have been read several times for it was very creased, and had worn edges. Some words were blotched and difficult to decipher, as if they had been wet by something. *Could they have come from Father's tears?* She touched them reverently, and then proceeded to read the letter.

1 February, 1821

My dearest husband,

My love, how I have missed you so these past five months! I cannot begin to count the number of times I have yearned to see your kind face, your beautiful eyes, and your bright smile. When you are with me, I feel that all is well with the world. Oh, if it only could be! There is some important news to tell you. My father has recently suffered a stroke and is very ill. I came to Patras with Lily as soon as I found out. He is bedridden, and because of the seriousness of his illness, I feel I should remain awhile longer.

I am blessed that I have little Lily beside me. She reminds me of you, with her blue eyes and blonde hair. She asks for you each day and I remind her that you are away on business. She prays for you each night before going to bed. I know that you have business to take care of, but it would be good for you to come in time for Lily's sixth birthday, March 23. We probably will still be here in Patras.

I will anxiously count the days until I receive news of your safe arrival to England, for I know how treacherous the sea can be.

Love always,
Your wife Penelope

Lily reread her mother's letter several times, imprinting it in her mind. She then searched the pile. There were no other letters from her mother. After she was finished, she returned the papers to their proper place.

Later, as she lay in bed, her thoughts revolved around her parents. It was evident from the letter that her mother loved her father dearly. Thoughts of unfulfilled hopes and dreams that had turned into ashes spilled through her tears, one drop at a time. How very sorry she was for what happened to them.

✥ ✥ ✥

A few days later, while Mrs. Bennington was out shopping, Marianne suggested to Lily that they take a carriage to Regent's park with Amanda. The uncharacteristic blue sky and the park's luscious landscape were a temptation to Lily's young heart. Soon, their open carriage ambled into the green expansive park. They joined the parade of well-dressed couples and families in carriages. Just then, the strong wind ruffled her dress so that it flew out of its position. She swiftly bent to fix it.

"There is Sir Douglas Charleton, riding a beautiful black stallion, and that man riding alongside him, he is Charlotte's new beau. I just know it is him!" Marianne cried. "Oh, and there is Mr. Penbroke on that gray horse."

Lily sat up, her one hand keeping her dress down while her eyes combed the many carriages and horses in the park. "Where?"

"Oh, Lily, you missed him," Marianne settled back in her seat. "Remember the dress I wore last night to the assembly ball?" she asked dreamily. "Well, I think it brought me good luck. I was introduced to Mr. Penbroke and he didn't leave my side all evening. He danced two waltzes with me. He is fair and average height, and he made me laugh so much." She smiled, her eyes twinkling. "He even danced with Mother."

"Is he a younger son?" Lily teased.

"I never got around to asking. Mother will surely find out for me."

The following day, Sunday, they took the carriage to church. Lily had never been in a church before and stared at the saintly statues, the architecture, and the people. The women wore plumed hats and fashionable dresses while the men wore black suits and white cravats. The people looked solemn, and quietly listened to the sermon. Some even had their eyes closed, as if they were sleeping.

Marianne, who had been on her best behavior all morning and was holding a bible, nudged her. "Stop staring at everyone and pay attention!" she hissed. She shoved the bible in her hands.

Lily blushed at her cousin's remarks. She hadn't been aware of doing anything improper. She opened the bible and fixed her gaze on the pages. Soon, she was engrossed in the verses.

Later that afternoon, Mrs. Bennington met with some women from a charitable organization, so the two girls and their chaperone took a stroll outside. The weather was fair and breezy, as Marianne and Lily walked down the street decked in their fine Sunday dresses.

"This is *such* a lovely day. Let us go to the Serpentine," Marianne said.

In a short time, they meandered through beautiful, idyllic scenes of natural tranquility and peace. Lily took deep breaths, enjoying the lush green bordered by the curved line of the sparkling river. When they reached the river's bank, two men stood to the side, conversing. They turned and waved to them. Marianne excitedly waved back. She lifted her dress and hurried toward them, leaving Lily and Amanda behind. Lily stared at Amanda, who appeared helpless for a moment. Then, with a determined look on her face, Amanda lifted her skirts and charged after Marianne. Lily had no recourse but to follow them.

One man was fair-haired and the other, redheaded.

"Fancy meeting you here, Miss Bennington," the fair-haired man said to Marianne, flashing a dimpled smile. "I was just telling Mr. Wren what a fine day to go for a stroll, but the only thing missing was a lovely face to share it with. Now I cannot complain, for you have supplied that lovely face."

"We also thought it a fine day, Mr. Penbroke, and just happened to take a walk along the Serpentine," Marianne explained.

"May I presume that your companion is the lovely cousin you so delightedly talked about?" Mr. Penbroke asked.

Marianne had the grace to blush. "Yes. Miss Montgomery is visiting us from York."

Lily wondered how much her cousin had revealed about her past. Marianne made the introductions, and the two men bowed in polite succession while Lily presented a stiff curtsy.

Mr. Wren was the more serious of the two and did not say much. He had uncommonly pale features, red curly hair, and cool gray eyes. He studied Lily with interest, causing her to flush and glance away.

The men joined them and they strolled along the river. Marianne fell in with Mr. Penbroke, chatting merrily. Lily walked alongside Mr. Wren, feeling cross with her cousin. She glanced at Amanda, who was keeping a discreet distance from them. She sighed. Amanda was no more a chaperone than Lily was.

"How do you like London, Miss Montgomery?" Mr. Wren asked.

"It is like any large city," Lily replied, her gaze fixed on the couple in front of her. Something about Mr. Penbroke made her uneasy. "I mean, I have traveled to large cities, like Paris and Rome, and after a while, they all have that same fast pace, the noise, and bustling activity. So much life is concentrated into one place."

"For one so young you seemed to have done much traveling," Mr. Wren remarked.

Lily blinked at him. He seemed amused. She bit her lip. Without thinking, she had referred to her past.

Marianne turned around. "Did I not tell you, Mr. Wren? Her father is *Sir* Frederick Montgomery. He has traveled all over the world," she said, batting her eyelashes at him. "Have you had a chance to travel outside England, Mr. Wren?"

That prompted a discussion of the countries Mr. Wren had traveled to. He talked about his travels to Egypt and Europe, with Mr. Penbroke chipping in with his own travels to Europe.

Just then, Mr. Hartford rode by on a gray mare, lifting his hat civilly as he passed them.

On the way back to the house, Marianne reprimanded Lily. "You are such a baby! How were you going to explain traveling all over the world? No one knows you traveled with gypsies. No one but us and the Hartfords. I have been very careful about not telling anyone. I really have. So be careful next time."

Lily was quite penitent by the time they reached the house. She knew her cousin was right. It would not do to tell people about her colorful past. Mirela had even made her promise that she would not tell anyone about the gypsy camp. She must be more careful in the future.

That evening, Mrs. Bennington and Marianne entertained friends for dinner. They had invited Mrs. Hartford and her son, as well as several close friends.

After the party left, Lily heard Mrs. Bennington's raised voice coming from Marianne's bedroom. "Mrs. Hartford said her son saw you today in the park and you were with two young men. That will not do, young lady! It is improper!"

As a result, the girls were not allowed to walk in the park for a whole week.

Chapter 8

Initially dismayed by the disarray of his father's books for the London property, Edward devoted a considerable amount of time attending to them. He tackled the task with determination and persistence. With methodical precision, he took inventory of all the stock and straightened out the accounts. Piles of outstanding bills gathering dust in one corner of the desk were sifted through and organized. Many had not been paid in more than two years to several merchants.

When Edward finished his arduous task, he showed his father the books. "I am afraid that there were several missing entries in these books."

"After Mr. Benton, my manager, passed away two years ago, I became ill and did not have the energy to manage the books," Lord Peterborough explained wearily. "That is likely the reason."

"I fear that Mr. Benton was not doing his job properly, even before then. He was siphoning out funds without paying the merchants."

Lord Peterborough lifted an eyebrow; his intent eyes showed an alertness of character reminiscent of earlier years. "Are you sure about this?"

"Quite sure. When I discovered several unpaid invoices, I visited with the merchants and promptly paid them." Edward showed his father the corrected numbers in the books.

"That rascal!" Lord Peterborough exclaimed. "But now he has met his dues. It is so hard to trust anyone these days."

"These are small issues compared to Greystone Manor's books. Who is taking care of them?"

"Last year, Aunt Mabel suggested the local vicar's son, Mr. Pilford, so I hired him. She says he is doing a passable job." He broke out into a coughing session. "Now that you are here, you can oversee the accounts for both places. You have always enjoyed numbers," he rasped. He coughed. "Nurse, get me some medicine."

After the medicine was dispensed, his father's coughing subsided.

"What has the doctor said about your health?"

"He has ordered me to seek the country air. Says it is good for my lungs, but I have put it off. I do not look forward to the journey. The jolting of the rough road is painful to my old bones."

"It is time that you went, and I will come with you. I have missed seeing Aunt Mabel and Greystone Manor, and you would also benefit from having a companion along the trip."

"Your intention is to bring me comfort and make your aunt happy, I am sure, for she has been eagerly waiting to see you," Lord Peterborough said, "but do you think it wise to leave Miss Stanton so soon during your courtship?"

Edward chuckled at his father's matchmaking efforts. "Do not worry. Douglas and Gertrude have mentioned that they will be coming up to Yorkshire for Christmas, and Miss Stanton plans to do the same. We will see plenty of her there, I assure you." He stood up. "Speaking of Miss Stanton, I have an engagement with her tonight and must prepare for it. Goodnight, Father."

❧ ❧ ❧

During that week, Lily and Marianne remained inside. Even Marianne was not allowed to go out in the evenings with her mother. Lily used her free time to explore the books in the library. Several words were difficult to understand, forcing her to consult the dictionary often.

One afternoon, while Mrs. Bennington was out shopping, Marianne and Lily were in the dayroom. Marianne was drawing busily on her sketchpad, while Lily attempted to read Shakespeare's *Romeo and Juliet* aloud, having convinced Marianne that it was a story worth reading.

"What do you think, cousin?" Marianne handed her the finished sketch.

Lily studied the sketch. "Who is it supposed to be?"

"Do you not recognize him? It is Mr. Penbroke, silly!"

"I wish I could draw and paint like you," Lily said wistfully.

"It takes *years* and *years* to learn these things," Marianne said, appearing smug. "I had all kinds of instructors as far back as I could remember. You spent most of your time riding horses in the sun and selling trinkets, and dancing at fairs."

Just then, Mr. Tippins entered the room and announced that they had callers. "A Mr. Penbroke and a Mr. Wren."

"We can receive them in here," Marianne said, appearing pleased. "Oh, and call for Amanda." She put aside her materials and arranged herself on the sofa, sitting upright and smoothing her dress. Then she looked at Lily. "Don't let them see that you were reading."

Lily tucked the book underneath her dress.

The two men entered the room dressed in formal attire.

Mr. Penbroke presented a bouquet of crimson roses to Marianne. "Please accept my heartfelt present. Beautiful roses for a beautiful lady."

"Oh, these are lovely!" Marianne exclaimed. She called for the maid to place them in a vase.

Mr. Wren presented Lily with a bouquet of white and red carnations. "I thought you might like these." His gray eyes were warm as he gazed into her eyes.

Lily hesitated. She did not know what to do. Marianne nodded her approval. Just then, Amanda came in and sat discreetly to the side.

Not wanting to offend Mr. Wren, Lily thanked him, taking the bouquet of carnations and handing them to the maid.

"I hope we did not come at an inopportune time," Mr. Penbroke said.

"No, not at all. My mother should be arriving any moment," Marianne replied.

The two men stayed for a while, listening to Marianne chatter about various topics while sipping tea and enjoying an assortment of small cakes reserved for such occasions. Lily was quiet, as was expected of her. She glanced at Mr. Wren and caught him staring at her. She blushed and steered her eyes toward her cousin, who was having an animated discussion with Mr. Penbroke. Lily wondered how Mrs. Bennington would react when she saw the young men there.

"Maybe we will see you at the soiree, Mr. Penbroke," Marianne was saying, procuring a prompt promise from the young man that he would surely attend the function.

Mrs. Bennington arrived at that moment and paused at the door when she saw the young men. Lily recognized the familiar flush of color dotting her cheeks, which meant she was displeased. By the time that she entered the room, her face had resumed its composure and she chatted pleasantly enough with the young men. It seemed to Lily that all was well with her, but after the two men left, Mrs. Bennington's smile turned into a frown.

"It is inappropriate behavior to allow the two men to visit you without a proper chaperone," Mrs. Bennington snapped at Marianne.

"Amanda was here," Marianne reminded her. "Besides, I told them that you would be back any minute, and I was right. What do you think about Mr. Penbroke? Does he not have such a nice smile?"

"A nice smile does not make a good marriage," Mrs. Bennington retorted. Then a gleam appeared in her eyes. "However, I just learned from a reliable source that he has recently inherited an estate from a late uncle. He is well off."

"Oh, how wonderful!" Marianne exclaimed.

"Not so fast, my dear. He has been known to have a history of gambling debts. Even Lady Charleton, when she was single, wisely backed off from marrying him, and look at her now, she married well indeed."

"I would not listen to all that gossip," Marianne said, appearing offended. "Besides, he probably paid off his debts by now. I think he has good qualities."

"Marianne, you have flirted with so many young men this summer that people are starting to form an opinion of you, and it is not a good one, I am afraid. I learned from Mrs. Hartford the other day, in strictest confidence, of course, that her son has expressed an interest in you, but I suppose what is holding him back is your propensity for flirting with every man that looks at you."

Marianne blinked back her tears. "It is not my fault, Mother. When men seek me out to talk to me, I cannot ignore them. Mr. Hartford has never once engaged me in conversation or asked me for a dance." She struck the pose of a martyr, the tears shimmering in her eyes.

"Maybe he is shy. Some men are like that until they marry. It takes a wife to bring out the best in a husband." She paced the room with uncommon vigor. "And what do you think about Mr. Wren? He is not only gentry, but has five thousand pounds a year."

"I dislike his red hair. Besides, I think he is interested in Lily."

"Lily?" Mrs. Bennington stopped her pacing to stare at Lily. "How can this be?"

"Mr. Wren brought those flowers for her today." Marianne gestured towards the vase of carnations.

"This is totally unacceptable! She has not had her coming out yet," Mrs. Bennington said. "I am responsible for Lily until her father's return. I cannot have her meeting young men in secret. Tell me, what does he know about her? Does he know who her father is?"

Marianne's eyes looked down. She appeared penitent. "The other day he found out, in the park. It just slipped out."

Mrs. Bennington's mouth narrowed into a thin line. "Then we must act quickly to remedy this." She left right after their talk and was gone most of the day.

Lily's mood was unsettled the rest of the day. She could not focus on her reading while thinking about Mrs. Bennington displeasure with her behavior. What did she mean about remedying it? Somehow, it did not bode well. During lunch, she picked at her food and reflected on the visit by the two young men. It was an awkward moment for her when Mr. Wren presented her with the flowers. Not wanting to offend him by refusing them, she accepted them. What else could she do?

That evening, Lily was called down to dinner, which was a rare event. Normally she would sup in her room because there would be guests. Tonight, Mrs. Bennington and Marianne were the only ones at the table. Mrs. Bennington's mood appeared almost convivial, making Lily relax, but she soon found out the reason for her improved mood.

"Lily, I have been thinking about your lack of education and refinement for some time now. It would be difficult for you to mix with people of your father's status if we did nothing to repair this fault," Mrs. Bennington began, wiping the corners of her mouth with her handkerchief.

"But I know how to read," Lily countered. "I know three languages. I know my arithmetic--"

"It is more than that, dear. It is also about poise, mannerisms, playing music, dancing, and knowing what to say in public. You are lacking in these things."

Lily hung her head in shame. She knew there was truth in what Mrs. Bennington was saying.

"Today, I visited a dear friend of mine, a Mrs. Bodline. I learned through her that the Greystone School for Girls, in Yorkshire, starts soon for the Michaelmas term. Two of her daughters attended the school, and her youngest will be admitted this term. I hear they teach very useful subjects for a young lady, such as penmanship, bookkeeping, French, dancing, painting, and embroidery. That sort of thing. I have decided that is where you will go."

Lily set her fork down, unable to eat. This was not at all what she had expected to hear. Just when she was getting used to the idea of living here and seeing her father, she was being sent away.

"Oh, Mother! How could Lily leave us? And it so far away. Just when I was beginning to enjoy her company," Marianne exclaimed, appearing dismayed.

"It is for her own good. You must stop being selfish and start thinking about others for once."

"Mrs. Bennington, could you tell me how far Yorkshire is from here?" Lily asked, trying to appear calm. "I do not want to be too far away when my father returns."

"Do not worry. Although Yorkshire is several hours drive from here, it is actually near Montgomery Park, your father's country home. It will be a *perfect* arrangement for you. When your father returns, he will surely visit his country home in Yorkshire and you could see him during the holidays."

Lily felt some comfort in that thought. Then another nagging thought entered her mind. "May I ask, how will it be paid for?"

"Once the school finds out whose daughter you are, they will eagerly set up an account. I will send a letter with you, explaining your relation to Sir Frederick, and that he will make the payment after he arrives from his trip."

They ate the rest of their dinner in silence.

That night, Lily sat by her open window, gazing out at the moonlit night. She had come all the way to England to find her parents, and instead of meeting her goal, she was being sent away to a school just so she could act like a lady. Was it possible that the wise, all-knowing Mirela had made a mistake? Lily could not fathom that happening. Her grandmother cared about her, and so did the gypsies. They had been her family all these years and accepted her the way she was. They did not try to change her, as did Mrs. Bennington. A wave of nostalgia coursed through her young heart. Maybe she should never have come to England.

Feeling unduly perplexed, Lily arose and began to pack her bag as tears welled up in her eyes. What would she tell Mirela? That it was difficult to find her parents? That she was being sent away to a school where she knew no one? That she did not want to go and would rather be with them?

Lily held one of Marianne's dresses in her hands, staring at it. She could not use it where she was going. She set it aside, and then stopped her packing when she realized that she had given her gypsy clothes to Marianne, and besides, she did not know where the caravan was. Mirela had told her that they were to leave for Germany because Count Igor had a cousin there. She had forgotten about Count Igor.

Lily sat numbly on the edge of the bed, feeling helpless. She could never go back. *What should I do?* At least the school was near her father's country home. That thought brought a small measure of comfort into her young ailing heart.

A new thought assailed her mind. What if Mrs. Bennington was away when her father returned from his trip? How would he know where Lily was? She barely knew how to write, yet it was critical that she make contact with him somehow. With new determination, Lily advanced down the dark corridor to the library, walking barefoot so as not to make noise. Once there, she lit a candle and sat down at the large desk. With the help of the dictionary, she painstakingly penned a letter to her father.

> *21 September in the year 1831*
> *dear father i no this letter will come as a shock to you when you read it up until recently i thinkd i was a gipsy and just found out the trueth from the gipsy woman that took care of me she saw a vision and gave me the paper and loket and told me that ten years ago they faond me in Patras with theez and my doll she sayd there were fires and the gipsys took me away because the Turks had burnd down the buildeengs she sayd now it was time for me to find you and mother so i came to England looking for you but misses beneengtun said you were away on a trip she is sending me to grey stone girls school in york and says it is close to your home and i want to see you very much   please forgive my writeng, since i did not go to school*
> *i put this letter in the secret drawer so no one else sees it*
> *with love your dauter Lily*

There were smudges in the areas where the ink was too thick. Lily blew on it, helping it to dry, and then folded the letter and carefully placed it in the hidden drawer next to her mother's letter, hoping that one day her father would read her letter and come looking for her.

 భాఖాఖా

A few days later, Lily sat in the carriage with her cousins, heading for the coach station. Although she had made peace with the trip, her body was taut from the unknowns lurking in her mind. Yet at the same time; the idea of the school helping her to become a lady brought her some reassurance. She wanted to be worthy of her father.

"I wish you did not have to go," Marianne complained to Lily. "I will truly miss our discussions and strolls in the park."

"It is for the best, Marianne. You can write to each other," Mrs. Bennington reminded her daughter. She handed Lily a sealed letter. "You will present this to the Head Mistress of the school. I was told her name is Mistress Bates."

Lily placed it in her bag.

"Now Lily, there is a delicate matter I wish to discuss with you. It is about that document you have, with your father's signature. It might get lost at the school. I remember when I lost a very pretty brooch at my school and it cost me dearly."

"Oh, I will keep my eyes on it, I will," Lily promised.

"No, as your guardian, I believe you should leave it with me. When your dear father arrives, I will show it to him as proof that you are here. It will make him very happy."

"Mother is right, Lily. I also lost some precious jewelry when I went off to school. You do not know what the servants are like there."

So that is how the document was left behind in Mrs. Bennington's care.

Soon, their carriage was pulling up to the station. A group of people stood in front of the coach, ready to board.

"Come, follow me. I see Mrs. Bodline and her daughter," Mrs. Bennington said to Lily.

Lily was introduced to the stately matron and her petite daughter, Miss Bodline. She was a girl around Lily's age, with a round face, little hands, and bright eyes. Her chaperone was an older woman by the name of Mrs. White.

"All aboard!" the coachman shouted.

The last few minutes were a flurry of motion as Mrs. Bennington rushed to pay Lily's fare. Lily bade her cousins a tearful farewell and boarded the coach. She sat next to Miss Bodline and Mrs. White. Opposite them sat a young couple and their two small children. Lily leaned out the window, waving to her cousins.

"I will write you my news, Lily!" Marianne cried, as the coach pulled away.

Lily fixed her gaze on the fading image of her cousins until they dwindled away into specks.

Soon, they had left the city with its many buildings and congested streets, and ambled past lush, green pastures, heading for York.

"Is this your first term with the Greystone School for Girls, Miss Montgomery?" Miss Bodline asked Lily.

"Yes. I will be in the sixteen-year-old age group," Lily replied. "And you?"

"I will be in the same group. We can only afford two years, although students can go for three." Miss Bodline twisted her small hands. "Two of my sisters attended that school, and after they finished, within a short time they married well."

"Is that the reason your parents are sending you there?" Lily asked incredulously.

"Mother says I do not have the good looks of my older sisters and that the school will help prepare me for marriage. Men want women who look up to them, and are lady-like and dainty, you know, and speak well and dress well. That sort of thing. I am not like that at all. I like to read and Mother frowns upon it."

"I also like to read, although my cousins do not care for it, either. My favorite author is Shakespeare."

"I am familiar with his works. Have you read *Hamlet*?"

"Not yet, but I would like to. I just finished reading *Romeo and Juliet*," Lily said, recalling the book she had borrowed from her father's library. "It was quite good, but I did not care for the ending. It was sad, although it did show how deep their love was for each other."

"Oh, yes. Sad indeed. I think it would have been better if the couple married and let their families patch things up on their own."

Lily agreed with enthusiasm.

By the time they reached the inn, they had become good friends.

The innkeeper served them hot cabbage soup and crusty bread. Afterwards, they were led upstairs to a room to retire. Lily fell asleep as soon as her head hit the pillow.

The next morning, after a quick breakfast of hot coffee and freshly baked biscuits, everyone piled back into the coach. During the journey, the two girls discovered more about each other. Lily found out that Miss Bodline's father was a vicar and her mother a daughter of landed gentry.

"What about you?" Miss Bodline asked. "Do you have any brothers or sisters?"

Lily knew these questions would be coming. Her cousins had prepared her for them. She repeated what Mrs. Bennington had told her to say. "I am an only child. I never knew my mother. She died when I was very young. My father, Sir Frederick Montgomery, fifth baronet, travels a lot, and I rarely get to see him. I live with my cousins when he is away."

Chapter 9

By the time the carriage rolled into the town of Leeds, the sun was beginning to set. Its rays formed silvery stars that twinkled on the River Aire. They passed various stone buildings that graced the broad, well-paved streets. The carriage eventually stopped in front of a two-story brick building.

Mrs. White was to continue her trip further north. The girls bid her farewell and gazed around them expectantly. A lonely carriage sat across the road and a woman stood in front of it. She glanced their way, then lifted her arm and waved to them.

"That must be Miss Farfield," Miss Bodline said. "She is a Mistress from the school, who was supposed to pick me up. Let us go to her."

Miss Farfield was well into her late thirties. Dressed in gray, she was thin as a reed, and her movements were nervous and agitated. Her face and nose were markedly long, and she wore spectacles which encased her small eyes, and added to her unattractiveness.

Miss Bodline made the introductions.

"Oh, my, this is *quite* unexpected!" Miss Farfield said, sputtering, while her hand fluttered to her collar as if to smooth an invisible crease. "I was told to collect only you, Miss Bodline. I do not know whether the school will accept Miss Montgomery. Their standards are quite high, you know. We only accept students with references."

"Her father is Sir Frederick Montgomery, a *fifth* baronet," Miss Bodline reported.

"Oh!" Miss Farfield's eyes flew open. "Well, but we have not received any letter from him. How did this come about?"

"I have a letter from Mrs. Bennington, my acting guardian, that explains everything," Lily said, procuring the letter and handing it to her.

Miss Fairfield read the letter. "I see." She gave it back to Lily. "That is sufficient." She glanced down at her watch. "Now we must hurry for we do not have the advantage of a full moon tonight. The roads are narrow and one can get lost at night. Come. Come."

The girls settled into the carriage. Soon, they were passing rolling fields with sheep grazing on heather. In some places, the terrain became rocky and steep, causing a bumpy ride. Lily held on to her seat tightly.

"We have much rain, particularly this time of the year, so I hope you brought umbrellas with you," Miss Farfield informed them.

Up ahead, under the fading sunset, an impressive stone manor towered on the hill. Miss Farfield pointed to it proudly. "That is Greystone Manor. It is over two hundred years old. Lord Peterborough, the lord of the manor, is a baron and was also knighted by the late king. He is a widower, and owns the school, and the tenant buildings on this land." A smile flitted across her face, replaced by a look of consternation. "He typically arrives for Christmas, but due to his failing health, is expected to return sooner."

"How did the school come about?" Lily asked.

"Twelve years ago, Mistress Bates approached Lord Peterborough to convert the farmhouse on his land into a girl's finishing school, with the condition that she pay him rent. He agreed to the terms, and soon after it opened, Mistress Fence, the sister of Mistress Bates, joined her. They are both widows. I arrived five years ago."

Darkness had descended by the time the carriage wheeled in front of the school. Light shone from its many windows, like stars lined up in rows. A servant came outside with a lantern and helped them up the stairs and into the building.

The large lobby was empty except for the butler, who informed them that everyone was at supper.

Miss Farfield led the girls into a room and asked them to wait there. The girls stood near the fireplace, warming themselves. A few minutes later, the Mistresses arrived. They almost looked identical. Both were petite and slim, and dressed sternly in dark clothing. At first, Lily could not tell them apart, but upon studying them more closely, she noted that Mistress Fence appeared the younger and gentler of the two and had a proclivity for smiling.

After the introductions were made, Mistress Bates addressed Lily. "We do not normally take in students without recommendations. Your case is quite unusual. I heard from Miss Farfield that you are Sir Frederick Montgomery's daughter. You brought documents with you?"

"Yes, here is a letter from Mrs. Bennington, my cousin, that explains everything," Lily replied, handing the letter to her.

The Mistresses reviewed Lily's letter.

"Your father is away to the East Indies?" Mistress Bates asked, folding the letter and pocketing it.

"Yes," Lily said. "He travels often. He is expected back soon."

"Very good, then. This term lasts until Christmas. Typically, we would ask for the fee in advance, which comes to seventeen guineas. But given your background, we would be honored to open an account for you."

Lily's eyes grew large with wonder at the exorbitant fee. "Thank you," she mumbled, her tongue feeling thick. She had never owed money before, but if they were willing to accept her on the basis of her father's name, then she would follow through with it.

Miss Bodline was next. She gave Mistress Bates her information, and then pulled out her purse and proceeded to pay the fee.

Mistress Bates appeared pleased. "We are happy to have you, Miss Bodline. I have personally taught your sisters and they were exemplary students in our school. How are they faring?"

"Both have married well."

"Ah, good news. Now, I would like to briefly convey the rules here at the school. There are three mistresses in this school and each one has an assistant. We expect our students to present themselves in their best character at all times. This means no lying, no cheating, and no stealing. When you retire to your room, we expect you to remain there. There will be no visitors in your rooms. Male visitors will be received in the drawing room with the chaperoning of a mistress or an assistant. Any behavior not deemed worthy of the school's principles and teachings will constitute grounds for expulsion."

Lily learned that Mistress Fence was in charge of the fifteen-year-old group, while Miss Farfield was in charge of the sixteen-year-olds. Mistress Bates was responsible for the seventeen and eighteen-year-olds.

The class schedule and dress code were discussed, along with the times for meals and bedtime.

"From now on, you both will go to Miss Farfield if you require anything," Mistress Bates finished. "Do you have any questions?"

The two girls were quiet. Lily suppressed a yawn with her hand.

"I think they are a little tired from the long trip." Mistress Fence smiled. "Which room shall they use?"

"The Bailey twins will not be returning this term. They may use their room."

The girls groggily followed Miss Farfield up the central staircase. She held a lit candle. "There are four floors, and each floor has an east wing, which is the old part of the structure, and a west wing, which is the newest addition. In the back of the building is the courtyard and the gardens. The first floor is where all the classes take place. You will be in my classes."

They arrived on the second floor. Lily could hear chatter coming from the closed doors ahead of them. The strong scent of food hovered in the air.

"The dining room is located on the second floor. The girls are finishing dinner and should be out soon. A sitting room is located just to your left, where parents and guests can be received, and next to it, the library. On the east and west wings of this floor is where Mistress Bates and the older students in her classes have their rooms."

They continued up several stairs and turned down a corridor.

"The fourth floor is my jurisdiction, where you will reside. Your room is located at the far end of the east wing. I will be in the west wing if you need anything."

Miss Farfield led them past several doors to their room. It was simple, with lime-washed walls and a window, two twin beds, a table with two chairs, and a basin. Moments later, a servant brought the girls' luggage into the room, and then lit the fireplace.

"Since it is past dinnertime, I will order your meal to be sent to your room. It should be here shortly." Miss Farfield pointed to the table; on top were two candleholders with unlit candles. "You are allowed one candle each, per night. Mistress Bates charges a shilling for each extra candle."

"Oh," Lily said. One candle a night would not be enough for her.

Miss Farfield went to the door. "Prayers are at seven-thirty sharp, followed by breakfast. Do not forget to bring your own silverware. Good-night."

The following morning, the two girls entered the dining hall at seven-thirty. A high beamed ceiling with plasterwork and chandeliers overlooked three long tables with benches that spanned from one end of the room to the other. The tables were filled with students and there was much chatter and noise. Miss Farfield waved to them and pointed to the empty seats next to her. They advanced toward her and sat down. They were introduced to Miss Cray, the assistant, who sat across from them.

Miss Bodline leaned over to Lily and whispered, "My sisters told me that Miss Cray was a former student, who underwent difficult circumstances and could not pay her tuition, so the school hired her."

The din died down as Mistress Bates led the prayer. Next, the servants brought bowls of porridge, poached eggs, and small mugs of milk. Two students who sat across from them at the table were introduced as Miss Bradenton and Miss Lawrence, and had returned the second year. They were both friendly and cheerful, which made the meal a pleasant one.

Miss Farfield's class on needlepoint and sewing came after breakfast. Lily had to redo her stitches several times. By the end of the class, she was able to form a straight stitch without stabbing herself.

Next, Miss Farfield covered proper social etiquette and poise. "We will discuss what is becoming in the way of walking. Do not stride like a man, or bounce like a child, but walk with small, dainty steps." She showed them how, then asked Lily to arise.

"Now, I will place a book on your head, and you are to walk with it to the door without falling," she told Lily.

Lily commenced forward with mincing steps, but when she felt the book slipping, raced toward the door, grabbing the book just as it fell.

"Please, no running, Miss Montgomery!" Miss Farfield admonished her, while the others laughed. "You may try it again."

Next came the penmanship and bookkeeping class. The students filed into another room and sat at a long table. Mr. Smith, the instructor, was an older man with spectacles and a bushel of gray hair. He handed out sheets of paper, inkstands and quill pens, then lectured on proper penmanship, and showed them how to use the quill.

Afterwards, he pointed to the items located on the table, ranging from linen, to paper and ink, books, containers of tea, and candles. Next, he asked the students to write a list of the items neatly on paper. Any smudges or mistakes were to be rewritten. Lily glanced at Miss Bodline's paper, and then copied her. She had to redo her work twice before it was neat and legible.

A half-hour later, Mister Smith discussed the art of bookkeeping. "Bookkeeping is an important asset when you are mistress of the house and manage the household accounts." He lectured for a while longer, emphasizing the responsibility of being accurate and keeping logs. "You will be helping me keep the books for the school. Use the good penmanship we practiced earlier."

It was eleven-thirty when they entered the art room. Mrs. Green, their instructor, was a young woman with cinnamon red hair. She showed them some sketching techniques, and discussed shading and colors. "Since it is too wonderful a day to be closed up inside, we will take advantage of it. Observe how the sun's light plays upon colors. Gather your art supplies and follow me,"

The students were led outside to sketch the trees and landscaped grounds. Lily enjoyed that class immensely. Although it was windy, and she had a difficult time keeping her paper intact, her finished sketch was among those commended by the instructor.

An hour later, Miss Farfield arrived to take them for their walk. "Hurry, now. We are to join the other students and must not be late."

Lily and the others filed into the line of students that had formed in front of the school. Miss Bodline was chosen as her walking partner, while Miss Bradenton and Miss Lawrence stood behind them. Soon, the students trudged down the gravel lane, passing green fields, buzzing bees and bright-colored trees and chatting merrily along the way. The lane led to a larger road.

After some time, they came upon a tree-lined lane that wound its way up the hill to the imposing Greystone Manor. Rows of shapely bushes and traces of a pond were observed in front of the house.

"That is Greystone Manor," Miss Bodline told Lily. "Is it not wonderful?"

Lily nodded in silent wonder. It was larger than the school and could easily house several families. The walk ended there, and the students returned to the school.

After having tea, sandwiches and scones in the dining hall, the girls were ushered to Miss Farfield's piano class. Miss Farfield performed a piece by Bach, which inspired Lily greatly. They were taught a few notes and the proper placement of the fingers on the keyboard. Each student had a chance to practice afterwards, but by the time it was Lily's turn, the class was dismissed.

The French class was next and was taught by Madame Martine. Lily knew the language well and was able to understand what she was saying. She responded correctly to the instructor's questions with the proper diction, causing admiring glances from the other students.

Afterwards, Lily and Miss Bodline adjourned to their room for the afternoon rest.

"You play the piano very well, and I liked the way you embroidered. I traveled often, and did not get a chance to learn those things," Lily said.

"Yes, but your French was outstanding. Maybe I could help you with your music and embroidery and you could help me with my French."

Miss Bradenton and Miss Lawrence joined them a short while later in their room, and there was much laughter when Lily mimicked the instructors, her pronunciation exaggerated with inflections.

Dinner was quite a grand affair as compared to breakfast. The girls had to wear formal dress. The ample fare consisted of mutton, fish, kidney pie, overcooked vegetables, crusty bread, and bread pudding.

By eight o'clock, Lily and Miss Bodline were back in their room. There was very little talking, as the two girls fell promptly asleep, comfortably full from the meal and exhausted from their first day of school.

The days all blended together, filled with classes, and walks, and merry chatter. When Saturday morning came, Lily received a letter from Mrs. Bennington. Although it was brief, Lily read it with much effort, for Mrs. Bennington's handwriting was not the best. Apparently, they were in Bath and Marianne was going to write to her. There was no mention of Sir Frederick Montgomery. Lily tucked the letter in her pocket.

"Come, Miss Montgomery, or we will be late for breakfast," Miss Bodline said.

After their meal, they went to dance class. Their instructor was Mr. Bonito, a dark Italian of medium height with a small mustache and roving eyes. Miss Farfield played the minuet while he progressed around the room, instructing the girls on the steps. Lily stood near the piano, swaying, and swinging her arms in the air.

"Miss Montgomery, we do not dance with such abandon. Some reserve, please!" Miss Farfield barked, appearing flustered. "Miss Bodline, please show her the proper steps."

"Here, watch me," Miss Bodline said, taking her arm. "I learned this dance from my sisters."

In a short time, Lily had mastered most of the controlled, repetitive steps.

Afterward, they went to their room and caught up on their coursework. When it was time to leave for their riding class, Lily noticed Miss Bodline had changed into a riding habit.

"Did you remember that we have riding class today?" Miss Bodline asked her.

"Yes," Lily replied, feeling puzzled. She soon learned the reason behind Miss Bodline's question.

Mr. Gleeston, their instructor, was a stout man with a red face and loud voice. He covered the rules of riding, and the use of the riding gear, and how to handle the horse. They were told to stand in line before the mounting block, and one by one, each student was given a horse. When it was Lily's turn, she stepped up the mounting block, eager to get started.

When Mr. Gleeston approached Lily with her horse, he frowned. "You, young lady, are not properly dressed for riding and will not be permitted to ride."

Lily was dumbfounded. Several girls tittered behind their hands as she stepped down. Miss Bodline was next, and was given her horse. When all the students were mounted, Mr. Gleeston led them out of the stable.

"I am sorry, Miss Montgomery, that you cannot ride with us today," Miss Bodline called out as she rode away.

Lily managed a weak smile, trying not to show her disappointment. She watched the instructor lead the students into the field, then returned to her room, feeling unusually somber.

Where would I get a riding habit? Besides, even if she found one, she probably could not afford it.

Chapter 10

Each evening, Miss Bodline aided Lily with her embroidery, while Lily diligently spoke to her in French. By Friday evening, both girls had improved greatly in their respective areas. The topic came up about the riding class.

"I do not think that I will make it to the riding class tomorrow," Lily informed Miss Bodline.

"Is it because you do not have a riding habit?"

Lily blushed. "Yes," she admitted. "Mrs. Bennington did not mention that it would be one of my classes and I did not think to bring one with me."

The next morning before breakfast, Miss Bodline surprised Lily by presenting her with a blue riding outfit. "I have two others. This one used to be my sister's, who is much taller. I have not had a chance to alter it."

Lily was overjoyed. It was slightly worn, but was more than sufficient for her. "Are you sure you want to do this?"

"That is the least I could do for your helping me so much with my French."

"You are very kind, Miss Bodline."

"You can call me Jane from now on."

Lily hugged her new friend. "You can call me Lily."

During the riding class, Lily performed well. She maneuvered her horse with ease and was soon galloping across the open fields, feeling the wind against her face, astonishing everyone with her prowess. The instructor's face showed signs of respect for her, and by the end of the class, he had placed her in the front of the line as a leader. Afterward, her friends showered her with compliments.

The following week, Lily received a letter from Marianne. She took it to her room and read it in private.

> *My dear cousin Lily,*
> *So much has happened since we arrived in Bath. Mother has kept me busy attending social events here. I confess that I now have two more beaus. Any time now, there should be one, if not two marriage proposals. I am undecided, and Mother has already told me that Mr. Huntington, one of the beaus, is quite acceptable. He is a widower and has a big estate and fifteen thousand a year, but he is so old! He stoops and has infirmities, and comes to Bath often for the healing waters. I told her why didn't she marry him? She said she was not looking to marry.*
>
> *The surprising news is that we received a call from Mr. Penbroke. He visited us a week ago, when he arrived in Bath. Mother wonders why he is here. She does not like that I spend time with him, but he is such fun! Also, Mr. Penbroke mentioned that rumors had it that my friend Charlotte was ill. Some even said she might have typhoid, because she had not been seen in any events in the past few days. Anyhow, as soon as I heard this, I wrote to Charlotte right away, and just received a reply.*
>
> *Charlotte was ill, and did NOT have typhoid as it was rumored. I learned the name of her handsome beau. It is Edward Grant. He was leaving for the country with his father, Lord Peterborough, at that time. Charlotte is keen on Mr. Grant, you know, and I think she was upset because he was leaving so soon. The good news is that Sir Douglas Charleton and Lady Charleton are going there for the Christmas holidays with Charlotte, who is Lady Charleton's younger sister. You see, Charlotte's home is near Mr. Grant's home. Anyhow, Charlotte is*

*very excited and has asked me to accompany her. Of
course, I'd love to go! I am just waiting for Mother to
approve the trip. She has other plans for me (a Mr.
Huntington who is very wealthy). There is no need to
write back for I will probably have left already by the
time your letter arrives.*

> *Fondly,*
> *Marianne*

Lily reread the letter. She recalled Lady Charleton's
conversation with Mariette in the carriage at Caen. "So
Marianne's friend, Charlotte, is Lady Charleton's sister," she
whispered. She also thought about Marianne and Penbroke. It
seemed as if Marianne had feelings for him. If Marianne were to
come here for Christmas then Lily knew she would not be going
to London.

November arrived and with it, cold, windy weather. It was
icy cold at times in the drafty building and Lily added extra
layers of clothing under her dress to keep warm. One day, during
their daily walk, as they passed by the Greystone Manor's tree-
lined road, Lily sensed the pounding hooves of horses. She
looked up to see two carriages swiftly bearing down on them,
apparently traveling towards the manor house.

"Girls, move out of the way. Come, come now!" Mistress
Bates shouted.

The girls were shooed off the road as the carriages flew
past them.

"Those are Lord Peterborough's carriages. We must not
slow him down. He is an important person," Mistress Fence
announced, appearing flustered.

One sunny afternoon, after classes, Miss Farfield took her
class into town for shopping. Three carriages were reserved for
the trip. They passed endless rolling hills and meadows spotted
with grazing sheep, with an occasional grand house seen in the
distance.

In town, they followed Miss Farfield towards the market.
Many people had assembled there to buy and sell cheese, cattle

and sheep, grain, and milk. Several items were for sale, like pieces of local cotton cloths woven by hand, leather goods, local pottery, hats, shoes and farm tools. Lily had to be careful in making her shillings last. The cost of her London shoes, school embroidery materials, and candles had slowly eaten away at her funds.

Later that afternoon, as they were returning to the school, their carriage passed a group of dirty miners plodding wearily along the road, carrying tools.

Miss Farfield told them there were tin mines nearby and the landowner, Mr. Stanton, owned the land adjacent to Greystone Manor. "His family is gentry. They have been here for centuries, like Lord Peterborough's family. He is an important man."

Lily wondered where her family's home was located, and how far it would be from here. She could not ignore the nagging thought that something was terribly wrong if her father had not returned from his trip yet.

The days became even colder, shorter, and wetter, restricting the girls to the courtyard. Lily used her free time either to catch up on her music, or visit the library for new reading material, or to work on her embroidery. Her embroidery stitches were now uniformly tight, and she could play short tunes on the piano by memory. Her dark tan had faded into a healthy glow and her hair reached down to her shoulders.

It came as a pleasant surprise when, on a cold Saturday morning, Lily peeked out the window and was greeted by a rare sunny day with no cloud in the blue sky. After classes, the Mistresses informed them that they were allowed to go for a walk outside. Everyone was in a good mood, with much lighthearted chatter, as they marched down the lane away from the school.

Lily discussed with Jane the latest book she was reading, expounding on its merits. With rosy cheeks and high spirits, the girls passed the border of the Greystone Manor's tree-lined road. The wind twirled their dresses, and the sun had disappeared, but that did not deter them as they advanced forward. At some point, Lily glanced up at the sky. Dark gray clouds had formed. She furrowed her brows. "I think it is about to rain," she announced to Jane.

A loud clap of thunder overhead caused the mistresses to glance up in alarm. "Come girls, let us go back quickly!" Mistress Bates shouted. "Come quickly!"

Everyone made a wild dash back to the school as the raindrops fell. There was nothing ladylike about the way they ran. Lily, being a fast runner, reached the school first. It was just in time, for the raindrops became a torrential downpour. She wiped herself dry and waited for Jane, who had been right behind her, to arrive. But she did not appear. The rest of the drenched girls spilled in, shivering and wet, followed by the assistants and the Mistresses. The lobby emptied quickly as everyone disappeared to their rooms. Miss Farfield was the last one to enter the lobby, brushing her clothes and her wet face.

"Miss Farfield, have you seen Miss Bodline?" Lily asked.

"I am sorry. I cannot tell you at the moment. After I change into dry clothing, I will check on the girls. It is likely that she may already have gone to her room." Miss Farfield departed hastily up the stairs.

Lily had a strong foreboding sense that something was wrong with Jane. She ran outside into the howling wind and icy rain, retracing the path the girls took earlier that day. Barely able to see in front of her, she raced through the muddied road, sidestepping newly formed gullies. There was no sign of life anywhere. A clap of thunder made her flinch, but she pressed forward.

"Jane! Jane!" she yelled urgently. Her face and clothes were soaking wet and she was shivering from the cold rain. It seemed like ages before she reached the tree-lined path that led to the manor house. By now, she was panting heavily from the exertion. Moments later, her heart skipped a beat when she saw the dark shape lying on the ground near the side of the road.

Lily hurried towards her friend. She bent down anxiously and helped her sit up.

"I fell and cannot walk!" Jane wailed, clutching her ankle. "My foot, it hurts."

"We need to get back!" Lily shouted. With determination, she helped her up.

Jane gripped Lily's arm, leaning on her as she hopped on one foot. The rain pounded furiously on them and it was difficult to see. They inched their way forward. Lily heard the sound of thunder and looked around. She screamed. The dark shape of a horse was gaining on them. She pulled Jane swiftly the side.

"Whoa!" the rider shouted, pulling back the black stallion, causing his front legs to paw the air.

Lily watched in amazement as the man controlled his horse and then jumped off and strode towards them. He was dressed in a black cloak, and his face was hidden under his hat.

"It looks like you need assistance!" he shouted, amidst the thundering.

"Miss Bodline fell and hurt her foot!" Lily pointed towards the direction of the school, which was a considerable distance away. "We are from the school. I do not think that she can walk very far."

He quickly assessed Jane's situation. "The manor is much closer than the school. It is best to take you there," he told Jane.

Jane nodded thankfully.

The black horse appeared skittish, so Lily held on to his reins, stroking his mane. That seemed to calm him.

The man's strong arms gently lifted Jane and deposited her on the saddle. He helped her get settled. Then he turned towards Lily. "You are next!" he shouted.

Lily did not have time to respond, for in one sweep, he lifted her, easily placing her behind Miss Bodline on the horse. Lily felt slightly giddy from the power this man was emitting. He was definitely in control.

He removed his cloak and threw it over the girls. "Here, cover yourselves with it!"

Lily clumsily helped Jane drape the garment over their heads. Made of wool, and still warm from its previous owner's body, it smelled of sandalwood and spice. There was something soothing about that smell, something familiar. Lily could feel Jane's body shivering as she hugged her, burying her face on her shoulder.

The man took the reins and led the horse toward the manor. He walked relentlessly forward, his head bowed against the force of the wind and rain.

When they arrived at the manor, the servants scurried outside to assist them. The man lifted Jane and carried her into the comforting warmth of the house. Lily followed them into the lobby. Her eyes opened in wonder as she stepped on the marble floor.

The round lobby was very large and well lit. White, Grecian columns encircled it, and in the center stood a grand staircase. Lily glanced upward, impressed by the height of the ceiling and the immense chandelier. Their rescuer was climbing the stairs swiftly, carrying Jane. He shouted orders to the servants as if he were master of the house. Lily was intrigued.

"Please come with me, Miss," a maid told Lily.

Lily followed her up the stairs, staring at the family portraits that hung on the wall. They continued down a long, carpeted corridor, past more paintings. Several doors later, they entered a bedroom.

The maid introduced herself as Dotty. She was thin and cheerful, and her movements were brisk. "Please, Miss, let me help take these off."

The clothes were stripped off of Lily, and she shivered as Dotty covered her with wool blankets.

"I heard that you and Miss Bodline were rescued and brought here. Are you from the school?" Dotty asked. She took the wet dress and wrung it tightly, squeezing the water out into the basin.

"Yes," Lily answered. She explained what happened.

"You're lucky Lord Peterborough's son was around to help you," Dotty said. "He's a fine gentleman, he is. Good to us all. Not like his aunt, Miss Grant. She's a strict one." She stretched the wet dress on the chair to dry. "Now I better go and help Miss Bodline. She's next door." She curtsied and left.

Lily sat on the bed, staring at the rain streaming down the large window and listening to the howling wind. *The man that had rescued us was none other than Mr. Grant!* He was the much-talked about son of Lord Peterborough. The one that

Marianne had been raving about all this time and the one destined to marry Charlotte. She recalled the exhilarating rescue in every minute detail. Although she could not make out Mr. Grant's features in the rain, his tall height and remarkable strength had been evident.

Someone knocked on the door and Lily went and opened it, but there was no one there. Feeling puzzled, she shut the door and turned to see Jane standing in the middle of her room. Her straggly hair was wet and she was wrapped in a blanket.

"Jane! Where did you come from?" Lily asked.

"That door." Jane pointed to the side door. "It joins the two rooms. It is much bigger in my room and there is more furniture. I don't like being alone in that room. Please join me." She limped back into her room.

"Oh, here, let me help." Lily strode toward her and took her arm. "How is your foot?"

Jane grimaced. "Still sore, I am afraid."

Lily assisted her friend to her bedroom. It was grand and also included a dressing room. Lily helped Jane sit in the armchair near the fireplace.

Jane's face glowed as she described the bravery of Mr. Grant. "To think I was rescued by Lord Peterborough's son! He was so strong and able. It almost feels like I am living in a dream."

"We were fortunate that he happened to be there at the right time."

"I think he is quite handsome and strong," Jane said, giggling. "He carried me carefully up here, as if I were fragile."

Lily stared at her friend, seeing her in a different light. Was her friend falling in love with Lord Peterborough's son?

⌘⌘⌘

Edward entered his bedroom and rang for Herman. Droplets of water streamed down his face and shirt as he removed his wet boots and placed them near the fireplace. His valet came immediately and quickly stripped off his wet clothing and helped dress him in dry, clean clothing.

Later, Edward went to the library and sat near the fireplace, gazing at the cackling flames. He thought about the two helpless girls on the road, huddling together, wet and shivering in the storm. The school was a considerable distance from the manor. What would have happened if he hadn't been riding back to the manor at that time? He shook his head.

Someone knocked on the door. "Come in."

Aunt Mabel entered the room. "Herman said you might be in here." A tall woman with soft white hair, she carried herself with dignity. "I heard that you rescued two students caught in the storm."

"Yes. I was returning from visiting the tenants, and came upon them on the road. One girl had sustained injuries to her foot and the other was helping her. Given the severity of the weather and since the manor was closer I thought it best to bring them here."

"You did well. Where did you place them? I wish to see to their needs."

"Yes, of course. They are in the east wing, the rooms nearest my bedroom. I felt it would be better there, given that the one girl's foot might need attention and the east wing is staffed with servants."

"I shall visit them," Miss Grant said. "By the way, your father is asking for you. He wishes that you meet him in the drawing room for tea."

⌘⌘⌘

Lily was conversing with Jane when they were interrupted by the arrival of the maid with a tray of tea and some biscuits, followed by a well-dressed older woman. She introduced herself as Miss Grant.

"I understand from my nephew that he helped you during the storm?"

Jane explained what happened. "We are grateful for Mr. Grant's help."

"You are fortunate that he was traveling back at that time," Miss Grant said. "I will see what clothing I can find for you to wear until your clothes are dried. I suggest you rest here until the storm abates."

"Is there a way we can send a message to the school?" Lily asked anxiously.

"It is difficult to send anyone out in this weather. We will have to wait."

Lily glanced at Jane. She didn't seem troubled by it.

Miss Grant went to the door, then turned. "By the way, this is the east wing, where the family resides. My nephew felt that you would receive better service here, since the west wing was closed while Lord Peterborough was away. We are in the process of hiring more staff for that wing. Now I must go downstairs and explain all this to Lord Peterborough," Miss Grant said as she left.

A short while later, Dotty strode into their room, humming and carrying some clothes. "Miss Grant found some of these in the trunk in the attic. They might be old, but they're clean and dry."

"Thank you," Lily said, taking them.

Dotty picked up the basin. "I better be going or else the housekeeper will be pinching my ear, she will," she said, rolling her eyes and curtsying, her brown curls bobbing under her bonnet as she bounded out of the room.

After the two girls changed into the dry clothing, they sat by the fireplace and talked about the rescue scene in all its detail. They both agreed that if it weren't for Lord Peterborough's son, they would have had a very difficult time of it returning to the school.

Dotty returned with a tray. On it were two bowls of hot soup, mutton and bread. She placed the tray efficiently on the table without spilling a drop. "Look here, some nice, hot chicken soup I brought for you," Dotty said, "to warm you up. The cook just had mutton and bread for you, but I said in a nice manner, I did, it is soup that they need on a day like today, not cold meat! She didn't like it one bit, but she made the soup!" Dotty beamed. "Eat up, now. I heard Miss Grant saying you won't be leaving until the weather lightens up, and it don't look as if it'll do that anytime soon."

Chapter 11

The next morning, Lily changed into her dried dress, which seemed to have shrunk overnight. She pulled and stretched on it in frustration, buttoning it with difficulty. Finally finished, she peered into the mirror only to see a tangled mess of blonde curls encircling her face.

Not having a comb handy, Lily raked her fingers through her hair until there was a semblance of order. It will have to do for now. She then visited Jane in her room to see how she was faring. "Jane, are you awake?"

Her friend was still in bed and her eyes were closed, which surprised Lily. She called out to her once more, but there was no response. She touched her forehead. It was hot to the touch.

Lily frantically pulled the bell for the maid. She waited for a few minutes, but no one arrived. She ran out into the hallway, looking for anyone who could help. A man stepped out of his room in front of her. She blinked, for he was none other than the handsome servant from Caen. Her heart raced at the thought that he might remember her.

He grabbed her arm. "What are you doing here, little gypsy?"

Lily's heart sank at the angry manner of his tone. Evidently, he remembered her as the gypsy that danced at Caen. He was not the mild-mannered servant who had dropped coins in her tambourine. He was acting as if he ruled the house.

Lily flung her head back. "I am Miss Montgomery to *you*!" she retorted trying to wiggle out of his grasp.

He maintained his firm grip on her arm. "Miss Montgomery? Hah!"

"I *am* the daughter of Sir Frederick Montgomery. Miss Bodline and I both attend the Greystone School for Girls," she retorted. "It was I who went to Miss Bodline's aid yesterday in the storm."

He released her arm, appearing puzzled. "Explain yourself."

"We were going for our daily walk with the other students and mistresses when it began to rain. We all ran back to the school, but Miss Bodline tripped on something and hurt her foot. I returned to find her lying on the ground and tried to help, and, and we were rescued by the kind Mr. Grant." She stared defiantly at him. "If only he were here to see how you treat his guests, he would dismiss you immediately."

He cocked an eyebrow, appearing suddenly amused. "Ahhh. Have you seen this Mr. Grant?"

"No, but, oh please! Miss Bodline needs a doctor. She has a fever and is very ill."

His amused look vanished. He frowned. "I will send for the doctor. You will attend to Miss Bodline and do not leave her room."

Lily fled toward Jane's room. When she glanced down the hallway, he was already gone. She was trembling as she went and sat next to her friend's side. Nothing was going right this morning. First Jane's feverish state, and now this. How could this happen?

The servant from Caen was probably recently hired as a footman. He might decide to talk to his master about her. Once they learned that she was a gypsy, she would be expelled from the school, and then what would happen to her? If only she had brought the legal document with her instead of leaving it behind with Mrs. Bennington.

Soon thereafter, Miss Grant arrived with the doctor and Nurse Nellie, Lord Peterborough's nurse. Doctor Johnson was a middle-aged man with graying hair and a kind face. Nurse Nellie was plump, with brown hair and large, brown eyes. The doctor gently spoke to Miss Bodline, but the only response he got was a fluttering of her eyelids. He then touched her forehead with one hand while his other hand found her wrist. "She has a high fever and a rapid pulse. She needs to be cooled down. I will need cold water and clean linen."

"Yes, of course. I will have them brought right away." Miss Grant turned to Lily. "Dr. Johnson and Nurse Nellie will take over from here. We shall leave them."

They walked together through the side door and entered Lily's room.

"It is unfortunate that Miss Bodline is suffering like this. Since you missed breakfast, a tray of food will be sent to you," Miss Grant said before she left the room.

Lily was relieved that Miss Grant did not act as if she knew about her gypsy past. The footman had kept the information to himself.

Dotty arrived shortly with a tray of food. "I heard Miss Bodline was took ill," she said, her eyes large. "Lord Peterborough's nurse is right snippety. Mr. Grant asked her to come and help, but heard tell she told him she was milord's nurse, not a schoolgirl's nurse. But we all know that he'll get what he wants. She's in there, isn't she?" She placed the tray on the table.

Lily nodded. "Dotty, do you know all the servants here, especially the footmen?"

"The footmen?" Dotty asked, appearing puzzled. "Well, if it's Robert you are asking about, he's getting on in years, and he's a widower with two children." She tittered, rolling her eyes.

"No, I did not mean it that way," Lily said, swallowing nervously. She didn't want the maid to misunderstand her. "Are there any new ones? I met a footman in the hallway earlier, and he did not look like Robert."

Dotty shook her head. "They'll be hiring more soon, but he's the only one that I know of, Miss."

After she left, Lily thought about the servant in the hallway. She didn't even know his name. She picked at her meal, her mind on poor Jane. She wished Grandmother Mirela were here. She knew how to use herbs to heal. She would know what to do about

Jane. "She would know what to do about me," she mumbled miserably.

At some point, Dotty returned to her room. "Lord Peterborough has asked that you join them for tea in the drawing room."

Lily's heart sank. *I am going to have tea with Lord Peterborough.* He was going to expel her from the school. She was sure of it. Acutely conscious of her disheveled appearance, she nervously pulled the loose strands of hair behind her ears and followed Dotty downstairs.

They entered a beautiful drawing room. Dotty left and Lily gazed in awe at the large windows, elegant Chippendale furniture, exotic rugs on the Italian marble floor, and the large fireplace with a sculpted marble mantel. Seated in the center of the room, facing the fireplace, was an older man with his head bent slightly. He was probably Lord Peterborough. He was conversing with a man whose back was also turned toward her. To their right sat Miss Grant.

Lily stood at the door, listening and waiting for them to finish their conversation.

"I am afraid the Reform bill will not be passed and there will be a price to pay," Lord Peterborough was saying in a raspy voice.

"I don't expect the Peers to readily change the way they conduct business overnight. Some who have pocket boroughs are particularly against it," the man next to him replied. "There have been rumors of rioting if it does not get passed."

At some point, Miss Grant turned and saw Lily. She gestured toward her to come. "Lord Peterborough," Miss Grant interrupted him. "I want to introduce Miss Montgomery to you."

Lily walked up to him and curtsied, trying to remember how low and how long she must hold it. After a moment or two, she looked up at the older man. His features could have been called handsome at one time, but he was as white as the moon and there was hardly any flesh on his face. His large, black eyes twinkled as he observed her.

"Lord Peterborough, I am honored to meet you."

He nodded politely, and then coughed. "You can get up now. No need for all this formality. I am not the king, you know." He chuckled, and then coughed again. "I know of several Montgomery families. You met my son, Mr. Grant." He gestured to the young man to his right.

Lily turned and drew her breath in sharply. Silence reigned for a moment. Gazing at her with an amused air was none other than the handsome servant from Caen. She felt her face heat up with embarrassment at her mistake. *Now I am definitely in trouble.*

"We already met." Mr. Grant arose and bowed slightly towards her. "Miss Montgomery, please have a seat." He gestured towards the seat next to him.

Lily sat down, her knees feeling oddly weak.

"Miss Montgomery is the friend of Miss Bodline, the girl who has the fever," Miss Grant explained. "I doubt if she will be able to leave today or even tomorrow."

"I hope she is all right," Lord Peterborough muttered, shaking his head. He coughed slightly, and then studied Lily. "I heard from my son what happened. You were brave to go looking for your friend, Miss Montgomery. I like bravery, although some might call it foolishness."

"To save a life is anything but foolish, my lord," Lily countered.

Lord Peterborough lifted a brow. "Well said. How old are you?"

"Sixteen, my lord." Lily sensed that his scrutiny was a result of years of being a peer and dealing with all types of people. She sat up straighter, her hands folded neatly on her lap.

"Hmm. Too young," he murmured, keeping his thoughts close to his chest.

A servant arrived with the tea and cakes. Miss Grant served the tea.

Lily thanked her when she was served. She chose a sweet cake, trying to remember how she was to consume it. She was about to take a bite when she saw Miss Grant lifting a spoon from the tray. There were several spoons there. Lily blushed, placing the sticky pastry back on to her plate, about to lick the frosting off her fingers when she stopped, abashed by her uncouth behavior. She glanced nervously around for something to wipe her fingers on.

"I believe you were looking for one of these?" Mr. Grant handed her a linen handkerchief, his eyes hooded.

Lily bit her lip. She thanked him and wiped her fingers on it. She was about to hand it back, when he lifted his hand and said, "You may keep it."

Lily folded it and tucked it into her pocket, feeling distraught by the whole incident.

Lord Peterborough drank his tea, oblivious of what had taken place, his mind elsewhere. "So, which side of the Montgomery clan are you from?"

Lily blinked at him. *What did he mean by that question?*

"Well, speak up, girl! Who are your parents?" Lord Peterborough asked. He coughed, grabbed his cup and downed some tea, and then sputtered.

"Now do not get excited, my dear," Miss Grant admonished him. "You always cough when you do. Take deep breaths. There."

Lord Peterborough attempted to do as she said, but his hacking cough escalated. He rang for his nurse. "Where is she when I need her?"

"She is with the doctor and Miss Bodline," Miss Grant reminded him. "Let me help you to your room. Indeed, you have been up too long."

The servants arrived and Miss Grant excused herself as she assisted Lord Peterborough back to his room.

After they left, Lily arose, blushing. She did not want to be alone in the room with this man. "I should also be going."

"Now, now. You must not desert me, too," Mr. Grant said, sipping his tea and gazing steadily at her. "It is quite all right. We do not need a chaperone. You are too young and besides, we know each other quite well by now, do we not?" He patted the seat next to him. "Please, sit down."

Lily bit her lip as she complied with his request, sitting down with her back straight like a rod. She stared ahead, avoiding his amused look.

"I wish to ask your pardon for my behavior earlier today. I was not aware of, I mean, I thought you were a servant," she said.

"I wonder how that came about," he mused.

"In Caen, at the festival, you were wearing servant's clothing."

"Oh, that," he chuckled. "I happened to save a girl the night before from a fire." He paused, flashing her a knowing look. "It is amazing, but she looked exactly like you."

Lily blinked, feeling disconcerted. Her mind raced back to that event. *He had been my rescuer.*

"As a result of the smoke, my suit was ruined and I did not have an extra change of clothes, so my valet graciously lent me some of his. They did not fit as well as I would have liked them to, I admit."

"I truly am sorry for what happened," she muttered.

"That is quite all right. Now, let me ask you a question." He leaned towards her, his eyes gleaming. "I have an excuse for converting from a servant to a son of a peer. How did you miraculously change from a gypsy overnight into *Miss Montgomery?*"

Lily leaned back, her heart racing, astutely aware of his closeness. His voice had dropped to a low growl by the time he pronounced her name, implying that he was very serious. She gulped.

"My father is Sir, Sir Frederick Montgomery, fifth, fifth baronet."

"Sir Frederick?" Mr. Grant snapped, appearing stunned. "We have known the family for many years. His wife and daughter were lost during the Greek war more than ten years ago. How could this be?"

"I'm afraid it is a long story," Lily began, hoping he would not pursue the topic.

He crossed his arms and his brows. "I have nowhere else to be at this time. Please proceed."

Resigned to tell him her story, Lily recalled her capture by the gypsies, and Mirela's dream and how she learned about her identity only recently. "Because Count Igor wanted to marry me and take hold of my inheritance, Mirela helped me escape. She told me what to do," she finished.

"Who is this Count Igor?"

"The leader of the gypsy caravan," Lily said, opening up under his show of interest. "I felt that he was too old for me, and besides, Sultana loves him. They were meant for each other."

"Tell me what happened next."

Lily was piqued by his interest. "I, uh, I came to England looking for my father. That is when I met Mr. Hartford. I showed him the legal paper and he sent me to his mother, Mrs. Hartford, who knew my father. She contacted Mrs. Bennington, a cousin of my father's and she came and took me to live with her. I was very disappointed to learn that my father was away in the East Indies." She stopped, realizing that she was rambling on, something she rarely did.

"Have you thought about returning to the gypsies, then?"

"Oh, no! I could never go back. I am *not* a gypsy."

"Hmm. How did you come to be at Greystone?"

"Mrs. Bennington sent me to the school here, until my father's return. She has kept the legal document with her."

"Ahh, how interesting." He stroked his chin. "Without that document, there is no proof of your identity. If the Mistresses found out that you were lying, or even Lord Peterborough, you would be expelled."

"It is true. She has it!" Lily retorted, arising with agitation, her hands clenched. "You do not believe me?"

"I will reserve judgement on your character. That remains to be seen. But you should keep this quiet, if I were you. People have a tendency to look for the worst in others."

Slightly mollified by his response, Lily relaxed. "I do have a locket which holds my parent's portraits, but it is at the school."

"In that case, I shall very much like to see it next time I visit the school, mostly to make sure we are talking about the same Frederick Montgomery." He was quiet for a moment, tapping his foot. "I must write to Mrs. Hartford and find out more. Meanwhile, we must keep this quiet. Neither my father nor my aunt shall know about this. Father expects all the girls attending the school to be of the highest caliber. There is no middle ground with him. If he asks, I will tell him that you are distantly related to Sir Frederick Montgomery's side of the family." He arose, as if excusing her. "That is sufficient for now. I have some affairs I need to attend to."

"I thank you for not mentioning it to anyone."

The rest of the day, Lily sat in her room, in silent contemplation over the encounter she had earlier with Mr. Grant. She admitted that she was still reeling from the surprise that he was Lord Peterborough's son. If he had not seen her in Caen dressed as a gypsy, maybe he would have readily accepted her as Miss Montgomery. But it was not so. His skepticism over her identity was causing the inner turmoil she was feeling. She was still trying to accept the fact about what had happened to her, and now she had to convince others of her identity.

Mr. Grant was not only handsome, but also wealthy and of noble birth. He was civil, strong, and quite the dashing rescuer. These were all admirable traits sought after by every young woman she knew at the school.

Lily asked herself if she had exposed too much of her past to him in order to convince him of the truth, thus presenting a problem that she had not foreseen. How was she to maintain a formal, respectful stance with such a distinguished, almost unapproachable person, who now was privy to every detail of her past? She had broken the foremost rule of social etiquette by remaining alone in the room with him, and conversing with him as if they were equals. He had an irresistible magnetism to him, which made it easy for her to open up to him. No wonder Jane appeared dazzled by him.

Unwilling to have another encounter with Mr. Grant, Lily feigned feeling tired and asked that she take her meal in her room that evening.

The next morning, Jane's fever was gone and the doctor left her under the care of the nurse. Lily was called to help Jane when Nurse Nellie left to serve Lord Peterborough.

"Be sure she gets enough liquids," the nurse said before leaving.

Lily served Jane some tea with honey. "It looks as if you are doing better."

"Thank you," Jane said hoarsely. "I have a tendency to catch colds. I should have been wearing warm clothing to begin with. That is why Mother had me bring several coats to wear."

Miss Grant entered the room, accompanied by Miss Farfield, who anxiously rushed to Jane's bed.

"How are you Miss Bodline? I came as soon as the weather permitted," Miss Farfield said.

"Better, thank you. The doctor and the nurse were here to help me, as well as Miss Montgomery."

"Yes, I was told what happened. Miss Montgomery, you have done a good deed for Miss Bodline, I am sure, but you are to return to the school with me. Lord Peterborough kindly offered to have Miss Bodline remain here until she is well enough to return. His nurse will see to her needs."

Chapter 12

Thursday evening, while Lily was mending her dress, she received a surprise visit from Jane. Her constitution appeared healthy, and her limp was barely visible. The two friends exchanged warm greetings.

"I have missed you so. How was your stay at the manor?" Lily asked her.

Jane recalled how well she was treated and how Miss Grant paid her daily visits. "I felt special there, and had everything I needed. Yesterday, I even had tea with the family in the drawing room, and later dined with them."

Lily opened her eye wide with wonder. "Oh!"

"Mr. Grant spoke to me at length, inquiring about my classes," Jane continued, her eyes shining. "He is very learned, you know, and has traveled to many countries. He knows Shakespeare well and even recited several passages from *Hamlet* beautifully. *To be, or not to be! That is the question!*"

Lily smiled at Jane's exuberance. "It is encouraging to see a man who likes to read."

"I also thanked him for rescuing us. He said that your actions were courageous, fighting that storm to come to my aid."

Lily was surprised and secretly thrilled by the compliment, and at the same time, disturbed by her feelings. *I must put Mr. Grant out of my mind.*

Someone knocked on the door, and before Lily could answer it, Miss Bradenton and Miss Lawrence slipped into the room. They were both happy to see Miss Bodline. She filled them in on her news.

"It is now official. I heard that Lord Peterborough is going to throw a masquerade ball the third week in December and the whole school is invited," Miss Lawrence announced.

"Yes, but only the older girls are allowed to stay until midnight. We have to leave earlier," Miss Bradenton reminded her.

"Some girls say that Lord Peterborough is trying to marry his son off, and that this is an opportunity for him to meet eligible girls," Miss Lawrence said.

⚜⚜⚜

One sunny and breezy afternoon, Edward rode around the estate with his cousin. Sir Douglas had chosen one of his recently purchased stallions to ride. He was passionate about his horses, and kept them in good shape to race in various events. They discussed the sheep business and how much wool they made each year. Sir Douglas was keen on expanding his textile business and increasing his wool production, and was eager to involve Edward.

Edward felt that he needed to prioritize his father's health and his own marriage before becoming involved in a complex operation that cost time and money. Being a diplomat at heart, he decided to forgo the decision. "I will consider the options," he said, as they rode back to the manor.

Along the way, they saw the line of students and the Mistresses going for a walk.

"Let us stop for a moment," Edward said, slowing down. "I wish to speak to the Mistresses."

⚜⚜⚜

Mistress Bates called out to the students, "Please move to the side. Come, girls."

Lily dutifully moved back with the other students and peered at the riders. Periodically, they would come across a rider and dogcart with supplies heading towards the manor, but these men had stopped to speak to the Mistresses.

"It's Mr. Grant," Jane whispered to Lily. "He is talking to the Mistresses."

"Whatever for?" Lily asked. She preened her neck to have a better look. Mr. Grant was conversing with the Mistresses.

"I think he has seen us. Oh, look. The Mistresses are waving to us. Come, Lily."

"Me? Why me?" Lily asked, panicking. She did not want Mr. Grant to pay attention to her in Miss Bodline's presence. "He probably wants to see how you are doing. I have nothing to do with Mr. Grant."

"Oh, all right," Jane said, hurrying towards them.

Lily turned around, looking for a way to escape, not wanting him to see her. With alacrity, she bounded to her right and slipped behind a tree. She bent down, pretending to fiddle with her stocking, in case anyone came looking for her. With relief, she heard the sound of the horses' hooves moments later.

"Lily, Lily. Oh, there you are," Jane said, appearing flushed. "I searched all over for you. The girls have already marched on without us. Come, we must hurry."

The two girls sped forward and fell into the back of the line.

"What did Mr. Grant want?"

"You were right. He wished to see how I was doing," Jane said brightly. "He commended me for feeling well enough to walk with the girls." She was silent. "He also asked about you, and where you were."

Lily's heart raced. "He did? Whatever for?"

"He said you had left something behind at the house and he was returning it. I told him that you were in line, but when he looked, you had disappeared."

"I had to fix my stocking, so I slipped behind the tree. Did he give it to Miss Farfield to give to me?" Lily asked, wondering what it was that she had left behind.

"No, he did not. He just excused himself and left. Oh, if only I were seventeen," Jane said, starry-eyed. She sighed. "I could stay longer at the ball. I would love to dance with him. Oh, I almost forgot. I heard him tell the Mistresses that he will visit the school tomorrow to represent his father, Lord Peterborough. He might even come to our classes."

The next day came too quickly. Lily did not feel like rising from bed. Her thoughts were preoccupied with Mr. Grant. He was supposed to appear at the school today. Although she was curious what it was that she had left at the manor, her inclination was to avoid him, if possible.

Today was also the day she was supposed to lead the dance with Mr. Bonito and her heart wasn't into it. Every Saturday, he chose a different student to perform the dance steps in front of the class, and today it was Lily's turn for the waltz. She planned to arrive later than usual to class, forcing him to inevitably choose someone else.

Jane took extra care in her dress, humming softly, while going over every little detail. "Come, Lily. You need to get up. It is getting late."

"I did not sleep well last night. You go ahead," Lily mumbled to her friend, pretending to yawn. "If I do not make it to breakfast, I will see you in dance class."

When Lily finally arose from bed and dressed, breakfast had passed. She slipped the locket in her pocket as an afterthought, and then headed to the dance class.

Miss Farfield was seated at the piano playing a waltz, while Mr. Bonito danced with an uncomfortable looking Miss Cray in front of the class. Lily's eyes widened when she spied the distinguished Mr. Grant seated to the side observing the couple dance.

Mr. Bonito stopped dancing when he saw Lily. He dismissed Miss Cray, thanking her and strode toward Lily. "Did you forget, Miss Montgomery? It is your turn to dance the waltz today."

Lily blushed as he took her arm and led her toward the center of the room. She felt everyone's eyes on them.

"Now, Miss Farfield, one more time, please." Mr. Bonito smiled joyfully as the music began. He twirled Lily around the room. "We must show Mr. Grant how well our students perform."

Lily moved with natural grace and poise, and Mr. Bonito was a smooth dancer. Soon she was enjoying herself, immersed in the dance, twirling around the room, while the onlookers became a blur. When the music finished, she was almost disappointed. She curtsied to the sound of the clapping.

"Magnificently done. Now let us all take partners and practice the steps. Mr. Grant, would you like to join us? I am sure any student here would be delighted in dancing with you. Miss Bradenton, you will dance the next waltz with me."

"I would be honored to dance." Mr. Grant arose, gazing at the girls, his eyes twinkling. His dark eyes rested on Lily.

Lily held her breath, and then looked down. She knew how Jane felt about Mr. Grant and did not want to encourage his attentions.

A moment of silence ensued.

"Miss Bodline, would you like to dance the waltz?"

Jane beamed back at him as they stepped into the dance.

The other girls paired off, dancing and giggling to the waltz. Lily stood awkwardly to the side, watching them dance. Her eyes kept landing on Jane and Mr. Grant. Although her friend was petite, she appeared a perfect partner for Mr. Grant, moving smoothly and effortlessly with him.

Lily wondered how it would feel dancing with him. There was something thrilling about watching him move to the music, his head erect, his profile so clean and chiseled. The dance ended too soon and he returned Jane to her former place.

The country-dances followed and Lily joined the other girls, focusing on her steps. When she looked around for Mr. Grant, he had already left.

Lily thought she would rest in the riding class, but Mr. Gleeston asked her to lead while he attended to some students at the back of the group.

Fifteen minutes into the ride, Lily spied Mr. Grant galloping towards them on his black steed. He slowed down and pulled alongside of her.

"So, you are leading here, too," Mr. Grant commented wryly.

"It is not what you think. I did not choose to lead, but was asked to by the instructors. I would have been just as content being in the back," she replied smartly, staring straight ahead. She knew that a dozen pair of eyes were glued on them.

He leaned toward her. "You dance and ride well, as I expected," he teased, "but to become a lady requires much more than that. A legal paper will not do it."

"And how is your father doing these days, Mr. Grant?" Lily asked, feeling stung.

"As well as he could be, given his ailment," he replied tightly.

Lily spurred her horse abruptly around and left Mr. Grant, riding to the back where the instructor was. "I am not feeling well," she said, desperately trying to avoid Mr. Grant's barbs. "Could you excuse me? I wish to ride back to the school."

Mr. Gleeston appeared concerned at the news, and was ready to appoint someone to accompany her, but she said she did not need assistance. He complied and she rode away from the group.

Lily sped through the meadow, eager to leave Mr. Grant behind. He was too handsome, too strong and virile, and even worse, knew too much about her past. In a few moments, she heard the pounding of hooves behind her. She glanced behind her. It was Mr. Grant, and in a short time, had caught up with her.

The two raced forward. When they reached the boundary of the forest, she slowed down, skirting the edge of trees that stood like a barrier to her escape.

He slowed down with her. "You show off your riding ability very well, Miss Montgomery."

"Mr. Grant, you are mocking me."

"On the contrary, since Mr. Gleeston said you were not feeling well, I offered to escort you back to school. I was only doing my duty. I did not expect you to ride with such enthusiasm."

They both burst out laughing.

Lily bowed her head slightly. "Then I am much obliged for your thoughtfulness in escorting me, sir."

They cantered silently for a few minutes in a rare moment of unison. Lily relaxed, listening to the sound of the fallen leaves rustling under the horses' feet, and feeling the cool breeze against her skin. "I find it wonderful being outside this time of the year," she sighed, gazing at the bucolic surroundings. "I so love it, with the leaves glistening in the sun, and looking almost like jewels. It's so beautiful."

"But it also can be dangerous," he reminded her. "As you quite well know, one minute it can be calm, and the next, stormy. One must always be on their guard."

Lily nodded, remembering Jane's plight. "You are right, indeed. By the way, Miss Bodline is doing much better; well enough to dance the waltz with you, and doing an admirable job of it."

"I hope my dancing also met your approval," he remarked dryly.

Lily blushed, feeling confused by his remark. "Oh yes, of course," she replied. *Why was he interested in my opinion of his dancing?*

"You did not seem too eager to want to dance with me, though."

"It would not have been fair to Miss Bodline and the others if I danced a second time."

He appeared thoughtful after that.

They had reached the fork in the road. One lane led to the Manor, while the other led to the school.

"Would you happen to have your locket with you?"

Lily nodded, stopping her horse. She pulled it out of her pocket and handed it to him. "The portraits of my father and mother are in it."

He examined the images, his eyebrows furrowed, and then he studied her face. "You do have the coloring of your father." He gave it back to her. "But many people have blonde hair and blue eyes."

"You still do not believe me!" she said hotly. "I know why. Gypsies have been labeled as being notorious liars, and it is difficult to trust them. I did not choose to be a gypsy. It was something thrust upon me a long time ago."

"You are mistaken. I was not referring to my feelings on the subject. For some odd reason, I do believe you, but I fear that others will think differently."

Lily quietly digested his words.

"Now I have something for you." He removed something from inside his coat and unfolding it, gave it to her. "It is a Greek cap that I brought back with me from my trip to Greece. I thought you might like to have it, seeing that it comes from your country."

Lily stared at it in wonder. The red cap had a black tassel attached to it. "Oh, this is wonderful. Thank you. I have never worn one before."

"I will help you put it on. Go on."

Lily blushed. She removed her bonnet and watched as he slipped the Greek cap on her.

"I think the tassel hangs down on the one side," he said, moving it to the side, brushing some gold curls away, his eyes resting on her wide, solemn eyes. Just then his horse nipped her black tassel, pulling on it.

Lily laughed delightedly and pulled away. She removed the cap and replaced her bonnet. "Thank you. I will cherish this gift." Then she looked up. "But I have nothing to give you in return."

"Your pleasure at my humble gift is more than sufficient reward, I assure you, my beautiful, Greek maiden," Edward said lightly, his eyes twinkling.

Lily blushed at his compliment, and then sped away with her horse amidst his roar of laughter.

≈≈≈

Later that day, Lily noticed that Jane was subdued. That evening, Lily did not get a chance to ask what was troubling her, because as soon as they adjourned to their room after dinner, Miss Bradenton and Miss Lawrence joined them.

"I saw Mr. Grant follow you when you left the riding class," Miss Bradenton said. "We were all wondering why he left."

"He said he felt obligated to escort me because I was not feeling well."

"He is gallant, is he not? He helps everyone," Jane said.

The discussion turned to the masquerade ball, which coincided with the end of the school term and their holiday plans. All sorts of costumes were suggested for the event.

Jane decided to go as Juliet, from Shakespeare's story. "I only have to sew a few things. I will need to go to town to get some supplies."

"What have you decided to be, Miss Montgomery?" Miss Lawrence asked Lily.

"I have not thought about it," Lily admitted.

"Why not go as a Greek maiden?" Miss Bradenton suggested.

Lily shook her head. She could not afford the material for the costume. "I do not have a blue skirt, or an embroidered red vest, the way I have seen it in Greek books. Besides, my fair hair will give me away."

"I have *just* the skirt you could borrow," Miss Lawrence piped in.

"I have some red velvet left over from a sewing project. You could embroider it," Jane offered.

"I was going to cut my hair," Miss Bradenton said, pulling her long dark hair that hung below her waist. "You could wear it under a Greek cap."

Lily smiled, touched by their generosity. "You all have been too kind. I will go as a Greek maiden and I will use the Greek cap that Mr. Grant gave me."

"Was that what he was supposed to give you?" Jane asked curiously.

"Yes. It belonged to my father, from his travels to Greece. Mr. Grant felt that I could have more use of it than he did," Lily said.

"May I see it?" Jane asked.

Lily retrieved it and handed it to her. "It even has a tassel."

"So that was what he wanted to give you," Jane murmured, eyeing it enviously.

"Oh, how authentic," Miss Lawrence said. "May I try it on?"

Lily helped her put the cap on. "You look more Greek than I do, with your dark looks."

"I wonder why he singled you out," Miss Lawrence said thoughtfully, giving it back.

Lily shrugged, feeling self-conscious. "Do not read too much into his actions. His nature is to be kind to everyone, and he was only being kind to me."

"I think you should be careful," Miss Bradenton warned. "I hear he is practically engaged to the Stanton girl. They have been neighbors for years and years and always marry each other. It keeps the wealth in the neighborhood. He may just be toying with you."

"Really, Miss Bradenton, he has been a perfect gentleman. There is nothing to worry about," Lily said, feeling her face heat up.

That topic was not approached again, and once the girls finished discussing their costumes, they retired for the evening.

Chapter 13

December 1831

Several days before the end of the term, Lily approached Miss Farfield and asked if she could stay with her for the Christmas holiday.

"My father is away in the Indies, and I do not have a place to stay," Lily told her.

"Miss Cray is expected for the holiday. Our home is not large enough for another guest. You *do* understand," Miss Farfield explained. "However, you may remain here at the school. I will inform Mistress Bates."

The day of the masquerade ball at Greystone Manor arrived quickly. It was unseasonably sunny for a winter day. A certain feeling of elation followed Lily throughout her morning classes. No one seemed to be paying any attention in the classes, neither the students, nor the instructors. Everyone was talking about the ball. Since this day marked the end of the school season, the classes ended early, with some of the students leaving in the morning for the holiday.

As the sun was beginning to set, Lily carefully dressed into her Greek costume. It consisted of a blue satin skirt, white blouse, and red velvet vest with decorative embroidery. She combed her golden locks and twisted them under the Greek cap. She had sewn Miss Bradenton's long hair inside the cap so that it looked like her own hair when she put the cap on.

"Oh, Lily, you look lovely. I would not have recognized you with that black hair!" Jane exclaimed when she saw her.

"And you are the perfect Juliet," Lily replied, smiling at her friend's Shakespearean attire.

They assembled downstairs in the lobby. Miss Bradenton was dressed as a shepherdess, while Miss Lawrence was dressed as an angel with wings. Her wings kept flapping behind her as she moved, causing giggles to erupt from the other students.

Miss Farfield had not changed into any costume, but wore her typical dress. It was a constant reminder that her role would not change and that she would be chaperoning them throughout the evening.

"Now remember, young ladies, once we arrive at the ball, you must wear these at all times," Miss Farfield said, handing them their masks. "Also, only the seventeen and eighteen-year-olds will remain until midnight. The younger students will leave at half past ten."

Groans came from the students in her group. "Why can we not stay until midnight?" someone asked.

"You must remember that you have not come out in society yet and it is improper to be introduced at midnight," Miss Farfield replied sharply.

Miss Farfield's comment initially dampened the girls' spirits, but soon they were back to their bubbly, cheerful selves, as they were bundled off in carriages that transported them to Greystone Manor. When they arrived, they slipped their masks on amidst bursts of laughter.

Lily and the other girls were ushered into the grand mansion. Boughs of green holly and elaborate ornaments decorated the lobby, giving it a festive air. Miss Grant, dressed in Renaissance style clothing, greeted the guests. Next to her stood Lady Charleton, who wore an eighteenth-century costume with powdered wig and much jewelry. It seemed as if they had raided their ancestral trunk, for there was a decidedly musty smell surrounding them. They did not wear masks.

"Welcome to Greystone Manor," Miss Grant told them, smiling graciously. "I suggest you partake of the meal first, which is in that direction. Then go to the hall to dance it off. There are plenty of young men to dance with, and the unveiling will take place at midnight when everyone will remove one's masks. Enjoy yourselves."

The dining room was crowded and on the table sat silver trays laden with an assortment of delicious food. Several guests were already there, dressed in various costumes, chatting merrily and partaking of the food, while servants stood discreetly to the side, ready to assist the people.

"Did you see that man standing there to your far left?" Jane whispered to Lily. "The tall one, dressed as a naval officer. He looks handsome with that uniform and those boots, does he not? He must be Lord Peterborough's son."

Lily glanced curiously toward the naval officer. He bantered with a woman dressed as Marie Antoinette. Two other men were with them. The shorter one was stout and dressed in Shakespearean style clothing while the taller one was dressed as a potbellied pirate with a striped red bandanna tied over his pony-tailed head. Soon the group dispersed and left the room.

"Come, young ladies, now do not gawk. Let us approach the dining table with delicacy of spirit. Remember to not pile food on your plates. We are not here to show how hungry we are," Miss Farfield reminded them.

After the quick meal, the girls were ushered into the great hall. The room was enormous, with its peach silk lined walls and rows of long mirrors that reflected the candlelight, giving the room an ethereal appeal. The floor was polished with beeswax and shone well under the light of the numerous candles. The high ceiling had crown molding and intricate plaster designs. There was an aura of enchantment in the air.

The girls stood near Miss Farfield, murmuring and casting covert glances at the costumed people. The orchestra members positioned in the far corner tuned their instruments with ardent strokes. Soon, the cacophony stopped and the organized, constrained notes of a minuet began. The dancers with their medley of colorful costumes, ranging from ancient times to current, moved in perfect harmony with the music, casting a surreal feeling on the scene, as if the minuet had existed even in ancient times.

"Do we need formal introductions if someone asks to dance with us?" one student asked Miss Farfield.

"It is not necessary in these types of balls. People wait until midnight to do that. However, if you plan to have a conversation with any gentleman, please do so in my sight. We do not want the school to be criticized for improper behavior."

Soon, the young men arrived, and one by one, the girls left to dance. Miss Bodline accepted an invitation to dance from a shy young man dressed in a monk's robe. "Not quite my Romeo," she whispered to Lily as she was being led to the dance floor.

Lily watched them, and then mulled over her outfit, her hand smoothing her skirt. She and another student remained behind with Miss Farfield.

"May I have the pleasure of this dance?" a man asked Lily. She turned and faced the highwayman dressed in black with dark eyes that twinkled underneath his mask. She curtsied with dismay, recognizing Mr. Bonito. He led her to the dance floor.

"Miss Montgomery, I would have known you anywhere!" Mr. Bonito exclaimed. "You are like a beautiful flower ready to--"

"Mr. Bonito," Lily interrupted, feeling flustered by his attentions. "Please do not--" She was spared her response, for he was pulled away by the steps of the dance, unable to complete his sentence.

Lily turned to face the naval officer.

"What are you supposed to be posing as? A Greek maiden?"

"*Ne, eimai Ellinida,*" she affirmed in Greek, noticing that his eyes were blue, and not dark like Mr. Grant's. If he were not Mr. Grant, then who was he? She moved out of his sight to face her next dance partner, the pirate with the ponytail, who had been in Marie Antoinette's party in the dining room earlier. Up close, his big red nose glistened under the candlelight and his face was covered with dark stubble. Lily cringed, wondering who invited him to the dance.

"I heard ye speak Greek, me lovely," he said in a roguish manner. His broad smile revealed several black teeth.

Lily gulped, thankful that she was unable to respond, because he moved on. Her next dance partner was none other than Mr. Bonito.

"We dance so well together, you and I," Mr. Bonito said. "What grace. You not only dance with your legs, you dance with your arms."

"Please, do not continue any further, Mr. Bonito," Lily countered. "I am not used to such fancy language." She noticed that several other dancers were glancing their way. Feeling flushed, she turned and faced the mysterious naval officer.

"Fancy language?" the naval officer intervened, sounding amused. "I seem to be arriving at interesting passages in your conversation. Humor me with your Greek, little Greek girl, *sas parakalo*."

Lily smiled, unwilling to continue speaking Greek. "I assume you know Greek?" she asked, but he did not have time to answer, for he moved on to the next part of the dance. When she returned to her group, she found Jane and Miss Lawrence discussing the various costumes in minute detail and deciding which ones they liked the most. They agreed that Marie Antoinette's costume was the most beautiful and that the pirate's costume was the ugliest.

"I wonder who the pirate is," Jane said.

"He is probably some uncouth farmer that pretended to be invited by Lord Peterborough," Miss Lawrence said, shuddering, gazing around. "Oh, look who is coming! The vulgar pirate himself. Which one of us do you think he is going to ask?" she whispered fiercely. She scurried towards the safety of Miss Farfield, her large wings flapping behind her.

Jane stared at Lily. Lily blinked, and then followed Miss Lawrence to the corner to stand with Miss Farfield. She was determined not to dance with him. When she heard his deep voice, she was surprised, for it sounded like Mr. Grant. She turned her head a notch, just enough to see sideways. It was the pirate asking Miss Bodline to dance. Jane curtsied and went with him, her head lowered.

The naval officer materialized in front of Lily. "I see you escaped the clutches of the infamous pirate. Would you honor me with the next dance?"

Lily hesitated, and then nodded, allowing him to lead her to the dance floor. His voice was deep, yet his sentence ended in a drawl.

"You intrigue me," he said, his lips curling. "What made you dress in that delightful costume?"

"I am partly Greek and my classmates suggested I dress the part."

"Ah, that explains it. I studied the language at Oxford and found it to be a bore, until now."

Once again, their dance did not provide them with the opportunity to speak. He was a good dancer and moved gracefully through the steps. She was unnerved when she found his gaze fixed on her every chance he could get. He was too bold. She blushed and looked away each time.

When the music ended, he led her back to Miss Farfield. "I look forward to seeing your face, my Greek maiden, when you are unveiled at midnight. I know I will not be disappointed."

Lily watched him blend into the crowd, fascinated by his charm. He must have thought she were older if he expected her to be there at midnight.

Soon, the couples were forming on the dance floor for the waltz.

Lily sensed the pirate before she saw him. She cringed as he asked her for the next dance, holding out his hand. This time she did not turn her back, for it would be obvious that she was shunning him. Instead, she curtsied and allowed him to lead her to the dance floor. As they danced to the music, Lily found her uneasiness abating. He was a good dancer, moving fluidly and with finesse, although his large stomach seemed to get in the way. As long as she did not look at him, she enjoyed being in his arms.

"Ye dance well, me lovely," he said, with his roguish accent. He leaned forward. "Like a true lady. Ye are one of the students here?"

"Yes," she replied, feeling the warmth of his breath, moving back slightly. She felt he was too close.

They passed by the naval officer who was dancing with Marie Antoinette. They made an attractive couple and danced close together. Marie Antoinette glanced at them as they passed them by.

"Did ye enjoy dancing with that officer there?" the pirate asked Lily, whisking her away from the couple. Lily was impressed by the pirate's agility.

"Why, yes," Lily admitted. "I believe he is a good dancer."

"Not like me, I am afraid," the pirate said, smiling at her. "Me stomach, it always gets in the way."

Lily was surprised by his perceptive comment. It showed sensitivity. "No, no, you do dance well," she assured him. His dark eyes seemed to have a glint in them, which she could not interpret. Feeling awkward under his gaze, her eyes moved down and settled on his bulbous nose. She swallowed her distaste and looked away trying to find something nice to say. "You have managed not to step on my feet," she mumbled.

The pirate roared with laughter. "I am thankful Lord Peterborough invited me and some others, ye know. There weren't enough men to go around for all you girls. Hehe. Mr. Grant has his hands full, I gather."

Lily blinked. So the pirate had been invited after all. "Do you know who Mr. Grant is dressed as?"

The pirate chuckled, his dark eyes twinkling beneath the mask. "Now, now. If I told ye that, missy, then it would not be a surprise at midnight, would it? All in due time, all in due time."

When they finished, he led her back to Miss Farfield and the group, bowed, and left with a flourish. Lily felt flushed from the encounter.

Jane arrived with a gypsy girl. Lily's eyes opened in wonder. Was that Marianne wearing her discarded gypsy outfit with the black wig?

"Miss Bennington said she was related to you," Jane told Lily. "So I brought her here to speak with you."

"Marianne?" Lily squeaked.

Marianne pulled Lily to the side. "Dear cousin, how are you? Do not look so astonished. I did write to you that I would be here. I came with Uncle Charles. He's dressed as the naval officer," she proclaimed. She turned around and gazed boldly at the people in the dance hall, trying to act the gypsy part to its fullest. "Did you see my friend, Charlotte? She was dancing with him just now. She has much nerve dressing up as Marie Antoinette, but she is very much the belle of the ball, so she could do what she pleases. Well, how do you like my costume?" She twirled around, her black hair flying behind her.

"What can I say?" Lily said, furrowing her brows. "You look authentic, more so with the black wig."

"Yes, and guess who mistook me for you? Mr. Grant himself. He took me to the side and called me Miss Montgomery, and then said he was surprised I had the audacity to wear the gypsy outfit." She laughed loudly. "I told him I could wear anything I wanted. He did not sound too happy. He said he plans to personally expose me come midnight." She grabbed Lily's arm. "Oh Lily, he knows! You should not have told him anything. Now everyone will know."

"It was not my fault!" Lily cried. "He recognized me from the Caen festival where I danced. Did you not tell him the truth, who you really were?"

"Of course not!" Marianne laughed. "It would be too easy. Let him get a good look at me at midnight. I cannot wait to prove him wrong." She was off with her next dance partner before Lily could ask her further questions.

Lily felt uneasy about Marianne's conversation with Mr. Grant. She wished she knew whom he was dressed as, so she could explain to him Marianne's deception.

"Come girls, we must leave," Miss Farfield said to her charges. Like a protective hen, she rounded up the students and herded them into their carriages.

There was much chattering and discussion among the students as Lily settled in the carriage and removed her mask.

"Did anyone learn who Mr. Grant was dressed as?" Jane asked around. Most of the girls shook their heads.

"Lady Charleton informed me that he was the pirate," Miss Farfield answered.

Exclamations of surprise rippled throughout the carriage.

"The pirate!" Lily cried in dismay, staring at Jane. They laughed all the way back to the school.

Chapter 14

The day after the ball, there was an exodus of students from the school, which kept the halls and rooms humming with noise. Friends hugged and bid their good-byes before embarking on their journeys home.

By dinnertime, the school was eerily quiet as only the two Mistresses, Lily, and a couple of other students sat in the dining hall. Even the lights had been dimmed so as not to waste the candles.

Lily sat next to Francis Holton, a student from her classes. Her plain face, spectacles, and brown hair pulled severely back made her appear much older. She sat next to her sister, Gloria, who was seventeen and more attractive. They lived with their father in Devon, and since it was too far away, they did not go home for the holiday.

After the prayer, Mistress Bates mentioned about the extra cost to the girls for their stay there during the holiday. "We must charge you each a guinea for your meals, candles, and use of the facilities. It will be added to your accounts."

Then, the Mistresses discussed the affairs of the school between them, leaving the girls to talk among themselves.

When the dinner was finished, Mistress Bates arose. "This will be the last meal we will eat together in the dining room. From now on, you will eat in your rooms. It is too costly to heat and light the dining room for so few."

The next morning, as Lily ate her porridge in her room, the quietness was unnerving. She thought about what her friend Jane would be doing now. Afterwards, she worked on a new pair of mittens, redoing the stitches several times, unable to concentrate, for her mind was on the ball and all that had transpired there. She wondered what Mr. Grant's reaction was when he found out that the gypsy was Marianne after all. She also thought her cousin Charles Montgomery was not one to observe proper etiquette. He not only showed interest in her by his bold talk, but also danced very closely to Miss Stanton during the waltz.

That afternoon, Lily visited the library. Sunshine from the large windows mixed with the distinctive smell of leather-bound books greeted her as she entered the spacious room. Bookshelves lined the walls, while rows of freestanding bookshelves stood in the middle of the room. Feeling content at the peaceful setting, Lily browsed the books until she found the novel. She settled in one of the chairs near the window and began to read.

A short time later, the Holton sisters entered the library carrying books. They sat next to her.

Francis peered at her book. "Which book are you reading, Miss Montgomery?"

"Victor Hugo's new novel *Notre Dame*, and is about a gypsy named Esmeralda." Lily saw her blank stare. "It is written in French and was recommended by our French instructor," she explained. "I am almost finished. I plan to read Shakespeare next."

There was a sign of respect from the two girls. Gloria recommended the Shakespearean book of sonnets that she was reading. "I find the sonnets quite beautiful. I could give you the book after I am finished."

Lily thanked her. Soon, silence reigned as they dipped their heads into their books.

Francis shut her book. "The school is so quiet now that everyone is gone," she complained. "I do not like being all alone in my room. They would not put me in the same room as my sister. What about you, Miss Montgomery? Do you feel lonely?" She removed her spectacles and began to clean them.

"Yes. I miss my friend, Miss Bodline. We shared the room together. We would stay up at night talking sometimes."

"Lord Peterborough's son was very gallant in rescuing her from the storm. I wonder if he will choose her to marry," Francis said, appearing starry eyed. She put her spectacles back on.

"I assure you, it is *not* going to be Miss Bodline," Gloria countered. "At the ball when he unveiled himself, I saw Miss Stanton, who happened to be Marie Antoinette, standing next to him. She was with him all the time."

"You cannot be too sure," Francis persisted. "I saw her dancing very closely with the naval officer. Also, remember that day Mr. Grant visited the school? He chose Miss Bodline to dance the waltz in dance class, and another day, when we were walking he stopped with his horse and asked for her."

"It will be a matter of time before he announces his engagement to Miss Stanton," Gloria insisted, glowering at her sister. "Mark my words!"

One afternoon, while sifting through her clothes, Lily came upon a white handkerchief with the blue letters EDG stitched in its corner, the very same handkerchief that Mr. Grant had lent her. She stroked the letters thoughtfully, remembering the conversation between the Holton sisters regarding Mr. Grant and Miss Stanton. Their words made her think seriously about her own thoughts about him. She realized that he represented all that was good in her life, but she could not say the same for Miss Stanton.

A week had passed since the beginning of the holiday. On a cold, windy Monday afternoon, Lily visited the library. Finding the book of Shakespearean sonnets, she settled in her favorite chair nearest the window. The fireplace in the library had remained unlit since the students left. For the first time, she felt the cold draft from the window seeping through her bones.

Lily must remember to wear extra clothing next time. She toyed with the idea of returning to her room where it was warmer, but instead, began to read. Her fingers were soon cold and numb as they turned each page. She blew into them, warming them.

A polite cough made her turn her head. It was not the high, soft cough of a female student, but a deep and mellow tone. *It was a man's voice.*

"Hello? Is anyone there?" Lily called out, bolting up, her heart racing.

In the far corner of the room, out of the shadows, emerged Mr. Grant. He was dressed in riding gear and his handsome face appeared healthy and ruddy. There was an attentive look on his face, an intensity of purpose about him as he strode towards her.

"It's a pleasure to see you again, Miss Montgomery," he said, bowing.

Lily curtsied. A thrilling feeling enveloped her, as if there was something special about this meeting. She sat down, trying to remain calm. "Mr. Grant. I did not expect to see you here."

"I was visiting with the Mistresses, and I observed you entering the library. I wished to speak to you about something." He turned and looked at the unlit fireplace and frowned. "Why do they not light the fireplace? It is too cold to sit in here. I must speak to them about this."

Without waiting for Lily's response, he strode out the library.

Lily anxiously stared at the door, wondering what he wanted to speak to her about. She sat down and resumed her reading, only to be interrupted once again with Mr. Grant's entry followed by the maid, who went about lighting the fireplace.

After the maid left, Mr. Grant stood by the fireplace, warming his hands. "I assure you this is a much better place to be than near that drafty window."

Lily hesitated, observing the warmth of the fireplace and Mr. Grant's inviting look. Throwing all caution aside, she joined him. Slowly lifting her hands, she extended them toward the crackling fireplace. She could feel the heat thawing her frozen fingertips and warming her whole body.

"You had nowhere else to go to for the holiday?" he asked quietly.

"My cousins live too far away."

Edward leaned toward her, his dark eyes intent on hers. "Did you enjoy the masquerade ball?"

Lily was mesmerized by his closeness. For the first time she noticed that his beautiful, dark eyes had long eyelashes. Realizing that she was staring, she blushed and looked down at her hands. "Very much. I have never attended anything so grand before," she admitted.

"I am pleased that you liked it. So you played the part of the Greek girl, and not the gypsy!" he said, his eyes dancing. "I was relieved to learn the truth from Miss Bennington at the unveiling, although I was disappointed that you did not stay until the end." He was silent. "Yours was a much preferable costume, in my opinion."

"Thank you, although your costume was quite authentic, I must admit that you played the part of the pirate *too* well."

"I agree with you. All the young ladies were running from me!"

As they laughed together, the room seemed to take on a life of its own, becoming warm and cozy, and full of energy. It was at that moment that Lily's comfort level took a dive. She moved away from the fireplace, and returned to the safety of her seat by the window.

Edward followed her and sat across from her. "I have some good news to share with you."

"Yes?" Lily asked.

"I received a reply from Mrs. Hartford. She confirmed what you had told me about your background. You have a loyal supporter in Mrs. Hartford." He took her hands in his. "*Dear Miss Montgomery, I want you to know that you also have a staunch supporter in me.*"

"Thank you." She felt unexplained emotions course through her body and pulled away her hands.

Edward stood up appearing slightly agitated. "You are so young, and so vulnerable." He searched for the right words. "Promise me that if you ever need help, that you will come to me."

Lily's eyes flew open in alarm. "What do you mean?"

"You are at the mercy of your cousins until your father's return," he replied, and then paused when he saw her startled look. "I do not wish to frighten you, but Mrs. Hartford feels that they do not have your best interests in mind."

Lily felt her face flush in anger. "They have been very kind to me, I assure you."

"Mrs. Bennington had no business in keeping a document that belonged to you," he retorted. He paced the room, his face troubled.

"It was because she thought it would be stolen or lost."

He stopped to glare at her. "We have *never* had an incident in all the years the school was open. Indeed, does this school look like a place where such a thing could happen?"

Lily was quiet. He was right to be offended. Everything was in its place where she had left them since she had been there. "You speak as if Mrs. Bennington does not care about me. If that is the case, then why did she send me to boarding school to become a lady?"

"The boarding school was a convenient means of removing you from their presence. You were a constant obstacle to what they wanted, which is your father's entire estate in the event of his death."

"How could you say that?" Lily cried. She arose in indignation and faced him. "I do not believe it."

"I overheard Charles Montgomery boasting to his friends, which included Mr. Penbroke and Mr. Wren, at the ball, that if Sir Frederick were to be lost at sea, and that was a good possibility, and since Sir Frederick had no survivors, he would become heir to the Montgomery fortune."

Lily was stunned. "It is true that he would be the next heir, but he said there were no survivors? Why was I not mentioned?"

"For all I know, that legal document you gave to Mrs. Bennington may have found its way into a fireplace. They would not want to have proof of your existence, now, would they?" He appeared apologetic. "I am sorry to be the bearer of this news. But you are young, and I wanted to prepare you for the worse."

Lily felt numb. "I thank you for your concern, Mr. Grant."

"Now I must be going, for I have several things I need to attend to. Good-bye, Miss Montgomery," he said, bowing.

"Good-bye, Mr. Grant," Lily said, curtsying.

The days that followed were filled with fear and trepidation about her future. Each day that Lily did not receive news about her father reinforced the chances that he would never return into her life. Her funds were almost gone. She had only a couple of shillings left.

Lily had been dependent all this time on her father's return to pay for the school tuition, and if he didn't return, what would happen to her? How would she pay for her school supplies? She struggled daily with these issues. Finally, a plan had developed in her mind. She could exchange her jewelry for money at the jewelry shop in town.

There were no more visits from Mr. Grant. Often, when Lily was in the library and heard footsteps outside the door, she expected him to enter, but it would inevitably be the other students.

Christmas was a few days away when Lily and the other two students were summoned to a meeting with the Mistresses.

"Lord Peterborough has invited us to Greystone Manor for Christmas dinner. It will be a small affair. There will be the five of us with some other guests," Mistress Bates said. "Tomorrow we will go into town for shopping, so dress well. It will be cold. We will leave here nine o'clock sharp."

Lily accompanied the Mistresses and the Holton sisters into town the next morning and was able to exchange her jewelry for cash, for which she was thankful.

The day of the Christmas dinner arrived, and Lily had dressed warmly, wearing extra clothing under her dress. She felt excited to be visiting Greystone Manor and particularly Mr. Grant. When they arrived, they were taken to the drawing room. Miss Grant greeted them, speaking to the Mistresses.

Lily glanced around the room with expectation, her eyes searching for that one person who evoked dear feelings in her. Her eyes rested on the tall figure that stood near the fireplace, his sculptured countenance appearing calm as he pleasantly conversed with Lord Peterborough.

Sir Douglas Charleton and Lady Charleton were nearby, speaking to a distinguished looking couple that Lily did not recognize. Miss Stanton stood to the side, speaking with Marianne. Miss Stanton wore a light blue dress, which accentuated her shape and matched her clear blue eyes. Her pale blonde hair was done up in the latest fashion. She was beautiful, yet carried an indifferent air about her, as if it did not matter whether or not she were there. Marianne was also dressed well, and fit into this elegant environment.

Lily suddenly felt dowdy in her old clothing that she had mended several times.

Marianne rushed to Lily and hugged her. "I thought you were going to stay at one of the Mistresses' house for the holidays."

"There was not enough room since she had already committed to having her assistant join her." Lily saw Miss Stanton staring fixedly at them. "I do not think that I was formally introduced to your friend, Miss Stanton."

"Oh, of course!" Marianne led her to her friend and made the introductions.

"I have heard so much about you," Miss Stanton said, inclining her head to the point that she appeared to be looking down at her with one raised eyebrow, although Lily was taller. "With the way Marianne raved about you, one would think that you two had grown up together all these years rather than having just met."

Lily's eyes widened. She wondered how much Marianne had told Miss Stanton. She saw Marianne blink with astonishment. "I assure you, it is as if we had been raised up together. Is it not so, Marianne?"

Lady Charleton joined them and Lily was introduced to her.

"Ah, the lovely Miss Montgomery that we have heard so much about. I feel as if I've seen you before. Maybe it is because you resemble Marianne with your fair looks."

Miss Stanton turned and set her gaze on Mr. Grant. "Mr. Grant, have you met Marianne's cousin, Miss Montgomery?"

Edward strolled toward them. "Yes, we have met," he replied. He bowed. "She was one of the young ladies I rescued during the storm. Is that not right, Miss Montgomery?"

"Miss Bodline and I are very grateful for it. We had no idea that the weather could change so abruptly," Lily said.

"The weather can be fickle this time of year," Lady Charleton said. "But at other times, the country is the most enchanting place to be."

"I love the country, too," Marianne said, appearing bright-eyed. "It provides such picturesque scenery and a peaceful environment, so different from London."

"I find this place too far away from London, and gets secluded in the winter, for the roads are typically impassable during that time," Miss Stanton admitted. Then she gave Mr. Grant a coy look. "But when you are with the ones you love, what does it matter?"

"Well said, Miss Stanton," Edward said, appearing pleased. "And you, Miss Montgomery, what do you think of the country?"

Lily noticed Miss Stanton's sudden sharp look turned her way. "I enjoy riding in the country with the wind against my face, and also the country walks," she said. "Yet, I also like London. It provides the diversion and culture that is lacking in the country."

"Ahh, but you are mistaken Miss Montgomery, we do have diversion and culture in the country," Lady Charleton said. "You have not been here long enough to witness it."

"Miss Montgomery is correct. There is something good to be said for both the city and country living," Edward said.

They were called in to dinner, where everyone was seated according to rank. Lily sat at the far end of the table with the other students. The meal was fit for royalty, with all the various dishes of soups, meats, fish, vegetables, pies, and delicious puddings. The rest of the dinner was uneventful as the two sisters occasionally offered some mundane gossip, then spent the rest of the time gazing raptly at Mr. Grant. Meanwhile, he was indulgently attentive to Miss Stanton. One time, Lily caught him bestowing a penetrating glance her way when Miss Stanton turned to speak to Marianne. She blushed and looked down at her plate wondering if she had made an error in the use of her silverware.

◦ఌ◦ఌ◦ఌ◦

Edward found it difficult to focus on Charlotte's constant prattle. How could he, when Miss Montgomery's presence captured his interest. She was appealingly fresh, dressed in simple elegance and not aware of her effect on him. What was it about her that attracted his eye? Was it her golden curls that glowed like a halo around her head, or her delicate oval face and large, blue-green eyes? Was it the way her fine lips curved when she smiled, revealing perfectly formed white teeth? No, he had seen many lovely faces before. Was it the fact that she was a gypsy with many faces? He could not tell. Whatever the reason, she had become an intriguing challenge.

"Edward, did you hear what I said?" Charlotte asked.

He turned his attention on her and politely replied to her question.

Chapter 15

Several days later, on a cold January day, Lady Charleton and Sir Douglas departed for London due to some unavoidable business they had to take care of, and Marianne left with them. Charlotte and her family remained behind at Stanton House.

Edward was in the study later that day, reviewing the books and discussing the management of the estate with Mr. Pilford, the vicar's son. Mr. Pilford was in his early twenties, of average height, with light brown hair and a pleasant constitution.

"We have yet to receive payment from the Lowry group for the wool we supplied them. Please check into this," Edward said, closing the book. "In the future, make sure that they pay at least half the amount up front when they receive the wool, and that we bill them for the rest of the amount within a month, or else it will take them forever to pay us back."

"Yes, Mr. Grant."

After Mr. Pilford left, Edward rummaged through his letters, looking for a particular business letter. He encountered Mrs. Hartford's letter in the pile. He reread it, taking great satisfaction in her enthusiastic reply. She painted a picture of Miss Montgomery as she remembered her, a beloved grandchild of her dear friends, Sir Frederick and Lady Montgomery.

Often, there were invitations from the Stanton House for dinner, and Edward and his aunt would attend. Lord Peterborough did not join them on these visits to the Stanton house. Not wanting to travel in all that cold, he remained home, under the care of his nurse. Occasionally, Greystone Manor would also invite the Stantons for dinner.

Stanton House was a sizeable mansion and held considerable wealth. Every room was decorated with taste and style suitable for nobility. In comparison to the extravagant surroundings, Mr. Stanton was an average looking man, portly and dressed simply. He kept a careful watch on his wealth and had done well over the years. Mrs. Stanton, on the other hand, was petite and vivacious and wore the latest fashions. She was also generous of heart and entertained lavishly whenever she could.

One evening, Edward attended a dinner at Stanton House with his aunt, and the topic of discussion centered on the increasing acts of aggression against nobility and gentry due to the Reform bill not being passed.

"People are restless," Mr. Stanton said. "Just this morning, word came that there was a riot in the tin mine, resulting in some men being hurt. I had to send men in there to break it up."

"I have heard rumors of similar happenings throughout England," Edward said. "People want their vote to be counted. They think the nobility is not allowing this to happen by not letting the Reform bill pass. The common people want representation, which in a number of places is not the case."

"Could the passing of the Reform bill solve everything? Will the rioting stop if it passes, or are we to have another French revolution on our hands?" Charlotte said, shuddering. "I would rather not to be here right now. Give me London any time."

"Dear, do you not think it would be better if we were back in London?" Mrs. Stanton asked her husband, appearing worried.

"I cannot leave now," Mr. Stanton said. "There is too much work to be done." He turned and looked at Edward. "Mr. Grant, please inform your father of the incident at the tin mine. He needs to know of such happenings."

Afterward, Charlotte played the pianoforte, singing in her fine silvery voice. After she finished, Edward went to her, while the others applauded.

"Did you like it?" Charlotte asked him, tipping her head prettily to one side.

"Very much," he said, smiling. "You honored us with your excellent performance. It is a shame Sir Douglas and Lady Charleton were not here to witness it."

"Yes, if only I were in London!" Charlotte sighed and complained pettily how she missed her friends, the balls and theatre, and the idle gossip. "I wanted to leave with Gertrude and the others, but Father said--" She stopped, as if catching herself in saying something she wasn't supposed to, then lowered her lashes, concealing her thoughts. "You are still here, so that is enough for me."

"Thank you for the compliment, but when I was not here, how did you ever manage?" he asked dryly.

"I have spent much time with Gertrude and Sir Douglas, and they are almost always in London." She shrugged her pretty shoulders. "You know how time flies there when you are having fun."

The following evening over supper, Edward mentioned to his father the discussion he had with Mr. Stanton. "Given the volatility of the situation, I think we should leave for London," he concluded.

"You know I do not like to travel," Lord Peterborough began, and then hesitated before saying, "but I fear you are right. It may not be safe here." He turned to his sister. "Mabel, what do you say about all of this?"

"I also do not like traveling, but I do not want to be here given the state of affairs."

They discussed the option further, and decided that they should leave soon.

A servant rushed into the dining room, panting. "There is a fire, milord, at the Stanton House! Mr. Stanton is asking for your help!"

Edward jumped to his feet and strode out the door. He rounded up several servants and headed for Stanton House. Part of the house was ablaze with fire. Luckily, the Stantons were not hurt. He found them outside, shivering from the cold and appearing dazed. He arranged to have the women transported to Greystone Manor. Everyone pitched in and fought the blazing fire all night. A line of workers had formed, carrying buckets of water that were slopped on the flames continuously in hopes to lessen the damage.

It wasn't until early morning when Edward dragged himself home and to bed. The fire was almost out. The next day it rained, helping put out the last remnants of fire at Stanton House.

Mr. Stanton and his family stayed at Greystone Manor. They showed great consternation and sadness. Much wealth had been lost in the fire. That evening, there was discussion around the dinner table. Lord Peterborough said that his sources told him that the Stanton House had been targeted because they were landed gentry.

"It seems to me you should dismiss your servants," Lord Peterborough told Mr. Stanton. "They should have been protecting you and they did not do their job."

"I have been a fair and generous employer. This does not make sense," Mr. Stanton complained.

"For some reason you were targeted," Lord Peterborough replied. "It can get ugly when people are in that mood. We may be next."

"My *dear* Mr. Stanton, we must not remain here, but leave for London immediately! It is not safe here!" Mrs. Stanton said hysterically.

Mr. Stanton agreed. "I will put my manager in charge while I am away."

They all left the following day for London.

જાજાજા

The second term at the Greystone Girls' school had begun. The corridors and rooms were once again filled with exuberant chatter and laughter. Classes were resumed, and the studies began.

One day at dinnertime, Lily learned about the fire at the Stanton House and that both Lord Peterborough's family and the Stanton family had left for London. Because of the rising instability in the country, the students were not allowed to journey into town to shop.

March arrived, and Lily received a short letter from Marianne informing her of her recent engagement to Penbroke. The wedding was scheduled to take place that summer. There was no mention of Lily's father or of her attending the wedding. "So, she will marry Penbroke after all," Lily said aloud.

Lily continued to improve in her classes. Her penmanship now equaled that of the other girls. However, her few dresses were becoming threadbare in certain places. During her free time, she mended and patched them the best she could. She had spent most of her coins on candles and school supplies, and was saving her remaining money in case it was needed later.

Lily's birthday arrived in March, a spring day like any other. The classes were the same, but she felt different, as if her birthday marked a turning point in her life. During the day, Lily sensed an anticipation of sorts, as if something was about to change in her life. When she shared the news about her birthday with her friends that evening at the dinner table, they became jubilant.

"Congratulations! Now that you are seventeen, you could have your coming out this summer and go to all those dinners and balls in London," Miss Bradenton exclaimed.

"My father is away on one of his long trips. I do not know if he will be back in time for the season," Lily replied pensively.

"If he does not return in time this year, you could always have it when you turn eighteen," Jane said.

Miss Farfield overheard them. "Miss Montgomery, I will recommend to Mistress Bates to have you moved to her floor. You have done well in your courses and I feel you are ready to move to the next level."

That evening, Lily and Jane sat talking about her impending move and what it would mean to both of them.

"I will truly miss your company. How will I get by with my French?" Jane said, her face downcast. "I wish I were seventeen so I could be in your group. My birthday is in August. I have to wait until Michaelmas to be in your classes."

"I will miss you, too. I hope they find a roommate for you."

The next morning at breakfast, Mistress Bates summoned Lily to her section of the table.

"From now on you will attend my classes and will be eating here, with students of your own age." She turned and gestured toward a student seated across from her. "Meet Miss Livingston, who will be your new roommate. She will show you to your room."

Miss Livingston was quiet and pale, and her light brown hair was pulled back tightly. After breakfast, she dutifully led Lily to her room and was silent along the way, preferring to focus on some obscure item in the distance than to talk. Lily glanced at her a few times, trying to catch her attention, but Miss Livingston was in her own little world and did not even look her way.

The room they entered was slightly larger than Lily's previous room and when she went to the window, saw that it faced the stables.

"This will be your bed," Miss Livingston said, gesturing toward the bed closest to the door.

"What happened to your roommate?" Lily asked, gazing around the room.

"She received a proposal of marriage during the Christmas break and decided to accept it," Miss Livingston snapped. She looked at her watch and frowned. "I am to take you to our classes. We already are late."

During tea break, Lily gathered her meager belongings with Jane's help and carried everything to her new room. She hung her dresses in the closet.

"Miss Livingston has many beautiful dresses. She must be wealthy," Jane said, eyeing the colorful dresses in the closet. "She will surely get many proposals of marriage."

"What matters wealth?" Lily asked. "She is as cold as a fish. No one will ask for her."

Jane giggled. "It is known that wealth makes up for any insufficiencies. I have heard of arranged marriages based on wealth alone. Oh, Lily I will miss your cheerful company!"

Chapter 16

April 1832

The Greystone Girls School was closed for the Easter holiday. Once again, the rooms and corridors were quiet. Lily felt a sense of relief at the chance to rest from all the schoolwork, but was sorely disappointed that she had not been able to bid Jane farewell before she left. That evening at dinner, Mistress Bates reminded Lily and the Holton sisters about the extra cost for staying there, and that they would be eating their meals in their rooms.

That night, as Lily rested in bed, she thought about her future. Where was she going to go for the summer when her term finished? There had been no letter from Mrs. Bennington for a long time. Was she to continue the school next season? How was she going to pay for her tuition and extra costs? It was a sleepless night for her.

The next morning, Lily penned Mrs. Bennington a letter, informing her that the term would finish in June. Would they send for her then? She also asked her if she had heard anything from her father. She sent the letter off that day.

Afterwards, she took a stroll in the garden, for it was a sunny day and she sorely needed some comfort from her troubled thoughts. A line of cherry trees bordered the garden, displaying magnificent white blossoms. Lily spied the Holton sisters in the garden and joined them. The three girls strolled among the rows of red and yellow tulips and lilac bushes, chatting about their sewing projects and other topics.

The garden soon became their meeting place, and when it rained, they met in the library.

Two days before Easter, Lily met the Holton sisters in the garden. The two girls were subdued and told her that they had received news from their father that they would not be returning to the school next term.

"I'm sorry to hear that," Lily said.

"Our father's health has been ailing lately and he cannot afford to have us both in school," Gloria explained. "Oh, I forgot to mention, did you hear the latest news about Mr. Grant?"

Lily became alert. She had missed seeing him all these months. After he left for London, there had been no news about him, leaving a void in her life that was difficult to ignore. "No, I have not."

"One of my friends, Miss Dorsey, receives newspaper clippings from her mother in London, and passes them on to me when she is finished. Anyway, a few days ago, we learned that Mr. Edward Grant is engaged to none other than Miss Charlotte Stanton," Gloria announced.

Lily's stomach plummeted as she stared in dismay at the bearer of the news. He *never showed more than a kind interest in my plight. Even worse, poor Jane would be devastated from the news. So why am I feeling so bad?*

"Miss Bodline appeared disenchanted when she learned the news, as did several other hopeful young women," Francis piped in, giving her sister a knowing look. "What do *you* think, Miss Montgomery?"

"What Mr. Grant does is none of my business. He can do as he likes." Lily's hands trembled as she smoothed her skirt. "I have some sewing I need to finish. Good-bye." She fled from the garden before the girls could respond.

Later that night in her bed, Lily's thoughts were centered on Mr. Grant. His image shifted from the handsome servant at the Caen festival, to the mysterious footman in the hallway of the Greystone Manor, to the bawdy pirate at the masquerade ball. Then she remembered his gift of the Greek cap, and the library conversation where he told her the truth about her cousins.

She felt as if she had just lost a dear friend. Everything swam together as her tears fell down her face. *How could he even think about me now, or offer any assistance if I needed it? He would be too involved in his marriage. I would have to rely on myself from now on.*

cΩΩΩΩ

On Easter morning, the Mistresses, Lily, and the Holton sisters rode to church. The ceremony was long, for the vicar took the opportunity to expound on the importance of that day and what Christ's resurrection meant. She listened intently, but the sun's rays warmed her into a drowsy state. She suppressed a yawn, for she hadn't eaten breakfast.

Afterwards, they ate the traditional Easter meal in the dining hall that adjoined the church. The vicar, his family, and several other parishioners also attended. Lily sat next to the vicar's son, Mathew Pilford. On the other side of her, was Mrs. Pilford, a plain, simple woman dressed in somber clothing and Miss Louisa Pilford, the vicar's spinster daughter.

Mr. Pilford was a friendly young man who conversed smoothly on a number of topics. He asked Lily about her family and she told him what she had told everyone else before.

Lily learned that young Mr. Pilford was managing the Greystone Manor estate.

"Mr. Grant is such a fine man, and very smart," Mr. Pilford said. "His father had left the books in shambles after his manager passed away, so I was hired during that time, but it was a daunting task, to say the least. When Mr. Grant returned from his tour, he helped make things right."

"I understand that he is now engaged to Miss Stanton," the vicar offered.

"She has beauty and wealth," Mrs. Pilford added. She turned and stared at her plain daughter and sighed. "Not everyone is blessed with good looks."

Lily stared at the downcast features of Miss Pilford, and realized that she might also have had hopes in marrying Mr. Grant.

"I hear she is bringing twenty thousand into the marriage," a parishioner offered.

The meal seemed to go too fast, for Lily and the other girls were whisked away to the school just as she was beginning to be on friendly terms with Mr. Pilford.

The next day, while Lily was in the library, reading a favorite novel, Mistress Fence brought young Mr. Pilford to her. There was a gleam in his eyes and he seemed pleased to see her. There was a moment of awkwardness as Lily scrambled to her feet, blushing at this unexpected visit.

He bowed and she curtsied.

"I was riding by and thought I would stop and see you," Mr. Pilford said.

"That is kind of you, Mr. Pilford."

He asked her if she liked to ride. She admitted that she did.

"Tomorrow I will ride around the estate. Maybe you could join me." He turned to Mistress Fence and asked if it would be all right.

"I do not see why not, providing that she is chaperoned," Mistress Fence replied. She then moved to the other side of the room to allow them to speak more freely.

Lily asked him about his father and family. Mr. Pilford's countenance became gloomy. He complained about his father's stern character and talked about how it affected the spirit of his sister and mother. He then talked about his work and soon, he was smiling again. By the end of the visit, Lily felt more comfortable with Mr. Pilford.

Mr. Pilford was true to his word. The next day, he came with his sister, and Lily joined them on their ride around the Greystone estate. First, they visited several cottages to collect the rents. The tenants were friendly and offered them refreshments. Then they went to the dairy farm, where milk and butter were made. They were treated to scones and clotted cream from the dairy master's wife. Then, they passed by the farmland where the farmers and their helpers were hard at work, tilling the land.

Mr. Pilford was called to help solve a problem that had arisen. He rode away while the two women stayed behind. They dismounted and strolled along the meadow, holding the reins of their horses.

"My brother tells me that your father is away, in the East Indies. I understand that he is a baronet?" Miss Pilford inquired.

Lily nodded, not wanting to say too much on the topic. "He trades spices."

"And your mother?"

"She is no longer living."

"I am sorry to hear that. Has your father remarried?"

Lily shook her head. "No, and I don't think he ever will. He loved my mother too much."

"That is so beautiful to hear," Miss Pilford said, her eyes glistening unshed tears. "It is difficult to find a love match like that. I think Lord Peterborough would make a good husband, for he is kind and gentle." She paused, stopping to pick a wildflower and smell it. "All the Peterborough men loved their wives. The woman he marries will be lucky indeed."

Silence reigned for a few moments as they became immersed in their own thoughts.

"I wonder why my brother is taking so long," Miss Pilford fretted, gazing around her.

An older man rode toward them and greeted them. "Mr. Pilford is busy and will not be able to return right away. He asks that you kindly return without him," he said.

In two days, the classes resumed once again. Miss Livingston did not return to school, so Lily had the room to herself. Everything was going well for Lily. Her penmanship was excellent, she knew all the dances and played the piano passably, and could carry on a socially acceptable conversation. She walked in a subdued ladylike manner and refrained from making frank and thoughtless remarks.

A week later, Mr. Pilford visited Lily on a Sunday afternoon, after they had returned from church service. He wore his dark Sunday outfit, which gave him a distinguished air.

They strolled in the garden where other families were also visiting. The garden had become a popular place for the visitors. Therefore, there was no need for a chaperone.

"I apologize for what happened the other day. Unfortunately, problems arise when one least expects them," he began.

Lily smiled. "That is all right. I understand."

He seemed pleased with her answer. "How are your classes coming along?"

Lily told him about her schoolwork and the teachers. She then asked him about his family.

"Always the same. My father's stern character has taken the spirit out of my family. My sister is still unmarried, and my mother is afraid to live," he said bitterly. He was quiet, then turned and looked at her. "I, however, have plans to run my family differently. I plan to have several children, at least seven or eight, all running around and having fun. It will not be as stern and cold an environment as my father has it. Also, my wife will be free to express herself, and she will have pretty clothing to wear and ribbons in her hair." His eyes shone. "What do you think?"

Lily blushed, her gaze settling on a cluster of rose bushes nearby, afraid to look at him. *Was he intending to propose?* "Well, that sounds like a n-nice large family," she stammered.

Luckily, Lily was saved from having to say anything else, for they ran into her friend, Jane, who seemed happy to see her. They hugged.

"I saw you from the window and I had to come down to talk to you," Jane said to her, smiling. "It has been so long since we saw each other."

"I am glad you came." Lily introduced Miss Bodline to Mr. Pilford. "Mr. Pilford is the vicar's son. He is also the manager of Greystone Manor."

There was a sign of respect in Jane's eyes as she assessed him. She lowered her eyes, and her normally pleasant demeanor froze into a timid smile.

"Miss Bodline is one of my best friends," Lily proclaimed. "She is the gentlest, kindest person I have ever known. She is also a vicar's daughter." She locked her arm around her friend's arm affectionately.

"Miss Montgomery is too gracious," Jane said, blushing. "If there were a person who was ever so kind or gentle, it would be her."

Mr. Pilford's eyes rested with appreciation on Jane. "I can understand how you could feel that way about Miss Montgomery. The feeling is mutual."

Jane's eyes grew large with wonder at his compliment. She stared at him, and then at Lily.

Jane strolled with them, and Mr. Pilford asked her a few polite questions about her family. It wasn't long before Jane blossomed under his gentle probing, chatting away and laughing with them.

His visit was short and pleasant. After he left, Lily hummed to herself as she and Jane continued walking in the garden.

"So tell me all about it," Jane said. "Are we to hear wedding bells soon?"

"He hasn't asked me," Lily retorted, smiling. She thought about what would have happened if Jane hadn't appeared. Would he have proposed? What would her answer have been? She, shook her head. "I do not think he is the one for me."

"He seems taken in by you."

"Do you think so?" Lily said, sighing. "He is more like a brother, or close kin. He is kind and considerate." She was quiet, trying to listen to her feelings. "He is also quite logical, and can rattle off numbers easily. But there is no excitement, no thrill that the thought of him might provide, as does Mr.--" She stopped before she could say Mr. Grant's name. She bit her lip. She had been a second away from blurting out her secret.

"Oh, so there is someone else," Jane teased her. "A secret love?"

"Dear Jane! Do not talk about me. More importantly, I thought about you when I heard the distressing news about Mr. Grant and Miss Stanton. He surprised us all, for he had showered his attentions on you so much, that he had us all believing that it was you he loved!"

A shadow passed over Jane's features. "Yes," she replied. She turned slightly away from Lily, looking in the distance. "I was foolish to think that he would return my love. He did show considerable attention toward me, but in all truth, no words of affection were spoken between us." Jane turned her sad gaze on Lily. "He did everything that was worthy and in good form, like a true gentleman. I could not fault him for loving another. I was the one at fault. My imagination formed associations in my mind that did not exist."

They walked for a while without saying a word.

"It is a good match, I hear," Jane continued. "Miss Stanton is twenty-one, beautiful and exceedingly wealthy. I am a plain vicar's daughter. It is only fitting that I set my cap on a more suitable match."

"You have a beautiful spirit, Jane, and even Miss Stanton, with all her beauty and wealth, cannot match that!" Lily said. "Indeed, you will find your true love one day, and all this will be a distant memory."

Jane smiled at Lily and squeezed her hand affectionately. "Thank you for your good wishes. I have missed talking to you. I also hope you will find your true love one day."

Their walk ended soon after that and Lily returned to her room, pondering on Jane's painful admission of love for Mr. Grant. He *was* good, as Jane said, for Lily had witnessed his gallant rescue of Jane as well as other good acts. Could it be possible that Lily had also been falling under his spell, mistaking his gentlemanly acts of kindness as signs of affection? Yet she could not put him out of her mind. He had become a part of her, buried deep in her psyche; his image represented all that was good, no matter how unattainable he was.

Mr. Pilford, on the other hand, was kind and gentle, and occasionally, Lily would picture herself as a manager's wife, running the house and taking care of a large family. Little did she realize that it would be the last time she would see Mr. Pilford in that capacity, for life was to change drastically for her in the coming weeks.

Chapter 17

13 June, 1832

It rained all day on Thursday, only two days away from the end of the term. That day was to become imprinted in Lily's memory for a long time. That afternoon, she received the fateful letter from Mrs. Bennington.

Lily,

It is with deep regret that I am writing to you. We received a letter just the other day from the East Indies shipping company. They stated that your father was traveling here, on a ship from the East Indies, when the ship was lost at sea. It is presumed that he has met with his maker. Given the unfortunate circumstances, I went to the attorney, Mr. Hartford, with this news and he read me the will. The will does not mention you at all. By law, everything will pass over to my brother Charles. He has left him everything, including the town home in London and the estate in the country. Unfortunately, I have received no monies and it will cost me a considerable amount of funds to sustain your schooling. In addition, Marianne will be getting married and the wedding will deplete our funds further.

Given these circumstances, I will not be able to meet the financial demands of the school. I will write a letter to the Mistresses stating the case. You will have to earn your own keep from now on.

Mrs. Bennington

Lily reread the letter, feeling numb all over, unable to accept the news of her father's death. The dream that she had been holding on to all these weeks was her father's image, greeting her. Now that dream was shattered. Now she had no one to love her. What was she to do? She did not go to dinner, but stayed in bed, rocking to and fro, silently mourning the father she did not remember.

The next morning was dreary and wet and Lily felt too miserable to get up for her classes. When Mistress Fence stopped by, Lily explained that she was not feeling well. She was told that if she felt better, she should resume classes.

Later that morning, Lily finally sat up in bed, still feeling morose. Her thoughts were in turmoil. She knew what would happen. It was just a matter of time before Mistress Bates received her cousin's letter and would summon her. She had to design some plan.

Mr. Grant had said to turn to him if she ever needed help, but he was in London busy with Miss Stanton. She did not even know his address in London. There wasn't even Mirela to turn to. She was in Germany. Lily wept, missing her. Mirela always knew what to do.

At least Lily knew Mrs. Hartford's address. *Kind Mrs. Hartford.* Sobbing and choking on her tears, Lily penned a letter to her telling her the news and asking for her advice. She also requested that she inform Mr. Grant about her situation. After her tears subsided, Lily arose to mail her letter.

That evening, a servant by the name of Franny came to her room and said that Mistress Bates asked to speak to her.

"Please tell her that I will be there shortly."

Lily dressed for the meeting, her anxiety mounting. She had not met formally with Mistress Bates since her arrival to the school last September. Had Mistress Bates received her cousin's letter, and if so was she going to dismiss her? Where would she go? How would she pay back her tuition? All kinds of terrible thoughts assailed her young mind.

When she arrived at the office, Mistress Bates was there. Her features were pinched.

"We received a letter today from Mrs. Bennington, informing us that your father has passed away," Mistress Bates announced.

"I also received such a letter." Lily searched for a handkerchief in her pocket and dabbed her eyes with it, feeling the pain of her loss once more.

"Please control yourself. We also learned about your true circumstances of the past. We first heard rumors back in December, during the ball, about your gypsy past, spread by your cousin Miss Bennington, who said she was disguised as you. Of course, we discussed it with Mr. Grant and he dismissed her quibble as being part of the disguise she wore, but this letter," she thrust the document in Lily's face, "coming straight from Mrs. Bennington, we *cannot* ignore!"

Lily read the words in shock. It stated that Lily was a gypsy that had shown up claiming that she was Sir Frederick's daughter and that they believed her story, expecting Sir Frederick to return shortly to verify her identity. But when he was presumed dead, and there was no mention of her in his will, then they could not vouch for her true identity. Due to insufficient funds, she would ultimately be responsible for her fees.

Lily trembled with rage at her cousins' betrayal. "I am the rightful daughter of Sir Frederick Montgomery!"

"So you say. We maintain the highest caliber in this school and your hidden past, the life of a gypsy, would have sooner or later inflicted a bad influence on the other students." Mistress Bates shuddered. "To think that we were harboring a gypsy under our roof!"

"It was no fault of my own that I was raised up as a gypsy," Lily began, but was interrupted by an imperious stare from Mistress Bates.

"I do not care whether or not it was your fault." Mistress Bates tapped her foot nervously on the wood floor. "You will not be permitted to further your education here, and you must pay the thirty-six guineas that you owe us."

Lily's fingers shook as she pulled out her purse and gave her all the money she had in her possession. "Here are five guineas towards the cost. That is all I have."

"Huh! That is not enough." Mistress Bates paced the room, causing the keys hanging from her waist to rattle with each step she took. "You must pay the rest of the money."

"I can be an assistant to Miss Farfield," Lily cried. "I have done well in my studies, I have."

Mistress Bates stopped and gave her a horrified look. "Given your gypsy past, you are quite unqualified." She resumed her pacing. "We have recently lost a maid who left to get married. You will take her place. It will take you two years' worth of work to pay back your debt."

Lily's pride was shattered. She had wanted to become a lady, one that her father could be proud of, but it was not meant to be. In such a short time, she had lost everything, her father, her chance to become a lady, and her pride. She could see no other way to procure the funds than by working.

With a determined look, Lily pulled herself upright and straightened her back. "I am not afraid of work. When do I begin?"

"Immediately. Gather your belongings. I will send a maid to take you to your room."

Lily slipped into her room, thankful that everyone was still at dinner and did not see her humiliating exit. She numbly pulled her clothes from the closet and folded them into the bag, the tears streaming down her face. She had worked so hard to become a lady, to please her father, and now she had lost everything.

Minutes later she was done. She sat on the bed and waited, her heart racing at what was before her. Should she just leave everything behind, and risk going back to the gypsies? *No, you can't do that. That will surely label you a gypsy for the rest of your life.*

By the time Franny, the servant, came to get her, Lily had recovered her composure.

"Miss, you are to come with me to your new room."

And that is how Lily found herself that night on the fourth floor, all alone, in a tiny attic room crying heartily.

The school was quiet the next day, as most of the students had left for the summer. There was not a moment of rest for Lily. She was given a simple gray cotton dress with a white apron and her hair was severely pulled back and hidden under a gray bonnet. She worked with Franny Rothbee, the maid who had come to take her to her new room.

Franny was twenty years old, with a homely face and a sturdy body. "We are to clean all the bedrooms, including hallways, classrooms, and closets, before the students return in the fall," she told Lily.

"There are so many rooms!" Lily cried.

"Do not worry." Franny laughed. "We do not have to do them all in a day's work. We have the whole summer."

Each day, Lily helped Franny remove the bedding, linen and curtains from several bedrooms. They dumped everything in a pile at the end of the hall, and then later carried it downstairs to a back room for washing. Lily hauled several buckets of heated water to the back room, filling the five large wash basins. Then they sat and scrubbed the bedding and linen clean with soap, rinsing them in fresh water, and hanging them outside to dry.

In the evenings, Lily and Franny ate with the other servants, downstairs in the large wooden table in the kitchen. There was Mr. Caldor, the aging butler who never married and minded his own business, except whenever he barked out an order. Once in a while, Susan and Minnie, Franny's younger sisters would join them if they were called in that day to help with the chores. Then there was crabby Mrs. Durham, the housekeeper, and the nosy Mrs. Brewson, the cook. Both appeared old and overweight, with wrinkled faces, and they filled the dinner table conversation with complaints about their ailments, like Mrs. Brewson's rheumatism, or Mrs. Durham's weak heart.

Lily's dinner often consisted of watered-down tea, a bowl of vegetable or meat stew and some bread. Other times, they had only plain bread and cheese or a piece of boiled mutton. In the mornings, there would be fresh milk and bread.

In her small attic room at night, Lily would often stare out the tiny window at the black, star-studded sky, thinking about the elusive Mr. Grant, with his handsome features. He would arrive on his horse, his face ruddy and his dark hair rustled by the wind, and he would sweep her away. They would ride off together, far away from the Mistresses. Then Lily would turn her face away from the window and look around the small room, remembering where she was and sigh, wondering for the hundredth time if Mrs. Hartford had given him the letter.

One day, while washing clothes, Franny asked her about her past.

Lily told her the truth, holding nothing back. She even included Mrs. Bennington's letter. "That is why I am here," she finished.

"With kinfolk like that, who needs enemies, huh!"

"What about you?" Lily asked. "How did you come to be here?"

"We've lived in a cottage on Lord Peterborough's land for many years. The Rothbees have always been farmers, and my father is one, but he's sick with his heart and can't farm, so we all have to help in some way. There are seven of us children. Me older sister, Victoria, worked here, and when she left for York with her husband, I came in her place. You've met Minnie and Susie who come once in a while to help."

"Do you stay here?"

"Oh, no. I go home to sleep and come early in the morning to work," Franny said, busy washing the sheets. "It's good that they feed us here, for there ain't much food at home." She told Lily about her beau, Samuel, who was a farmer. "We plan to marry in August. He says he'll not have me working here once I'm his wife."

"Oh, that is nice."

"Yes, it is. We'll have our own house and I'll be the perfect wife," Franny said starry-eyed. "Do you have anyone special?"

Lily stopped what she was doing and thought for a moment. Mr. Grant's image came to mind. She blushed. "No one has proposed yet, but there is someone who is a friend. He is the young Mr. Pilford, the vicar's son."

Lily resumed her work. Sadly, these past few weeks, she had heard nothing from Mr. Pilford, and now had begun to wonder that maybe he did not even care for her.

Two weeks later, Mr. Pilford paid the school a visit. Lily was outside hanging up clothes to dry with Franny when she saw him riding down the path towards the school. She dried her hands quickly on her apron and ran and hid behind a tree so he wouldn't see her.

"Lily, what's the matter?" Franny asked her.

"Sshh!" Lily hissed, pointing frantically toward Mr. Pilford.

Franny looked, and then shrugged, resuming her task. "Can't understand why she does not want to see him," she mumbled.

Mr. Pilford dismounted from his horse and sauntered towards the school whistling. He was dressed in his Sunday suit and carried a bouquet of flowers. Lily had not been to church since she began her work. She waited for the defining moment, and it wasn't long in coming. He left the school, looking dejected. The flowers were still in his hands as he rode away.

"Well, how do you like that?" Franny said, her hands on her full hips. "Your suitor comes with flowers and all you do is hide behind the tree."

"He thought I was a lady," Lily said. "If he saw I was a maid, he wouldn't be interested in me."

"Do not hold yourself up too high!" Franny spat, shaking her wet finger at her. "T'aint nothing wrong to work and make a decent living. If he were a true friend, he wouldn't stop seeing you."

Lily knew that Franny was right, but there were no more calls from Mr. Pilford. She wondered what the Mistresses told him. She brooded over what happened as she went about her work. Although she felt betrayed that he did not reappear, she also felt somewhat relieved. She did not want to marry him, and if he had proposed to her, she might have felt obligated to accept. But another part of her was disappointed. If he were a true friend, he wouldn't have stopped visiting her.

Other days, Lily dusted the rooms, wiped the fireplace mantels and polished the furniture, and helped scrub and wax the floors. There were new candles to make from the wax drippings, as well as inkwells to fill. There were many closets to clean and cupboards to empty, clean, and restock. It seemed as if every minute of Lily's waking moment was dedicated to paying back the debt she owed to the school, and she loathed it. There was no time to read, to ride a horse, or to even walk. She knew that Franny and the other maids had the day off on Sundays, but she was not even allowed to leave the school.

While scrubbing the stairs one afternoon, Lily complained to Franny. "They work us too much, and hardly give us enough food to eat!" she cried. "They act as if they are better than us."

"That's the way it is," Franny said simply.

Lily was also told by Mrs. Durham that she was to bathe on Saturday evenings, and that she had to use the water in the bathtub after the other maids took their baths in it first, since it cost money to heat up the water. Disgusted at that, Lily secretly hauled a bucket of cold water to her room. Then, using the soap scrubbed herself until her body tingled. The bath was as cold as the creek water, but she was used to it. She preferred washing in clean cold water than in lukewarm dirty water.

At night, Lily would be so exhausted and hungry, that when she entered her tiny room, she would crawl into her cot, too tired to change into her nightgown.

Chapter 18

One sultry evening, Lily sat down in the servants' kitchen with Franny to a humble meal consisting of day-old bread, a hunk of cheese and watered-down tea. Mr. Caldor, Mrs. Durham, Mrs. Brewson and Debbie were already seated at the kitchen table, eating hearty leftovers from the Mistress's meal.

It had been an exceptionally hot day, and Lily felt exhausted from the tiring work. As the school term approached, their chores increased considerably. They needed to have everything ready before the students arrived. Lily felt the perspiration running down the middle of her back. She scratched the back of her neck, something she would never have dared attempt in school. How she had changed from that ladylike image she had been trying to attain a few months ago. It seemed so far away, as if in a dream. *How I wish I could go into a creek and wade in the cool water!*

Franny stared at the other servants' generous portions, and then frowned at her own plate, mumbling. "This ain't enough for a working girl, it aint."

Lily knew that her friend's large shape required more sustenance than she did. She could get by with much less. Without a second thought, she broke off portions of her bread and cheese, and placed them in Franny's plate. "Here is some mutton, and bread pudding," she said grandly.

Franny's face broke out into a smile at the joking gesture. She winked at her. "Are you sure you don't want the mutton? It looks *so* delicious."

Lily giggled, rubbing her stomach. "I feel so full that I do not think I could finish it all."

Franny burst out laughing. "Ahh, all right!" She helped herself to Lily's share.

The others stopped and stared at the two girls.

"And who gave ye mutton and bread pudding?" Mrs. Durham asked imperiously.

"We were only joking," Lily muttered, feeling her face flush. She raised her plate for them to see. "See? It is only bread and cheese."

"I'll give you something to joke about. You'll wash the dishes and pots after this meal!" Mrs. Durham retorted. She and the others resumed their eating, mumbling amongst themselves.

Franny wrinkled her face and stuck her tongue out at them while they weren't looking, causing Lily to giggle.

It wasn't until midnight when Lily returned to her little room. The stifling heat of the attic room was so great that the open window did not bring any respite. She lay awake, thinking gloomily about her past and her future. For the hundredth time, she thought bitterly of Mrs. Bennington's abandonment of her upon her time of need. She could never have imagined such heartlessness coming from her cousin. There also had been no reply from Mrs. Hartford, ever since Lily sent her the letter over a month ago. And where was Mr. Grant, who had promised he would help her if she needed it? Mr. Pilford never visited again since that one time. It seemed as if Lily were alone in the world, with no one to help her.

Something from her past surfaced and beckoned her outside. Unable to sleep, Lily arose and ventured downstairs and out the back. She knew that she might risk seeing someone, but luckily, she did not. Her bare feet skimmed over the carpet of the cool grass, into the textured darkness of the garden. She inhaled deeply and without thinking, spun around under the starlit sky, dancing her gypsy dance in her nightgown. She twirled and whirled, and then fell on the grass, exhausted. But it did not matter. She felt joyous. In this rare moment of expression, she was able to experience some semblance of joy in her life. No one could take this feeling tonight away from her. A short while later, she slipped back into her room, and in no time, fell peacefully asleep.

꧁꧂꧁꧂

Since the announcement of Edward's engagement to Miss Stanton in the papers, everyone of importance had invited them to dinner. They had been together almost daily, attending social events and dinners. Charlotte blossomed in this environment and had become quite popular with both the ladies and men. The fact that she was engaged to Edward did not inhibit her dallying with other men. His male friends flocked around them at dances and balls, and she flirted with them as if it were a game.

One particular evening at a dance, Edward had finished dancing with Charlotte and was conversing with his old, school friends, Mr. Mansfield and Mr. Beaumont, both sons of nobility. At one point, he spied Charles Montgomery dancing a waltz with Charlotte. He did not feel comfortable having an old rival dancing with her.

"Grant, have you heard a word I said?" Mr. Mansfield asked. His features were boyish, and he had a good-natured, lopsided smile.

Edward tore his gaze from the couple and focused on his friend. "Hm? What was that?" he asked. Without waiting for a reply, he turned a bemused gaze back on the couple.

"I say, he is keeping watch on Old Monty," Mr. Beaumont explained to Mr. Mansfield, nodding towards the dancing couple.

"Just look at that, Grant," Mr. Mansfield said, staring at the couple. "Old Monty will not sit still. He always wanted to be first at Oxford, whether in classes, or boat racing, or fencing. Now he has to go after your woman too."

"If she were my fiancé, I would be challenging him to a duel!" Mr. Beaumont exclaimed.

"Come now, it is just a dance," Edward said, touching his friend's arm to reassure him.

"Monty could never match your caliber," Mansfield said. "You were the best athlete in the school."

Mr. Beaumont appeared appeased, but Edward's stomach churned as he recalled Montgomery's competitiveness. He had caught him cheating once in college, just so he could be victor. No, he did not like Charles Montgomery's crafty character at all.

When Charlotte finally returned to him, Edward took her arm and excused himself from his friends. His grip was firm as he marched her towards the refreshments. "You know I do not like you dancing with Charles Montgomery," he muttered.

"Do not be so stuffy," she said, laughing at him. "I know him well. He will not bite."

Edward clenched his jaw. "You trifle with me. You do not care what I think?" he growled.

Charlotte's eyes flew open. "Do not start a scene!" she hissed. "I do care what you think, but--" she glanced around her to see who was looking at them.

"Yes?"

"I have a reputation, you see," she retorted, her blue eyes flashing. "I am considered the belle of the town, and given that, it is expected of me to dance with everyone."

"Not if you are to be married to me."

"Edward Grant, I think you are jealous," she replied, laughing gaily into her fan.

⁂

On a Saturday afternoon in August, Edward rode in Hyde Park with Charlotte. The grounds were filled with people of all types either walking, riding, or in their carriages. They stopped often to chat. Later that afternoon, he dropped off Charlotte at her house. She appeared to be in a good mood. Afterward, she was to attend a charitable function with her sister.

When Edward returned to his London residence, he browsed through the calling cards. They included invitations for dinner from an earl, a marquis, and a viscount.

The last card in the pile was from Mrs. Hartford. He wondered why she would have called there. Could this have something to do with Miss Montgomery? He slipped the card in his pocket. It will have to wait. First, he must visit his ailing father.

His father's room was dark and smelled of medicine. Nurse Nellie sat in a chair near the bed, reading a book. His father appeared to be sleeping. Edward strode into the room and pulled the curtains wide to allow the light to pour in. He never did like dark rooms. "How is my father?"

"His coughing was so heavy today that I had to sedate him."

Edward nodded, feeling a nagging sense of guilt. It seemed that while he had been enjoying his travels through Europe, and his engagement with Charlotte, his poor father had been battling with this illness. "I wish to be alone with him."

After the nurse left, Edward sat by his father's side, holding his cold, limp hand. Lord Peterborough's once lively eyes were now sealed shut, and he appeared emaciated and pale.

"Although we cannot converse like in the old days, I do think about you, Father," Edward said. "I have been busy with Charlotte and wherever we go everyone asks about your health." He paused, thinking. "I hope I am making the right decision by marrying her."

Lord Peterborough's eyes fluttered open. He stared at Edward for a moment, breathing shallowly, as if he wanted to say something, and then shut his eyes again. His hand squeezed Edward's, confirming his blessing to the match.

Knowing that his father was listening, Edward spoke to him in a low, soothing voice, reminiscing about the life at Greystone Manor, about his happy childhood and Aunt Mabel's charitable acts, and his father's honorable standing with the community. Edward rambled on, recalling everything he could think of that was uplifting, and trying to fill the void that was creeping in and replacing the dear father he once knew.

When he was finished, Edward was rewarded by another squeeze of the hand and a weak, raspy "Thank you," from his father. He stayed there for another hour, and then called the nurse.

That evening, Mr. Mansfield and Mr. Beaumont paid Edward a visit. They planned to visit White's club and after much badgering, convinced Edward to join them.

The topic at the club was the Reform bill. It was heard in every corner of the club, the conversations being either in whispers or in loud voices, or in angry or soothing replies. The Whigs and Tories both had their reasons for voting for or against it.

"My father voted for it. What could he do? There was pressure from the people and King William," Mr. Beaumont cried. "Now he does not even have a borough any longer."

"I think it will not be as bad as some say it will be," Edward said. "There will be more representation for those places that needed it."

"We will get much more commoners involved in politics," Mr. Mansfield said with raised eyebrows. "Who knows where that will lead us?"

"Let us be flexible about the whole thing. Time will iron out the differences," Edward replied.

Just then, Charles Montgomery entered the club with Mr. Penbroke.

"Old Monty is now Sir Charles Montgomery of Castleford," Mr. Mansfield whispered into Edward's ear. "He inherited a vast fortune from his cousin Sir Frederick, I hear, who recently died."

Edward was stunned to learn the news. Sir Frederick Montgomery was dead and Charles Montgomery had inherited his estates. That meant Miss Montgomery was surely on her own. He wondered if that was the reason why Mrs. Hartford had called upon him.

The next afternoon, Edward paid a visit to Mrs. Hartford. He was led into the drawing room, where she was seated.

"Oh, Mr. Grant! I am so glad you came. Please, sit down. Would you like some tea?"

"No, thank you."

"I am expecting Mrs. Elkins and Mrs. Lincoln to arrive shortly, so we must cover this delicate topic quickly."

"What is it you wish to speak to me about?"

"Over a month ago, I received urgent news from Miss Montgomery. Unfortunately, I was away at the time, in Bath, and did not read the letter until I returned just a few days ago," Mrs. Hartford said, appearing distressed. "She asked that you be notified of the change in her circumstances, since she did not have your address in London."

"This is in reference to her father being dead, I presume?"

"Yes, and now she is no longer accepted as a student at Greystone Manor and owes the school a considerable sum for her tuition. It appears that her cousins did not have the funds to support her any longer, and her father's will did not include her at all. She is hopeful, the poor dear, that she will be offered employment as a teaching assistant to pay for her tuition."

"I see."

"Poor Sir Frederick and poor Miss Montgomery." Mrs. Hartford sighed. "I had hoped that the two would get together, but it is not to be. Her cousins have abandoned her and she has no one to look out for her best interests. We *must* do something!"

Edward was silent, assessing the situation.

"You see, I have a fondness for the girl, for I was *very* good friends with her grandmother, Lady Montgomery, and I know that you being the good gentleman, would do the right thing by her."

"Do not worry, Mrs. Hartford. I will check into her status."

The butler announced the arrival of Mrs. Elkins and Mrs. Lincoln with their daughters.

"Now I must leave you to your party. Good day," Edward said, bowing, as he left the room. He passed the women in the hallway and exchanged polite greetings with them as he left the residence.

Edward felt troubled by Mrs. Hartford's news. He would write to the Mistresses to inquire about her status.

Charlotte was waiting for him when he returned home. She was already dressed in evening clothing and wore the diamond brooch he had given her when he proposed.

She tapped her foot nervously. "You are late. Did you forget that we had the theatre to attend today?"

"I apologize, but I had some business to attend to. I will be just a moment," Edward replied. He went upstairs and with Herman's help, prepared for the evening.

"All these social events," Edward grumbled, watching Herman shave his face. "I cannot get a day of rest. How I miss the country."

He spent the evening with Charlotte, Sir Douglas and Gertrude at the theatre, followed by a midnight dinner party at an earl's palatial residence. Edward returned home in his carriage, in the wee hours of the morning.

When Edward entered the lobby, he found all the servants hovering around, whispering to each other. A few of them appeared to have been weeping.

"Lord Peterborough," they greeted him.

Edward's heart sank at his new title. "Has my father passed?" he demanded, feeling his head suddenly throb horribly, somehow dreading to hear the news. In that infinitesimal moment of waiting to hear the answer, his aloneness was never more apparent.

"About an hour ago, my lord," Herman replied. "The nurse informed us that he is no longer with us. God rest his soul."

Edward choked back the cry that surged through his every being, and instead, mumbled something polite to them, his tongue feeling thick. He headed upstairs, his breathing heavy, as the impact of his grief threatened to overwhelm him. All he wanted was to be with his father one final time.

Behind him, he thought he heard the words muttered, "He went peacefully, milord."

Chapter 19

August 1832

A week later, on a Tuesday morning, amidst the gray clouds and drizzling rain, Lord Peterborough was laid to rest in the family grave next to his wife, with Vicar Pilford presiding over the ceremony. Many local people attended, including the gentry, villagers, tenants, farmers, and other folk in the surrounding area. After the funeral, everyone was invited to Greystone Manor for refreshments.

Edward returned to the house with his aunt, Sir Douglas and his wife, in a somber mood and preoccupied. He thought about all the social commitments in London that had to be cancelled, and when the news about his father's death had reached the elite, countless of calls poured into their London home. The relatives, noblemen, and gentry duly paid their respects, which continued until the day Edward left for the country.

The attorney in London had read his father's will. Edward was now a very wealthy Baron. He inherited the country estate, which included the school, all the expansive land used for agriculture, sheep raising, wool making, and several rented cottages. There was also the London property and countless stocks and bonds. He was also responsible for the wages of twenty-eight servants in Yorkshire and ten servants in London. His Aunt Mabel was to remain at Greystone Manor and continue receiving seven thousand pounds a year.

In a short time, lines of people of all ages, sizes, and varying occupations filtered into the lobby of the mansion, paying their solemn respects to Edward, his aunt, Sir Douglas and his wife. From there, the servants ushered them into the large ballroom and served them drinks and pastries. They spoke in hushed tones.

"He was a fine man, Lord Peterborough was," people kept saying.

Edward heard many stories that day from farmers, tenants, and locals about his father and the charitable deeds that he had done in his lifetime. Lord Peterborough was a dashing young man some said. Others said his good looks had broken many a young woman's heart.

One widow said, "What a shame that such a handsome man like your father never remarried."

"Apparently, he still loved my mother," Edward replied dryly.

Vicar Pilford and his family came to pay their respects. "Your father was a just and kind man," the vicar told him.

"We thought very highly of him," young Mr. Pilford added.

"Thank you," Edward replied resolutely. "Please, have some refreshments." He gestured towards the table laden with food.

The young Mr. Pilford stayed behind. "I do not wish to impose upon you during your time of duress, but would it be possible if I showed you the books tomorrow morning, my lord? There are some pressing issues that we need to discuss."

"Tomorrow at nine would be fine."

After the visitors left, Edward informed the staff that they would not be receiving any more visitors. He found his aunt in her room. She told him she preferred the solitude and did not want to see anyone, but he coaxed her into having tea with him in the parlor. "It will just be you and me. Please join me."

Aunt Mabel complied, and they made their way to the dayroom. She was unusually quiet as she poured the tea and handed him a cup. Her face appeared tired, as if she hadn't slept well.

"How have you been handling the loss?"

"Frankly, my dear, I feel drained. I knew it was a matter of time, given what the doctor said, but I still miss him," she replied. She took a deep breath, as if trying to calm her emotions. "How about you? You seem to be handling the loss of your father well."

"Only on the surface. Father's condition had been deteriorating for quite a while and I thought I had braced myself for the inevitable." He stopped, trying to control the emotions that rose to the surface. "Yet, I still look for him, waiting to hear his voice, that commanding tone, which made everything all right. But he is no longer, and that has left a void in my heart," he replied sadly. "I think of him with Mother, and that brings me some consolation."

They drank their tea in mutual silence.

Edward noticed that there was something else on his aunt's mind. "What is it, Aunt Mabel?"

"You are perceptive," she admitted. "I have been feeling lonely lately, and old, particularly these last few days. I was hoping with your coming marriage, that there would be new life in this old, large house. I suppose now, you probably had to change your wedding plans to a later date."

He thought about Charlotte and tensed. The day she visited him, they had an argument. He was leaving for York the following day to bury his father and requested that they move their wedding day to a later date due to his father's death, but Charlotte balked. She said that she and her family would be arriving there in November, when the repairs to their house would be finished, and she would give him her answer then. He insisted that she give him an answer before then. Charlotte lashed out in anger at him and left the room. The next day when he left for Yorkshire, she did not appear. It was bad enough losing his father, and now he had Charlotte to worry about.

"We have not settled on the new date yet. The way Charlotte loves being in London, you probably will not be seeing much of us here."

"I suppose I could get a companion to keep me company. Gertrude suggested it today before leaving for Stanton House. What do you think?"

"That seems a good idea," he said slowly.

಄಄಄

On the day of Lord Peterborough's funeral, Lily was overwhelmed with work. Franny stayed home, tending to her father, who had recently suffered a stroke. Not only did Lily have responsibility for her tasks and those of Franny, but was expected to fill in for the cook and her assistants who were away at the funeral.

As Lily waxed the hallway floor, she thought about Lord Peterborough's death. She had been saddened by the news and couldn't help thinking about poor Mr. Grant. He had lost his own father, just as she had lost hers.

"Lily, come help cut the vegetables. There's no help around here today!" Lorrie, the cook's assistant, shouted from the kitchen.

"Coming!" Lily washed first, and then hurried into the kitchen. She cut the turnips and beets, picturing poor Mr. Grant alone in his grief, with no mother or father. While stirring the stew, she pictured herself being with him and consoling him, making him feel better. Then the image shifted, and a searing pain cut through her as the truth reared its ugly head. *He is no longer Mr. Grant, but Lord Peterborough, the lord of the Manor. What would it matter to him, a lord, to worry over me, a lowly maid?*

"Lily, wake up, girl. Get the bread out of the oven before it burns!" Lorrie shouted.

Lily ran and pulled the pan out of the oven. "Ouch!" she said, having touched the edge of the hot pan. She rubbed her burned finger and looked at the dark brown bread in dismay.

At the dinner table, Lily heard all about Lord Peterborough's funeral from the servants.

"It was well attended. Besides the young Lord Peterborough, his cousin Sir Douglas, and Lady Charleton and Miss Grant, there were several gentry and many locals," Mrs. Brewson said.

"The young Lord Peterborough looked so handsome and dignified," one of the young female servants said.

"But we were drenched from the rain and the wet ground muddied all the women's dresses! Even the Mistresses got soaked!" Mrs. Durham retorted.

"This bread is brown as a cow!" Mrs. Brewson said, holding a burned piece. She turned and looked at Lorrie. "What is the meaning of this?"

Lorrie cocked her head in Lily's direction. "It's her fault, it is. She was supposed to be watching it and it just about burned. I caught her dreaming again. Thinks she's going to be a lady one day."

Everyone laughed.

"Huh, she's only a maid, and can't even cook at that," Mrs. Brewson said bluntly.

Lily blushed, biting defiantly into her dark, crusty bread, and chewing every bit of it.

Someone asked if Miss Stanton had attended the funeral.

"Miss *high and mighty* Charlotte Stanton did not attend the funeral," Mrs. Durham replied, smacking her lips. "She's too good for the likes of the country. My cousin, who was the nanny at Stanton House, said there was always trouble where Miss Stanton went. She couldn't sit still until she got her way. A pure rebel she was. Always wanted to go to London for the excitement. Now her older sister, Miss Gertrude, was always good, never getting into any trouble. She came to the funeral."

Lily was surprised to learn that Miss Stanton did not attend the funeral, which was a very important event in her mind. The servants also did not speak well about Miss Stanton's character.

"God help us once Miss Stanton becomes mistress of Greystone Manor," Mrs. Brewson muttered darkly. "The family is planning to come in November, and the wedding is in December. Too soon after the funeral. They should move the date, I say."

"No saying what that Miss Stanton will do," Mrs. Durham said, shaking her head.

❦❦❦

The next morning, Edward sat in the study, gazing outside the window at the rainy afternoon, seeing the lawn and rolling hills, thinking about the loss of his father. Everything appeared the same, the house, the servants and beautiful garden, and yet, everything was different.

At nine o'clock, Mr. Pilford arrived for their meeting, carrying a stack of books. He smelled of dampness, and his coat was wet, a sign of his having ridden in the rain to come here.

They leafed through the books for Greystone Manor, going over everything, including the prices of goods, the inventory, and the wages of the servants. The dairy farm was providing sufficient milk and butter. The farmers and their crops were discussed next. It seemed as if the rotation plan that Lord Peterborough followed was working, and there was enough wheat and corn to sustain them for a year.

"Also, all the rents have been collected," Mr. Pilford continued.

"That is good. Now what was the urgent business you needed to discuss?"

"Due to the heavy rain, it has damaged and rotted the wood in a couple of cottages. I need your permission before we began the work." He described the damages in detail. "I think it would be good for you to inspect them first."

"Very well," Edward said, nodding. "How about tomorrow at two, weather permitting?"

When they finished, piles of papers lay on the desk for Edward to review and sign.

As Mr. Pilford closed the books and put them away, Edward asked him about the happenings of the locals. Edward's father always believed in being up to date with the news of the tenants and farmers, and anyone else who lived on the land. Edward had promised him that he would continue that tradition.

Mr. Pilford told him about the latest birth, and who had died. "We also had a marriage, one of Farmer Mike's daughters. Her name is Heather, I believe."

"Farmer Mike mentioned her marriage and thanked me for something, but I did not catch what it was."

"Greystone Manor supplied them with a wedding gift of one hundred pounds," Mr. Pilford explained. "That is part of the tradition."

"Ahh, now I remember. Thank you." Edward nodded. "Any other marriages?"

"Well, one other marriage almost took place," Mr. Pilford began ruefully. "It would have been a union with me and a student from the school. We saw a bit of each other, and I attained feelings for her. Thinking that she felt the same towards me, I decided to tell the Mistresses of my intention to propose to her, as I thought it would be proper. But they were upset when they heard it, and said she would definitely not be in a position to accept me or have anything to do with me." He appeared agitated. "The reception they gave me was humiliating."

"Did you not try and speak to the young woman yourself, to discover the reason why?"

"One rejection was enough. I did not want to risk another rejection from Miss Montgomery herself."

Edward blinked when he heard the girl's name. His jaw clenched. Overwhelming feelings of possessiveness consumed him. They were not that of a detached observer, but more like that of a jealous lover. "So you were thinking of proposing to Miss Montgomery and it did not work out."

Mr. Pilford nodded. "Do you know of her? She is a student at the school."

"I am aware of her."

"She is so innocent, so refreshing and so unique. Alas, it was not meant to be." Mr. Pilford paused, turning red. "I have not seen her since then, and I noticed that she did not come to your father's funeral."

Edward was puzzled as he sifted through his mind the events of the funeral. He also had not seen Miss Montgomery there. She should have come with the Mistresses if she were employed at the school. *Then where was she?*

"And what about you, my lord? I heard there was to be a wedding, with Miss Stanton. Congratulations are in order."

"Thank you," Edward replied tersely. He arose, signaling the end of the meeting. "Remember to meet me here tomorrow afternoon. We will ride out to the cottages and inspect the damage."

After his steward left, Edward could not focus on his work. Thoughts of Miss Montgomery invaded his mind. He could not live with the guilt that was gnawing at him. He had not kept his promise to Mrs. Hartford and to Miss Montgomery. He had failed his duty as a gentleman. Because of his father's untimely death.

Could it be that Miss Montgomery refrained from attending the funeral because he had let her down? He also realized that Mr. Pilford's love for the girl was shallow, for he did not pursue her after the encounter with the Mistresses. She had been let down twice, not only from his promise to help her in her time of need, but also from Mr. Pilford. Feelings of sympathy for the girl swept over him. "When did I begin to have such feelings for her?" he muttered aloud in growing astonishment.

Unable to sit still, he strode out the door and down to the stables. Mounting his horse, he galloped into the woods to his favorite haven. There, he stayed for a while, leaning against a tree, contemplating on things. After what seemed like a long time, he finally arose and left, knowing what he needed to do.

Chapter 20

Edward strode into the Mistresses' office with mounting impatience. He must get to the bottom of this. The two women appeared flustered by the unexpected visit.

"Lord Peterborough," Mistress Bates said, curtsying. "Our deepest condolences on the loss of your late father."

"May he rest in peace," Mistress Fence finished.

"Yes." Edward paused, trying to remain calm. "I actually came to inquire about Miss Montgomery's status since the death of her father."

The two women tensed.

"She owed the school money for tuition, but only paid a portion of it," Mistress Fence began, and then looked at her sister for verification. "I forgot how much it was."

"She only paid five guineas, my lord, and still owes thirty-one. Since no one from her family came forward to pay her tuition, we were forced to hire her," Mistress Bates reported.

"As a teaching assistant, I presume."

"Oh, no! That would not do." Mistress Bates shuddered. "She works here as a maid."

"Did I hear you correctly? She was hired as a *maid?*" Edward shouted. He had never raised his voice to them before. "It is bad enough that the girl suffered from the loss of her father, Sir Frederick, and to employ her, a peers daughter, as a maid is totally unthinkable!"

Mistress Bates' face turned several shades of red.

"Do you have anything to say for your actions?"

"We heard rumors about her gypsy past, my lord," Mistress Bates began. "At first, we thought nothing of it, a rumor, that was all," she said, her voice high pitched. "But then we received Mrs. Bennington's letter."

"Mrs. Bennington's letter?" Edward echoed, raising an eyebrow.

"Her letter cast doubts upon the girl's identity and eligibility, stating that she was raised by gypsies, and the fact that no one came forward to pay her tuition, made us seriously question her credibility," Mistress Fence finished.

"Let me see the letter," Edward demanded.

Mistress Bates pulled her keys out of her pocket and unlocked a drawer from her desk. Sifting through a pile of letters, she pulled one out and handed it to him.

As he read it, his disbelief grew stronger and stronger. The girl's situation was more serious than he had imagined. The smirch on her family's name would never be erased if it were known publicly that she had been a gypsy.

He folded it and stuck it in his pocket. He glowered at them. "You will not speak to anyone ever about her past. *Do you understand?*"

"Yes, my lord," the two women squeaked in unison.

"Send for the young lady. I wish to speak to her," he commanded.

❦ ❦ ❦

At that moment, Lily was in the washroom, scrubbing the linen that she did not have time to do yesterday. She noticed for the thousandth time her reddened hands, her patched maid's uniform, the mended stockings and old, scuffed shoes. Her battered bonnet hid her pinned up hair, but a few long strands had come loose, and with a wet hand, she tiredly pulled them behind her ear. She sighed, wondering when this work would ever end.

Becky, one of the maids, ran towards her. There was an excited look on her face as she gestured wildly. "Lily! Lily! Come quickly."

Lily stood up, feeling puzzled.

"Come quickly! The Mistresses are asking for you, and I think it has to do with Lord Peterborough."

Lily wiped her hands, hurrying behind Becky. All kinds of terrible thoughts assailed her. She wondered if the young Lord Peterborough was upset that she did not attend his father's funeral. It was not her fault, for she had to stay behind and help. Maybe she was going to be scolded because the bread last night was burned.

Lily entered the office and saw young Lord Peterborough, as majestic as could be, with a brooding look on his fine features. The two Mistresses appeared terrified. A shadow crept over his face as his eyes swept over Lily's simple maid's dress. He bowed.

Lily curtsied in return, her knees feeling weak. "I was sorry to learn about the loss of your father, my lord."

"And I, yours," he said, gesturing toward a chair. "Please have a seat."

Lily sat down. Her heart was beating fast. What was he going to do?

Lord Peterborough remained standing, his hands behind his back, staring at her with brooding brows. "I learned about your plight only recently, as Mrs. Hartford, the source you wrote to, had been away to Bath and did not get to me until a few days ago."

Lily blinked in astonishment. So that is why he had not responded to her plea. Could it be that he had come at last to save her? Her heart began to beat wildly.

"I understand from the Mistresses that you owe money to the school, and they felt the best way for you to pay it back would be to work as a maid."

He turned towards the Mistresses, viewing them with a look of distaste. "I vehemently disagree with their treatment of your condition, given that you are a nobleman's daughter. I have therefore revoked that condition." He turned his gaze back to Lily. "Now, I place before you, Miss Montgomery, two other options to pay back your debt. It is up to you to decide which one you will accept."

Lily could not believe her ears. She waited to hear what he had to say with abated breath.

"One option is for you to work here as a teaching assistant, allowing you to pay off your debt in about a year," he said. He then paused, as if weighing his words. "The other option, and I believe, more suitable to a person of your stature, is to become a paid companion to my Aunt Mabel, who is getting on in years. Since the pay will be much higher, you could pay the debt off much sooner. Once your debt is taken care of, you will be free to do whatever you wish."

Lily was speechless. He was giving her a chance to choose what to do with her life. The decision came swiftly. "If it be all right with you, I will accept the offer of being a paid companion to your aunt."

Edward flashed her a special smile. "Go and get your clothes together. I will send a carriage to take you to the manor."

"Yes, my lord!" Lily sang out, curtsying. "Thank you, my lord!" She hurried out of the office and ran through the lobby and raced up the stairs, two steps at a time, singing out "I'm leaving!" to the servants she passed along the way. To think that he came to help her after all this time was like a dream come true.

Through a flurry of movements, Lily sped through the necessary steps. After a quick wash, she stuffed her clothing into her bag, and then threw on a simple white dress that had been mended many times. In a matter of minutes, she was flying out the door. She did not want to have anything more to do with the school.

Like magic, the carriage was there, waiting for her. She ran outside and a liveried servant helped her into the carriage. She did not look back as the carriage whisked her away towards Greystone Manor.

⸎ ⸎ ⸎

At that very minute, Edward was conversing with his aunt. The discussion was about Miss Montgomery.

"You think Miss Montgomery would make a good companion?" Aunt Mabel echoed, appearing surprised. "Is she not a little young? I thought she was still in school."

"Her father, Sir Frederick Montgomery, recently died, and she is penniless. She cannot remain at the school."

"Sir Frederick Montgomery? Did you say Sir Frederick Montgomery?" Miss Grant whispered, looking suddenly pale. She clutched her chair as if she were going to faint. "I knew Sir Frederick's father well."

"What is the matter?" Edward asked, going to her side.

She looked up in a daze, and nodded, a glimmer of a smile hovering over her lips. "I never told anyone this, but I was once in love with the late Sir Frederick and we almost married."

Edward shook his head, feeling surprised. "What happened?"

"It was not meant to be. When he married Judith, I vowed never to marry." She was pensive. "I remember his son when he visited once or twice here. He was young then. Now Sir Frederick's son is gone. How terribly sad."

Edward digested the news. He had always wondered whom his aunt had pined for all these years that caused her not to marry. Now he knew.

"So the young Sir Frederick married and had a daughter," Aunt Mabel continued. "What happened to her mother?"

"I understand that she died when Miss Montgomery was young."

"One would think that her father would put her in his will."

"His death was untimely," Edward said, not wanting to go into the girl's past.

"Yes, now I see it all. She has no one, and is essentially an orphan, and I need a companion. It might do both of us good," she said. "Oh dear, I forgot. Gertrude mentioned this morning that she was going to see about finding a companion for me."

"It is too late now. I sent the carriage to fetch her. Miss Montgomery will be here soon."

"Very well, then."

"When she arrives, could you see her to her room?" Edward asked. "Maybe one close to yours in case you need her? I will be out visiting the estate."

"Will you be back in time for dinner?"

"It is unlikely, for there is much work to be done. You have dinner without me."

When Edward rode away from the house, he recalled what happened at the school when he inquired about Miss Montgomery. It had never occurred to him that she would be hired as a maid. To think that all these months, she had suffered this insult without complaining to Mrs. Hartford or running away showed she had backbone.

He had also been appalled at how thin and pale she had become. There was no glow, no life in her, as he remembered her. Instead, it had been replaced by a melancholic look in her pinched features that he had not seen before. The guilt hung over him at her plight. He only hoped he hadn't been too late, and that her spirit was not broken under that harsh environment.

When Miss Montgomery chose to be his aunt's paid companion, a feeling of gladness had leapt into his heart. It was as if she had forgiven him for not coming to her aid sooner and now was offering herself as a gift.

He wondered what Mr. Pilford would do once he found out Miss Montgomery was living there. If the man loved her, he would find a way to propose to her.

"And if he did? How would you like it?" Edward said aloud. A knot formed in his chest. "You fool. You would be against it because you have been in love with her all this time."

He could not understand himself. He was now her benefactor, and she trusted him. Yet, the feelings he had for her were not that of a benefactor. Instead, the urge to hold her in his arms, to feel her close to him, to protect her, could never have been stronger. He had never felt this way for any woman before. Not even the woman he was to marry.

When Lily entered Greystone Manor, she followed the butler into the drawing room where Miss Grant was seated.

"Welcome to Greystone Manor, my dear. Please sit down. We will have tea together and become better acquainted," Miss Grant said warmly. She rang for more refreshments.

Lily expressed her condolences for Lord Peterborough.

"It is a difficult time for me, because I not only lost my brother, but also my companion. Lady Charleton and my nephew both felt that a female companion would do me good."

"I understand what you are going through, for I recently lost my father."

"I was saddened to hear the news. My condolences on your father's passing away." Miss Grant paused. "I have a confession to make. I knew your grandfather Sir Frederick, well. We were almost married."

Lily was struck by the news. "Then you might have been my grandmother!"

"I had not thought of it that way," Miss Grant chuckled, showing a rare sign of being amused. "Your father looked like him, and you do, a little."

"In what way?"

Miss Grant had a soft look on her face. "You have his blue eyes, light hair, and firm chin, although your nose is smaller. Sir Frederick had a longer, aristocratic nose."

The maid arrived with the tea and sweet cakes. Miss Grant dutifully served the tea.

"I dare say. You look rather thin, and too pale. Have they not been treating you well at the school?"

Lily placed her teacup down, feeling uncomfortable from the older lady's astute comment.

"Never mind. We will fix that quickly. Now let me see how you could help me." Miss Grant was silent, thinking. "I like to spend my mornings in my room, having breakfast and taking care of correspondence. You could get involved with that. I also supervise the housekeeper and staff during the day, and like to keep the house running smoothly, so there will be plenty to do there. When the weather is fine, I like to occupy my time in the garden. A couple of hours before dinner, I rest in my room. On

Sundays, I typically attend church services, and once in a while, will entertain guests. If there are any charitable cases, we handle them as they come. You could help there also. I do like to read, although my eyesight is not as it used to be."

"I would love to read to you."

"That would be fine. It is quite a sedentary existence. I hope it is not going to be too boring for you."

"Oh, no," Lily said, shaking her head. "I would enjoy this very much."

"Good. In the afternoons, when I take my naps, you will have some free time. You could make use of the library, or the music room. We have a nice piano. Also, if you wish, you could go out riding, although I would not go too far because the weather can change so suddenly."

"Yes, my lady."

"My nephew will be marrying soon, and his fiancé is from Stanton House, as is Lady Charleton. They are sisters and their family is wealthy, but they have no title and thus are not as honorable as peer. So it is to their best interests that they marry into nobility." She paused. "You probably know that in every household there are secrets, and whatever you hear will be kept within these walls. You *do* understand."

"Yes, Miss Grant," Lily replied. "You can trust me with your secrets."

Miss Grant leaned forward with a conspiratorial look in her face. "I am going to tell you a secret. Oh, this is so much fun! I have not had a soul to talk to about this," she said, her eyes twinkling. "Lady Charleton always had a soft spot for Edward. I could tell, but after he left for college and showed he was not interested in her, she settled for Douglas, his cousin. I felt for her, because she reminded me of when I was young. I too was in love once, with Sir Frederick, but it did not work out."

Lily nodded, spurring her on. It looked as if Miss Grant needed to talk with someone.

"Now Gertrude has pushed her sister Charlotte, to marry Edward. You know, keep it all in the family. She always said the nicest things about Charlotte in front of my brother and, of course, Lord Peterborough succumbed to the idea of having her as his son's bride. Hence, he also pushed Edward in that direction. I believe that is why Edward asked her hand in marriage."

Lily caught her breath. "Does the young Lord Peterborough not love Miss Stanton?"

"I do not know, for he has not confided in me."

A brief lapse of silence ensued as they sipped their tea, absorbed in their thoughts.

Lily was disturbed by the news. "Given that the young Lord Peterborough has decided to marry Miss Stanton, it would seem to me that he *must* be in love with her."

"When the Grants fall in love, we love fiercely, and for life. It has always been that way. Time will tell if he has made a good match."

They finished their tea.

"I would like to rest before dinner. You also look like you could use a nap," Miss Grant said. "By the way, you will eat with us at the dining table, and will join me when we have guests."

"Oh!" Lily's eyes flew open. "My clothing is not appropriate for such fine dining. I only have student dresses, and they have been mended so many times. Please, could I be allowed to dine in my room?"

Miss Grant was astonished. "That will not do. We should correct that immediately. I will have the seamstress take your measurements tomorrow. You need proper clothing if you are to be my companion."

Lily winced at the supposed cost. "Thank you, my lady. Only it will take me time to pay it back."

"I like you already. That will not be necessary. It will be a gift from me to you." She paused. "Now that you reminded me, I need to think about your pay." She coughed slightly appearing somewhat disconcerted. "Frankly, I do not know what the right amount is to pay. I have never had a paid companion before. Would three hundred pounds a year do? You could be paid quarterly. Would that be all right?"

Lily's eyes widened with surprise. She had never made that much money before in her life. It meant that she could pay off her school fees very soon. Her face broke out into a brilliant smile. She nodded. "Why yes, of course, that is fine, my lady."

"That is better. I like to see you smile. You are quite beautiful when you smile, you know. You must smile more often."

Lily thanked her, beaming.

"Now, we will go to our rooms and rest," Miss Grant said. "Dinner is at seven. Since it will be only you and me tonight, you do not need to dress up. My nephew is out seeing the estate and will not return in time. And Sir Douglas and his wife are at the Stanton House."

Chapter 21

Lily was already up and dressed the next morning when Dotty, the maid, came to her room.

"Welcome back to the manor, Miss Montgomery," Dotty said, curtsying. "I'm supposed to help you with your dress and your hair from now on."

Lily recognized the saucy maid from the year before when she stayed there with Jane, but sensed a more respectful attitude in her behavior than last year. It was as if Dotty had placed her on a higher pedestal than a mere student. "Thank you, but I have already dressed."

"Aint no problem, Miss. You can call for me whenever you need me," Dotty said, smiling. "Miss Grant is breakfasting in her room and asks that you join her when you're ready."

Miss Grant's suite was large and cheerful. Its four-poster bed sported a white silk bedspread with a flower design. Peach colored satin curtains graced the two tall windows, while a Persian rug lay in the center of the room. Miss Grant sat at a round table in the center of the room, wearing a blue, silk dress and having a breakfast of tea, hot scones, eggs and ham.

"Ah, there you are, my dear. Come, have breakfast with me."

After a leisurely meal, and listening to Miss Grant chatting about her likes and dislikes, they went over some correspondence together. Lily helped her write a few letters. Miss Grant complimented her on her writing. It seemed that the penmanship classes at the school had been successful.

When they went down to the drawing room, Miss Grant showed her two large baskets filled with a variety of colored cloths. "I get these scraps from Lady Charleton every time she visits. They come from their cotton textiles." She took out some samples and stroked them. "These will be used to make Christmas items. The finished products are placed in a basket with food and given to the needy."

"What do you make?"

"Mittens and stockings, and handkerchiefs; those kinds of things. Would you like to help?"

"Yes, of course." Lily sifted through the pile of cotton fabric, remembering that the previous day she was scrubbing linen and waxing floors.

They talked about different topics while working on their sewing projects. Lily told her about the school life and the teachers, painting funny scenes with her colorful words, and causing Miss Grant to laugh with glee.

"I have not laughed like this in a long time," Miss Grant admitted. "To think that they have dance instructors who talk and walk that way is hilarious. I admit that I never went to school, but had a governess."

"What was it like, having a governess?"

Soon, Miss Grant was reminiscing about her younger days. She told her about her studies and her governess, Miss Gracely. "She was ladylike and strict, yet I loved her dearly. She never married, you know, and after she left, we kept in contact. She died a few years ago."

Edward entered the drawing room late morning.

"Ah, there you are," he said, his eyes twinkling. "I am heading to the stables and thought I could help Miss Montgomery choose her mount. I remember that she likes to ride."

"Why of course," Miss Grant said. "Lady Charleton should be returning today from the Stanton house and I should have company then."

Lily followed Lord Peterborough down the hallway. A feeling of happiness enveloped her. "I would like to thank you for everything you have done for me."

"I should not take all the credit. You also had help from Mrs. Hartford and my aunt, who agreed to this."

"Yes. I feel as if I found a friend in Mrs. Hartford, although at one time, I thought-" she floundered.

"It was not her fault," he interjected. "She told me that she was away when your letter arrived and did not read it until recently, and felt guilty about it. I believe that she is fond of you, you know."

Lily blushed at his comment. "I think it has to do with her being good friends with my grandmother."

They reached the end of the hallway.

"You also are doing some good around here," Edward remarked. "My aunt was feeling lonely after my father's death, and from what I've seen so far, your company has pleased her."

"I like being with her." She smiled brightly.

"I am glad it is working out" His eyes dipped to her curved lips. "Would you like to see our portrait gallery? It is on our way."

"Yes."

They browsed the impressive array of paintings, all portraits of handsome men and beautiful women.

"That is my father, and there is my mother."

Lord Peterborough's virility and dark handsome looks were apparently inherited from his father, although his fine nose seemed to come from his mother. His mother was dressed attractively in the Georgian period style dress and had delicate, fair features.

"How beautiful your mother looks. You come from a handsome family."

"Thank you. It was expected that Father would marry a Stanton girl, but he fell in love with Mother and married her instead. It is well known that when the Grants fall in love, it is forever." He gazed at the portraits, appearing to be deep in thought. "Father never remarried after Mother passed away."

"Neither did my father." Her eyes went to the next portrait. The woman appeared to be a younger version of his aunt. "Is that Miss Grant?"

"Yes, and over there is Aunt Dorothy, Sir Douglas's mother. Her husband was an admiral in the navy. Both of them died when Sir Douglas was young, so he grew up here."

ৡৣৡৣৡৣ

Edward became reflective. After he graduated from Oxford, he bought a commission in the navy with his cousin, Sir Douglas. A year later, in 1827, their ship fought for the Greek cause in the battle of Navarino. The loss of life he witnessed that day devastated him. Edward realized he was not destined for military life and sold his commission soon thereafter. His father suggested that a grand tour would be good for him, to forget the past, and that is what he did. Three years he was gone, travelling through Europe with his valet.

"Does Sir Douglas and his wife live here all the time?"

"Only when they visit the country, and that is a few months of the year. Because of their business in textile goods, they divide their time between London and Paris. They have homes in both countries."

They continued their walk.

"All the Grant wives were beautiful, young, and healthy, and had heirs," he observed with a partial air.

"Shall we be going to the stables? I do not wish to leave your aunt for too long."

"Yes, of course."

They entered a doorway and walked downstairs. Miss Montgomery warily held on to the rope banister, for it was quite dark. When they reached the bottom of the steps, she looked around in awe. They had entered a large lobby depicting another era. On the one side, hung various armor, while ancient tapestries depicting battle scenes and pastoral settings hung on the other side. The tall ceiling had wood beams.

"This is the oldest part of Greystone Manor," Edward explained. "The house was given as a gift in the seventeenth century from the king to one of my ancestors for services rendered. Luckily, there have always been males to inherit Greystone Manor, that way it has stayed in the family all these years. On the surface, it does not look its age. About a hundred years ago, when the original structure was beginning to crumble, parts of it were torn down and remade, with new buildings and modernized rooms. There were once two turrets, but they were also torn down. Much of the furniture in the manor is the original, and if you go down into the dungeons, one can see the real age of the building."

"You have dungeons? Is that not the dark place where they kept the prisoners?" Miss Montgomery shuddered.

"Do not let that scare you," he said, laughing. "In the old days, they were used as a hideout to escape from their enemies." They entered a hallway. "This corridor leads to the outside, to the stables."

They passed several doors. "That door leads to the kitchen, and those stairs to the right lead up to the dining room and grand ballroom. It is an unusual layout, I admit. The servants use these back stairs often." Edward spoke in a low tone.

They wandered outside. The path led through the large garden, which had a gravel pathway in the center, and a manicured lawn on each side, lined with boxwoods. Rows and rows of blooming flowers and climbing roses were on each far end of the garden, providing a splash of color and luxuriant beauty. Up ahead, in the center, was a small pond with statues encircling it. The gardener greeted them as they passed by.

When they entered the stables, Edward looked around for the stable boy. "Roger? Are you here, Roger?" No one answered his call. "It appears that the stable boy is not around. I will have to choose a mount for you."

He pointed out the different mares and stallions. Each one had a name. Some were frisky, neighing loudly and shaking their heads, while others quietly gazed at them with lucid eyes.

"Oh, hello *Night Dust*," Miss Montgomery said, stroking his mane. The horse nipped her curls and she laughed. "I do not have any apples for you today."

Edward was surprised by the girl's familiarity with the horse. "You know the horse?"

"*Night Dust* was raised by Count Igor to sell, and *Tsingana*, his mother, was our horse." She turned back to the horse, her face next to his. "Are you happy to see me?" she whispered. She turned towards Lord Peterborough. "Did you buy him from Count Igor?"

"No, Sir Douglas bought him, for racing. He does not allow anyone to ride him, not even myself," Edward commented dryly. He stopped in front of a dappled gray horse. "Victoria is young and lively, but trained well enough to give a good ride. She is the favorite of the women who visit here."

"Victoria." Lily stroked the horse's mane, smiling. "That name has distinction."

Edward gazed at Miss Montgomery's expressive features as she whispered endearments to the horse. It seemed as if overnight her exuberance and spirit were revived. It was good that he had brought her to Greystone Manor. His eyes fell on her long golden curls that spread about her shoulders. A warm feeling enveloped him and he had an urge to touch them.

"Now my name, Lily, is only a nickname. My real name is Judith. It is not as dignified as Victoria."

"Judith," Edward said in a low voice. "Indeed, there is dignity in that name. I, for one, like it."

Miss Montgomery turned and blushed, gazing at him with those large, beautiful eyes. "You are too kind, my lord," she murmured, and stepped back, trembling like a frightened does. She turned to leave.

"Do not go yet," he murmured, suddenly feeling forlorn.

She smiled at him in that special way. "As you wish."

He smiled back.

The sound of footsteps on the gravel alerted him that someone was coming.

"Edward? There you are!" Lady Charleton called out. She approached him, smiling. "Aunt Mabel told you would be in the stables," she said gaily. Then she saw Miss Montgomery and her expression changed. Her eyes searched Edward's face, and then the girl's.

"I was showing Victoria to Miss Montgomery," Edward said matter-of-factly, masking his emotions.

Gertrude grimaced. "Oh, Victoria is Charlotte's favorite. Is it wise for Miss Montgomery to ride her?"

"Charlotte is away, and since no one else rides her, I felt it would be good for Miss Montgomery to exercise her. They were just getting acquainted."

"I came to tell you that I will be sending letters off to my parents, and to Charlotte this morning. The repairs at Stanton House are finished and I am letting them know that they can return. Did you want me to include anything from you to Charlotte?"

Edward tensed. "It is not necessary, but thank you for the thought. Now I must be going. I have an appointment to attend to." He tipped his hat, and moments later, mounted his thoroughbred and left.

❧❧❧

Lady Charleton hooked her arm into Lily's arm as they walked slowly back to the house. "This house is so big, that we should go back together so that you do not get lost."

Lily was led through the garden and into the house.

"I was surprised to learn that you are to be Miss Grant's companion. I thought you were at school. Tell me, how did you come to be here?"

"My funds ran low after my father's death, and I needed to work. Lord Peterborough found out about it through the school and hired me."

"It is unfortunate that all this happened without my knowing about it. You see, I had already picked out a woman for Miss Grant, a Mrs. Liston. She is exceedingly qualified for the task. She is a widow, much older, and does not require to be chaperoned." She gazed steadily at Lily. "Lord Peterborough is young and handsome, and engaged to be married, and you are rather young for the task. You know how the servants talk."

Lily tensed, realizing the direction the conversation had taken. Lady Charleton wanted her sister to marry Mr. Grant, and she was not about to let a young, single woman interfere with her plans.

They entered the lobby.

"I will have a talk with Lord Peterborough, and I do not think Miss Grant will mind. If he decides to hire Mrs. Liston, do not worry, for I have already found a position for you." She smiled. "A friend of mine in Bath is looking for a governess for her two children. She would be willing to pay fifty pounds a year. What do you think, my dear?"

"I would prefer staying here, but it is up to Lord Peterborough whether he wants to keep me or not."

They entered the drawing room. Miss Grant was there, with the seamstress.

"Ah, there you are, Miss Montgomery," Miss Grant cried out. "Come to get your fittings."

Lady Charleton's eyebrows raised when she saw the seamstress. "What is going on here?"

"Miss Montgomery is going to be fitted. Oh, do not worry! Lord Peterborough has agreed to it," Miss Grant said gleefully. "Were you in need of any alterations, my dear?"

"Oh, no, no," Lady Charleton said in a condescending manner. "I have a French woman who sews all my clothes. I will leave you to your work. I have some letters to write."

They discussed the patterns and dresses with the seamstress. They finally settled on a white day dress with small satin roses, a blue evening dress, and a more formal white silk dress with gold trim. All the dresses were to be in the latest style, with large sleeves and ribbons, and matching accessories.

It was a busy afternoon, for after the seamstress left, the housekeeper and cook came and talked with Miss Grant about needing certain supplies for the kitchen. Then, a couple of older women who lived in Leeds, visited. They had formed a charitable association for the needy in town and were asking for donations for Christmas.

"Where are you located? I will see to it that funds are sent there," Miss Grant said to them.

They gave her their card and thanked her. "May God bless you, my lady."

Shortly after, a few other visitors arrived. They were local gentry, who had not been able to attend the late Lord Peterborough's funeral and were calling to express their condolences. Miss Grant introduced Miss Montgomery as her companion, and then offered them tea and refreshments. They stayed for a while, reminiscing about Lord Peterborough.

The flow of callers continued until five o'clock when Miss Grant told the butler that they were no longer receiving callers for the day.

"I want to rest a little before dinner," Miss Grant explained. "I rarely receive more than one caller a day, so this has been tiring for me. Why don't you rest also, my dear? You do look a little tired."

Lily returned to her room and lay on her bed, going over all the details of the last two days. Her emotions were in turmoil. She went over the interaction with Lord Peterborough and the effects he had on her emotions. She could not stop thinking about him, about the way he looked, what he said, and how he had helped her. What was happening to her? Was she falling in love with him? She recalled Lady Charleton's conversation. Was she right in taking these measures to send her off to Bath? Lily felt miserable with the thought of leaving Greystone Manor.

Shortly after, she called for her bath. It was a luxurious feeling not to have to work so hard, and to relax before dinner. She chose one of her old student dresses to wear. Dotty came and helped her with her dress and hair.

When the dinner bell sounded, Lily was ready. She was worried in case Lady Charleton would bring up the subject of Mrs. Liston during dinner. If she did, what would she say in return? What would Lord Peterborough say?

She entered the drawing room. Everyone was dressed in formal attire. Lord Peterborough and Sir Douglas were deep in discussion about farming, while Lady Charleton conversed with Miss Grant. Miss Grant gestured for her to join them. Shortly, they were called into the dining room. Lord Peterborough sat at the head of the table with Miss Grant to his right. Lily sat next to Miss Grant and Sir Douglas and Lady Charleton sat across from her.

The two men resumed their conversation.

"One of my top farmers has been ill, and as a result, we will not produce the typical harvest," Edward said.

"What about the rest of the land that is not being used?" Sir Douglas asked. "You can raise more sheep there."

"I prefer to grow crops on that land. I could double my output if we were to hire more farmers to work that unused portion," Edward reminded Sir Douglas.

"It would be much better to buy more sheep and focus on the wool industry rather than on agriculture," Sir Douglas insisted. "It will raise more revenue that way."

"What makes you think we will earn back our costs so easily?" Edward asked, appearing wary.

"I have two businessmen from France eager to buy wool from us. Our focus has been on cotton and more recently, silk. Yet we do not have a steady supplier for wool. That is where you come in. I tell you, our business is booming."

Lily ate her meal quietly, listening to the others talk. Lord Peterborough glanced at her a couple of times, but did not speak to her during the dinner. Miss Grant spoke a few words to her, and then was silent.

"Edward, you must think about it," Lady Charleton said. "You have nothing to lose. You'll be making more money."

The subject of Mrs. Liston did not come up.

Chapter 22

September 1832

The following day marked the beginning of September. Dotty arrived that morning to help Lily get dressed.

"Is this all the clothing you have, Miss?" Dotty asked, fingering the old dresses in the closet.

"Yes. I've already ordered new clothes. I'll wear the white dress today."

"That is a good choice, Miss." Dotty removed the dress from the closet. "White always looks nice, no matter how old it is."

As Lily dressed, she learned that Dotty had connections with the school, and that the school term would be starting in a couple of weeks. She also learned that Franny never returned to the school, but was to marry in a week, after having postponed the wedding to care for her father. Her two younger sisters had replaced her at the school.

"Here, let me comb your hair, Miss. I'm very good at it."

Lily sat down in front of the mirror.

"How soft and pretty it is, and just like the color of the sun," Dotty said, combing it.

"Thank you," Lily said, smiling and watching Dotty from the mirror as she deftly pulled her hair back, securing it, and then formed perfect rows of ringlets on each side of her head.

"I heard that Lady Charleton approached Lord Peterborough this morning about employing Mrs. Liston as Miss Grant's companion."

"She did?" Lily asked, trying not to sound too anxious. She battled the urge to show any interest. It wasn't ladylike to gossip with the servants.

Dotty grinned as she finished her task. "There, you look quite nice, I might say. Now I must go and help Lady Charleton. She doesn't like waiting and should be up around now." She hurried toward the door.

Unable to contain herself any longer, Lily said. "What *did* Lord Peterborough say?"

"Lord Peterborough said that if you wanted to stay, you could," Dotty said as she flew out the door.

Lily spent the morning with Miss Grant, having breakfast and then going over correspondence. Miss Grant confirmed what Dotty had said. She asked her if she'd like to remain as her companion.

"Yes, I would like that very much, thank you."

"It pleases me that you wish to stay here, my dear," Miss Grant said, patting her hand.

After breakfast, they spent the rest of the day in the drawing room, working on the Christmas projects.

Later in the day, Miss Grant went for her nap, and since it had begun to rain, Lily ventured to the library, intent on finding a good book to read. These were her favorite times, when she could immerse herself in a good story. She was surprised to find Lord Peterborough seated at the desk, appearing to have been wading through a book. He stood up and bowed.

"Lord Peterborough." She curtsied, feeling flustered. "I came to get a book to read."

"By all means." He sat back down.

She browsed the shelves, conscience of Lord Peterborough's eyes on her.

"How do you like our library, Miss Montgomery? Is it to your satisfaction?"

"It has many wonderful books. I do enjoy reading them, particularly the novels." She turned around. "My father also had an interesting collection of books in his library in London."

Lord Peterborough closed his book. "I would be interested in knowing what he had."

She mentioned a few books on geography and the classics. "The collections of Shakespeare are also one of my favorites."

"Yes, he was a gifted writer. *Hamlet* always fascinated me. *To be or not to be, that is the question,*" he began, and then stopped, his noble features looking sad. He looked up. "Excuse me, but I was just thinking about my father. I still feel the loss." Lily said. "To work and play, and have families, and in the end to leave all this behind. Grandmother Mirela would tell me that when we leave this earth God still takes care of us. The spirit never dies."

"She is a wise woman," he said. "What other books did your father's library contain?"

"Oh, there were books on politics, history, and philosophy. I read some works of Aristotle and Socrates in Greek. They were quite dense and it would take years before I could understand them completely!"

Lord Peterborough smiled at her. "Scholars have plowed through them and are still interpreting them. I admire your attempt to read them."

"I guess I was attracted to them because my mother's family is from Greece."

"Greece is a great country and has contributed much to civilization in the way of ancient philosophy, mathematics, and beautiful architecture. You *should* be proud of it." He picked up the book he had been reading and handed it to her.

She leafed through the pages, gazing at the scenic pictures. The book was about the history of Greece.

"As you can see, I am a Philhellene, like your father."

Lily handed it back to him. "I wish I knew more about him."

"Yes, I can understand why," he said, placing the book down. "You had been expecting to see him, and now--" he paused, as if searching for words.

She leaned against the desk, her fingers brushing its edge. *Something about this desk reminds me of Father.*

"I can't," she finished, unable to continue, the tears welling in her eyes.

Edward was quiet.

"He had a desk in his library, in London, just like this one," she said, her voice trembling. "I wrote him a note, telling him I was leaving for the school, hoping he would read it one day. I left it in one of the drawers of his desk. Now, no one will read it," she mumbled. She looked down at her hands, feeling suddenly vulnerable at revealing her secret.

Lord Peterborough rose purposefully and went to a bookshelf, and pulled a slim volume from it. He handed it to her. "Here is a journal, written by my mother before she died. I think you might find it interesting, for there is a reference to your family in it."

Touched by his action, Lily smiled. "That is kind of you, my lord. I will certainly read it."

"I like to see that smile of yours. It lights up your face. Let me know what you think about the journal."

That evening, in the privacy of her bedroom, Lily read the journal. Dated 1814, it included mostly the daily life of Lord Peterborough's mother. She mentioned her son in an affectionate manner, calling him Eddy, and noted how quickly he was growing up. He was school age and had a tutor, but would soon be attending Eaton. She appeared happy and content with her life, referring to Lord Peterborough in an adoring manner and mentioning Miss Grant fondly.

It wasn't until August of that year, that Lily saw the reference to her parents in the journal.

20 August, 1814
Today we visited Montgomery Park in Castleford, to attend Sir Frederick Montgomery's son's wedding. For some reason, Mabel did not want to attend, but feigned illness, so only Lord Peterborough and I attended. This was my first time there. The house was built a hundred years ago, and is grand in style with luscious gardens and a well-stocked pond. It was a memorable event and the bride and groom were quite attractive. Their son, Frederick, was tall and blonde, with blue eyes. This was the first time I laid eyes on him, as he had been away to school followed by his grand tour during the times that his parents visited us. His wife,

Penelope, was a Greek maiden in the true sense. She was very beautiful with large, exquisite eyes and was dressed in a white satin wedding dress. I was surprised to hear her speak English so fluently. I understand that they met in Corfu a couple of months ago and have already been married in Greece, where her parents live, but Sir Frederick wanted them married in the English tradition. We stayed for two days, enjoying the merriment and festivities. During that time, the young Mrs. Montgomery and I became good friends. She was poised and graceful, and spoke with intelligence. I also learned that she liked to paint. I felt that Frederick had made a very good match. We invited them to Greystone Manor in the near future.

Lily found another entry in November, where her parents visited them for the weekend.

The men occupied their time with hunting and riding, while Mrs. Montgomery and I caught up on our news. I was delighted to learn that she was in the family way and expecting a child sometime in the spring.

Lily's heart beat rapidly when she realized Lady Peterborough was documenting her own entry into the world. She noticed that the entries stopped abruptly in December, after Lady Peterborough complained of coming down with a fever and not feeling well. Lily shut the journal, wondering sadly if that was when Lord Peterborough's mother passed away.

The following afternoon, while Miss Grant was resting, Lily decided to go riding. Lady Charleton joined her.

"It is better we ride together, for you might get lost. The estate is so vast," Lady Charleton said.

During their ride, Lady Charleton talked about fashion and clothing, and about how much money it cost to rebuild Stanton House. "Thankfully, my family is exceedingly wealthy, so they had more than enough to pay for it."

The next day was cloudy and Lily spent it mostly with Miss Grant, reading to her, and later sewing the Christmas projects in the company of Lady Charleton. There were no visitors, and the day went slowly.

That afternoon, during Miss Grant's rest, it rained, and Lily visited the library to return the journal, hoping to see Lord Peterborough again, but he was not there. Afterward, she went to the music room, where she played compositions by Bach and Mozart on the piano.

ৎৡৎৡৎৡ

Edward returned to Greystone Manor. He had been riding with Sir Douglas and had visited a farm in York to see about buying sheep. The rain caught them on their journey back.

Tired and wet, he trudged up the stairs to his room. His only intention was to take a warm bath and to rest. As he passed by the ballroom, he heard delightful music. Someone was playing the piano.

Curious, Edward opened the door and peered inside. Miss Montgomery sat at the piano, performing a piece by Mozart. He forgot his untidy state and stood there, listening with intense pleasure.

She was bewitching, with her golden ringlets cascading about her shoulders as her lithesome figure and slender arms moved to the sound of the music. When she finished, he clapped, pleased with her performance.

She arose, blushing at her unexpected audience.

"You *must* play for us sometime after dinner," he said.

"It would be my pleasure."

He gestured toward his clothing. "As you can see, I just returned from the trip and must go and change."

"Please, before you go, I wanted to thank you for your mother's journal. I was sorry to hear about her fever."

He was silent. "Yes, that happened just before she died." He excused himself and left, not wanting to show his emotions.

ৎৡৎৡৎৡ

Dinners had a routine of their own. Everyone dressed formally and ate with decorum. The delicious and plentiful food varied each evening, as the cook made sure to change the menu daily. Lily rarely spoke, but listened to the conversations between Lord Peterborough and his cousin, covering several issues. Lady Charleton and Miss Grant would occasionally enter the conversation.

One evening, after dinner, Lord Peterborough asked Lily to play the piano for them.

Although Lily felt nervous, she had secretly been preparing for it. She dutifully performed the music that she knew. She chose two Mozart compositions and one Bach composition. When she finished, everyone clapped.

Lily smiled and rose, feeling pleased.

"Well done, Miss Montgomery!" Miss Grant cried. "I did not know you played so well. You should do this more often."

"I am afraid that you will get bored quickly, for this is the only music I know."

"Then we should remedy it," Lord Peterborough replied promptly. "There are several sheets of music in the library that you can choose from."

"It is a shame that Charlotte is not here," Lady Charleton complained in a condescending manner. "She knows many more pieces and could entertain us the whole evening."

⛧⛧⛧

Lily received her dresses in the middle of September. She was delighted with the color and the fabric and eagerly tried them on.

"They certainly make you look attractive, and with your hair up like that, one would think you were older," Miss Grant remarked, after Lily paraded around the room, wearing the new dresses.

Lily learned from Miss Grant that day, that Lady Charleton and Sir Douglas were away on a business trip to York and would be gone for a few days.

After Miss Grant went for her daily nap, Lily ventured outside. She rode her horse across the fields, feeling free as a bird, flying with the wind against her. She inhaled deeply, enjoying the scent of the grass and flowers, and not wanting this to end.

When she spied the school in the distance, she slowed down, gazing at it, and feeling a bittersweet emotion. Although she had enjoyed her lessons there and her friends, she had suffered miserably under the harsh treatment of the mistresses. If it weren't for Lord Peterborough, Lily would still be there, cleaning rooms, washing linen, and scrubbing floors.

She spurred her horse onward, picking up speed and sweeping through the fields filled with red poppy and wild heather, occasionally passing a cottage or two. She slowed down as she approached the woods, remembering her gypsy past. She had grown up spending much time in the woods and being close to nature. The forests had been a shelter for her gypsy caravan, away from civilization, and a place to rest.

On impulse, Lily sauntered into the woods, slowly weaving her way through the tall trees. She stopped at a clearing, near a stream. She let Victoria quench her thirst, and then tethered her to a tree, enjoying the serene and secluded atmosphere.

Lily lay on the grassy bank, staring up at the sky, trying to gather her location from the sun. The sound of the stream's running water was soothing and rays from the sun warmed her. Birds chirped overhead and a pretty butterfly landed nearby as she watched in dreamy amusement.

She thought about Lord Peterborough, feeling warm inside. He was so good to her, and she always felt thrilled in his presence. Lily knew that if she had a choice, she would want to be near him for the rest of her life, but the image of Miss Stanton decked in her French wedding dress intervened in her thoughts.

A melancholic feeling descended upon her. Would she end up like Miss Grant, who loved her grandfather and watched him marry someone else, and never marry? She plucked listlessly at the grass, picturing herself becoming an old, withered maid. What kind of life would *that* be?

A rustling sound, followed by a horse neighing to her right, startled her and caused her to jump up. She had not expected to see anyone here. A rider came out of the woods, ambling toward her.

Lily brushed away the grass from her clothing and hair, peering anxiously at the rider. It was Lord Peterborough. His tall, broad-shouldered body sat upright on his steed. She was surprised to see him.

"Miss Montgomery," he called out. "It is a surprise to see you here."

"I came out for a ride. It was such a nice day," she called back. "I had never come this way before. It is so beautiful here."

"Yes, it is one of my favorite spots. I come here often." He dismounted, tethered his horse and joined her. "You should not be out here alone, though. Would you have remembered how to get back?"

Lily pointed the way. "It is in that direction. South."

"Good," he said, nodding. "I keep forgetting your past. How do you like Greystone Manor?"

"I like it very much. Miss Grant is nice to me, and quite pleasant. I have everything I want, including the nice dresses, thanks to you."

"A very ladylike remark. I commend you for it," he said, appearing amused. He stooped down and picked up a few stones, and then hurled each one into the stream, watching them skim the surface. "I have never heard a complaint coming from your lips, no matter how difficult your circumstances."

Lily picked up some pebbles and joined him. "Grandmother Mirela used to say that life is filled with ups and downs, and we just have to go with the flow, like this stream. Sometimes you land on a rock, and other times, you swim freely away."

"Well said, little mermaid," Lord Peterborough said teasingly. "Let us see how many times your stones can bounce off the surface."

Lily flung a pebble as expertly as she could. It bounced four times before sinking.

"You probably succeed in everything that you attempt," he said, his eyes twinkling.

Lily thought about her futile search for her parents, and how she was losing the man she loved to another woman. "Not all the time," she said, assuming a serious air. She looked at him. "How do you like being the lord of Greystone Manor, my lord?"

"It has its responsibilities. There is much to be done, but unlike you, I do have a complaint."

"Yes?" Lily asked, the blood rushing to her face. Did he have a complaint about her? Was she too bold in coming out here alone?

"My complaint goes towards someone who unwittingly coerced me into a situation for which I am beginning to deeply regret."

"Is it something that you can get out of?"

"When a gentleman gives his word, he is expected to honor it. But my heart is bound elsewhere," he said enigmatically.

Lily gazed into his dark, beautiful eyes, wondering what all this meant. "My grandmother used to say that nothing is impossible in this world, my lord."

Lord Peterborough burst out laughing. "Come, let us take a walk. I want to show you something."

He took her hand and led the way.

Lily was acutely aware of his warm touch, glancing often at his handsome profile. He appeared absorbed in thought. *Maybe he is still mourning his father.*

"Do you ever miss your gypsy life?" he asked softly, looking ahead.

Lily blinked, surprised by his question. "Not lately. Although I used to dream of it sometimes, when I would be working as a maid, I mean--" she blushed, not wanting to say more.

"I understand," he said, squeezing her hand gently.

Lily felt elated and flushed from his response. "I like it here very much where I am now."

He turned, and taking both of her hands in his, gazed warmly into her eyes. "I am pleased."

Lily stared back, fascinated by his proximity. He was so powerful, so vibrant, and his magnetism drew her to him, ever so closer, ever so closer. She could feel his breath upon her face as he leaned toward her. Her breath became shallow and she trembled, knowing that he was about to kiss her.

An urge to melt into his arms, to be loved, and to love, overcame her, but she knew better. *I could never expect him to love me as long as he was married to another woman.* She had seen the results from Grandmother's clients. There was only pain and suffering for the other woman.

With reserve and maturity far greater than her age, Lily withdrew her hands and stepped back. "What was it you wanted to show me?" she asked, trying to ignore the raging feelings coursing through her body.

With great difficulty, he tore his gaze from hers, and pointed towards a tall oak tree. "See there? That was my tree house when I was young. I would go there to hide when I wanted to be alone. It is barely visible from here."

"That is quite high, and there are no lower branches to reach it," she said, shielding her eyes with her hand as she looked up.

"I found it a challenge to go up there, but I love challenges," he admitted, gazing at her uplifted face. "The secret is that the trees adjacent to it have branches, so one climbs up to it that way, and then crosses over. No one knows about it. Not even--" he stopped, sweeping his hair back with his hand nervously.

Lily waited for him to finish his sentence, but he didn't.

He sighed. "Let us go back. It is getting late and I must prepare for tomorrow."

She walked with him back to the horses. This time he did not hold her hand.

"You ride ahead, so as to not cause any gossip. I will be on the lookout to make sure you have reached the house safely."

Lily mounted her horse. "Thank you, my lord." She turned her horse toward the direction she was to go, trying not to show her disappointment. It would always be like this from now on, if they ever wanted to talk, she thought sadly. She would always be worrying if anyone saw them alone, because there would be a Miss Stanton in the background, or a Lady Charleton, or whomever.

In no time, Lily found her way to the clearing and cantered away from the woods. From a distance, Greystone Manor looked splendidly large and magnificent. When she reached the manor, she turned and looked behind her. Lord Peterborough sat on his horse at the edge of the woods, looking on.

She knew now without a doubt that she loved him, no matter what the obstacles.

Chapter 23

The previous two Sundays, it had rained, and they had not gone to church because of the bad roads. This Sunday, it was sunny, and the sky was clear, and the church was full. The vicar gave an impassioned sermon about fire and brimstone, raising his voice several times and rousing Lily from her thoughts.

Later, as they were leaving the church, they ran into Mr. Pilford and exchanged greetings. He appeared at a loss for words. His face was unusually solemn. Lily stood there, feeling awkward at this unexpected encounter while Miss Grant climbed into the carriage.

"I hope everything is well with you, Mr. Pilford," Lily said politely.

"Yes. I heard that you were no longer at the school," Mr. Pilford replied. "I did not know you were at Greystone Manor."

"After my father passed away, I had to work, so Miss Grant hired me to be her companion."

"I am very sorry."

"It is all right. I am managing," Lily said, flushing under his concerned look. She excused herself and hurried into the carriage.

That evening, Sir Douglas and Lady Charleton were away at a house party that would last a few days. Lily chose her white, silk dress to wear for dinner. It had a low neckline, and she wanted to look particularly good tonight. Her hair, swept up by Dotty, emphasized her slender neck.

Lily gazed at herself in the mirror, amazed at the transformation. The dress brought out the highlights in her blue-green eyes and showed off her creamy-white skin.

Her entrance into the drawing room caused Miss Grant to exclaim. "Oh, how lovely you look, my dear!"

"Miss Montgomery, you have chosen well your dress," Lord Peterborough said, eyeing her intently.

"Miss Grant is deserving of the compliment, not I, my lord," Lily said, blushing. "She helped choose the dress."

"I always love to see beauty around me," Miss Grant admitted. "I believe that if I had attempted to learn to paint, that I would have become good at it."

It was time for dinner and they went into the dining room.

The meal was quiet at first, for both Lord Peterborough and Miss Grant appeared to be in reflective moods tonight.

"Edward, what have you decided regarding the proposition by Sir Douglas?" Miss Grant asked.

"Hmm?"

Miss Grant repeated her question.

"He makes a strong case for converting the land for raising sheep," he replied. "We visited a farm in York not long ago to see about prices."

"I personally feel he wants to take over, and use the land for his own profit. He was not always that way. He has changed since he married. I think his wife is pushing him on," Miss Grant complained.

"Are you not being a little hard on them?"

"Then why did they not approach your father with the idea? It is because they knew he would not go for any changes," she retorted. "They know you are too kind to say no."

"Miss Montgomery, what do you think?" Lord Peterborough asked. "Currently, under the program we use, the sheep and agriculture share the land. When the land is not being used for farming, the sheep graze there, fertilizing it. However, Sir Douglas wants to raise sheep on the land rather than use it for agriculture."

Lily felt a little thrill running down her spine when he asked her. *He cares about my opinion.* "First of all, the crops provide sustenance, and given that the farmers and tenants have worked the land all these years, their livelihoods depend on it," Lily replied. "They would have to find other work."

"She is right!" Aunt Mabel crowed.

"I have a suggestion," Lily offered.

Lord Peterborough's eyes were riveted on her. "Yes?"

"Could you add more sheep to an area that is not tillable? That way you still maintain the farmland, and still get more wool, and over time, you can decide whether to continue with one or the other."

"I have thought about that also. Taking the incremental approach appears to be the less risky path."

After dinner, Miss Grant surprised Lily with her suggestion that they go to the music room. "Lily, will you please entertain us a little with some of your playing?"

Lily played old and new pieces on the piano, with Lord Peterborough turning the pages for her. He congratulated her on how well she played, his dark eyes shining brightly. Lily beamed under his compliments and attention, thinking that this must be one of the happiest moments in her life. *If only this could last forever.*

⌘⌘⌘

Two mornings later, as Dotty helped Lily to get dressed, she was harboring a concealed excitement that was difficult to hide. Lily soon found out the reason.

"You might be interested in learning that the Stantons arrived yesterday morning at the Stanton house," Dotty informed her. "Miss Stanton is with them. That is why Lord Peterborough was invited to dine with them last night."

"Oh," Lily said, feeling a sinking feeling in her stomach. She remembered how disappointed she was last night when he didn't show up at dinner. She had spent a considerable amount of time with Dotty, dressing to perfection, with her hair piled up with ringlets, wanting to look beautiful, wanting to repeat the dinner and piano performance from the evening before. But it did not happen.

Miss Grant was alone and had smiled briefly when she saw her, but was not in a talkative mood, so the dinner finished quickly.

"There, all done. You do look fine, Miss," Dotty said, gazing at Lily with admiration.

"Thank you, Dotty," Lily said, managing a smile. "You do wonders with your hands."

Lily found Miss Grant in bed, moaning and complaining of a headache.

"Lady Charleton, Sir Douglas, and Lord Peterborough left this morning to visit the Stantons and I was also invited but did not feel well enough to go," Miss Grant informed her. "You have your breakfast without me. I am not hungry."

"I am sorry to hear that you are not feeling well. Shall I ring for the nurse?"

"I have done that already. She should be here any minute."

As Lily sat down and ate her meal, her thoughts were on Lord Peterborough and Miss Stanton.

A few minutes later, Nurse Nellie arrived.

"Nurse, get me something for my headache," Miss Grant said, touching her head.

"This will make you sleep," Nurse Nellie said, administering the medicine.

"I will not be needing you. I will remain in my room and rest," Miss Grant told Lily.

"I will stop by later to check on you," Lily promised.

The weather was fine, so Lily dressed in her riding habit and rode out on her own. Her thoughts were troubled as she pictured Lord Peterborough with his fiancé, enjoying her company in her parent's large mansion. A burning desire to see Stanton House made her turn and head toward its direction.

When Lily reached the border of the Greystone estate, she stood perfectly still, for up on the far hill she could see the large, stately mansion. She pictured Miss Stanton with her parents, enjoying the comforts of family life. Just then, two riders left Stanton House and made their way down the hill. Upon closer observation, it appeared to be Lord Peterborough and Miss Stanton riding together.

Lily sped away, her heart racing. She did not want them to see her. By the time she entered Greystone Manor, she had calmed down.

She visited Miss Grant in her room and asked how she was faring.

"I feel a little better, although I will remain in bed today," Miss Grant replied, sighing. "Please get another love story from the library to read. I seem to have formed a passion for them these days."

Lily went to the library and perused the shelves, browsing the books until she made a suitable choice. She secretly wondered if Miss Grant's sudden inclination for love stories might have been prompted by her memory of Sir Frederick.

The sound of the door closing behind her alerted her that she was no longer alone. Lily flushed at the thought that it might be *him*. She must leave and not stay; he was practically a married man, but her feet were heavy like lead. She could not make herself move. She clutched the book protectively against her chest.

"Miss Montgomery."

Lily turned and curtsied, staring at his riding boots, while the image of him riding down the hill with Miss Stanton was still fresh in her mind. She had promised herself that she would not make the mistake again in loving him.

"Lord Peterborough."

"I visited Miss Grant, and she told me you came to fetch her a book. She fell asleep as I was leaving." His face became thoughtful as he studied her. "It seems that a little quiet might be better for her."

"Oh," Lily said, placing the book back on the shelf, feeling confused. What should she do next? *I do not want to be alone in the room with him.* "I must go. I forgot something that I need to do."

She brushed past him and opened the door, wanting to leave before he could see her raw emotions.

"Can it wait?" he asked in a puzzled voice.

Lily turned, unable to resist his request. Keeping her eyes down, she nodded slowly.

"Please have a seat. I wish to share some news with you."

Lily went and sat down on the edge of the chair, feeling shy and nervous.

"I was invited last night to Stanton House for dinner. Sir Charles Montgomery was also there. He traveled from London with the Stanton family."

"Sir Charles Montgomery?" Lily echoed, looking up at him, forgetting her resolve not to imprint more of his image in her mind and not to converse alone with him. This bit of news is serious, indeed.

"As you probably know, he is now heir to your father's estate and resides at your family's home in Castleford. It is less than two hours from here."

Lily was silent, feeling the anguish of the loss of her father all over again.

"Lady Charleton mentioned to him last night that you are staying with us and strongly recommended that he meet you. Apparently, he was aware of your whereabouts for he readily consented. The result was that he has invited us all to Montgomery Park for a house party."

"I, I do not know what to say," Lily stammered. "Is Miss Grant going?"

"She does not like to travel," Lord Peterborough replied. "Sir Charles specifically asked that you be invited."

Lily's strong dislike for Charles Montgomery and Mrs. Bennington after her father's death could not be ignored. "I do not know what I should do," she mumbled.

"I am not the best person to ask," he replied, combing his fingers through his hair. "But I believe that it would be good for you to see your familial home, even if someone else lives in it."

"Then I shall go."

The following day, Lily sat with Miss Grant in the drawing room, sewing mittens and socks. Miss Grant was feeling better.

They received a visit from Mrs. Stanton and her daughter, Miss Stanton. Miss Stanton wore a lilac walking dress with matching plumed hat. Her blonde hair was pulled back in ringlets, emphasizing the elegant curve of her neck. She eyed Lily with cool animosity.

"My dear Miss Grant, I heard about your headache," Mrs. Stanton said, gliding towards Miss Grant. "I hope you are feeling better."

"Quite better, thank you," Miss Grant said . "Please join us for tea."

The two older women began chatting about various topics.

"Miss Montgomery," Miss Stanton said, sitting near Lily. "I have news from your cousin, Marianne." She removed a letter from her reticule and handed it to her.

"Thank you," Lily said, taking it.

"She and her husband, along with her mother, Mrs. Bennington, plan to visit Montgomery Park for Christmas."

"I see," Lily said, fingering the letter. She was not enthused about meeting her cousins again.

"Sir Charles journeyed with us from London. He is your cousin, I believe. Such a distinguished and interesting man." Miss Stanton paused. "Anyway, he wishes to make your acquaintance, having heard so much about you from his niece, Marianne."

"Yes?" Lily stared at Miss Stanton, wondering what Marianne had told him.

Miss Stanton leaned over and whispered in Lily's ear. "Is it true that you were once a gypsy?"

Lily blinked in surprise at the question. She moved away, feeling greatly distressed.

"Oh, do not look so stricken. Marianne could never keep a secret. If only you knew how much you are the rage now, my dear girl," Miss Stanton said slyly, a glint in her eye. "Even Sir Charles is interested. *Everyone* wants to see the gypsy."

Lily arose, feeling hot and bothered. "Please excuse me." She went to Miss Grant and told her that she left something in her room. She blindly ran upstairs to her room, feeling the shame of what she just heard.

She lay in her bed crying. *How could Marianne do this to me?* Why did Miss Stanton find her past so intriguing? Then she remembered the letter from Marianne. She tore it open. It was brief. Her cousin Marianne was to come to Montgomery Park with her husband, mother, and grandmother for Christmas. She hoped to see her then. She was the same silly cousin that Lily remembered. It was as if nothing had changed between them.

When Lily returned downstairs an hour later, she was much calmer. To her relief, the Stantons had already left.

"Is everything all right, Miss Montgomery? You left so urgently," Miss Grant said, studying her. "Was it something Miss Stanton said?"

Lily felt her cheeks heat up from the older lady's astute remark. "She gave me a letter from my cousin, and I wished to read it in private. I had not heard from her for a long time. She will be coming with her husband and family to Montgomery Park for Christmas and wishes to see me then."

Miss Grant appeared skeptical, but did not pursue the topic. "Sir Charles has invited us all to Montgomery Park for a couple of days," she said in a tired and restrained voice. "You should go, given that he is your cousin and that is your family home."

"Would you like to come?"

"Unfortunately, I do not like to travel these days. I am ill as it is and traveling does not agree with my general constitution."

Once again, that evening, Lord Peterborough was away at Stanton House for dinner.

Chapter 24

The day of the trip to Montgomery Park arrived quickly. Lily and Dotty accompanied Lady Charleton, and Mr. and Mrs. Stanton in the Stanton carriage, while Lord Peterborough and the others followed in the other carriage.

The ruts in the road and rocky passages caused a considerable amount of joggling and jerking of the carriages, which resulted in an uncomfortable ride.

Throughout the journey, Lady Charleton conversed with her mother on the intricacies of the reconstruction of Stanton House. Mrs. Stanton found a few things that still needed to be done, and Lady Charleton tried to convince her otherwise, reminding her of the cost. After a while, the effort to converse died down when the worsening roads and bouncing carriages competed for their attention.

"I say, these roads are quite nasty!" Mr. Stanton huffed, after a particularly fierce bounce caused him to knock his head against the window.

"We are almost there, dear," Mrs. Stanton reassured him, holding on tightly.

"I can see Montgomery Park!" Dotty cried, looking out the window.

Lily peered outside and was rewarded by the sight of the grand stone mansion looming up ahead.

Soon, the carriages rolled down the long gravel drive that led up to the majestic house. A pond graced the front of the house and the carriages pulled around it to finally park in the front entrance.

Two liveried footmen materialized from the house and escorted them inside. They entered a cool, marble floored lobby, with Grecian columns stationed at the corners and a central staircase, with carved banisters, rising up to the next level.

Sir Charles Montgomery strode into the lobby, greeting them cheerfully. Lily was mesmerized, for she remembered him from the masquerade ball a year earlier. He was tall, like Lord Peterborough, and had similar broad shoulders and slim hips. His hair was dark and wavy and he had the lightest blue eyes. One would have called him handsome if it weren't for his mouth. He had a twisted smile, almost as if he were constantly amused by something.

"Ahh, we meet at last, little cousin," Sir Charles said, his eyes gleaming.

"I am pleased to meet you, Sir Charles."

"We finally brought you two together," Miss Stanton said, coming up to them. "Well, what do you think about your long-lost cousin? Does she look like a Montgomery?"

"No Montgomery compares to her," Sir Charles said boldly.

Lily blushed at the compliment.

Lord Peterborough came and took Miss Stanton's arm. His eyes rested upon Lily. "Maybe the ladies would like to freshen up from the trip."

"Of course." Sir Charles called for help.

Lily and the other women were led up to their rooms. She was pleased with her bright and cheerful room. It had tall windows and partial views of the glimmering front pond and the garden. She gazed out the window nostalgically, picturing her parents and her grandparents living here.

She had come home.

That afternoon, Sir Charles gave a tour of the house, covering the well-stocked library, drawing room, dining room, game room, and ballroom. There was even a small chapel.

"Many rooms are still shut after all these years," Sir Charles told the group. "I am still looking for maids."

Miss Stanton's eyes rested on Lily in an amused manner. "Maybe Miss Montgomery could find some for you."

Lily felt her cheeks burning from the stinging remark.

Lord Peterborough placed his hand on Miss Stanton's arm, as if to silence her.

They reached the gallery of portraits.

Sir Charles focused his attentions on a handsome male portrait. "This is my uncle, Sir Frederick, who was fourth baronet, a title handed down from his ancestor's service in the navy. His beautiful wife, Judith Gray, was the granddaughter of a Viscount. She is the lady to his right."

Lily observed the paintings with a proud feeling, admiring her handsome grandparents.

"Sir Charles, am I to understand that your father and the late Sir Frederick's father were brothers?" Lady Charleton asked.

"Yes. Sir Frederick's father was the eldest, and my father was the youngest. There were also two daughters. My father married my mother, a French noblewoman, during the time of the war. Mother lives in Bristol part of the year, and the other times in France."

"We have a place in Bristol," Mrs. Stanton commented. "It is so lovely there."

Sir Charles promptly invited the Stanton family to visit his family in Bristol next time they were there. There was some more discussion along that vein before they adjourned to the drawing room for tea. Afterward, the men played a game of pool in the game room while the women took a stroll in the garden.

The garden was a labyrinth with its many small gravel paths jutting out from each end of the main path. Untended red, pink, and white perennial flowers and roses, green weeds, and untrimmed bushes fused together forming a sea of vivid colors everywhere, while sturdy, olive green ivy crept along, covering everything it could find, including the benches.

Lady Charleton hooked her arm around her sister's, whispering to her, while Mrs. Stanton studied the different flowers, complaining about the lack of attention given to them.

Lily quietly strolled behind them, picturing her family living here, and her father's sorrow at his loss and the subsequent neglect of the house. Somehow, she didn't notice where she was going, and at some point, meandered away from the group. She entered a charming passage that was lined with trees on each side.

At the end of the path, stood a life-size, marble Grecian statue of a handsome, athletic Adonis. She blushed upon observing that the only clothing he wore was the ivy that had wound itself around his midsection. A shiver went through her when she observed his face; it was similar to Lord Peterborough's chiseled face. A sparrow was perched on top of his shoulder, chirping merrily away. Lily smiled at the bird and felt peaceful. She heard footsteps behind her and turned.

"So we find you here, my Grecian maiden." Sir Charles smiled. "Do not look surprised. During the unveiling at the masquerade ball, my niece informed me of your identity. I was sorely disappointed that you did not stay."

"The school did not permit us to remain until midnight," Lily explained. She turned and gazed around. "It is so beautiful and peaceful here."

"Over there is another pond, a smaller one than the front entrance pond, and nearby, an interesting folly of an ancient Greek building." He pointed in a certain direction.

"Really?"

"Yes, I think you will be interested. Come, I will show you." He took her hand and led her. "I discovered it myself as I was touring the garden the other day."

They walked slowly down the path together. Lily was acutely aware of his grip on her hand. It wasn't gentle, but possessive.

"Tell me, my dear cousin, more about yourself. How is it that you are employed as a companion to Miss Grant?"

"It is quite simple. I owed money to the school and needed to pay it off."

"Tsk. Tsk. It is just like my sister to send you off to boarding school and dump the cost on you," Sir Charles said, shaking his head. "I only found out recently. I am surprised that Lord Peterborough did not play the gallant and pay off your debt."

"Oh, no. That would not do!" Lily cried, stopping and pulling her hand away. "It is my responsibility, not his."

"Nevertheless," Sir Charles said, placing his long, tapered finger over his mouth, apparently thinking. "There is something I must discuss with you. It pertains to your future." He stopped and gestured ahead. "But first, let us enjoy the view. Over there is the Greek folly."

The folly resembled the architecture of the ancient Parthenon. The marble columns jutted up to the blue sky in white lines of perfect harmony, a veritable contrast to the lime-green, knee-high grass that surrounded the building with impunity.

"It is beautiful! Like the one I saw in a book on Greece."

"Do you like it here?" Sir Charles asked.

Startled by his question, Lily looked at him, gauging the sincerity of his words. His lips were curled and a shrewd look had settled in his eyes. "I like it very much, mostly because it was my family's home. I still think Father is alive and will return one day."

"Do not deceive yourself," Sir Charles retorted. "You must accept the fact that he has passed away!"

Lily blinked back the tears.

Sir Charles calmed down and smiled, and then took her hand once more. "Come, let us not discuss morbid things. We are here, in this beautiful setting, so let us enjoy our walk."

She was conscious of the possessive hold his hand had on hers. It was as if he was leading her somewhere, but she did not know where.

"I will now divulge what I have done, and what I plan to do concerning you. When I recently learned about your debt to the school, I took it upon myself to pay Lord Peterborough the total amount," Sir Charles announced.

Lily stared at Sir Charles in speechless surprise.

"He was pleased, of course, saying it was a noble thing to do," he continued in a smug tone. "From now on, you are not obligated to that family nor to the school."

"I must admit that I did not expect this generosity coming from you, especially after--"

He gave a hearty laugh, revealing strong, white teeth. "I may not be a saint, and I know my sister is definitely not one." He smirked. "But one thing I do have, is Montgomery pride."

"Really, Sir Charles, there is no need--" she began.

"You are a Montgomery!" he interrupted her, "and I do not want the name to be bandied about from person to person. Also, it was not right for you, a single young lady, to be living at Greystone Manor with an eligible bachelor. Already, gossip has reached my ears that your reputation may be at stake."

"I was under the chaperone of Lady Charleton and Miss Grant. I did nothing wrong."

"Nevertheless, it is out of the question that you remain at Greystone Manor. I have decided to be your guardian until you are of age. From now on, you will live here, at Montgomery Park."

Lily was silent, digesting the news. "I feel as if I am dreaming. If this is really true, then I thank you, Sir Charles."

"You are not dreaming." He paused. "We must also find you a respectable companion."

Lily thought for a moment. "I would like to keep Dotty, my personal maid from Greystone Manor."

"That is fine with me," he replied, his eyes elsewhere. "Ahh, there are the others. Come, let us join them."

Miss Stanton approached them, her blue eyes flashing. "I see that Sir Charles found you. We were beginning to think that you might have been lost on your father's property."

Lily felt her body trembling with rage at the snide remark. "I assure you I was not lost. I was just enjoying the walk."

"I am sorry that you missed her company. We had a little family chat," Sir Charles said, patting Lily's arm. "Now you go and rest, dear cousin. Dinner will be at seven."

⋘⋙

Lily stayed in her room the rest of the afternoon, pondering on Sir Charles' proposal. Her heart felt heavy at what lay before her. She realized that she had grown fond of Miss Grant and Greystone Manor.

Those few months there, had been the most peaceful in a long time. She also knew that she loved Lord Peterborough with all her heart, and wished to be near him. *If I remained at*

Greystone Manor, what would I do once he married? Become a governess to his children, or a paid companion to Charlotte, his soon-to-be wife, who clearly dislikes me? She sighed at the thought.

Then she remembered Sir Charles' words. By paying her fees and acting as her guardian, he had shown signs of decency and righteousness. The idea to remain here with him was becoming more and more attractive, yet no matter how much she tried, she could never see him filling the void left from her parents or replacing the goodness of Lord Peterborough.

Dotty arrived at six o'clock. Lily listlessly chose the silk white dress with gold trim to wear.

"I love this dress," Dotty said, helping her into it. "It looks so beautiful on you."

"Thank you," Lily said absentmindedly.

"You're awfully quiet, Miss, and your eyes are red," Dotty remarked, with raised eyebrows.

Lily sighed. "Too many memories of my family."

"I'm sorry," Dotty replied. "It is a big house, I must admit. I had no idea your family was so rich, Miss."

"I have a question for you," Lily said, looking at her. "I am to live here from now on and will require a personal companion. Would you like to remain with me?"

Dotty appeared pleased. "Oh, I would love that, Miss!"

When the dinner bell rang, Lily made her way downstairs to the drawing room, where everyone had assembled, including two French guests.

Sir Charles gave her an admiring look, and then took her arm. "You look lovely, my dear. Come, we will lead the group."

They proceeded forward into the dining room, while the others followed. He positioned himself at the head of the table. "Sit here, next to me, cousin," he said, patting the empty chair to his right.

Lily blushed as she sat down. To her right sat Lady Charleton and her husband and the two French guests, the Fondieu brothers, who dealt in textiles. Across from her sat Lord Peterborough, who appeared tense, and next to him sat Miss Stanton, followed by her parents.

When the drinks were served, Sir Charles stood up, holding his glass of wine. "I would like to propose a toast, to the reunion of my cousin with the Montgomery clan. As of today, Miss Montgomery will be under my guardianship, living here at Montgomery Park. To the beautiful Miss Montgomery."

He saluted Lily, and then drank his wine.

Lily felt her face flush at the compliment and the public disclosure of her situation. She raised her glass along with the others, feeling her hand tremble as she took a small sip. *Why do I feel suddenly so miserable?*

"A generous gesture on your part, Sir Charles," Sir Douglas said. "I commend you for it."

There were similar positive responses from around the table.

Lady Charleton leaned toward Lily. "You are much better off here," she whispered, appearing pleased. "I was worried about all that gossip, my dear."

"What about Miss Grant? She will be waiting for my return," Lily fretted.

"Do not worry," Lady Charleton replied. "A few days ago, I had the foresight to mention to her the possibility of your departure. At first, she rejected the idea, not wanting to part with you. I admit she is fond of you, but I reminded her of maintaining proper decorum, and a few other things, and she graciously consented to the idea." She inclined her head and tightened her lips, emphasizing her stance on the issue.

Lily was thoughtful. "Is that when she had her headache?"

"She is already over it," Lady Charleton said. "Mrs. Liston will arrive at Greystone Manor tomorrow."

Lily was amazed at the sudden turn of events. It seemed as if everyone was moving her around like a pawn in a chess game.

At some point, Sir Charles asked Lily, "Is everything to your satisfaction, dear cousin?"

"Yes," she said. "Except that I have not had a chance to ask Lord Peterborough about keeping Dotty."

"Do not worry. I have informed him of the decision and he agreed to it."

The rest of the dinner was spent on various topics. Miss Stanton kept up her share of the chatter, including Lord Peterborough and Sir Charles into her conversation.

Lily stole glances at Lord Peterborough, trying to decipher what he was thinking about, but his tight face was like a closed book, unreadable.

⚜ ⚜ ⚜

When Edward returned to his room that evening, he was in a somber mood. A feeling of emptiness descended upon him, one that he could not shake off. It was as if he were mourning a death. No matter how much he tried, he could not forget Miss Montgomery's forlorn look at the dinner table when Sir Charles claimed she would be staying with him.

The only reason he came to Montgomery Park was to see about her welfare, and it seemed as if after today, she would be taken care of. She was like that small bird with the broken wing that he once nurtured back to health when he was ten years old. He tended to it, day by day, watching it slowly heal until he set it free. Since her arrival to Greystone Manor, the pale and thin Miss Montgomery had blossomed into a beautiful young lady.
It had become more and more difficult to keep his feelings concealed when he was alone with her. Lately, he had avoided her by going to Stanton House.

When Lady Charleton recently dropped the warning, "It is not proper to have a young, single woman staying at Greystone Manor, especially now that you are engaged to my sister. The only solution is for her to leave," he realized that she was right. Montgomery Park provided the opportunity for her to leave, and now that it was happening, he did not like it one bit.

He had deliberately left Herman behind, for his valet had a nasty habit of picking under his skin.

"You're only going because of Miss Montgomery, isn't it?" Herman said, as he was preparing his white cravat that morning. He gave it a tight twist. "I know how you loathe Sir Charles."

"You know, you are becoming a little pest," Edward replied playfully, loosening his cravat. "The man invited us all to his house, which included my fiancé and her family. I had no other choice but to go."

Earlier today, Sir Charles took him to his study where they discussed Miss Montgomery's debt in private. Edward had been surprised when he promptly paid him the amount due, saying it was his duty.

Edward also admired Charles' move at the dinner table. By claiming his guardianship of the girl in public, he sealed her fate as a Montgomery. She was accepted into a titled and wealthy family.

Edward had no more to do with her as he did with the bird that healed its wing and finally flew away. Yet, a nagging thought haunted him. Anyone other than Sir Charles would have been a better choice of a guardian for the girl.

⋘⋙⋘⋙⋘⋙

The next day was like no other that Lily had experienced before. Everyone's behavior had changed toward her, ever since Sir Charles's announcement the previous night. Even Dotty took more time in the morning, dressing her and doing her hair, making sure she was impeccably dressed.

"I'm wondering if you could do me a favor, Miss," Dotty said. "I need to get a message back home, to let them know I'll be staying, and to send me my belongings, but I don't know how to write."

"That is no problem." Lily penned a note for Dotty.

"Thank you, Miss," Dotty said excitedly. "I'll hand this to Fred, the coachman, to take back with him." She curtsied as she left the room.

Lily took the opportunity to write a note to Miss Grant to let her know of her decision to stay. She also mentioned that she enjoyed being her companion and hoped to see her sometime soon. She folded the note, planning to give it to Lord Peterborough before he left.

After breakfast, the men rode out on the property to examine the estate while the women took another stroll around the garden. It was a sunny and calm day, with no clouds in the blue sky. This time, Lady Charleton hooked her arm with Lily's and included her in the conversation, with her sister and mother trailing behind.

"We can be on a first name basis from now on, dear. You can call me Gertrude, if you wish," Lady Charleton said.

"And you can call me Charlotte," Miss Stanton called out.

"Thank you. You may call me Lily," Lily replied, feeling surprised.

"What do you think about adding some red velvet curtains in the dining room, Miss Montgomery?" Gertrude asked. "I have a wonderful set that I have not had a chance to use. You may have them."

"That sounds interesting," Lily said.

"You and Sir Charles must come and visit us at Stanton house once you are settled, my dear," Mrs. Stanton said.

"Soon, it will be hunting season, and Father always gathers a party to go hunting. I'm sure he will invite Sir Charles along with the others," Miss Stanton added.

Lily thanked them and said that she would be glad to visit them. She was pleasantly surprised to see this show of respect coming from the Stanton family.

"Of course, you will have a personal maid with you. For it is not conducive to a young lady's impeccable reputation to live all alone in this house with a young bachelor and no chaperone," Mrs. Stanton pointed out.

"Dotty will remain behind with me," Lily said.

"Yes, my dear. It is better that way," Mrs. Stanton said.

Even Miss Stanton remarked on her silk white dress. "Was it made by a French woman?"

Lily shook her head. "She is a local seamstress. Miss Grant found her."

"How interesting, I should get a hold of her. Her style is so refreshing," Miss Stanton remarked.

Lily showed them the pond and Grecian folly, which caused exclamations of delight from the women.

"What exotic architecture! Your mother must have influenced your father to build this," Mrs. Stanton raved. "We have wanted to travel to Greece. It is so beautiful, I hear, but the war has kept us away all these years, I'm afraid."

"Sir Douglas told me that Greece is not the same as it was years ago. The ravages of war will be felt for a long time," Lady Charleton announced. She spied the tree-lined path with the statue at the end. "Oh, let us see what that is about!"

They strolled toward the Adonis statue.

"To think that the Greek men looked like these statues," Miss Stanton said, sighing. "I wonder what is underneath the ivy." She tittered.

"Charlotte, really," Mrs. Stanton said, admonishing her daughter. "You will have to wait until you marry to find out."

"It resembles Edward, does it not?" Lady Charleton asked, studying the handsome face.

"Yes, now that you mention it," Miss Stanton said.

After the group returned to the house, the women ordered tea in the drawing room. The room was bathed in sunlight and the light beige curtains and saffron damask walls gave it a cheerful feeling. Scenes of the garden could be viewed from the tall windows.

"It is easy to see myself as a mistress here," Miss Stanton said, her face glowing. "I would love to stay and help Miss Montgomery decorate the place. What do you say, Lily?"

Lily did not know how to reply to her question.

"You always wanted to be a mistress of a wealthy chateau, Charlotte," Lady Charleton chided her.

"I see no objection to it, my dear," Mrs. Stanton said. "But we are expected for dinner at Greystone Manor, and I do not think Edward would approve of your staying behind."

After the men returned from their ride early that afternoon, everyone sat down to lunch before their departure for Greystone Manor. The meal was plentiful and accompanied by animated discussion as the men talked about horses and hunting, while the women continued their discourse on how to decorate Montgomery Park.

The group dispersed to their respective rooms to prepare for the impending trip and Sir Charles retired to his study to interview a local couple interested in working for him.

Lily decided to wait in the drawing room to bid the group good-bye. She was feeling unusually solemn. Her mind said that it was right and proper to stay with Sir Charles who would replace her parents as her rightful guardian. Yet she could not deny the fact that she would miss Greystone Manor, the kind Miss Grant, and particularly the noble Lord Peterborough.

Lily would always remember his acts of kindness and must try to forget the deep, yearning feeling gnawing inside her that bespoke of a love that he could never satisfy, for he was betrothed to another. She blinked back her tears of frustration.

"Miss Montgomery."

Lily shot up in confusion when she heard *him* call her name, collecting her emotions together. She turned and gazed at his beautiful form.

"Lord Peterborough," she said, her knees feeling weak as she curtsied.

He approached her, his hat in his hands. "I wished to see you before I left." When he reached her side, he smiled. "I hope you will be happy here."

"Given my circumstances, this is the right thing to do."

Lily pulled out her note from her pocket, trying to remain calm. She handed it to him. "Please give this to Miss Grant for me," she said. "Everything came so suddenly, and I did not know I would be remaining here. Please tell her that I will always think fondly of her and of Greystone Manor."

He fingered the note thoughtfully. "And what do you think of me, Judith?" he said softly.

Lily's heart raced at his endearing use of her name. She looked up into those beautiful, expressive eyes, and felt an inexplicable burst of joy run through her body.

In one fluid movement, his large, warm hand encased her hand.

His steady gaze was mesmerizing, and his touch revealed an intentness of purpose. She felt as if she were entering a secret world where only they existed. At that moment, she knew in her heart that if he were ever to love her, she would be the happiest woman in the world. *How wonderful it would feel to keep my hand in his and never let go.*

Lily blushed at her bold thoughts, remembering he was betrothed to another. With as much dignity as she could muster, she withdrew her hand. "I will never forget your kindness to me. I am grateful for it," she replied. "I also hope you are happy, wherever you may be, Lord Peterborough."

A shadow crossed his features. "Thank you. I will write to you our news whenever I have a chance. If there is any need for assistance, do not hesitate to ask." He bowed, and then whispered, "Goodbye, Miss Montgomery."

"Good-bye, Lord Peterborough."

Lily watched him leave with abated breath, trying to memorize every part of him as he strode out of the room and out of her life.

Chapter 25

Sept – Oct 1832

The next morning, Lily joined her cousin in the sunlit breakfast room.

"I want you to feel comfortable here," Sir Charles told her, patting her hand. "Was your room to your liking?"

"Oh, yes, thank you. I particularly like the view from the window."

"Good. Today I thought I would come down for breakfast and keep you company. You see, I normally take it in my room," he continued. "During the day, I will be busy with the estate. We will typically dine together at dinner. Seven o'clock each evening."

He filled Lily in on the duties of running the mansion, and also talked about the servants. There was Mrs. Kindle, the housekeeper, and Mrs. Brady, the cook and her daughter. "We also have two footmen, two maids, and the stable boy. We still need to hire more people, but all in due time."

"Are these the original staff?"

"Oh, no, no. That would not do!" Sir Charles laughed ironically. "I am the lord of the manor now. The few that were here I let go. Start with a clean slate, I say."
He told her that his mother would be arriving in December and he wanted to have the place ready for her. "Now I am off to Leeds, to see about more supplies and servants."

"What should I do?"

"I want you get to know this place well. Open the rooms and see what needs to be done. Do not be afraid to talk to Mrs. Kindle and Mrs. Brady, and give them instructions. Inform me if any supplies are needed. Can you keep records?"

"Yes. I learned it at school."

"Good. You will keep the books from now on until I find a steward." He paused, his light blue eyes gazing at her keenly. "We will show the Grants and the Stantons that we are better than them."

After breakfast, Lily visited the kitchen. The scent of freshly baked bread and pudding assailed her senses. It was blistering hot with its big stoves working in full force. The overweight cook, whom Lily decided was Mrs. Brady, contentedly peeled the vegetables.

"Hello, Mrs. Brady," Lily said.

The cook looked up. The beads of sweat ran down her wide, pasty ace. She smiled. "Hello, Miss. Did you like my cooking?"

"Oh, yes, very much."

"Good! Me daughter has been helping me with the cooking, but I need someone to take care of the pots and pans and dishes."

"Sir Charles is planning to get more help." Lily glanced around the kitchen. "If you have a moment, could you show me around?"

After wiping her hands with her apron, Mrs. Brady showed her the kitchen and pantry, and then led her down a flight of steps into cold and dark area quarters that held the wine cellar, cheese room, and the large spice room with its multitude of fragrant containers.

"These are expensive spices. From India, I heard."

"Yes," Lily said, remembering that her father worked in the spice trade.

Afterwards, Lily wandered upstairs and found the music room, but the piano needed tuning. She tinkered with it for some time, playing a couple Mozart pieces, but it did not provide the same satisfaction as the Greystone Manor piano.

The ballroom was next, with its many mirrors and chandeliers. Lily twirled around the room, pretending to be dancing with Lord Peterborough, but it did not have the same enchanted feeling as Greystone Manor's ballroom.

The little round chapel was off to the side, with its lead windows encircling it and a few chairs lined up in it. The sunlight rested on the altar table that sat at the front. There was a wooden cross on it. Lily had never been much into praying, but today for some reason, she knelt down and prayed.

During her tour, Lily met the housekeeper, Mrs. Kindle, a thick, middle-aged woman with a loud mouth and tremendous energy. She seemed to be everywhere all at once, giving orders to the two maids who were scurrying about.

"Welcome to Montgomery Park, Miss," Mrs. Kindle said.

"Thank you. Are you new here?"

"Oh, I've known Montgomery Park all me life," Mrs. Kindle said, tittering. "I didn't tell Sir Charles, but me mother worked here long ago, and I used to come up here when I was a child to help her out. Such a grand place. Those were the days when fine folks would visit from miles around when they had those grand balls!" She smacked her lips with satisfaction.

"I would like to hear about it one day."

"Fine," Mrs. Kindle said, beaming. "Is there anything you be wishing, miss?"

Lily instructed the housekeeper that all the bedrooms, including the linen, curtains and bedding needed to be cleaned.

"Of course. That is my duty."

⚯ ⚯ ⚯

The following day, Lily discovered a well-lit room that held several painted canvases piled to the side. In the center of the room stood a long table, and on top of it sat more canvases along with tubes of oil paint and a palette with caked oil paint and paintbrushes, causing her to believe that this was a painting studio.

Lily leafed through the stack of paintings. Some were finished while others were not. The signature P. Montgomery was at the bottom of all the finished paintings. A feeling of wonder enveloped Lily. *These must be Mother's paintings.*

One illustration portrayed Montgomery Park during springtime, with the magnificent pond and luscious landscaping, while another was a portrait of her father on a horse, smiling benevolently. The third painting was that of a little girl, about three or four years old, playing with an exotic doll. Lily was spellbound. The girl was none other than herself, for she recognized the blonde hair and blue-green eyes. Was she that beautiful? There was something familiar about the doll's porcelain white face and delicate features with its vivid red dress.

Lily saw herself holding the doll, feeling its sturdy chubby arms and its dress, and running through the corridors of the house, crying about something. Then her mother's beautiful face appeared as she reassured her and hugged her.

Lily sat there in a daze, reliving her childhood memories that came rushing back in a fury.

She was in Patras, holding her yiayia's thin hand, and dressed in her birthday dress. They visited her ill Greek grandfather who was in bed, yet austere looking and darkly handsome.

After Lily returned to her bedroom with her grandmother, her mother visited her.

"My Lily, you've been a good girl today, and now I have another birthday present for you."

Lily's eyes opened wide. This definitely was a special day. First, her new doll and dress, and now this.

Penelope showed her the locket, opening it. "Look. Look what I have for you. Pictures of Mama and Baba. I want you to wear this. Keep this always with you and do not give this to anyone. It is important."

Her mother then snapped it shut and looped the chain around her neck, securing it.

"Does my koukla (doll) also get one?" Lily asked, fingering the locket.

"I do not have an extra one for your doll," Penelope replied.

Lily's little fingers fumbled desperately to open it so she could see her parent's portraits again, but it remained firmly closed. She pouted at first and after a second or two, began to whimper. Her small hands formed into fists as she rubbed her tearful eyes.

"You must not play with it. It is not to be opened except by an adult," Penelope commanded. "Wait here, Lily. I have something else to give you."

Lily's attention was caught momentarily by this new present. She watched in wonder as her mother slipped out of the room, and then fumbled once more with the locket.

"See, my love, this is how it opens." Yiayia Sophia showed Lily how to open the locket. "But remember what Mama said. You must not play with it."

Penelope returned, carrying a small silk purse. "Look at this, Lily. I want you to keep this purse in your pocket. Remember the game we played last week, where I gave you something to keep in your pocket and if you kept it in there all day without losing it, you got a little present?"

Lily nodded, the locket forgotten.

Penelope opened the purse, revealing its contents. "Inside is an important paper and some coins. Do not lose them or play with them. Do you understand? Not until the game is over."

Lily nodded solemnly, watching her mother put the purse in her pocket. She wondered if she should ask if her doll was going to get a present. But the stern look on her mother's face stopped her. She would have to explain to her doll why she didn't also get presents. She reached for her doll and kissed her apologetically. "Do not cry. When I am older, I will get you presents."

Stavroula, the maid, entered the room. "Kyria Sophia, o Kyrios se zetai (Mrs. Sophia, your husband is asking for you)."

"Now I must go to your father," Sophia said, kissing her daughter, then her granddaughter. She tiredly walked out of the room.

"Mama, may I go outside with my doll and play?"

Penelope sighed, hugging her daughter. "My Lily, I am expecting your father to arrive today to take us home, and I need to prepare for the trip."

"Kyria Penelope, I can take her outside," Stavroula offered.

"Thank you. She's only to stay in the courtyard. Now I need to go finish my packing." Penelope kissed her daughter on the forehead and hurried out the door.

Stavroula took Lily's hand and they went down the back stairs into the kitchen. They walked outside where it was cool and breezy. The square courtyard was encased by a cement wall, which formed the front boundary of the estate. A stone path led to the front gate and on each side of the courtyard were red geraniums, gardenia bushes, and lemon trees. An archway connected the back of the house with the front and was covered by a grapevine. Even though the sun had begun to set, a surreal glow had formed in the horizon, like a harbinger of what was about to happen.

Lily let go of Stavroula's hand and ran around and around in the courtyard with her doll, and then swooped and ran gleefully towards the front. "Try and catch us!"

Stavroula followed her. "Do not run too fast. You might fall."

Lily sped under the archway, towards the back of the house.

"Do not go back there!" Stavroula called out.

Lily stopped, expecting Stavroula to come after her, but she didn't. Manolis, Stavroula's husband, had arrived and stood in front of the gate. "Stavroula!" he called. "Come quickly!"

Stavroula fled through the gate to talk to him.

Seeing that Stavroula was busy, Lily ran to the back, singing to her doll, "I will get you nice presents once we get to Corfu, and many, many sweets." After a few minutes of playing in the back yard, she returned to the front, looking for Stavroula. She was gone.

The gate was open, and Lily peeked outside. "Roula must be out here somewhere," she said.

She thought she saw a woman running down the street, wearing the same clothes as Stavroula. "Roula?" she called out, following her.

"Now this is the road that takes us to the market," Lily told her doll, pretending to know the way. She walked for a while, but already it was getting dark, and she was getting lost. She reached *the bottom of a hill, near the woods, and she did not know where her house was or how to get back.*

Fear filled her young heart. There was shouting in the distance, and she could smell acrid smoke, hot and thick, surrounding her. She could not breathe.

Just then, dirty hands snatched the doll out of Lily's hands, startling her. She watched numbly, too shocked to say anything, as two, dirty girls dressed in rags dashed away from her and ran up the hill, into the woods, carrying her doll with them.

Lily's yelled at them, "Give me back my doll!" She chased them, but in a matter of minutes, lost them. Panting, she slowed down and looked around her, feeling bewildered. The trees were many and close together, and it was dark. Then the girls darted out from behind some trees, taunting her, before running away again.

"Come back here!" Lily yelled, resuming her pursuit.

The woods became thicker and darker, and Lily faltered, having lost sight of the girls. She stopped, for she did not know in what direction to go. She could not see the town from here. Feeling frightened she buried her head in her small hands, and wailed for her mother.

Lily's tears flowed as she sat there in a daze, gulping in air, feeling the sadness engulf her.

After what seemed like a long time, she arose on unsteady legs, wiped her wet face, and promised herself fervently that she would ask Sir Charles to have these paintings framed and placed around the house. They were an invaluable part of her life.

Adjacent to the studio was the nursery. To her amazement, Lily found the porcelain doll that was in the painting. Its red satin dress was a little tattered, but the face was intact. Lily touched the doll's pretty face in awe, feeling as if she were a child again, joyful and content. Taking the doll with her, she hurried up to her room, overwhelmed by all the feelings storming through her.

The next few days brought more revelations as Lily discovered several artifacts from her youth. She took them into her room and placed them all around her so she could be surrounded by the memories.

When Dotty saw them, she commented on them, and Lily opened up to her, sharing her memories of her past, accompanied by Dotty's sympathetic nods and smacking lips.

"You have much to be proud of, Miss."

Lily felt as if she found a friend in Dotty.

Mrs. Kindle spoke to her daily about supplies, and Lily would relay it to Sir Charles at dinner.

One day during dinner, Sir Charles mentioned to her that she could order more dresses. "You look like you need some more."

The following day, the seamstress was called in and Lily was fitted for new dresses.

Each day, Lily kept herself busy, diligently plowing through the record books, logging all the supplies that Sir Charles bought, and noting those that needed replenishing. She also had the piano tuned and began to play it. When it rained, she spent time in the library, browsing and reading the books, and on good days, she took walks in the garden.

It was there that Lily often daydreamed about Greystone Manor and Lord Peterborough. She wondered what he would be doing and if he thought about her at all, since she had received no news from him. That part of her life was beginning to feel unreal, as if it were a dream.

Chapter 26

October arrived, and on that day, Lily received three evening gowns, a maroon riding outfit, two dresses for the day, and a sturdy walking dress. Each garment was beautifully tailored and fit her well, emphasizing her small waist.

"You look grand, Miss Montgomery," Dotty said, helping her try them on.

"Aren't they beautiful?" Lily replied.

Observing the way Dotty was eyeing her dresses, she became thoughtful. She recalled how her cousin Marianne gave dresses to her personal maid. Lily took two of her gowns that she had brought with her from Greystone Manor and gave them to her. "These are yours now. You could tailor them to your size."

"Oh, thank you. I surely will!" Dotty crowed, clasping her hands and admiring them.

Lily dined in the evenings with Sir Charles and used those opportunities to wear her evening gowns. She looked forward to the evenings because most days she spent them alone and spoke to no one other than the housekeeper or Dotty.

Sir Charles had a lively mind, and they would discuss a number of topics. Sometimes he would invite guests for dinner, which made it for interesting discussions, although she rarely spoke then, since officially she did not have her coming out yet.

One day, Sir Charles visited Stanton House to see about servants. When he returned that evening, Lily asked him about framing her mother's paintings. "I feel that they have value and should be framed."

"Yes, yes, that would be fine. I have been meaning to get a carpenter to frame them."

"You are kind, Sir Charles," Lily said, feeling content. He seemed in a good mood. "Also, may I have a horse to ride?"

"Of course, my dear cousin. You may join me tomorrow on my ride around the estate. We will find a horse for you then."

The next day, Lily rode with Sir Charles around the property. He talked about his plans for the land and pointed out to her that it had been abandoned all these years. He also mentioned that there were no sheep grazing the land, nor farmer to farm the land.

"Sir Douglas mentioned to me that his business is doing well and recommended that we grow sheep. I am seriously considering it," he said.

"He was trying to talk Lord Peterborough into it, too."

Sir Charles became alert. "What did Lord Peterborough say?"

Lily shrugged her shoulders. "He had not given him an answer."

They ambled quietly for a while. Sir Charles appeared preoccupied.

Lily spied a cottage in the distance. "Who lives over there?" she asked, pointing to it.

"That is one of four inhabited cottages on the property," Sir Charles told her. "The tenants are all old and previous employees of the manor. If they had not been paying rent, I would have gotten rid of them."

Lily drew in her breath sharply at his callous remark.

As the days progressed, Lily was becoming more and more friendly with Dotty. One day, Dotty confided in her that she was an only child of a veterinarian. Her mother died when she was young and her father raised her. She knew all about sheep, horses, and animals. Her father passed away when she was sixteen, and left her with little funds, so she ended up working at several menial jobs.

"I have worked fourteen years as a maid, and honestly admit that being your personal companion has been the most enjoyable," Dotty said, smiling.

Lily thanked her. "Did you not find anyone to marry?"

Dotty rolled her eyes. "Not everyone is blessed with your good looks, Miss," she said, smirking.

"You underestimate yourself," Lily remarked. "You are kind and good, and have a nice shape. And when you dress up nicely, I believe that men will notice you."

Dotty stopped what she was doing and gazed into the mirror. "You really think so?" she asked wistfully.

That evening, Lily told Sir Charles that Dotty also needed a horse so she could accompany her when he was away. He willingly obliged her. After that, the two women rode almost daily on the estate.

One day, Lily and Dotty visited the families in the two cottages, bringing baskets of food to them. The first family was the Sutherlings, an elderly couple. Mr. Sutherling used to be the steward at Montgomery Park. They had one married daughter and a son who worked in Leeds and was still single. "My Donald is almost forty and good with the books, just like Mr. Sutherling was. We cannot find a willing bride for him!" they said, guffawing and looking at Dotty.

After a short visit, Lily arose to leave. "It was nice meeting you. If you need anything, let me know."

"Thank you, Miss Montgomery. You come back soon."

The second cottage held Mrs. Burton, an elderly widow who lived alone. She was grateful for their visit.

The following day, Lily and Dotty visited the remaining two cottages. Both of them had elderly occupants that were happy to tell their stories of their years with the Montgomery family. It seemed as if all the houses needed to be repaired. On the way back, they discovered two deserted cottages.

"So, there are six cottages," Lily said.

"It looks like they were abandoned, Miss".

"Maybe we could fix them and put tenants in them."

Lily mentioned what she saw that day to Sir Charles in the evening.

"It is time I got a steward," he said. "This is too much for your little beautiful self to handle."

Lily mentioned to him the Sutherlings and their son, Donald, who was good in bookkeeping.

A few days later, they had guests for dinner. One of the guests was Donald Sutherling, a big-boned, hearty looking man. Lily learned later that he was to be their steward. The other guests were a young couple interested in renting one of the abandoned cottages, a Mr. and Mrs. Hanison, and their young son Harry, whom Sir Charles had met that day in Castleford. Mr. Hanison was a carpenter and was willing to repair the cottage for a lower rent. He also was willing to frame the paintings of her mother for a small fee.

It took Mr. Hanison several days to finish framing the paintings. When he was done, Lily was amazed at the transformation of the paintings. She went around the house, feeling emotional as she searched for places to hang them.

⋘⋙⋘⋙⋘⋙

One early morning in November, as Lily ate her breakfast, Sir Charles strode into the room. She was surprised to see him there, for he rarely joined her for breakfast. His traveling clothes suggested that he was going out. His face was pinched and he appeared agitated.

"I received urgent news this morning from my attorney. I must be off to London this very morning," Sir Charles informed her tightly.

Lily put down her fork. Her cousin appeared angry. "Is everything alright? How long will you be gone?"

"I should not be longer than two weeks. You have Dotty to keep you company while Mr. Sutherling will take care of the books," was his short reply as he strode out of the room.

It was even lonelier now with Sir Charles gone. Lily ate her meals alone and spent most of her time keeping busy. Often, the days were gray, cold, and wet and Lily did not ride out as before, but stayed in more often. On a rare sunny day, Lily and Dotty took the carriage to town. They browsed the shops, buying several supplies for the house. Lily also found a potter who sold her some paints. When they finished the shopping, they headed back to the carriage.

"What do you plan to do with those paints, if I may ask, Miss?" Dotty asked her.

"I will do what my mother used to do. I will paint," she replied. "I will paint portraits of my parents the way I remembered them."

Later that afternoon, back at the house, Lily dressed into some old clothes that she found in the attic, and spent a considerable amount of time preparing the canvas, and then sketching the portrait.

The next morning, she was up early, dabbing paint onto the canvas, using the techniques she had learned from her painting class. Her father was to be painted first, and then her mother. She relied on her recent memories from her childhood and the paintings from her mother to help her. Her father's features were to be kind and peaceful.

The days flowed together, with Lily spending much of her time painting. A peaceful feeling descended upon her as her brush stroked the canvas, filling it with vibrant colors. She would often pause, her thoughts traveling to Greystone Manor, Miss Grant, the school, and Lord Peterborough. Often, she would recall the little details of Lord Peterborough, his eyes, his laugh, and his magnetism.

Lily entertained the idea of writing to Mrs. Grant, but she had not even replied to the letter she had sent with Lord Peterborough. She was disappointed that she had received no word from Lord Peterborough or his aunt. It had been almost two months since she had left Greystone Manor. It was as if all ties with that place had vanished.

Ten days after Sir Charles had left for London, Lily decided to go for a brisk ride with Dotty. The sun peaked from under the clouds, beckoning to her, and she was eager to be outside. She felt invigorated from the exercise and upon her return to the house, found a letter waiting for her.

It was from Jane. She eagerly read it.

Dear Lily,

I hope you are doing well there at Montgomery Park. It took me several attempts to try and find you. A few weeks ago, I saw Mr. Pilford in church and he stopped to speak to me afterward. He mentioned that you moved to Greystone Manor! I was surprised to hear that. When I inquired into the reason why you left, he stated that you had lost your father and were required to work. I am so sorry, Lily, for what you've been through! I wish I could have been there for you.

I then penned a note to Greystone Manor to your attention and learned from Lord Peterborough that you no longer resided there. He visited me at the school and I learned from him that you live in Montgomery Park with your cousin, Sir Charles. I hope you like it there.

Now, for my news. I had my coming out ball in August and was very busy with much to do. My dress was quite beautiful and I danced all evening and received many compliments. Unfortunately, there was no Romeo for me, so I will remain at the school to finish my last year here.

Please write back with your news. Maybe we could get together before Christmas?

Your friend,
Jane Bodline

Lily promptly penned her a letter, dreaming about the good times she had spent with her at the school. A nagging thought returned. *Why hasn't Miss Grant or Lord Peterborough written to me all this time?*

The following day, gray clouds had settled in, threatening rain, and Lily stayed inside. Late that morning she was in the art studio, painting, when someone knocked on the door. It was Mrs. Kindle, and she appeared excited.

"There is a gentleman to see you, Miss. He goes by the name of Lord Peterborough."

Lily was struck by the news. She wondered what it was that brought him here so unexpectedly. There had been no formal letter to prepare her of his visit. What was she to do? Sir Charles was away and Dotty was in Leeds for an afternoon outing. *I could not turn him away, not my very own Lord Peterborough.*

"Please, send him to the drawing room. I will be there shortly."

After Mrs. Kindle left, Lily bolted out the door and ran to her bedroom to change. Her dresses required that she wore stays, but recently she had gone about without them. "Where did I put them?" She searched frantically for them.

Ten minutes later, and panting from her exertions, Lily finally finished buttoning the back of her fine, white dress with its light blue, satin ribbons and white lace. No wonder one needed a maid to get dressed.

She slipped out of the room and flew down the steps, feeling flushed, her heart beating hard. When she reached the drawing room, she took deep breaths, counting to ten until she calmed down. She must not let him see her affected so by his visit.

Applying all the rules of posture and decorum that she had learned in school, Lily calmly pulled herself together. Lifting her head high, she knocked with gentle precision on the door, and then entered.

Lord Peterborough was not seated, but stood at the window brooding, for when he turned to gaze at her, his eyebrows were furrowed and his lips were pressed together. He wore a dark riding habit with black cape and his cheeks were ruddy, suggesting that he had ridden here on his horse.

"I apologize for this unexpected visit, Miss Montgomery." He bowed, and then gazed at her with an intensity that was unnerving.

Lily dipped him a curtsy, her heart beating wildly. "It is a pleasure to see you, my lord, but Sir Charles is away to London, Dotty is in Leeds, and I--"

"Do not worry about formalities." he interrupted, striding toward her. "I needed to see you."

He stopped a few inches from her.

"Please, have a seat," she said, sitting down on the sofa, and trying to remain composed.

He sat next to her.

"Is everything all right with Miss Grant?" she asked.

"Yes, fine." Lord Peterborough's lips formed a glimmer of a smile as he glanced down at her hands. "I hope I did not interrupt you in whatever you were doing."

"No, no. I was just painting," Lily explained, looking down at her hands. Her eyes flew open. They were smudged with blue and yellow paint. In her haste to come down, she had forgotten to wash.

"Yes, I can see that." His lips quivered in amusement as he gently pulled a strand of hair from her head, curling it around his finger, smiling in that charming way. "It looks like you missed this one," he said in a hoarse voice.

"Oh!" Lily watched in fascination as his fingers gently scraped the blue paint off the tip of the strand. Then he bent down, his lips kissing the strand. *What is he doing?*

His dark eyes met her blue-green eyes, challenging her to respond. "Why did you not reply to my letters?" he demanded suddenly.

"Letters?" she asked, feeling thrilled that he wrote to her and perplexed at the same time. "I did not receive any letters from you, my lord."

He furrowed his brow. "That explains your silence. I had an inkling that your cousin had been snooping into your affairs," he said, sounding annoyed. "He has his motives."

"How could you say that?" Lily cried, standing up. "He has been the perfect gentleman."

"If that is the case, then why haven't you received any of my letters?"

"The only letter that came for me was from Miss Bodline, and I wrote back to her." She sat back down. "You wrote me letters?" she prompted.

Lord Peterborough appeared troubled. "It is nothing much. The first one was brief and simply asked as to how you were faring. Also, I mentioned that Miss Bodline had inquired about you." He cleared his throat. "I am curious to find out your reply, Miss Montgomery, if you had received my letter?"

Lily chose her words carefully. "Dear Lord Peterborough, I have been treated well here at Montgomery Park and all my needs are met, although it is not the same as Greystone Manor." She looked down, not wanting to reveal her true emotions. "I often wondered why I had not received news from Greystone Manor," she whispered. "You said there were more letters?"

"I wrote another one a couple of weeks later, thinking that the first one might have been lost en route." His fingers combed his hair. "Meanwhile, I wrote to my solicitor in London to check on Sir Charles. I learned that he received your father's inheritance, but had not filled out the guardianship papers for you."

Lily sucked in her breath, realizing the implications. "Then he is not my guardian?"

"No, he is not. I wrote a letter to Sir Charles, informing him that he needed to file the papers for you, otherwise, he was keeping you here with total disregard of your reputation."

"Did he reply back?" Lily whispered. She held her breath, already knowing the answer.

Lord Peterborough slowly shook his head. "No. Did he tell you the reason why he left for London?"

Lily's mind raced through all the events that had happened since she came to Montgomery Park. "He said he needed to see his attorney, but he did not tell me the reason why."

"My, my," Lord Peterborough said, going to her. "Sir Charles is a smart fellow, is he not? He takes you away from Greystone Manor with the promise of being your guardian and all this time, he has been keeping you here for himself. Tsk, tsk."

Lily's eyes flew open. "That is not so. He has done nothing that is improper."

"I have known him since college years. He always wanted to be the first in everything," he retorted. "And now he wanted the prize, and that was you. It was just a matter of time before you found out the truth."

Lily was indignant. "You must be jesting, Lord Peterborough, when you consider me as a prize for him. I do not have anything to offer him. I am beholden to my cousin for all that he has done for me."

Lord Peterborough shook his head, appearing bemused. "On the contrary, you have much to offer him. You do not know where his intentions lie, my sweet, but this is not the time to talk about him."

Lily was puzzled. "Why are you concerned about my welfare? Are you not to be married soon to Miss Stanton?"

A shadow passed over his handsome features. "I broke off the engagement a week ago, for I realized she was not my true love." He paused. "My heart is bound to another."

Chapter 27

Lily blinked back her tears, astounded by the news. He had broken his ties with Miss Stanton because he loved another. "Is that why you came here, to tell me about it?"

"Come now. There is no need for that." Lord Peterborough put an arm around her shoulders, and pulling a handkerchief from his pocket, wiped the tears from her eyes. "I hope these are tears of joy, for my happiness as well as--"

The loud banging of the door behind them startled Lily. It was none other than her cousin Sir Charles, and he appeared angry.

"Unhand her this instant!" Sir Charles commanded from the doorway.

Lily broke away from Lord Peterborough, trembling with shame. Her cousin wore a fierce expression she had not seen before. Was it because he had found them together and without a chaperone?

"Lily, come here, right now!" Sir Charles barked at her. He waved a paper in the air. "I have a marriage license in my hand. She is to become my wife."

Lord Peterborough stared at Lily in astonishment. "Tell me this is not true!" he said vehemently.

"No, no!" Lily cried, her hands covering her mouth in astonishment. "It is not true I do not love him."

"She is lying!" Sir Charles said with a shout, waving the paper once more in the air. "Lily, come here this instant."

Lily began to weep uncontrollably, unable to move. "It is not true, I tell you."

A show of disgust emerged on Lord Peterborough's face as he stared at her, his eyes blazing with anger. He turned and strode out the door. "I will not be party to this madness!"

"Please, I am telling the truth!" Lily cried after him, watching him leave. She turned against her cousin. "How could you do this to me?" With all her might she hurled herself past Sir Charles and sped up to her room, where she flung herself on her bed, sobbing.

Dotty magically appeared and handed her a handkerchief. After much sniffling, Lily arose and thanked her, wiping her eyes with the handkerchief. She paced the room, telling Dotty what happened.

"So, you love Lord Peterborough and not Sir Charles?" Dotty asked.

"Yes!" Lily wailed. "But he loves another. Now he is gone."

Someone pounded on the door. "Lily, I must speak to you at once," Sir Charles called out.

"I do not want to see him," Lily cried, gesturing towards the door dramatically.

Sir Charles barged into the room. "I wish to speak to you alone."

Dotty stood there, not budging, being protective of her mistress.

"Lily, dear, I know that you were probably shocked to hear me say what I did," he said pleadingly. "I was going to ask your hand in marriage in the near future, waiting for you to turn eighteen. I just lost my nerve when I saw that man handling you and couldn't control my anger."

Lily stared at him, her eyes wide with wonder at his change in behavior. "Lord Peterborough was not handling me, as you say. He was just wiping something from my eyes," she informed him. "If you did not plan to marry me now, then why did you have a marriage license on you?"

Sir Charles's lips curled slyly. "It was not a marriage license. I grabbed a letter that was in my pocket and waved it about. It did scare him off, I must admit." He chuckled, and then patted her hand. "I must find out one thing. Why did he come here? Was it to propose to you?"

"Propose to me? No," she replied sullenly. "He came because he had not received any reply to his letters and wanted to make sure all was well here."

Sir Charles smiled. "Good, I mean, that was thoughtful of him, but there was no cause for him to worry. I have taken good care of you, have I not?"

Lily was baffled by his transformation. He had changed from the raging ogre of a man just a few minutes ago to a kind, caring person. She nodded slowly, sniffling.

"You do like me a little. Say it, dear cousin," he needled, his eyes glinting.

"I like that you have been kind to me," she said cautiously. "And I thank you for it."

Sir Charles seemed pleased. "I am your family now." He paced the room. "I know what. Why don't you get dressed, and we can go to Greystone Manor and apologize to Lord Peterborough? Would you like that? He will surely calm down and everything will be all right. But we need to leave right away, so we can return before it gets dark."

Lily cheered up. "I will be dressed in ten minutes!"

"Good. Bring an extra dress, just in case we have to stay an extra day. You know how the weather can change so quickly. I will meet you downstairs."

"Oh, Sir Charles, can I take Dotty with me?"

"Come now. Not for such a short visit," he admonished her.

"Oh," Lily said. Somehow, she would have felt better if Dotty had accompanied them.

After he left, Dotty helped her dress.

Lily chose the silk, white dress with the gold trim to wear. She wanted to look her best for Lord Peterborough.

"I don't trust Sir Charles," Dotty hissed, shaking her head. "He's up to something. I just know it in my bones."

"I think he regretted his outburst and wants to make amends with Lord Peterborough. That is gallant of him," Lily remarked. "Oh, please hurry! We have to leave soon."

"There, that should do it," Dotty said, putting the final touches on Lily's curls.

"I need another dress, in case it is needed," Lily said. She chose another white dress, with matching gloves, which Dotty stuffed into a brown satchel.

"Don't forget your purse," Dotty reminded her, handing her the satchel.

Lily thanked her. She thought about wearing the white dress in the carriage with Sir Charles. Mindful of its dazzling effect on men, she bit her lip. She did not want him staring at her throughout their journey. It would be too uncomfortable. "I will wear my brown coat and the matching bonnet, in case it gets cold."

Dotty nodded knowingly, running to the closet and procuring the mantel and bonnet. "You don't want to catch cold, now, do you?"

∽∾∽∾∽∾

Edward's anger knew no bounds as he rode furiously home. He wanted to be as far away from Montgomery Park as he could. He had spent countless days and nights thinking about Miss Montgomery, and wondering why she had not responded to his letters. He had ruminated over her welfare, picturing her suffering under Sir Charles' cool indifference. Edward's love for her had driven him to break his ties with Miss Stanton. His journey to Montgomery Park was to seek out Miss Montgomery and to find the peace that had been missing in his life ever since she left.

He had planned to offer her a proposal of marriage.

Only it did not happen, for she was to marry Sir Charles.

It wasn't until halfway to his house that he cooled down. By now, his logic had kicked in. He slowed down. He reran the scene in his mind several times. The fact was that Miss Montgomery said that she did not love Sir Charles. He could not refute that. *She did state it.*

Also, Sir Charles's behavior was incongruent with Miss Montgomery's reaction. She surely would not have denied what

Sir Charles stated unless it was not true. Could he be sure that what the crafty Sir Charles had in his hand was a marriage license? It could have been any document for he was too far away to have a good look.

I need to find out the truth.

With renewed determination, Edward turned around and sped back to Montgomery Park. He knew one thing for sure, that he had more faith in Miss Montgomery than he had in Sir Charles. She would not lie to him. He could not desert her now.

When he arrived at the house, the butler told him that Sir Charles and Miss Montgomery had already left. "About a half hour ago, my lord."

"Did they mention where they would be going?"

"Dotty heard him tell Miss Montgomery that they were going to Greystone Manor to straighten things out with you, and Dotty thinks that's the reason why she went willingly."

"So, they are headed towards Greystone Manor."

"No, my lord. I think they went somewhere else." The butler paused, turning red with embarrassment.

"Speak up, man!" Edward knew that servants had a reputation for knowing the private business of their masters. There were no secrets where servants were concerned.

"I think Sir Charles was planning to take her to Gretna Green to marry her."

Edward was instantly alert. "What makes you think so?"

"They were headed north," the butler said knowingly, winking at him.

"Greystone Manor is west of here. The scoundrel!" Edward knew what that meant. Gretna Green was several hours away, and it would be dark soon. They would surely stop at an inn to sleep overnight and her reputation would be compromised, and she would be forced to marry Sir Charles.

With a fury that he had never felt before, Edward mounted his steed and rode north, hoping desperately that he would make it in time.

Lily sat in the carriage, daydreaming and wondering how Lord Peterborough would react when they visited him at Greystone Manor. Although she knew he loved another, she was anxious to see him and to explain to him the truth. She stared out the window, reliving her conversation with Lord Peterborough before he left.

Sir Charles was unusually quiet on the trip, reading a newspaper he had brought back with him from London. Periodically he glanced at Lily to ask how she was doing, and then continued his reading.

An hour into the trip, Lily started to pay attention to her surroundings. They should be arriving soon. She was sure she would see something familiar in the landscape. It wasn't until the sun began to peak through the clouds that she realized the northerly direction they were heading. "Are we not a little off?" she asked Sir Charles.

Sir Charles looked up from his reading. "Hmm?"

Lily repeated her question.

He peered outside. "The driver knows the way," he said absentmindedly. "He probably is using a shortcut that will take us there quicker."

His answer satisfied Lily and she lapsed once more into a daydreaming mood, thinking about Lord Peterborough and the mysterious woman that he chose over Miss Stanton.

It had to be Jane that he really loved. It made sense to her, for not only was Jane a kind and gentle person, but also Lord Peterborough had inquired after her health several times. Didn't he dance with Jane in the dance class? Also, didn't he say that Jane had contacted Greystone Manor regarding her whereabouts? They may have been meeting regularly, with the school so close to the house.

If Lord Peterborough loved Jane, then Lily was happy for her. At the same time, a miserable feeling crept in her heart. *I also love Lord Peterborough.* All of a sudden, she didn't feel so enthused in going to Greystone Manor.

Lily gazed outside, feeling mixed emotions about this trip. She noted the forest to her right. The thicket of trees reminded her of that time she had gone into the woods and Lord

Peterborough had found her. Maybe these were the same woods. Maybe they were close to Greystone Manor.

The sound of thunder in the distance caused Lily to wrinkle her brows. Gray clouds were quickly forming overhead. "It looks like it is going to rain," she announced.

Sir Charles put his newspaper down and peered out the window. "It seems that you are right. I will have a talk with the driver to hurry. Otherwise, the roads will be impassable."

He tapped the top of the carriage with his cane for the driver to stop, and then went outside and had a talk with him.

Lily waited, wondering what they would do if they were caught in the rain. She stuck her head outside to listen to what her cousin was telling the driver.

"I want you to go faster. We must get to the inn before it gets full for the night."

"But Sir, I think one of the horses has caught a stone in 'is shoe. I don't know whether we can go much faster."

"Let me have a look at him."

Lily was shocked. They were not going to Greystone Manor but to an inn. How could she have fallen for this trap? He had lied to her. He intended to trap her into marriage by taking her to an inn, and here she thought all along that they were going to Lord Peterborough. She must do something quickly before Sir Charles returned.

In desperation, Lily grabbed her satchel and slipped out of the carriage. She glanced behind her. The men were busy with the horse. With determination, she sprinted towards the woods, running as fast as she could. She did not feel the drops of rain until some moments later. She was thankful for her mantel and bonnet. They not only protected her from the rain, but also were brown, helping her to blend well with the surrounding trees that had shed their autumn leaves.

A shout came from the direction of the carriage. It was Sir Charles. He must have seen her.

Panting, Lily raced into the woods, her feet scurrying over leaves and broken twigs. She did not know where she was going, just that she did not trust Sir Charles any longer and did not want to go with him, wherever he was headed.

Her rapid pace did not slow down until she was deep into the woods. It had become dark and cold. A fierce wind pulled her dress about her. The rain continued to beat a steady path on her face and body. Lily stopped and looked around, shivering. *I am frightened.*

Lily searched for an evergreen tree, one that she could hide in. Finally finding one, she climbed up its sturdy branch and settled there, using her satchel to rest her head on.

She continued shivering, unable to stop. A fear gripped her heart. Where would she go? Whom could she trust anymore?

Sir Charles, who was supposedly her guardian, was no longer to be trusted, and she could never go back to live with him at Montgomery Park. Lord Peterborough had left with so much anger, thinking that she had lied to him, that she was sure he would never want to see her again. She had never felt so miserable and alone in all her life.

ﺔﻔﺳ ﺔﻔﺳ ﺔﻔﺳ

Edward's horse's hooves pounded the road as he raced against time, heading north. When the first raindrops fell on his face, he pulled up his coat sleeve, slowing down, for the roads could get treacherous in the rain. He maneuvered his horse to the side of the road, favoring the firm ground and avoiding the ruts. Within minutes, he spied a carriage ahead that had stopped.

As he approached it, he realized it was none other than Sir Charles' carriage. Sir Charles was in the front of the carriage, mired in mud as he tried to help his driver push it out of a muddy rut.

Edward roared with laughter when he saw him.

"Well, do not stand there, help me!" Sir Charles shouted, gesturing for help.

Edward dismounted and the three men pushed with all their might until the carriage was loosened.

"Thank you," Sir Charles said wearily.

"There is no need for thanks. I must know what your plans are for Miss Montgomery," Edward demanded.

"I did not have a marriage license. It was only a letter, to scare you off." Sir Charles swiped at his wet coat. "She will have none of me, I am afraid."

Edward peered inside the carriage, expecting to see Miss Montgomery. What he saw made him turn and grab Sir Charles by the coat. "Where is she? What have you done with her?" he shouted.

"She ran off into the woods and disappeared, that is what she did," Sir Charles said tightly. "I searched for a considerable amount of time but could not find her."

Edward was stunned. "If anything happens to her, you will pay for this!" he growled, shaking him, and then pushing him away with disgust.

With determination, Edward mounted his horse.

Sir Charles appeared shaken. "Where are you going?"

"I must find her tonight. We cannot leave her in the rain or she would surely die of cold!" he cried.

"What is she to you?" Sir Charles spat.

"I intend to make her my wife. Do you have any objection?" Edward gave him a challenging look.

Sir Charles crossed his arms. "Only if she objects."

Within moments, the two men rode towards the woods, an uneasy truce having been reached.

Chapter 28

Lily lay curled up in the tree, shivering and unable to move, and overcome by the terror that had gripped her heart. Although she was sheltered somewhat, the howling wind and pouring rain seemed to reach deep into her bones. There was something dreadful about being here alone in the dark woods. She had never felt this way before, or had she?

She was a child of six again, lost in those woods in Patras. The two gypsy girls had snatched her doll from her and she was alone, and it was dark and scary. She could not find her home, or her mother. Where was her mother to take her into her arms and make things all right? She sobbed uncontrollably. "Mama!"

"Miss Montgomery!"

Lily stopped her weeping, suddenly alert. Someone had called her name. She rubbed her eyes and lifted her head trying to hear the voice, but there was nothing but the howling wind.

Lily remained silent, waiting and listening. If it were Sir Charles, she did not want him to find her. Her heart beat wildly with fear.

☙☙☙

"Miss Montgomery!" Edward called out once more. He was cold and wet and growing tired, yet his concern for the girl's safety pushed him forward. Surely, the girl would catch her death of cold if she remained out here tonight. "It is Lord Peterborough calling! If you hear me, call out, please."

Edward stopped to listen. Sir Charles was marching nearby. Edward stopped him with his hand. "Sshh. I think I heard something. Listen."

There was silence.

"Where are you?" Edward called out desperately. "Miss Montgomery, where are you? It is Lord Peterborough. I have come to help you. Please, tell me where you are." He stopped to listen.

"Up here, in a tree," she replied faintly.

Edward was relieved to hear her voice. "Keep talking, so we can find your position."

"I am sitting in the tree. I will come down now, so you can see me," she said. "I am wearing my brown coat and am carrying a satchel."

"Keep talking, your voice is getting louder. Do you have a handkerchief, or something we could see?"

"I cannot see you, Lord Peterborough, but I can hear you. Can you see my white dress? Please answer me."

Edward spied something white in the darkness. "There it is. I am almost there!" he shouted, heading in that direction.

Within moments, he had reached the girl. Sir Charles was behind him. She stood leaning against the tree, holding a white dress. She was soaking wet and muddied, and sobbing.

"Miss Montgomery," Edward said with relief, taking her wet, shivering body into his embrace.

When Lily saw Sir Charles, she tensed, ready to bolt. "I do not want to go back with him," she cried weakly, pulling away.

"Please, do not run away again. Sir Charles will not harm you. I will take you back to Greystone Manor," Edward said soothingly, taking her arm.

"Lily, I am sorry," Sir Charles said penitently.

Lily did not respond, for she had fainted in Edwards' arms.

Edward lifted her gently. Her limp body felt soft and supple. "Take her satchel and dress and follow me," he ordered Sir Charles. "We will use your carriage."

కపు కపు కపు

As soon as he arrived at Greystone Manor, Edward awoke his aunt. She immediately took charge, summoning the servants to help. They stripped the wet clothing off the girl and dressed her in dry clothing.

By the time that Lily was placed in bed, she was hot to the touch. They notified the doctor and nurse.

After changing into dry clothing, Edward entered the girl's room. His aunt was seated by Lily's side, nodding off, not having slept all this time. It seemed as if Miss Montgomery had affected his aunt also, for he had never seen his aunt so attached to someone before.

"You go and rest, Aunt. The doctor will be here any minute. I will keep watch."

"Are you sure?" Miss Grant asked, hovering over the bed anxiously.

"Yes," Edward replied. "Please go and rest."

"You need it more than I do."

"I will not rest until the doctor arrives."

After his aunt left, Edward sat by Lily's side.

Her eyes were shut and she appeared to be sleeping. He thought about what had transpired. Her drastic measures had shown that she did not care for Sir Charles after all. He reached over and held her hot hand.

She stirred in her sleep, gripping his hand tightly. "Lord Peterborough! Please help me. Lord Peterborough!" she cried, her eyes sealed shut.

Edward became alert. He bent over her, stroking her forehead. "I am here, my darling, do not fear," he replied gently.

She was silent, as if appeased. A few minutes passed, and she stirred again. "Lord Peterborough! Lord Peterborough, where are you? Do not go away. I am frightened," she cried out, groaning and twisting her head to the side and back.

Edward stroked her forehead thoughtfully, murmuring soft endearments each time, which seemed to calm her considerably.

෴ ෴ ෴

Lily awoke at the break of daylight. Her mouth felt dry, like parchment paper. She licked her chapped lips. Her eyes combed the dimly lit room. Nurse Nellie sat by her side, placing a cool cloth on her forehead.

"Nurse Nellie? What happened? Where am I?" Lily asked weakly. She struggled to get up.

"You are at Greystone Manor," Nurse Nellie replied, pressing her back. "Please lie down. You have a fever and are too ill to get up."

Lily lay back, breathing shallowly. "What day is it? What has happened to Lord Peterborough, and Sir Charles?" She tried to get up.

"Please do not get up. It is Sunday. You have been ill for two days. Lord Peterborough has been here often to see you. Sir Charles left yesterday. The doctor has left some medicine for you to take. It will help you sleep. You are weak and need to rest. Now take this slowly."

Lily swallowed the liquid and shut her eyes. In a short time, she fell asleep.

⁕⁕⁕

A while later, Edward entered the room. "How is she?"

"She awoke briefly," Nurse Nellie replied. "Her fever is gone, but she is still weak."

"Good. The doctor said that she is young and strong, and should pull through it."

"Yes. Meanwhile, I have given her some medicine to help her sleep."

"You go and rest now, for you have been up all night tending to her."

The nurse smiled thankfully. She went to the door. "If she awakens, please give her plenty of liquids to drink."

"Thank you." Edward sat by Miss Montgomery's side. He rang for tea.

He observed her features. Even though she was pale and weak, she was still beautiful to him. He stroked her hand affectionately, murmuring endearments.

The tea arrived and Edward poured the hot brew for himself and for Miss Montgomery.

Her eyes fluttered open. She stared at the ceiling at first, and when her eyes settled on him, they opened wide. "Lord Peterborough," she murmured, shyly pulling her blanket closer to her chin.

"Miss Montgomery. I am glad to see that you're awake," he said, smiling.

She smiled weakly. "Thank you for everything."

"Sshh, do not speak. You have had quite an ordeal these past few days. Sir Charles and I agreed to put the whole thing behind us. It will become our little secret. All right? No one shall know what really happened. Not even my aunt knows the truth."

She blinked in surprise. "All right," she finally said.

"If anyone asks what happened, they are to be told that you were caught in the rain and came here."

She shut her eyes.

He noticed her parched lips. "Are you thirsty?"

"Yes," she whispered, falling promptly asleep.

Edward smiled, and drank the tea by himself.

When his aunt arrived, he told her the good news.

"Oh, I am grateful that her fever is gone and she is recovering well. I was so worried!"

"Did you notify Miss Bodline of her friend's situation?" he asked.

"Yes. She replied and said she will be here after church. It is good you thought if it. It would do Miss Montgomery some good."

Edward nodded thoughtfully. "That was my intention. Now, I will leave you, for I need to prepare for Mr. Pilford. I am to meet with him this afternoon. There is some business that needs to be addressed."

⋘⋘⋘

Later that morning, Lily awoke. She was feeling stronger and was able to sit up in bed and drink her tea with the help of Miss Grant. She even nibbled on some toast.

"We notified Miss Bodline about your situation. She is to arrive anytime soon. Meanwhile, I brought a book to read to you." Miss Grant raised it up in the air for her to see. "It is the same romantic one you read to me, just before you left for Montgomery Park. We never finished it."

"That is a nice one. Thank you." Lily listened to the soothing sound of Miss Grant's voice as she read to her. She drifted off once in a while, and then resumed her listening. "Can you repeat that last passage? The medicine is making me drowsy," she whispered, shutting her eyes.

"With pleasure."

‿❀‿❀‿❀

Miss Bodline arrived that afternoon at Greystone Manor with Miss Farfield.

"I came as quickly as I could," she told Edward. "How is she?"

"She was caught in the rain, and had a fever, but she is doing better."

"Lord Peterborough, I have some news that I think might be helpful to Lily."

She told him the news.

Edward was stunned. "Then I must be away this very afternoon," he said, rising to leave.

Just then, Mr. Pilford entered the dayroom. When he saw Miss Bodline, he appeared pleasantly surprised. He bowed politely. "Miss Bodline."

Jane blushed prettily. "Mr. Pilford."

‿❀‿❀‿❀

Lily was awakened by a knock on the door. It was Jane. Lily smiled as Jane rushed into the room, still wearing her coat, her features flushed from the cold weather.

"Lily! I heard about your illness and wanted to see you."

"Good afternoon, Miss Bodline."

Jane turned and saw Miss Grant seated in the nearby armchair and blushed. She curtsied politely. "Good-afternoon Miss Grant. Oh, I have interrupted your reading."

"Not a problem. I can read to her another time," Miss Grant said, rising. "She is still weak and has taken medicine that helps her sleep, so she might not be fully awake."

Jane embraced Lily, and then gazed at her with tenderness.

"Jane, it is so good to see you," Lily said weakly.

Doctor Johnson entered at that moment. Jane and Miss Grant moved out of his way, as he examined Lily.

The doctor appeared satisfied with the results. "You should be up in a day or two." He turned and spoke to Jane. "Were you not that girl with a similar situation about a year ago? It was around the same time."

Jane blushed. "Yes, Doctor Johnson."

"This is not the time of the year to be bandying about outside," he warned. Then he smiled at Lily. "Well, it is good to see you doing better."

"Thank you, Doctor Johnson."

After he left, Miss Grant excused herself. "I am sure you two will probably want to catch up on your news," she said before leaving the room.

"So, Lily, tell me what happened?" Jane asked. "I heard you got caught in the rain."

"Yes, that is what happened," Lily said, feeling sudden drowsiness. She shut her eyes. "I feel a little sleepy. It is from the medicine. How have you been? I wrote back to you after I received your letter."

"Thank you, I received your letter also," Jane said. "This is my last year and they keep us busy, as you know."

"Has Lord Peterborough visited the school again?" Lily asked.

"No, but once in a while we saw Lord Peterborough riding with Mr. Pilford during our walks." Jane blushed. "I just met Mr. Pilford downstairs with Lord Peterborough. He was courteous as usual."

Lily felt a rush of dismay when she heard her friend talk so knowingly about Lord Peterborough. "Yes, he is nice."

"I admit that he has been paying court to me recently, and we have formed an attachment."

"Is that so?" Lily asked, feeling very alert. "You have feelings for him?"

Jane nodded. "I do not know how to explain it. It just happened. He is comfortable to talk to and makes me laugh. He still talks fondly of you, though." She saw her Lily's downcast face. "I hope you do not mind."

"No," Lily said slowly, wondering how Lord Peterborough could pay court one minute to Miss Stanton, and then to Jane, and at the same time, take care of her. "And what about our old friends? Have they returned this year?"

Jane filled her in on the news of their old classmates. "Everyone misses you," she said. She paused, appearing doleful. "I heard some rumors about you at the school, and what happened after your father died. Everyone thinks the mistresses were quite cruel towards you. I am glad you did not stay long there."

"Lord Peterborough and Miss Grant were kind enough to hire me, and then my cousin, Sir Charles Montgomery, took me in as my guardian."

"Your cousin?" Jane asked, looking puzzled.

"Yes, Sir Charles Montgomery was the handsome naval officer at the masquerade ball."

Jane's eyes grew wide with wonder. "I almost forgot," she cried, appearing excited. She pulled a newspaper clipping out of her pocket. "Miss Dorsey, who is in my class, gave me this. She receives news from her family in London and that is how we learn the happenings there."

"Oh?"

Jane unfolded the paper carefully and read the news to her. "It states here that an unnamed nobleman, presumed dead from his travels to the East Indies, has suddenly appeared in London, claiming that all his estates had erroneously been inherited by a cousin."

"A cousin?" Lily echoed, her heart beating wildly.

"Yes. A cousin," Jane looked at her knowingly, and then continued reading. "It says that the nobleman wishes that his name be kept confidential." She beamed at Lily. "Do you know what that means?"

Lily was stunned. With all the strength that she could muster, she sat up. "Could it be?" she whispered. "Let me see that." She took the newspaper and read it. It was dated November 1, 1832. She stared at it.

"Oh, Lily, would it not be wonderful? If it is your father truly returned, then everything will be all right and you could go to London and have your coming out ball!"

"Please, could I keep the newspaper?" Lily whispered.

"Surely."

That evening, Miss Grant informed Lily that Lord Peterborough had left for London that very afternoon. He did not give a reason why. Lily had been hoping to share the news with him about the nobleman's return and was disappointed that he had left without telling her.

Lily spent the next day mulling over things and wondering about Jane's relationship with Lord Peterborough. It seemed as if her friend had significant sentiments toward him.

On Tuesday morning, Lily was well enough to get up. After she dressed, she visited Miss Grant in her room, surprising her. Mrs. Liston, the personal companion of Miss Grant, was also in the room. Lily was introduced to her. She was an older woman, dressed in somber clothing.

"You do look so much better, my dear," Miss Grant said, rising and coming to Lily. "I was going to visit you after breakfast. Now that you are here, you may join us. Just like old times."

Lily sat down and enjoyed the breakfast, for she had not eaten a solid meal in days.

"We thought it best if you remained at Greystone Manor a while longer, until you were well and strong," Miss Grant informed her with a smile.

Lily returned her smile. "I would like that very much."

"Now finish your meal. I have a surprise for you."

After breakfast, Miss Grant took her to a room at the end of the hall. There, Lily was delighted to see the unfinished canvas of her father. Her paint supplies were on a chair in the corner.

"This will be your room for now. Lord Peterborough has had a few of your things brought here from Montgomery Park. He felt that they would make your stay here even more pleasant."

"Oh, how wonderful! You are so kind," Lily exclaimed.

"It was mostly his idea. Dotty also brought your clothes. They are in the closet. I have kept her busy until you needed her."

Touched by their kindness, Lily's eyes welled up with tears. "Thank you."

"You go right ahead and paint," Miss Grant said, smiling. "I have some correspondence to finish with Mrs. Liston. I will send for you when it is time for tea. We can spend it together in the drawing room."

"Thank you. May I have an old servant's outfit to wear? I do not wish to dirty my clothing."

"Of course. I will have it sent to you right away."

Chapter 29

November 1832

A couple of days later, as Lily was painting, she stopped and paused, staring at her father's handsome image on the canvas. She smiled, feeling pleased that she had successfully captured his smile and twinkling, blue eyes. The room was well lit from the sun's rays that poured through the windows. She was content.

"Only a few more strokes on your hair, and I'll be finished," she said to the painting. Lily continued her work, dabbing the golden hues on her father's blonde head of hair.

She heard footsteps in the hallway and wondered if it were Miss Grant. For she often came to check on her progress.

Someone knocked gently on the door.

"Come in, Miss Grant."

Silence greeted her response, and Lily whirled around, her heart beating wildly, thinking it might be Lord Peterborough. It was not. Instead, a middle-aged man stood at the door. He was a stranger, but he was no stranger to her. His blonde hair, piercing blue eyes, and firm chin were similar to the portrait she had been painting.

A cry of joy escaped her lips. "Father!" She rushed into his open arms.

"Lily!" he cried, his tired face beaming. He embraced her with joy.

Lily was overwhelmed by emotions that she could not put words to. He smelled of soap and spices, and his voice was low and sweet as he spoke endearments to her. She felt as if she were dreaming, as if she would wake up any minute, and he would no longer be there.

When he finally released her, his eyes glistened with tears. They were the clearest blue color she had ever seen.

"Am I dreaming, Father?"

"No, you are not dreaming, my dear, darling Lily! I am alive," he said with emotion, gazing at her in wonder.

"I feel as if I am seeing your mother again. You have her looks, and you are even dressed in old clothes for painting, just as she always used to be." He brushed a speck of paint off her cheek, a faraway look on his face.

"Father, I believe that she might still be alive," Lily said. "If I am alive, then why not Mother?"

Several emotions passed over his face. "We will talk about it some other time when we are settled. I came here as fast as I could from London with Lord Peterborough and am tired from the trip," he replied heavily.

"Lord Peterborough?"

"Yes, darling. I owe him so much, for he is the one who told me about your whereabouts," he said. "Apparently, a student from the school showed him a newspaper clipping, and after he read it, surmised that it was me. He left that very same day for London."

"It was Jane who told him," Lily whispered, feeling a sudden pang of jealousy.

"Hmm?"

"Jane, I mean Miss Bodline, is my friend from school. She showed me the same article. She must have shown it to him also."

"She sounds like a good friend. I must meet her sometime."

"Yes," Lily said. She remained silent, remembering Jane's confession of love for Lord Peterborough, swallowing her disappointment. "What happened to Sir Charles?"

"I understand that he is in Bristol with his family. Unfortunate business, this," he said, shaking his head. "It all began when I wrote to my attorney in London that I was returning within the fortnight, and he sent him a letter, informing him of my arrival. Sir Charles immediately tried to clear up his actions. He had been in much debt and had used some of my wealth to pay it off. What a mess."

Lily nodded. "He even tried to marry me."

Sir Frederick's face darkened. "When did this happen?"

"A couple of months ago. He took me in as my guardian, and when he was away in London, Lord Peterborough visited me at Montgomery Park, having sent letters and not receiving any reply." She relayed the rest of the story.

"Sir Charles must have been desperate after he learned of my return. By marrying you, he could retain some of the wealth."

"I do not understand."

"You are wealthy in your own right, from your mother's inheritance. There are funds in the bank that are rightfully yours. He must have found out after he received the inheritance. If he married you, whatever was yours became his."

"I could never see myself married to him."

"Quite understandable, my dear. I distrust that man. I would never have consented to that marriage. But we shall talk more about this later. We must become better acquainted, then, all right?" He patted her gently on the back. "I am sure you have many things to tell me, as I have to tell you. Now go and wash, and prepare for our journey home. We will meet downstairs for tea."

He limped out of the room with the help of a cane.

With Dotty's help, Lily changed into one of her dresses and had her hair done in that special way that only Dotty knew how to do.

"There you are, Miss. All pretty with this fine pink dress. Lord Peterborough won't be able to take his eyes off of you."

Lily gazed at herself in the mirror, at the soft pink dress with white satin ribbons and lace that made her appear quite attractive. How could she continue to love Lord Peterborough after what Jane had said? "For your information, I am *not* dressing up for Lord Peterborough," she announced. "I am dressing up for my father."

Dotty's eyebrows shot up in surprise. "Yes, Miss."

Lily pointed to the paint supplies and canvasses. "Please have all these, along with my clothing, sent down to the carriage. We will leave shortly."

Lily found her father, Lord Peterborough and Miss Grant already seated in the drawing room. She curtsied, and they exchanged greetings.

"Ah, my lovely Lily, come, sit next to me. I have been waiting for you to take tea," her father said.

Lily joined him on the sofa, conscious of Lord Peterborough's eyes on her. The tea tray sat on the small table in front of them, so she poured tea, handing a cup to her father.

"Your daughter is a delightful girl, Sir Frederick," Miss Grant said.

"I am seeing that," Sir Frederick smiled, looking at his daughter. "I am indebted to the gypsies that saved her life and helped bring her back to me."

"So, you know my story?" Lily asked, her eyes wide with wonder.

"Lord Peterborough graciously filled me in on the trip from London," Sir Frederick said. "It seems that God was with you, my dear. Many Greek people did not survive that ordeal with the Ottomans. Everywhere the Ottomans attacked, there was total destruction."

Lily was silent.

"What are your plans for the future, Sir Frederick?" Miss Grant asked. "Will you be staying at Castleford?"

"We will stay there for a few days, then off to London. I must straighten my affairs with the attorney. Given the complexity of the situation, it might take months."

Lily noticed Lord Peterborough studying her with a pensive air, as if something was bothering him.

After some polite conversation, Sir Frederick arose to leave. "Please forgive us, but we must leave before it gets dark, for we have some way to go."

Lily arose. "I also wanted to thank you, Lord Peterborough and Miss Grant, for helping me. You both have been very kind to me."

"Yes," Sir Frederick said. "I am indebted to both of you for assisting my daughter in her time of need. If there is any way to repay you Lord Peterborough--"

"That is not necessary. A gentleman always helps a maiden in distress," Lord Peterborough replied, gazing steadily at Miss Montgomery.

Sir Frederick eyed him with keen interest.

Miss Grant arose and went to Lily. She smiled as she took her hands in hers and leaning closer, whispered, "Your father is the spitting image of his father. It brings back memories of my youth." She turned and gazed fondly at Sir Frederick, then patted Lily's hand. "But everything has worked out for you, has it not? You have your father now, and he will take good care of you."

"Yes. I am very grateful for all your help also," Lily said, smiling.

Lord Peterborough joined them. "Miss Montgomery, you are in good hands now."

"Yes," Lily replied. Her father joined her, and smiled. They made their way outside.

"Write to us with your news," Miss Grant said.

Shortly after, Lily and her father were settled in the closed carriage, while Dotty sat outside with the driver. Lily waved to Lord Peterborough and Miss Grant as the carriage rolled away.

On the journey to the house, Sir Frederick peppered her with questions. Lily told her father everything that had happened to her up to the moment that he found her at Greystone Manor.

After she finished, he smiled in a way that would become special to her.

"All this is behind you. No one will ever dare to label my daughter a gypsy, and Charles will not be a bother, either. I will make sure of that! From now on, we will be together."

"Tell me, Father. What happened to you?"

"In September of last year, I was travelling back from the East Indies on one of the spice ships, and a month into the journey, we were caught in a bad storm. The ship tossed and turned and was overturned by the storm. I barely survived, hanging on to some cargo in the sea. For days, I floated without food or water. By the providence of God, a fishing vessel spied me. I must have been unconscious when the fishermen carried me to shore, for I do not remember it. I was very ill by then, and had several broken bones, including this leg that requires me to use a cane."

"What happened then?"

"The good fisherman and his family kept me in their home, tending to me." He was silent. "Laying in that cot, often I thought about my life, and how I had lost your mother and you. Sometimes I wondered if it were meant for me to die that way. But the good Lord had planned for me to get well, so I could return to you." He smiled at her. "You wouldn't think that your father would become a fisherman, but while my leg was healing, I began to think of ways to return to England. No ships ran along that course. I convinced the fisherman to take me fishing with him, knowing that he sold fish to the neighboring islands. In September, a ship stopped at a neighboring island while we were there, and I found out it was going to England. That is how I returned home."

"How did you learn about me?"

"I learned about you when Lord Peterborough visited me in London. To my astonishment, he claimed that you were alive and staying at Greystone Manor, in Yorkshire. I did not believe him at first, but when he pointed out that you confided in him about a note you wrote to me and placed it inside the library desk, then I went and had a look. Your letter touched me deeply."

"I am so glad he remembered!"

"Yes. It made a difference, for now I had someone to live for," he replied, his voice cracking.

"So, Lord Peterborough helped you find me," Lily said, her face shining. "He is a good man."

He studied her face. "Yes, a very good man."

Chapter 30

Nov – Dec 1832

After Sir Frederick and Miss Montgomery left, Edward stayed with his aunt for some time, and then went upstairs to the study, trying to do some work. Once there, his thoughts kept drifting towards the beautiful Miss Montgomery. He wondered if she realized how deep his feelings ran for her.

He replayed the words she had spoken aloud, as she lay there in bed, sickly pale, and unaware of his presence. Her words had given him hope that she had feelings for him.

Miss Stanton and her family had been distant after he had broken off their engagement. Even Sir Douglas and his wife became reserved, preferring to stay at Stanton House lately. Gertrude felt that her sister needed her, and Sir Douglas complied by going along. It was as if all ties to Stanton House had been broken. However, he knew better.

The two families had lived peaceably as neighbors for many years. Miss Stanton could easily marry anyone of the several beaus that she flirted with, and her parents would still be happy. It was just a matter of time before the rift between the two families was repaired. Sir Douglas would see to it.

Unable to concentrate on his work, he arose and changed into riding clothes. Soon, Edward was heading for the stables. Moments later, he cantered through the fields, feeling the biting cold November wind on his face. It was becoming an increasingly gray day, with the clouds quickly rolling in, but he did not mind. It felt good spending time outside.

He recalled how he had told Sir Frederick about his serious intentions toward his daughter as they were returning from London. "I would like to make her my wife, with your permission, of course."

"Does she wish to become your wife?" Sir Frederick had asked.

"I did not have a chance to find out," Edward admitted. "The day I was about to ask, we were interrupted by Sir Charles' arrival. He forced me to leave by flashing that fraudulent marriage license. However, I have the impression that her feelings are similar to mine."

"I like you, young man," Sir Frederick said, smiling. "You come from a good family, and have all the fine traits that I would like to see in a son-in-law. However, she is young and has no experience in men. It is understandable that she would be in love with you since you appeared like the gallant knight, rescuing her."

Edward's disappointment knew no bounds when he heard those words. "I assure you that she would be in the best of hands once we married," he insisted.

"I believe you, but in all fairness to my daughter, I need to give her a chance to meet other young men in London during the season. By the end of the season, she will be in a better position to consider matrimony and if she still chooses you, then there will be no room for doubt in my mind."

Edward respected Sir Frederick's decision, knowing that it was the right thing to do. He wondered how she would handle being the daughter of a rich father. Once she had her coming out ball, he presumed that her beauty and wealth would attract several eligible young bachelors in London. Would it get to her head and change her, like it did with Charlotte, or would she still be the same, sweet girl he remembered? Meanwhile, how would he get rid of these obsessive thoughts about her? He would not see her for at least another five months.

⁕⁕⁕

Lily became engrossed with her father and his affairs. She devoted every waking minute to him, as if by doing so, she could recapture all those lost years she spent without him.

During dinner, one evening, her father mentioned to Lily how pleased he was with the portrait she made of him.

"You have much of your mother's artistic talents. We will have my portrait framed and hung on the gallery wall as soon as we return from London. All right?"

"Yes, Papa."

Lily learned that her father could be gentle when it came to her, but he had a firm tone and commanding manner when he dealt with the servants and business matters. One afternoon, Sir Frederick rounded up all the servants in the lobby to talk with them.

"Before I left on my trip last year," he said, "there were other servants in service. When I returned, I found that my cousin had hired new staff. Given that I am fond of my old staff, I am informing you that I plan to have them returned to Montgomery Park."

An uneasy silence ensued.

He paused and studied their solemn faces. "However, I believe in fairness. You all came here thinking that you had secure jobs. I will not turn you away so quickly. I will allow you three months to work hard, and during that time, if I find other uses for you, you may remain."

There was much cheering and everyone seemed happy.

The following day, Sir Frederick met Mr. Sutherling and went over the books with him. They also discussed the rehiring of the old servants. That afternoon, Lily rode with her father and the steward around the estate, visiting the tenants. They appeared happy to see them.

Within days, Lily and her father were traveling to London.

During their journey, they shared their news. Lily learned about her austere grandparents and her father's strict upbringing.

"Father was in the navy, and he was a foreboding figure when I was young," Sir Frederick said. "He instilled in me the importance of being heir to the vast Montgomery wealth, which has been handed down from our ancestors, who were in the spice trade."

"Is that why you are involved in trade?"

"Let us say I have followed in the footsteps of my ancestors," Sir Frederick replied. "Mother was the opposite. She was soft and gentle. I always went to her if I fell or scraped a knee."

"How did they meet?"

"Father had been away to college and then the navy. Upon his return to Castleford, he was invited to a dinner party given by mutual friends. Actually, it was at Greystone Manor. He saw Mother there and was smitten. It was a matter of time before they were married."

"Miss Grant told me that she was in love with him," Lily mentioned. "She never married after that."

His eyebrows lifted. "I did not know that. Her name was never mentioned in that manner. Her parents were probably upset that she did not marry."

"I feel sorry for her. She is such a kind person."

"Sometimes parents get too involved in this marriage business," he said dryly. "Your grandfather was outraged when he found out I had married your mother. He had wanted me to marry an earl's daughter, but it was too late. I was already happily married."

"What did they think of Mother?"

"They were charmed by her," he said. "She not only was beautiful, but sincere and accomplished."

He stopped talking, and stared out the window of the carriage. Lily recognized that faraway, hopeless look which always seemed to appear whenever he spoke of her mother.

"I've often wished that time had stopped and I had not left her to the hands of the Ottomans," he said, turning to look at Lily with a pained expression on his face. "If only I had been there."

"Please, Papa, it wasn't your fault. What is done is done."

"If only I could discover what happened on that day," he continued. "It was difficult to go back. Greece was in the middle of a war."

"Yes, I know."

"I shouldn't be reminding you of that atrocious time in your young life," he said ruefully, patting her arm.

"That's all right. Now I am here, with you."

"Yes, my dear, and I am grateful," he said, smiling. "The fact that you lived gives me hope that maybe your mother may have escaped somehow."

"I have been thinking about that," Lily said, nodding. "But she never contacted you, did she?"

He shook his head. "I wrote once to the embassy there, inquiring into the status of lost citizens, but never received a reply. The state of affairs for Greece has been chaotic since the Greeks declared their independence from Turkey."

"Why don't you try writing again?"

"Maybe I will," Sir Frederick said with a gleam in his eye. "Now we need to focus on you. I plan to present you officially to court right after your eighteenth birthday. You will need to prepare for that. It is an important occasion."

"Is it necessary?"

"Yes, and worth it. I am proud to show off my beautiful daughter," he said, smiling. "After that, we will plan a debutante ball in the spring. That way you can meet eligible young men. I do not want you to miss what the other young women have experienced. I will probably need the help of an older woman to coordinate all the activities."

"What about Mrs. Hartford?" Lily asked. "I think she likes me and would know what to do."

"Very good idea," Sir Frederick said, nodding. "She was fond of you when you were a child and is well immersed in London's society."

When they arrived in London, Lily became her father's right hand, helping him rehire all the former servants, and being in charge of the housekeeping staff. Her father was busy with his political and business affairs, and was gone much of the time. In the morning, they would have breakfast together and he would read the newspaper, and then be off.

Lily's daily walks with Dotty were restricted because of the cold, but she did not mind. She enjoyed the strolls in the park, for she looked forward to returning to the warm, cozy house. Each day, Mrs. Tippins would come to her for advice, and the cook also would give her a menu list, which she would approve or disapprove. Although the days were peaceful, Lily spent much of her time alone, reading, doing embroidery, or painting until her father would return.

In the evenings, Lily enjoyed having dinner with him. They discussed a number of things and caught up on their news of the day. Occasionally, he would be invited for dinner at some nobleman's house and she would eat alone with Dotty. Her father promised her that once she turned eighteen, she would accompany him to dinner parties and social outings.

One day, after breakfast, Lily found her father reading the newspaper with intensity.

"What is it, Papa?"

"Apparently, there are Greeks claiming that they have family members still being held as slaves in Turkey. This has caused British authorities to conduct investigations into the matter. As a result, these Greek families have demanded for their release, and it seems that the Ottomans are complying. This is wonderful news!" He was thoughtful as he left for work that day.

Lily picked up the newspaper and read it. She cut out the clipping and saved it.

The next morning marked the beginning of December.

During breakfast, Sir Frederick reminded Lily to write some letters. "We have been here a week. Write to Mrs. Hartford. I know it is early, but you need to see about booking the ballroom and beginning preparations for your coming out ball.

"Shall I write also to Miss Grant and Lord Peterborough?"

"Yes, let them know we are doing fine, and thank them again for all their help." He wiped his mouth with his handkerchief and arose. "Now I must be going. The stocks are keeping me busy these days. Oh, and please write to Mrs. Bennington and ask her where she put your mother's paintings. I miss seeing them."

"Mrs. Bennington?" Lily was dismayed.

"I am sorry, dear. I know you do not like her, and neither do I, after the treatment she gave you. Just keep it short." He bent and kissed her on her forehead.

After he left, Lily diligently read the newspaper, hoping to read some latest news about the release of the Greek slaves. There was no further news. She then sat down and wrote several letters, penning a thank-you note to Miss Grant and Lord Peterborough, telling them that they arrived safely to London. Then, she wrote to Mrs. Hartford to let her know she was in town with her father and asking that they meet one day.

Lily then wrote a terse note to Mrs. Bennington, asking her where her mother's paintings were. She paused in her writing, remembering her cousins and the time spent here. How naïve she had been then, trusting Mrs. Bennington until it was too late. Lord Peterborough had warned her, but she had resisted. She thought she knew all about human character from listening to her grandmother's clients, but she realized that she had been under her grandmother's protective wing all these years. She had learned her lesson with Mrs. Bennington and her brother. Her father was her protector and she felt so much better.

On impulse, she wrote to Jane, telling her what happened to her, and that she hoped to see her that summer. Even though she had misgivings, she could not be angry with her for long.

Two days later, Lily was pleased to receive a call from Mrs. Hartford. Mrs. Doonesbury, an elderly woman dressed in fine clothing, accompanied her.

"I was so delighted to hear from you!" Mrs. Hartford exclaimed. "To think that your father is here at last, and that you will be presented at court and will have your debutante ball. What great news!"

"Yes, I was so happy to see him," Lily agreed.

"Of course, my dear. And you *have* come a long way since I last saw you. You are quite a young lady now. You carry yourself with poise, and your hair is combed nicely, and your skin has a snow-white complexion. These are all to your advantage," Mrs. Hartford said, studying her proudly. "Is that not right, Mrs. Doonesbury?"

"She has great potential."

"Thank you," Lily said, blushing. "Only I do not have experience in being presented in court and being launched into society and I am glad you could help."

"Have no fear. You will have help from us. Mrs. Doonesbury has graciously consented in advising you. I'll have you know that she has launched several young women into society and they all have done quite well," Mrs. Hartford said, followed by a knowing wink.

"That is nice of you, Mrs. Doonesbury," Lily told the elderly woman.

"I was born a lady and have presented several young women to court and know all about it," Mrs. Doonesbury said in a nasal tone reserved for the upper echelons of society. "But there is much work to be done. We must start immediately."

They discussed the preparations over tea and small cakes. Lily learned about the intricacies of appearing at the Royal Drawing Room, including what she must wear, what to say, and how to curtsy.

By the time the two women left, Lily was overwhelmed with everything. That evening at dinnertime, she spoke to her father about their visit.

"That is kind of them," Sir Frederick said, his eyes twinkling. "You chose well with Mrs. Hartford. Now I have some news for you. I met some colleagues at the club last night. I told them about you appearing after all these years, and they were very surprised. We discussed the possibility of your mother being alive."

"Yes?"

"One colleague, who is connected with international affairs with Greece, said that the Ottomans had a habit of taking prisoners as slaves during the war. Through the help of recent investigations, several Greeks captured during the war have been returned back to Greece. He will look into the matter for me."

"Oh, it would be wonderful to have Mama alive and living with us!"

"Do not be too quick, my dear, in resurrecting your mother. He has not promised anything yet. Meanwhile, he suggested I write to the embassy in Greece informing them that your mother's been missing since 1821. Hopefully, I'll get a response this time."

A couple of weeks later, Lily received replies to the letters she had sent out. She was happy to learn that Miss Bodline was doing well and promised to see her in London once she graduated. Lord Peterborough wrote back, thanking her for her letter. He mentioned that his aunt missed her company. *Was his aunt the only one that missed me?* He and his aunt wished her well. She read his letter several times, remembering everything that transpired between them and feeling nostalgic.

A few days later, she received Mrs. Bennington's letter. She wrote that the paintings were in Bristol and she would bring them with her when she came for the London season.

When Lily relayed Mrs. Bennington's message to her father that evening, he was disturbed. "I do not wish to wait that long. Those are precious paintings. I will write to have them sent immediately."

Chapter 31

Within a week, her mother's paintings had arrived. After Lily had returned from her walk, she found them deposited in the drawing room. She carefully removed their burlap coverings.

Astounded by the richness and vividness of the paintings, she stood there gazing at them. It was as if she were seeing live people and live scenes. In one picture, Lily was a little girl and held hands with an older couple. They must have been her maternal grandparents, for they had dark hair and gazed lovingly into her eyes.

Another painting showed her around two years old, smiling and holding a ball. An older couple, both fair-haired, sat nearby smiling. She recognized her paternal grandparents.

Lily found a self-portrait of her mother, and a portrait of her proud father holding her as baby in his arms. She felt the love of her parents and family in these paintings, and was happy and sad at the same time.

Feeling emotional, Lily had Mrs. Tippins hang them back in their usual place.

When her father arrived that evening, she did not mention anything, wishing to surprise him. He kissed her on the forehead and went upstairs to change. After a few minutes, he returned, smiling. "The paintings came, and you wanted to be sure that I saw them?"

"Yes. Mrs. Tippins helped put them back in their places."

"They are where they should be," he said, nodding. "Your mother captured everything so well."

Christmas morning arrived, and Lily and her father had a scrumptious breakfast together. They talked about a number of things. Afterwards, Lily peppered him with questions about her past. He told her stories, ranging from his own childhood to the time when she was born.

"You were such a lovely and good baby. Not only am I saying this because I am your father; both sets of grandparents were happy with you."

Sir Frederick reminisced about Lily's mother, recalling several poignant moments he spent with her that revealed her good character and talents. He paused, absorbed in thought.

"Now you have her paintings to remind you of her," Lily said.

"Yes, and I am impressed by your own love of painting. I would like to see it develop," he said. He rang for the maid, who returned with several large packages.

"Merry Christmas, darling." Sir Frederick handed the presents to Lily.

Lily unwrapped the packages to find new canvasses and paint supplies. She was delighted with her gifts and hugged him.

"Thank you so much! Now it is my turn," she said, retrieving her gifts from the corner where she had placed them. She handed him a set of embroidered linen handkerchiefs with his initials on them and a painting she had made of her mother.

"You have made me very happy," he said, kissing her on the forehead.

"It is not as good a quality as Mother's, but it is the best I could do."

"This is very good. Now, let us share this day with the others."

The servants were called to the ballroom, which had been decorated with festive ornaments. The refreshments and small gifts of scarves, gloves, and embroidered handkerchiefs were handed out to the servants, and then everyone sang Christmas carols to Lily and her father. They were pleased, and everyone thanked Lily and her father.

Dotty was the last to receive her present. It was a painting of Dotty. Her mouth hung open as she gazed at it in admiration. "You have made me beautiful," she exclaimed.

"That is how I see you," Lily said, pleased with her reaction. "I had a very difficult time hiding it, for every time I began to paint, you would always appear."

They both laughed.

"Now I have a present for you, Miss," Dotty said, beaming. "It will only take a minute." She left and returned shortly with a box. "It is something I found upstairs just the other day, in the attic when I was dusting under my bed."

Lily opened the container curiously. Inside were several pages of writing. "Who wrote these?"

"I could not read, so I hope you do not mind, but I asked Mrs. Tippins, and she told me they were your mother's."

"Thank you," Lily cried. "This is one of the nicest presents!" She hugged her.

Afterward, Lily went to her room and looked at the papers in the box. Most of them were about her mother's daily activities. She took one and read it aloud.

"On this day, my dearest Lily said the word Mama. I was so happy." Lily stopped reading, feeling choked from her emotions.

Her mother also wrote about the time Lily's first tooth came out, and when Lily began to walk and talk. She wrote extensively about Sir Frederick, and her words showed how deeply she loved him. There was even a passage in there regarding a visit to Greystone Manor.

By the time she finished reading them, it was time to get ready for dinner. She wiped the tears from her eyes, dressed, and took the box of papers with her.

She showed the box to her father.

Sir Frederick was very much moved when he saw the papers. "I will read them this very night."

January arrived and brought with it snow and ice, and windy days. Confined inside much of the time, Lily often gazed out the frosted window at the pure, white landscape. Each day, she read the newspaper, searching for news about the Greek slaves, but there was little news.

Mrs. Hartford and Mrs. Doonesbury visited her a few weeks later, when the weather was more amenable. They discussed the preparations for Lily's coming out event. Their visit was pleasant, with much discussion and gossip over tea.

One day in February, Lily was surprised to read in the newspaper that the seventeen-year-old Prince Otto of Bavaria had arrived in Athens to become its new king. That evening at the dinner table, she mentioned it to her father.

"Why did the Greeks choose someone from another country to rule Greece? Why not have a Greek citizen rule the country?" Lily asked, feeling confused.

"It is quite complex, I'm afraid. A few years ago, the three countries, Britain, France, and Russia, as self-appointed intercessors, signed the Treaty of London for Greece to be free, but I believe the Ottomans did not honor it. Meanwhile, I understand that Count John Capodistrias was elected Greek president. However, he made many enemies during his presidency and was murdered in front of a Greek church. This has caused much turmoil in Greece."

Lily shuddered. "How terrible."

"Several treaties were signed among the powers during those years. I forgot most of them, but I do remember The London Protocol. It called for a hereditary monarchy to be chosen outside of the three powers. That is how Prince Otto of Bavaria came to be chosen."

March arrived quickly, and soon it was Lily's eighteenth birthday. Her father presented her with a beautiful diamond necklace and matching earrings. Delighted by the gift, she hugged him.

"This is a family heirloom," he explained. "It is passed down from generation to generation. You must keep it in a safe place, for you will give it one day to your eldest daughter."

Mrs. Hartford and Mrs. Doonesbury paid her a few more visits, and discussed the details of her presentation in court, including what she was to wear, and how she was to enter and leave the room. She practiced her walk and curtsy several times.

When the day in May arrived for Lily to be presented to the court, she was extremely nervous. Mrs. Hartford and Mrs. Doonesbury arrived, and with the help of Dotty, prepared her with meticulous detail. The dress they chose for her to wear was tailored by a famous French seamstress, made to the specifications of the court. It was a white dress with a train trailing from the shoulders, and it had a tulle veil.

"You must not stand out from the other girls, you know," Mrs. Doonesbury said.

When she was ready, Lily approached her father wearing her new dress, with the two older women and Dotty trailing behind her.

"You are magnificent looking, my dear." Sir Frederick smiled and lifting her veil, kissed her on her forehead. "Do not worry, you will do well."

When she arrived at St. James Palace, Lily was ushered into the Long Gallery with the other debutantes, waiting for the summons. Her train was folded over her left arm and her wrap was left in the carriage. The other debutantes appeared nervous, like her. When her turn came, Lily handed her card to a lord-in-waiting.

He announced her name to His Majesty.

Lily held her breath as she walked slowly and regally to where the king was seated. Trying to remain composed, she curtsied very low, almost kneeling, and kissed the extended, plump hand of the sovereign.

When she arose, she noticed that the king nodded, appearing pleased. Curtsying slightly to the king and to the other royal members present, she backed out of the room without tripping on her dress, making sure not to turn her face from the king.

It was a momentous event for Lily. Her father was pleased with her. That evening, they invited a few close friends to dinner, including Mrs. Hartford and Mrs. Doonesbury.

A week later, Mrs. Hartford and Mrs. Doonesbury visited her. They proudly showed her the newspaper. Her name was included in a column listing the debutantes presented at court.

Sir Frederick arrived just then and they also showed him the newspaper.

Then they discussed possibilities of where to schedule her upcoming ball. Sir Frederick gave some suggestions, and this time offered to pay them for their services. Both women refused.

"I am doing this for my late friend, Judith," Mrs. Hartford said.

Mrs. Doonesbury said she also enjoyed doing it. "Sir Frederick, we will need a list of notable people to invite. Maybe we can invite an earl or two. That always gives a ball distinction. We should also invite enough men and women of caliber, of course, to round out the ball," she said.

"As you wish, Mrs. Doonesbury. I will make the list and get it to you shortly," Sir Frederick replied.

"Father, I also have several friends from the school that we could invite. They would be finished with the school term by then," Lily offered, feeling excited.

"Lily, dearest, you can invite as many friends as you'd like," Sir Frederick said, smiling at her.

The next few weeks, the two women and Lily channeled their energies in preparing for the ball. The date was set for the tenth of June. With her father's encouragement, Lily had several dresses made. The first was an expensive white ball dress with all the trimmings, while the other dresses were for dinner and party invitations that would inevitably come after the ball, including a couple of walking dresses.

As the days warmed, Lily and Dotty paid visits to the parks, strolling around, just as she used to with her cousin, Marianne.

One day, her father took her in the carriage to the park, and she wore one of her new dresses. Several people of nobility, who happened to be in the park, stopped to converse with them. Her father proudly introduced her.

"It seems that you are making a favorable impression, my dear," Sir Frederick said to Lily, as they were returning home.

"Everyone is asking about your ball. I've added at least fifty more people to the list."

Chapter 32

March - June 1833

The day of the ball arrived, and Lily was nervous as Dotty helped her into her white silk dress. Creamy-white lace and matching silk ribbons trimmed the large sleeves, while shimmering pearls adorned the front of the dress. The open neckline and small waistline emphasized her velvety skin and shapely figure.

Dotty brushed Lily's hair, pulling and twisting it until it was shiny. Using all her expertise, she swept it up into an elegant vision of finesse and golden curls. She finished by pinning a cluster of fresh, white lilies into her masterpiece. The lilies gave off a nice sweet fragrance that Lily found soothing to her nerves.

Next, Dotty placed the diamond necklace around Lily's neck, clasping it securely, and then helped her put on the dainty, matching earrings.

"The necklace dazzles the eye, Miss, and your neckline is not too low, and not too high. Just right for you," Dotty commented cheerfully. "You have a slim neck and with your hair up, it gives you elegance."

"Thank you, Dotty. I specifically told Mrs. Doonesbury that I did not want the neckline too low. I want the men to look at my face, not my neckline."

They both burst out laughing.

"Don't forget to take that extra pair of dancing slippers with you. You'll need them."

Lily threw the white slippers into a small bag, and then grabbed her long white gloves and small stole from the bed. "I am so nervous, Dotty."

"You'll be fine, Miss. It is your day to shine."

"Thank you, Dotty," Lily said, hugging her. "You've helped me so much."

Sir Frederick had been waiting for Lily downstairs in the drawing room. Dressed in a dark, formal suit and appearing very handsome, with his firm chin, blue eyes, and flaxen hair, he smiled warmly at her. "You look beautiful, my dear," he said. "Your mother would have been proud of you."

When Lily and her father arrived at the ballroom, they stood at the entrance, taking in the view. The grand room was decked with pots of fragrant white lilies, while gold-gilded mirrors on the walls reflected the goings on of the room. Large chandeliers hung from the tall ceiling and an orchestra sat in the far end of the large room tuning their instruments. A whir of voices, high-pitched and low, with strains of laughter, filled the large room that teemed with people decked in the latest fashions, all glitter and show. Lily's eyes searched the room for the tall, handsome Lord Peterborough. She had seen the invitation list and his name had been included. A small sigh escaped her lips, for there was no sign of him.

The short, stocky Mrs. Hartford, and the tall, thin Mrs. Doonesbury floated towards them, their faces radiant. They were dressed in their finest clothing and jewelry. They exchanged greetings.

"You look lovely, my dear!" Mrs. Hartford exclaimed.

Mrs. Doonesbury chimed her agreement.

"Thank you," Lily replied, blushing.

"You also look elegant, Mrs. Hartford, and you, too, Mrs. Doonesbury," Sir Frederick said, his eyes twinkling. "It would not surprise me if you both received proposals of marriage tonight. Several bachelors will be attending the ball."

"I assure you, we are *not* looking to marry," Mrs. Doonesbury retorted, flicking her fan open and fanning herself in apparent fluster.

"Pray, speak for yourself, Mrs. Doonesbury," Mrs. Hartford snorted. "I will have you know that I am still passable enough to earn a few admiring glances from elderly bachelors." She batted her eyes at Sir Frederick.

Sir Frederick cleared his throat. "I must commend you both for your remarkable job in making this event a success," he said, glancing around the room. "You have not only turned my daughter into a princess, but managed to evoke such excitement in London, that several families of nobility were eager to attend tonight's ball."

"We did our best, Sir Frederick. Mrs. Hartford said, flushing. "Come, follow us, Miss Montgomery. There is a chamber reserved for you."

Lily and the two women made their way down a hallway and entered a small room, which held a table, chair and mirror.

"You will freshen up here," Mrs. Doonesbury informed Lily.

"When your name is announced, you will enter the ballroom. Your father will escort you to the dance floor. The first dance will be a waltz, and you and your father will dance it," Mrs. Hartford said.

"We have discussed this in great detail with him," Mrs. Doonesbury added. "When you finish your dance, you will move off to the side, and it is expected that several young men will come forward to ask to dance with you."

Mrs. Hartford rummaged in her purse. She handed her the dainty dance card with a pencil attached to it by a ribbon. "You will carry this with you and are to write the names of the dance partners next to the dances on the card."

"Remember, you should not dance more than three dances with any man," Mrs. Doonesbury added.

∞∞∞

The moment came too quickly. The master of ceremonies announced her name. Taking a deep breath, Lily advanced into the ballroom. There was a sudden hush in the room as numerous eyes turned and focused on her.

Blushing, Lily's gaze fell on her father, as he stood waiting for her like a beacon. She would make him proud. With slow, steady steps, and her head lifted high, she walked with poise toward him.

He smiled at her, his face glowing with pride, and took her gloved hand, slowly guiding her to the center of the ballroom. The waltz began. Lily relaxed in her father's arms for he was a smooth dancer, even with his limp, whirling her around the ballroom as if they had been dancing together for years. Lily felt safe in his arms.

After the dance, her father took her to the side.

"I am pleased with you, my dear," he said, patting her hand. "I will stay by your side in case you need any introductions. But first, there are several good families here that I wish you to meet."

He took her around the room, introducing her to some important families of England, staying just long enough to converse a little and move on.

Soon, several young men surrounded her and her father. After the introductions, they asked Lily for a dance. She wrote their names in her dance card. She recognized Mr. Beaumont among the young men. He was a tall, husky man, with a mustache and a slight limp.

"Mr. Beaumont," she said.

"Miss Montgomery," he replied, bowing. "Please reserve the waltz for me."

Lily gazed at her half-filled card. Two waltzes were still available on the card. She wrote his name next to a waltz.

"Lord Peterborough, what a pleasure to see you again," Sir Frederick said.

Lily flushed when she heard his name. *He came after all.* She looked up, her heart clamoring.

He gazed at her, an enigmatic expression on his fine features.

What was it about him that always gave her an exciting feeling? Was it his broad shoulders, his height, or the way he was impeccably dressed in his formal black suit with white shirt and white cravat, or was it his handsome face with those beautiful eyes? No, it was his soul that impressed her, his kind and gentle soul.

He gazed at her, with an enigmatic expression on his face. "Miss Montgomery," he said, bowing. "Sir Frederick. Mr. Beaumont."

"If you are looking for a dance, old friend, you will have to wait," Mr. Beaumont said. "She is promised to dance with at least eight others before you."

"I would have arrived sooner, but was conversing with Miss Bodline. If a waltz is available, please reserve it for me."

Lily jotted down his name, her writing shaky. "Miss Bodline is here?"

"I can take you to her," Lord Peterborough offered.

Lily hesitated. The last thing she wanted was to witness any tenderness between Lord Peterborough and Jane.

Just then, the music began for the minuet and Mr. Falston, her first dance partner, came and offered her his arm. A red-faced youth, with blonde hair and blue eyes, he must not have been much older than Lily.

"I am afraid I had reserved this dance, Lord Peterborough," Lily said as she was led onto the floor.

Several couples had already formed groups. With delicate steps, she performed the dance, mindful of the admiring stares she was receiving from both sexes. It wasn't long before the dance finished. Soon, she was dancing with the next dance partner. At one point, she spied Lord Peterborough dancing with Jane, and her heart squeezed a few tears.

With some dances, Lily had time to speak to her dance partners. She learned that some men were younger sons and others, elder sons. They came in all shapes and sizes and she received many compliments. Lily was called a beautiful angel, a vision in white, lovely to behold, and so on, which made for a special feeling indeed.

It wasn't until the eighth dance, when she saw Jane advancing towards her, her round face beaming, that Lily plummeted from her lofty height to the depths of misery. The image was still fresh in her mind of Jane dancing with Lord Peterborough.

"Lily!" Jane cried. "You are quite the belle of the ball. I am so proud of you."

"Thank you. I am glad that you could make it."

"I have some wonderful news for you," Jane said. "I am engaged to be married!"

Lily felt a tightening in her chest and with all the strength she could muster, ignored it. She smiled and hugged her friend. *Jane deserves to be happy.* "I am so glad for you. When will it be?"

"Next month in London. Is that not wonderful?"

Lily was about to respond but was interrupted by Mr. Beaumont, who had just arrived.

"Miss Montgomery, I believe we have the next dance."

Lily introduced him to Jane, and then allowed herself to be escorted to the dance floor. They danced through the waltz. He was a commendable dancer, but more powerful than smooth, his arms pulling her rather than moving with her.

"You are the talk of the town, Miss Montgomery," Mr. Beaumont said.

Lily blushed. "I hope it is good talk, worthy of a young woman's ears."

He burst out laughing. "Yes, very much so."

After he returned her to her father, Mr. Beaumont thanked her for the dance, and then bowed and left.

"Are you enjoying yourself?" Sir Frederick asked.

"I have never danced so much in my life," Lily exclaimed, fanning herself. Her next dance partner arrived, and she was off again.

A half-hour later, Lord Peterborough approached her. She was bemused. She glanced at her card. He was her next dance partner. How could she dance with him knowing he was to marry her best friend?

"Lord Peterborough," she said, curtsying.

"Miss Montgomery, I believe I have reserved this next waltz," he said, taking her stiff arm and walking with her to the dance floor. "Is everything to your satisfaction? Are you enjoying this ball?"

"It is as expected," she said, trying to appear calm as they faced each other, poised to begin the dance. "Everyone wants to dance with me because it is my ball, even you."

"You have mistaken my intentions, Miss Montgomery," he said, his eyes hooded. "I do not wish to dance with you because it is your ball, but because it is *you*."

"I am sure that your good manners require that you use such fine words, but do not forget that you had the pleasure of dancing with Miss Bodline first," she retorted, and then clamped her mouth shut, embarrassed by her selfish outburst.

Lord Peterborough raised an eyebrow, but was too well bred to reply. Besides, the music began. They whirled around in smooth harmony. Lily's feelings of discontent were replaced by an overwhelming sense of exhilaration as she sensed him anticipating every move she made. They danced so well together, it felt as if they were one person.

Lily saw his eyes flash with pleasure every time she gazed into his face. She felt as if she were floating on a cloud of happiness. When the dance ended, they slowly walked back to her place.

"By the way, the reason I danced with Miss Bodline first was because she had not danced the whole evening and was without a dance partner, while you were busy dancing with every man in this room," Lord Peterborough said. "I did the gentlemanly thing and asked her for a dance."

Lily blushed, her previous feelings resurfacing. She felt cross for some reason. "I fear my reading of your character was mistaken. I beg forgiveness, Lord Peterborough."

He stared at her for a moment, his stern look melting into a crinkled smile.

The orchestra stopped for an intermission. Lily fanned herself, her eyes searching for her father. She was thirsty and hungry. It was time to sup. "I wonder where my father is?"

"I saw him heading for the supper room with a group of people. I would be pleased to escort you there."

"What about Miss Bodline?"

"Miss Bodline?" Lord Peterborough asked, giving her a puzzled look, his eyebrow raised. "Yes, of course, we can see about having her join you."

Jane was not alone. Miss Lawrence and Miss Bradenton from the school were also with her, along with Mrs. Bradenton, who was evidently the girls chaperone.

"Will you join me for supper?" Lily asked them.

Along the way, Lily and her friends caught up on their news, while Lord Peterborough and Jane followed them. While she listened to the two young women chatter about their coming out balls last year and how happy they were to have finished with their schooling, Lily was only too conscious of the quiet couple walking behind them.

The supper room was large and buzzing with people. Several people sat at the long tables, while others stood around, talking and eating. Lily's father sat at the far end of a table, with an empty seat next to him. He waved to her. Lily excused herself from her friends and Lord Peterborough, and went and joined him. A few places were still available at the other tables where her friends sat down.

Lily noticed that Lord Peterborough did not stay to sup.

"I want you to meet some good friends of the family," Sir Frederick told Lily. He introduced her to an earl and his wife, and her time was consumed with them.

After they were finished, they sauntered back into the ballroom where Lily continued her dancing and did not get a chance to speak to her friends or to Lord Peterborough the rest of the evening.

Chapter 33

The next morning, groggy and tired, Lily awoke late, so she breakfasted in her room. Dotty dawdled in her tasks, lingering and asking questions, and listening to what Lily had to say about the young men she danced with last night at her ball.

"Did you get a chance to dance with Lord Peterborough?" Dotty asked knowingly.

Lily stared at her. Lord Peterborough haunted her thoughts and dreams, but she did not want to talk about him because he was engaged to Jane, and Dotty would perk her ears and raise more questions about him.

"Yes, but there were so many others vying for my attention, I fear I did not give him that much attention," Lily said, sighing.

It was eleven o'clock, when Lily finally joined her father in the drawing room. A sweet fragrance emanated from the lilies that filled the room. They had been brought back from the ball last night.

"You have already had two male callers and two dinner invitations, and it is not even noon yet."

Lily immediately became alert. "Who were the callers?"

"Mr. Beaumont and Mr. Falston."

"Oh," Lily said, feeling deflated, hoping it would have been Lord Peterborough. "What about the two invitations you mentioned?"

"They were for two dinner parties from distinguished peer. You have impressed them, my dear, and they have eligible sons."

Later that day, Lily received a call from Mrs. Hartford and Mrs. Doonesbury. Lily had been expecting them. She served them tea and small cakes.

"Your ball was the talk of the town!" Mrs. Hartford exclaimed. "Everyone seemed quite pleased. Also, several people were asking about your cousins, the Benningtons. I told them a white lie, that I did not know whether they were in town or not, and that Sir Frederick had made the list."

"I have something for you, to show my appreciation," Lily said, retrieving two small portraits from a bag she had set to the side. She handed them to the women. "I painted them during my spare time."

"Oh, how wonderful," Mrs. Hartford cried, admiring her portrait. "You made me at least twenty years younger."

"You should see mine," Mrs. Doonesbury said, smirking. "I look absolutely divine."

The two women chatted excitedly as to whom was better looking.

"I am glad you like them. That was the least I could do for all that you did for me," Lily said, smiling at their display of happiness.

"If you did not have your rich father to take care of you, my dear, you would have made a fortune in painting portraits," Mrs. Doonesbury said.

They stayed for a short visit and then were off.

The next morning, Mr. Beaumont called on Lily. He offered to take her walking to the park, with Dotty tagging along.

As they strolled, Mr. Beaumont talked about his years in college and afterwards. He knew Lord Peterborough well and referred to him respectfully. "He saved my life during the battle of Navarino," he stated.

"Is that so?" Lily asked. "I remember reading about the battle. It was between the allies and the Ottomans for the Greek cause. Please tell me about it."

He grimaced. "It really is not fit for a young lady's ears, but I will say this. Lord Peterborough arrived just in time and freed me from the pole that had fallen on me. If he hadn't moved me to safety, the cannon shot would have finished me where I had been lying."

Lily shuddered at the thought. "That was very gallant of him."

"I have a limp as a result of that day, but I am thankful that I am alive." Mr. Beaumont's eyes shone with gratitude. "I owe him my life."

They arrived at the house.

"Miss Montgomery, I have enjoyed our walk immensely," Mr. Beaumont said. "You are a lily in its purest sense. A refreshing contrast to the other young ladies." He bowed and left.

Lily liked him, but not for a marriage partner. When she entered the townhouse, she found two suitors sitting in the drawing room. They had brought flowers.

That evening, Lily and her father attended a formal dinner party at a viscount's residence. Her father knew several people there. Lily recognized a few distinguished couples from her ball and politely listened as they talked at the dinner table. Afterward, they sat and listened to a music recital before adjourning for the evening.

Each day, Lily hoped Lord Peterborough would call, but he did not. Instead, she received a steady flow of male callers, along with invitations to social events. She conversed wittily and laughed often during the day with young male visitors, but her heart wasn't in it. Her evenings were filled with dinner parties, or opera, or theatre, yet she felt as if something were missing every time she returned home.

One week after her ball, Lily turned down two marriage proposals from two hopeful men.

Lily was in a reflective mood one morning as she returned from a morning walk in the park with Dotty. She was surprised to see her father in the drawing room reading a newspaper. He would usually be out. As she removed her bonnet, he informed her that she had just missed Miss Bodline, and Miss Bradenton and her mother.

"Your friends seem like nice young women, particularly Miss Bodline," he remarked. "They stayed for a while, hoping to see you, and then had to leave."

"Miss Bodline is the one who alerted me to the newspaper article about you," Lily said, holding her bonnet in her hand, feeling downcast. "She is engaged to be married to Lord Peterborough."

Sir Frederick shot up as if struck by a lightning bolt, his hand clutching the newspaper. "Lord Peterborough? Impossible!"

His startled response surprised Lily. "Why do you say that, Papa?"

Sir Frederick settled back in his seat, groping for the right words. "I admit that she is a fine girl, but with his title and wealth, he could choose higher. I would never have guessed they would make a match of it."

"That is probably why he has not called here, although they could have come together," she mumbled, feeling cross about the whole thing. "I have missed seeing him, I mean them." She was embarrassed at the slip.

Lily paced the room with nervous energy. "Oh, it is no use in keeping up the pretense. I am so tired of all these young men calling daily, and not leaving me alone."

Sir Frederick appeared surprised. "I was not aware that you felt that way."

"I did it to please you, because you had spent so much money on my dress and my ball. The men are all the same after a while. The same stories, the same compliments, and the same jokes. If I have to choose one among them to marry, then I do not ever want to marry!"

"I am rather surprised by all this," Sir Frederick said, blinking in consternation.

Lily stopped her pacing to face her father. "Maybe you should not have spent so lavishly on me after all. It's so much better in Yorkshire, with its fresh air and beauty. There, I could ride and laugh in the wind, and the kind people do not care what I wear or say. Oh, *why* can't we go back?"

A shadow passed over Sir Frederick's face. "Let me ask you a question, my dear," he said. "Are you in love with Lord Peterborough?"

Lily was stunned. *Father guessed my feelings after all.* "Yeeessss!" she wailed, rushing to him and burying her face in his shoulder. "But he never did propose. He loves Miss Bodline instead!"

"Oh, dear," he muttered. "Why do you not go and rest? All this excitement may have been too much for you." He walked her to the door. "I suggest you have Dotty stay down here, fending off your callers. You do not need to see anyone else if you do not wish."

"Really?" Lily said, sniffling.

"Yes, from now on, you will only be available to the people you want to see."

⚬⚬⚬

Edward sat in his study that morning, with a pile of work on his desk. He stroked his unshaved chin thoughtfully, absorbed with thoughts of Miss Montgomery. He had toyed with the idea of visiting her, but her unusually cold behavior at the ball made him hesitate. Besides, he heard from several friends, including Mr. Beaumont, how she was inundated with male callers and was invited to several dinner parties and social events, which reminded him of Charlotte.

The other night at the theatre, he witnessed Miss Montgomery and her father seated in the Fullerton box. The Fullerton family had titles and their eligible son would eventually inherit an earldom and vast wealth someday. He sighed, resuming his work.

A while later, the servant entered the room and informed him that he had a male visitor.

"Tell him I am not in!" Edward called out, intent on his writing. "No, wait. Who is it?"

"It is Sir Frederick Montgomery, milord."

"What would he want?" Edward said, feeling bewildered. "Tell him I will be down in a few minutes. Oh, and offer some refreshments."

Edward rang for Herman. "Sir Frederick is downstairs. I must make haste. Make me suitable for the visit."

"Right away, milord." Herman quickly gathered the materials together and began making the lather.

Edward settled into a chair and watched as his valet lathered his face with the soapy concoction.

"It's about Miss Montgomery, isn't it, milord?" Herman asked, his eyebrow cocked, as he began to shave him.

"I do not know."

"I wonder if he's had a change of heart and wishes to speak to you about matrimony."

"What?" Edward sputtered. His servant knew too much about his affairs.

"Please, don't talk, milord. I don't want to nick you. I'll be through in a minute." Herman said, finishing the last strokes, and then wiping his master's face dry with a towel. "All done."

"I will have you know that you try my patience sometimes, Herman," Edward said, sitting up and looking in the mirror. "But you do wonders with your hands. Get my dark-blue suit ready. I will go out afterwards."

Herman tied the last finishes to the white cravat. "There. Perfect."

"Why have you never married, Herman?" Edward asked him, fingering the tight cravat.

"It is a long story, milord," Herman said, smiling. "Women can be fickle. But another time, you have a visitor waiting."

Edward found Sir Frederick in the drawing room. He appeared cross for some reason.

They exchanged greetings and a few pleasantries before Sir Frederick came to the reason for his visit.

"My congratulations. I understand that you are engaged to be married, Lord Peterborough," Sir Frederick said ironically.

"I *was* engaged once, a while back, with Miss Stanton, but that has been called off."

Sir Frederick raised his eyebrows. "There is no one else?"

Edward was puzzled. "I assure you there is no one."

Sir Frederick appeared confused. "It is quite odd. My daughter believes you are engaged to Miss Bodline."

"Miss Bodline?" Edward asked, feeling confounded. "I have no interest in her. Besides, she is to be married soon to Mr. Pilford, my steward at Greystone Manor."

"How could my daughter make such a blatant mistake?" Sir Frederick cried.

Edward shook his head. "There is definitely a mistake," he replied. Now it was beginning to make sense, her coldness toward him that night at the ball, particularly every time he mentioned Miss Bodline's name. He burst out laughing, feeling an immense happiness and lightness of being.

"Please, this is no laughing matter!" Sir Frederick said. "I had a talk with her this morning, and discovered that she has feelings for you, but you have been removed from the growing list of eligible bachelors by a silly mistake. As long as she thinks you are engaged to someone else, she will not allow her true feelings to show. I must tell her the truth."

"If you tell her, then she will think there is reason to believe I am interested in her, and that would sway her judgement," Edward said, feeling amused. "Remember what you had said about her not having any experience with men and that I must wait for her to make up her mind?"

Sir Frederick eyed him shrewdly. "Yes, I did say that. But you have not been around, either!" he retorted. "You have more than fulfilled your part and allowed all the young fops of London to beat a path to our door. The plan has backfired. She does not want to marry any of them. Now she is ready to leave for the country."

"Your daughter is a smart girl, Sir Frederick," Edward said, liking what he heard.

"Let me ask you this. Do you still have feelings for my daughter?"

"Even more than before, Sir Frederick," Edward admitted. "I lose sleep over the girl, but you said--"

"Forget what I said before!" Sir Frederick shouted. "You have my permission to marry her."

Edward stared at him, surprised by his outburst.

"I apologize for shouting," Sir Frederick said wearily, "but I do not wish to see my daughter in pain. You may call on her this very moment and tell her the truth. Tell her how you feel about her."

Chapter 34

July 1833

That afternoon, Edward called on Miss Montgomery. He was surprised to learn from the butler that she was out. "In case it is relevant, please tell whomever is here, that Lord Peterborough has called."

"Lord Peterborough? Please wait here, my lord." The butler climbed the stairs and disappeared. Moments later, Dotty came rushing down the stairs, her thin face appearing flushed. "Lord Peterborough!" she exclaimed. "What a pleasure to see you."

"Hello, Dotty," Edward said, smiling. "I came to see Miss Montgomery, but I was told she was out. When do you expect her in?"

"To be honest, my lord," Dotty said. "She is resting. I'll tell her you are here. I'm pretty sure she'll want to see you." She led him into the drawing room. "Please have a seat, my lord."

෴෴෴

Dotty relayed the news to Lily.

"Lord Peterborough is downstairs?" Lily cried. She had been reading in her room, trying to calm down after the conversation with her father.

"Yes, Miss," Dotty said, beaming. "And he's all by himself."

"Lord Peterborough is downstairs," Lily repeated, dumbfounded, not sure what to do. Her mind raced through a number of reasons. "He is either here to personally see that I come to his wedding, or--"

"Or he's here to see you," Dotty said pointedly. "He doesn't look like someone getting married, if you don't mind me mentioning it. He looks like he's had a bad day of it, Miss."

She had that raised eyebrow look that Lily was beginning to know well. It meant that through her years of experience, she knew more than Lily did about men.

"Help me get ready," Lily said, feeling disconcerted. Maybe he needed someone to talk with. He had helped her through so many difficulties; the least she could do was reciprocate.

Dotty showed her several dresses.

"How about that one?" Lily asked, pointing to a white dress. Then she saw the pink one. "No, that pink might be better." As Dotty was putting them away, Lily saw another white dress, prettier than the first. "Oh, wait! Get me that white one, with the satin ribbons and flowers. Yes, that one."

"You still have feelings for him, I can tell," Dotty said knowingly. "Your hands are trembling and you haven't been able to make up your mind which dress to wear."

"I always have trouble choosing dresses," Lily retorted.

"*Hmmf!*" Dotty muttered as she helped Lily into her dress.

In ten minutes, Lily left the room with Dotty. When she reached the door to the drawing room, she paused, trying to calm down. "Where is he seated?" she whispered to Dotty.

Dotty opened the door and peeked inside. "He's standing by the fireplace," she whispered back.

They entered the room.

Lily stood there, mesmerized by his presence, her heart swelling with fond memories of him. His back was turned toward them as he stared into the fireplace. He was splendidly dressed, and he was alone.

Dotty went quietly to a side chair and sat down.

"Lord Peterborough," Lily sang out. Her voice surprised her. It was as if her heart, unable to contain itself and overflowing with the sweetness of love, revealed its deepest anguish through her voice.

Lord Peterborough turned and gazed at her, his dark eyes shining. He bowed. "Miss Montgomery," he said earnestly. Then he looked at Dotty. "Dotty, you may leave us. I wish to speak to Miss Montgomery alone."

Dotty's eyes grew wide as saucers. She sputtered apologies, and slipped out of the room, leaving the door open.

Lord Peterborough went and shut the door, and then turned and looked at Lily. "I need to speak to you on a serious subject."

Lily's confusion knew no bounds. "What about?"

He strode toward her, smiling that special smile of his. "I am here for one specific reason. Can you guess what it is?"

Lily swallowed, feeling that miserable feeling again, yet wondering how his irresistible magnetism could still draw her to him. "To let me know you are getting married?" she managed to answer.

"Yes," he cried, taking her hands in his. "So, you *do* know."

Lily straightened her back, feeling an inexhaustible sense of vulnerability. *Why does he have to look so handsome and be so unavailable at the same time?* "Of course. I wish you all the best," she replied civilly.

"I also wish you all the best," he whispered, squeezing her hands.

Lily stared at him. "You do?"

He nodded, his beautiful, expressive eyes glowing with some hidden passion. He pulled her close to him. "It takes two to have a marriage, you know."

Lily froze. They were very close, their bodies barely touching, and the familiar scent of sandalwood and spice that she had grown to love, greeted her. "It does?" She blinked. "I mean, it does."

"Have you not guessed to whom my heart is bound to?" he asked in a low, husky voice. He smiled in that enticing manner of his, and kissed the tip of her nose, then nuzzled her cheek. "Have you not guessed that I love you?" he whispered.

"What did you say?" she whispered back, unsure if she heard him correctly.

"I have waited so long to tell you these words. I love you, my dearest, *dearest* Judith!"

Lily's heart soared when she heard those words, and an immense joy swept over her as he kissed her with such loving tenderness that she melted in his arms. He murmured sweet endearments as he cradled her within the cocoon of security that she had craved all these years.

She knew that her dreams had finally come true. *Except a nagging thought needed to be put to rest first.* "What about Miss Bodline?" she mumbled.

He pulled back, his dark eyes glowing with passion. "My beautiful, dearest Lily, there was *never* a Miss Bodline. It was you all along. Am I to believe that my affections are returned?"

Lily blinked in amazement. Yes!" she sang out, her fingers touching his sensuous lips in wonder. "I do love you! I have always loved you!"

He leaned toward her and kissed her with such loving tenderness that she felt weak all over. She trembled.

"I am honestly overwhelmed. I did not know you felt this way about me," she said.

"I have loved you since that day I rescued you and Miss Bodline and brought you to Greystone Manor," he admitted. He kissed her again, slowly and passionately. "Will you marry me?" he asked.

"Oh, yes, my love! Oh, yes."

"You have made me very happy." He held her close to him. "Come, let us sit so we can talk further," he said hoarsely.

They walked to the sofa together and sat down, their hands entwined.

She gazed up at his handsome features in adoration, her happiness making her feel lightheaded. "All along I thought your actions were those of a gentleman helping a maiden in distress."

"I have been meaning to tell you my feelings for a long time now, but the opportunity did not present itself."

"Why did you not tell me sooner?" she asked. "I might have married one of those young male suitors that have been knocking on my door lately. For all we know, one might come barging in on us, demanding that we have a chaperone."

They burst out laughing.

"I had a sick father to contend with, and an engagement that should never have happened," he explained. "Afterward, you had your newly arrived father. However, I must confess, that the day I came to Montgomery Park, I was planning to propose to you."

"So, you were talking about *me*, and not Miss Bodline," she said, feeling delighted.

He nodded as his fingers toyed with the silky golden curls that cascaded down her back. "I do not know how you got it into your pretty mind that I had intentions with Miss Bodline. She is to be married to Mr. Pilford."

"Mr. Pilford? Oh, how wonderful. And here I was, thinking that--"

He placed a finger on her lips. "Sshh, that is all behind us. But you should have had more faith in me, my dearest. If only you knew how I spent countless nights losing sleep over you. I could not see a life without you."

Lily was awed by his intense feelings for her. "Will you forgive me?"

"Will you also forgive me?"

"For what?"

"For having talked you into going to Montgomery Park. If I would have known what that wolf Sir Charles was planning to do to you, I would have kept you at Greystone Manor."

Lily placed a finger on his lips. "Sshh, that is all behind us. But you should have had more faith in me, dearest," she said, lowering her voice and mimicking him.

He laughed heartily, embracing her once more. "We are going to be good for each other."

They discussed their wedding plans. Lily suggested they have it in London in three weeks.

"I do not know how I will last these three weeks. I want to marry you as soon as possible. Today, if we can," he exclaimed.

"Oh, dearest Edward. Would it not be better if we did it the proper way and shared it with our loved ones? That will give us time to send out invitations and prepare everything."

"I like the way you think." He kissed her once more, and then put his arm around her shoulder. "Would you like to go to Europe on our honeymoon?"

She snuggled up to him. "It does not matter, as long as we are together. Even if we went back to Yorkshire, I would be happy."

"Yes, but you will have Yorkshire the rest of your life. I want to make it special. We will travel to Paris, Italy and Greece," he promised.

As they were talking, Sir Frederick arrived. He appeared pleased when he saw the couple.

"Papa!" Lily cried, rising and rushing to him. "I have good news."

"Yes, I know," he said, hugging her. "I spoke with Lord Peterborough earlier. You both have my blessings." He turned and spoke to Lord Peterborough. "Have you made the date and location for the wedding?"

"In London, at the end of July."

Sir Frederick was thoughtful, his eyes speculative.

"What is the matter, Papa?"

"I received some news today. There is a business matter I must attend to," he said. "It is of utmost importance. I will be away these three weeks, but I *promise* I will have returned by your wedding."

Lily was dismayed. "Oh, Papa!"

He kissed her on the forehead. "Do not be disappointed, my Lily. You will see why when the time comes. Now I must prepare for the trip." He shook hands with Lord Peterborough. "I am proud to have you as my son-in-law. Do you have plans tonight?"

"I am at your disposal."

"Good. You will dine with us at seven, but come a little earlier so we can discuss the necessary details of the marriage, since I will be away tomorrow."

That evening, Edward visited with Sir Frederick. He had been elated all day, ever since Miss Montgomery's declaration of love.

Sir Frederick met him in his study. They discussed the money situation.

"Lily will be receiving an annual stipend of fifteen thousand," Sir Frederick said. "Ten will be from my estate and five will be from her mother's inheritance."

Edward told him what he had to bring to the marriage. "I assure you that my earnings alone will provide your daughter a very comfortable life."

"That is very good to hear," Sir Frederick said, smiling and shaking his hand. "Now that this is over, let us go to dinner. I am sure Lily is eager to discuss the wedding plans in more detail with you."

Sir Frederick was right. Lily eagerly discussed it at dinner.

"Maybe Mrs. Hartford could help me prepare. She is well versed in the proper way things are done here," she said.

"Have you considered which church and religion to attend to?" Sir Frederick asked.

"Not really," Lily admitted. "I know that you were married in the Greek Orthodox Church, and then you were married again in the Catholic Church."

Edward was surprised. "What was the reason for marrying twice?"

Sir Frederick smiled. "We were trying to please both families. My wife's family was Greek Orthodox."

"It is my mother's faith," Lily told Edward firmly.

"I like that idea," Edward said. "Why not do as your parents did and marry in both churches?"

They discussed it further, and it was decided that they would marry first in a Catholic church in London, and while on their honeymoon to Europe, marry in a Greek Orthodox church in Greece.

"I expect relatives from both sides of the families to attend the wedding. Therefore, after the ceremony, there should be a reception," Sir Frederick promised. "So, do not plan to leave for your honeymoon right away."

Chapter 35

July 1833

The days after Sir Frederick left were a whirlwind of activity as Lily prepared for her wedding day. Mrs. Hartford, her loyal friend, helped her every step of the way. They met almost daily to make plans. They sent out the invitations, for which Sir Frederick had given them the list of names. Then there was the wedding dress to be prepared and the church to be reserved.

Dotty also fielded any calls from male suitors until the engagement was officially listed in the newspaper. After that day, the calls from suitors dramatically dropped. One older suitor who had not heard the news came calling one day while Lily was out.

"Miss Montgomery is no longer available," Dotty said, eyeing the handsome, middle-aged man.

"I beg your pardon," he replied stiffly.

"She is engaged to be married, and I'm *not*," Dotty said, fluttering her eyelashes at him.

That was the end of Lily's suitors.

The invitations to social events steadily arrived. Although Lily and Edward attended dinner parties, balls, operas and theatres, they also made time for themselves. Lily cherished their walks in the pleasure gardens, and riding in the parks. His thoughtfulness touched her in so many ways, from the umbrella he held for her when it rained during their walk in the park, to the time he carried her from the carriage to the pavement so she wouldn't walk in the mud.

One day, they went to a poetry reading where Lord Byron's works were also read. Afterward, Edward told her that Lord Byron was a Philhellene and had gone to Greece during the war of independence and had helped toward the cause. After that, Byron's poems became her favorite.

Lily also wrote a letter to Miss Grant, informing her of the upcoming wedding. She replied promptly that she would come as soon as she could, even though she did not like to travel.

During her free time, Lily spent it painting a portrait of Edward and one day, she presented it to him. He was delighted.

The day of Miss Bodline's wedding came soon upon them. Lily and Edward attended the small wedding. The bride was radiant and the groom seemed very pleased. Lily was happy for the couple. Afterwards, at the reception, Lily met Jane's family and when Jane had a free moment, she spoke to her.

"I am so glad for you," Lily said to her friend, beaming. "Now we will be seeing more of each other."

Jane looked surprised. "What do you mean?"

"Lord Peterborough has asked me to marry him. Our wedding will be the end of this month."

"Oh, how wonderful! I sensed that he had a *tendre* for you," Jane exclaimed, hugging her. "You will become the Mistress of Greystone Manor and we will have to call you milady."

"It will always be Lily to you."

"It is too bad that we cannot come to your wedding, for we will not have returned from our honeymoon by then."

"That is all right," Lily said. "Your husband is the most important thing right now."

❧❧❧

Edward visited her daily, and they would go for strolls or rides in the park or attend social functions in the evenings where he introduced her to several distinguished people. He also introduced his male friends to her, and Lily enjoyed the witty conversations and bantering that went on between Edward and his friends.

When it rained, they remained inside, and she'd play the piano, or he'd read poetry to her. There was always something new to learn with Edward when it came to politics and philosophy. When the discussion veered to their travels, both had stories to share. He often liked to quote Shakespearean passages to her and over time, she memorized a few passages and surprised him with them.

One day, Lily showed him her mother's paintings and the picturesque house in beautiful Corfu. "That is where we will stay during our honeymoon."

One morning, Mrs. Bennington and Marianne paid Lily an unexpected visit. Mrs. Hartford was there, helping Lily with the preparations for the wedding. After they exchanged greetings, Mrs. Bennington came to the point.

"I wanted to congratulate you on your engagement to Lord Peterborough," Mrs. Bennington began.

"Thank you," Lily replied, feeling uneasy.

Mrs. Hartford arose to her rescue, appearing flustered. "It is such an inopportune time that you should come now. Miss Montgomery was *just* getting ready to leave. Were you not, my dear?"

"Oh, yes, I was," Lily said rising. "I have to--"

"Her wedding dress is to be fitted today," Mrs. Hartford finished.

"Then I shall come at a more convenient time," Mrs. Bennington said coolly. "Good-day."

After they left, Mrs. Hartford and Lily burst out laughing.

"She does not deserve to be in the same room with you, my dear," Mrs. Hartford said. "She has done damage enough. If I know her kind, she was probably fishing to get on your good side for favors later."

⋘⋙⋘⋙⋘⋙

The day of the wedding arrived quickly. Lily was nervous all morning. She hardly slept the night before, thinking about everything. She had received her father's letter two days ago promising that he would be at the church at eleven for the ceremony. She had hoped that he would be here already, but there had been no sign or word from him.

Dotty dressed her in her beautiful white satin wedding dress, with its pearl buttons that lined the back, white lace trimming, and low neckline. The sleeves were puffed yet not bulky. "Don't fidget, Miss," Dotty said, smiling as she buttoned up the back of her wedding dress. "There's fifty buttons back here."

"What will I do if my father does not arrive in time?" Lily said, fretting. "He is to give me away."

"He'll make it. Now let's get your hair next."

Soon, Lily's hair was piled high on her head.

"I must admit," Dotty commented. "You do make a beautiful bride."

"Thank you. It is love that you are witnessing."

Dotty was quiet as she placed small white roses on Lily's hair. "There. All done."

"I hope one day that you will also find your true love," Lily said to Dotty, hugging her.

"Don't I wish it?"

At eleven o'clock, Lily arrived at the church with Dotty. It was jammed with people. Her eyes anxiously combed the area for her father, while Dotty fixed her train neatly behind her. *Where was he? What if he hadn't arrived yet?*

"Now, don't be nervous," Dotty whispered to her. "If you're looking for your father, he's up front, next to Lord Peterborough."

Lily preened her head and was able to see Edward up front, tall and stunningly handsome in his groom's suit. He flashed her a special smile, making her feel much better. Lily smiled back, and then spied her father. He stood to the side, talking to the priest.

When Sir Frederick saw her, he strode toward her, handsomely dressed in a formal suit. She noticed that he did not use his cane. There was a glow about him that she hadn't seen before. Smiling at her, he reached her side and kissed her cheek affectionately.

"You look beautiful, my dear," he said.

"I am so happy that you could make it!"

"I promised you that I would be here."

Lily walked down the aisle with her father. Her hands felt clammy as she held the bouquet of pink roses, and her knees felt weak as they passed the rows of people. "I feel so nervous."

Her father patted her on the hand. "Do not worry. You are doing wonderfully," he whispered.

When they approached the front, she spied a thin and beautiful woman standing in the front pew, gazing steadily at her. There was something familiar about the woman's face, those beautiful expressive eyes, that endearing look. Lily's eyes were riveted on her. The woman smiled at her in a very special way, as if she wanted to say something. *There were tears streaming down her face. Why was she crying?*

Sir Frederick turned and smiled at the woman with a special look reserved for a loved one.

Lily's heart thumped hard, and she blinked back the tears at this revelation. *It is my mother standing before me. My mother!* She caught her breath, overcome by the onslaught of emotions that spilled through her. With a choking cry, she sobbed into her bouquet, unable to reign in her feelings.

Her father patted her hand and whispered, "It is all right, dear. It is all right."

When they reached Edward, Lily was weeping with joy. There was a hushed silence behind them as her father handed her to her beloved. Edward's eyes were red as he turned to face her. His lips mouthed an "I love you" to her and squeezed her hand. She managed a weak smile, her tears flowing.

They turned to face the priest.

The priest gave her a disturbed look. "Is everything all right?" he asked.

"Oh, yes!" she cried. "I am the happiest person here! My mother came to my wedding!"

The news rippled through the masses causing much commotion in the church.

The priest appeared confused.

Sir Frederick leaned over to explain. "Her mother was presumed dead, and now she is alive. She is here today. That is why my daughter is weeping."

The priest made the sign of the cross solemnly. "This is truly a special day." He then began the ceremony.

Lily took a deep breath and focused on the wedding ceremony. Soon, her heart was singing, as her thoughts were on her true love. The couple solemnly took their vows and when the ceremony ended, kissed tenderly. With wedding bands now on their fingers, they turned to face the congregation, ready to leave.

Penelope came up to Lily and embraced her, gazing lovingly at her, the tears brimming in her eyes. "My daughter. My sweet daughter. I thought I would never see this day," she said, her rich, lyrical voice shaking with emotion. She tenderly kissed her on the cheek. "I love you dearly."

"I love you. I had hoped so much that you were alive, and now my wish has come true," Lily cried. "This has been the best wedding gift I could ever have!"

"Thank you. You make a lovely bride." Penelope squeezed her hand. She turned and spoke to Edward. "I have heard so many good things about you, and am proud to have you as my son-in-law," she told him. She kissed him on the cheek.

Sir Frederick joined them and put his arm affectionately around his wife. "Your mother was so excited to see you. Now, you have obligations to attend to. We will meet up with you later." He took his wife's arm and they walked toward the priest.

Lily smiled up at Edward and he returned her smile, squeezing her hand. "I love you," he whispered.

"I love you, too, my darling."

Once outside, they were peppered with rice from eager friends. They laughed trying to duck from it. After they moved away, Lily prepared her bouquet.

"All the single women, here is your chance to catch the bouquet!" she called out. Several women formed a group around her. She counted to three, and then threw her bouquet up in the air.

The women scrambled to catch it. There were exclamations as Dotty, being the tallest, jumped up and grabbed the bouquet with her scrawny arm.

"This is my lucky day!" Dotty crowed, her thin face beaming.

Afterward, Lily and Edward stood to the side, exchanging greetings with everyone as they trickled out of the church. Lily recognized several people from her ball and social events. She also met Edward's extended family; they were very warm towards her. Edward's friends soon followed, including Mr. Beaumont and Mr. Mansfield.

"You finally did it," Mr. Beaumont told Edward, beaming and slapping him on the back. "You are a very lucky man."

"I know," Edward said, gazing with adoration at Lily, her lovely face glowing as she conversed with a dowager.

Sir Douglas and Lady Charleton soon arrived with Miss Grant.

"Congratulations, Lady Peterborough. You looked lovely in that dress," Lady Charleton said, gazing at Lily warmly. "Not only did you gain a husband, but a mother."

"Yes, I am very lucky," Lily admitted.

Sir Douglas was next and gave her his congratulations. She smiled back.

"We shall be seeing more of each other, dear," Lady Charleton promised Lily after she had congratulated Edward. They moved on.

Miss Grant was next. "Welcome to the family, my dear. What a wonderful surprise to have both of your parents at your wedding. I was quite overwhelmed," she said to Lily, her eyes shining with unshed tears. She left with the others.

Mrs. Hartford was the last to leave the church with her son.

"I was so pleased to see your mother. It was really touching. You do make such a beautiful couple!" she exclaimed with delight. She turned to her son. "You should be thinking about marriage, too."

He turned red and muttered something, and then they were off.

Soon her parents arrived. Her mother's look was hopeful, as she gazed with pride at her daughter. "My Lily, *agape mou* (my love)," she said. "How you have grown."

Lily smiled at her mother. Her large, blue-green eyes, delicate features, and graceful carriage all made her appear ageless.

"I brought her to you," Sir Frederick said proudly, placing his arm around his wife.

"Father, you are wonderful! Here I thought all this time you were away on business," Lily said. "If only I had known. I was fretting daily that you might not make it."

"I could not have said much, because your mother was in a delicate situation, and if she had not come at the time, it would have been more of a disappointment," he replied.

"I was fortunate to have Edward to calm me down. He kept saying not to worry, that you would be here," Lily said, smiling at Edward who had been standing quietly by, observing the family reunion.

"Edward," Penelope said, going to him. "I hope and pray that you and our daughter will have a blessed and happy life together. One filled with much love."

"Thank you for your well wishes, Lady Montgomery. Rest assured that your daughter will be in the best of hands."

"There is so much to tell you," Lily said to her mother.

"And I want to hear it all," Penelope said, patting her hand. "But let us go now to the reception. We cannot keep your guests waiting."

Two hours later, after Lily and Edward had finished strolling around the reception room, talking to everyone, Edward told Lily she should go and have her talk with her mother. "We will be leaving soon for the honeymoon."

"Thank you, dear," Lily said. As Edward drifted off, she searched for her mother. She did not have far to go, for her mother had seen her and was coming toward her.

"Come, my Lily. *Ela etho.* Let us sit over here and talk," Penelope said. They sat down in a quiet corner. "First of all, I wish to thank you from the bottom of my heart. If it were not for you, I would not be here."

"What do you mean?"

"First, you saved my life that fateful day, for when I found out you were missing, I was frantic. I ran like a mad woman out into the streets looking for you," she said, sighing. "I was so distraught when I could not find you, and when I returned to the house, the Ottomans had already set it on fire. It was terrible, for I had lost both of my parents that day and you. I did not care that I was taken as a slave by the Ottomans."

"A slave?"

"It was difficult at first, but not as bad as you think. I ended up living all these years with a wealthy Turkish family. They were kind to me, as best as expected, although I was never the same after that day. I was not allowed to leave the house alone and could not write to anyone, including your father. No matter how much I tried, I could never get over my loss."

Lily nodded sadly.

"You have also helped me a second time. If you had not returned to your father, he would not have started the search for me and helped release me from bondage," she said, taking a deep breath. "But I will not talk anymore about me. This is your day, my dear." She patted her on the arm. "Now I want to hear all about you."

Lily obliged her mother and told her what had happened to her and before she knew it, time had passed when Edward arrived with Sir Frederick.

"I apologize for intruding," Edward said, smiling at the two women, "but we have a honeymoon that cannot wait. We need to be off. We do not want to miss our ship."

Lily tearfully hugged her mother, and then her father.

"Now you have a husband to look after as I do, too," Penelope said, going by her husband's side. "Go, and may God bring you back swiftly to us."

Chapter 36

August 1837

On a sunny, breezy summer day, Lily, Edward, their three-year-old son Eddy, and Miss Grant visited her parents in Montgomery Park. Blessed with good weather, they spent that afternoon in the garden near the Parthenon folly, picnicking and enjoying their time together.

Lily sat next to Edward, chatting about a variety of topics, while Eddy frolicked in the grass with his grandfather, Sir Frederick. Miss Grant sat nearby, smiling at the scene from under her parasol and occasionally interjecting a word or two to Sir Frederick. Lady Montgomery was busy painting the bucolic scene on her canvas.

"Is this not wonderful?" Lily asked Edward, gazing into his dark, beautiful eyes. "Everyone being here together like this?"

"Yes," Edward said, smiling at her as he put his arm protectively around her. "And soon there will be a little one to play with Eddy."

"Hmm." Lily smiled back. She had confirmed her suspicions with the doctor a few days ago. She leaned against his shoulder and gazed at her son's sturdy features. "Eddy not only has your handsome looks, but he acts like you. He held my hand tightly when we walked down the stairs the other day. He did not want me to fall, he said."

"One day, he will become heir to Greystone Manor," Edward said, gazing proudly at his son. He turned and kissed Lily on the nose. "You have made me very happy, you know."

Lily beamed back. "The feeling is mutual."

"Lily, I am finished!" Penelope called out. *"Ela etho, na thees* (Come here and see)."

"All right, Mother." Lily turned to her husband. "Excuse me, dear. I need to finish the painting."

"Go right ahead."

"I have left a blank section in the picture where you will paint me," Penelope explained to Lily. "That way the picture would be complete."

Lily nodded, gazing at the pastoral scene before her; the handsome family enjoying themselves in their natural setting while the white columns of the Grecian folly stood distinctly in the background. The contrast between the Greek and English worlds was startling to witness.

Lily realized that love had brought everyone together and made this possible. It was a scene to be implanted in her mind forever.

"You have done a wonderful job. Now it is your turn. Please go and sit next to Father." Lily told her mother.

She waited until her mother was settled, and then with precision and care, dabbed blue paint onto the canvas. As she worked steadily, her thoughts drifted to her life ever since she married. Edward was a gentle and loving husband. Their honeymoon was a glorious one, first in Paris, with its multi-flavored life, and then the romantic strolls along moonlit beaches in Italy, and later, the gondola rides in Venice.

Corfu was especially exciting, because a local priest married them the second time in the local Greek Orthodox Church. It was a memorable service, filled with ritual and ceremony. Her parents' house stood on top of a hill and had breathtaking views. They spent many afternoons swimming in the beautiful waters, and then strolling on the beach holding hands. When they returned from their honeymoon, her parents were waiting for them in London.

Lily had spent much time with her mother, talking about the past. Her mother had many issues to resolve from the war. She had watched people die in front of her. Everything she cared for had been taken away from her, her husband and daughter, her family, her religion, and her heritage. Whenever Penelope spoke about it, she wept, seeming to relive the harsh past in her mind.

Over time, with the help of Lily and her father, her mother slowly was able to overcome the pain and hurt buried deep inside, eventually replacing it with peace.

Lily looked up at her family, and saw her father beaming at her mother as they conversed in hushed tones. Mother replied to something he said, and they laughed together. Father was still in love with his Greek maiden, after all these years. It was obvious that her parents adored each other. *They were inseparable.*

Lily studied her son's image on the canvas. Her mother had captured his playful spirit very well. When little Edward was born, he brought joy to everyone in the family, laughing and cooing often.

Her thoughts drifted elsewhere. Lady Charleton and Sir Douglas were expected to return from Paris in a few days with their one-year-old daughter, Henrietta. Last year, Lily learned that Lady Charleton had seen Mirela and the gypsies in Paris. It appeared that Mirela was doing well. One day, she hoped to see her again.

Miss Stanton's marriage to Charles Montgomery shortly after their marriage had come as a surprise to all. Soon thereafter, it was reported that the couple had left for America. Since then, relations with the Stanton family had resumed and they were invited over for dinner at the Stanton House often. Lady Charleton had also become more attentive towards Lily and they seemed to get along quite well.

Lily thoughts turned to Dotty's marriage to Herman, Edward's valet, two years ago. Dotty's happiness was complete.

Lily's mind drifted to Jane and her growing family. Dear Jane was very content with married life and raising her two-year-old twin daughters. They met often and caught up with their news over tea.

This was a very good life.

THE END

Author Bio:

Patty Apostolides is a biologist, author, poet and classical musician. She has written five novels and a poetry book. When she retired as a cancer biologist in order to stay at home and homeschool her son, her second career as a writer began. She holds a BA in Biology from Case Western Reserve University, with minors in music and theater, and an MFA in Creative Writing from National University. She is the director of the Hellenic Writers Group of Washington DC. In addition, Ms. Apostolides has performed as a violist for the Cleveland Philharmonic, the Cleveland Women's Orchestra, and the Fairfield Symphony Orchestra. More recently, she has played as a violinist for the Frederick Symphony Orchestra and the Eklektika String Quartet. She lives in Maryland with her son.

Other Books by the Author

Helena's Choice
The Lion and the Nurse
Lipsi's Daughter
It's A Date
Candlelit Journey: Poetry from the Heart

Visit the author's website: www.pattyapostolides.com